A GOBLIN AMBUSH

From opposite directions, the goblins burst from the bushes that hid them and dashed toward the pack. They looked like gray-skinned children with pointed ears, except that the nearest one's black hair was streaked with white. "*Moinay!*" the elder goblin shrieked. *Mine.*

The goblin seemed aware only of the pack and his rivals for it. Ayesh vaulted beside him and kicked his knee. He fell to the stony ground, shrieking this time in pain. His rival grasped the pack, and other goblins, sensing easy booty, stood out from their hiding places.

Better finish this quickly, Ayesh thought, *before it gets out of hand.*

Ayesh wasted no moves. This third goblin already had her dagger out, and she swung the blade in a wide arc, aiming for Ayesh's neck. Ayesh stepped into the swing, the last thing her foe expected, and ducked the blade. She clapped one hand on the goblin's shoulder to keep her spinning in the direction of her swing, then reached over the goblin's other shoulder to grasp her chin. With just the right leverage, Ayesh tugged hard.

The goblin's neck snapped.

MAGIC
The Gathering™

ASHES
OF THE
SUN

Hanovi Braddock

HarperPrism
An Imprint of HarperPaperbacks

HarperPaperbacks   *A Division of* HarperCollins*Publishers*
10 East 53rd Street, New York, N.Y. 10022

Copyright © 1996 by Wizards of the Coast, Inc.
All rights reserved. No part of this book may be used or reproduced in any manner whatsoever without written permission of the publisher, except in the case of brief quotations embodied in critical articles and reviews. For information address HarperCollins*Publishers*,
10 East 53rd Street, New York, N.Y. 10022.

Cover illustration by Nicholas Jainschigg

First printing: March 1996

Printed in the United States of America

HarperPrism is an imprint of HarperPaperbacks.
HarperPaperbacks, HarperPrism, and colophon are trademarks of HarperCollins*Publishers*.

❖ 10 9 8 7 6 5 4 3 2 1

For Brooks Clark ni Frett Vales, and all others who teach vacets of Diamond Mind.

Thanks to all my GEnie friends who cracked whips or offered reassurance, especially while Holly was away. For their daily enthusiasm, special thanks to Kathy, Mark, Billie and Patricia.

To Holly Arrow for reasons beyond numbering.

To first reader and in-house cheerleader, Mark S. Cole.

To Paul Wood, for teaching me that *Oneah fuit*.

To Juanita Simser, for Gynnalem's on-line Tarot reading.

Thanks, too, to my agent Shawna McCarthy, who teaches me patience; to Dave, who hooked me; and to Janna and Kathy, who reeled me in. Thanks also to WOTC readers Jessica, Rhias, and Michael.

Poystiiliin mpaydim.

The Houses of Mirtiin Hearth Colors

Liberal Houses

Grass-Above	Green and Gold
Iron-in-Granite	White and Ochre
Gems-in-Hand	Turquoise, Pink, and Black

Orthodox Houses

Shade-in-Ice	Purple
Ants-Below	Orange and Gray
Cups-Ashattered	Yellow and Black

Non-aligned Houses

Stones-Afalling	Gray and Sky Blue
Flame-in-Void	Red on Black
Horns-of-Gold	Gold on Brown
Rock-in-Water	Black and Midnight Blue
Sun-on-Forelocks	Tan and White

Myrrax-Who-Is-Mirtiin wears gray and the Robe of the Eleven. His guards wear gray and a sash of the Eleven.

In Stahaan, the minotaurs of all houses wear red, or red and white.

CHAPTER
1

AYESH STOOD A WHILE AT THE RAILING WITH her eyes closed, treasuring the sounds of the ship. The masts creaked; the sails luffed. From time to time she heard the rattle of pans down in the galley. The mate called to the men, and the men called back. From close by came Captain Raal's shrill whistle. He always whistled his commands.

Indeed, he hardly spoke during most of this voyage. "I use words when I need them," he had told her between two of his long silences. And it was true that he could often do without them. He was a man who said much with gestures and the gaze of his blue eyes.

Soon she would leave these sounds for the silence of the forest. And for a still deeper silence.

She gripped the rail. *It is not my destiny to stay,* she reminded herself.

Ayesh heard the captain's tread on the deck. She opened her eyes but did not turn toward him. Instead she looked out at the mountains that rose up from the sea. The shore was rocky and barren for a league, but beyond that, the slopes darkened with pine trees.

"We drop anchor," the captain said. Ayesh could smell the sweet smoke of tinderweed from his pipe. She heard him puff. "I ask you again, will you not take my advice?"

From the afterdeck came laughter. Ayesh looked at the shore, the silent forest. The sounds of the ship had grown familiar. She would miss them.

The sounds? she thought to herself. *Is that all you will miss?*

And then she thought, *I can't stay.*

He waited for an answer.

Summer in this far northern land was fleeting and chill. Ayesh clutched at her quilted jacket to keep out the cold wind. Her sleeves rode up on her wrists, revealing the pointed edges of her tattoos.

"I do what I must," she said.

"Turn and look at me," he said.

She would not at first. He put his hand gently on her shoulder. "Ayesh—"

She turned. She meant to avoid his gaze, but could not.

"Do not go," he said, and it was hard for her to break his gaze.

"I am the last of my people," she said. "I asked you for passage to the farthest reach of the Domains. If this is that place . . . "

He nodded, pointing with his pipe stem but not taking his gaze from hers. "It is." Then he did look toward the shore. "The Mirtiin Mountains. And beyond, the Stahaan."

"Then this is where I bring my story."

"You might tell your tales in better climes. I make better ports in the Voda Sea."

"Ports where I have told my tale already."

"It needs telling again. Did you not say that those who have heard you years ago now misremember? Let me sail you from shore to shore, to renew in each land your history of Oneah."

He's a generous man, she thought. But he did not understand her if he thought it would be enough to retell her histories until people remembered them aright. What she longed for was the land where her words would do the impossible. She wanted her tales of great, fallen Oneah to spark some nation to say, *Oneah, now that was glory! Mayhap we can build anew ourselves! Mayhap Oneah is not dead, if we ourselves become as the Oneahns were.*

An absurd dream, of course. The further she traveled, the more times she told her stories, the better she understood that there was only one Oneah. Twenty years had passed since the fall of Xa-On. The last of the Seven Cities could never be rebuilt. The backward people who must live near this barren shore could hardly dream of a confederation like Oneah's. *And yet . . .*

"I go ashore."

"If you will not stay aboard, then at least take my advice!" He pointed again with the pipe. "Let us sail to meet the merchant ships. They come at the half moon."

"No," Ayesh said.

He gave her a hard look. Then he turned his gaze to the shore. His hand was heavy on her shoulder.

"I am the last," she said.

"Aye," he said. His voice softened. "And your tales are a precious cargo."

Ayesh noticed that her hands trembled. She shut her eyes. Where was her mastery? Was she a child to tremble so? She said, "Lower me a boat, Captain."

His grip tightened, then he let his hand fall from her shoulder. "Woman, do you not hear me?"

"I hear," she said, and thought, *Have you met many men such as this one?* She found much to admire in Captain Raal. Honor and discipline mattered to him. All Orvadish captains were schooled in the philosophical and mathematical arts. Much about the man reminded Ayesh of her own race before the Goblin War, when Oneah was great. When Oneah *was*, for now the Court of a Thousand Thousands was in ruins. Of the Seven Cities of the Sun, little remained but ashes and memories. *Her* memories.

During the voyage here, the captain had listened to the notes from Ayesh's flute with his eyes closed, giving all his attention to the sound and feeling of the Oneahn music.

More importantly, he had listened to her stories without interruption, without once saying, "Now the way I heard it told . . ." He understood that from her he was hearing history, not tales. And he appreciated the difference.

From the start of the voyage, Ayesh had suspected that he fancied her, despite the poverty and road dust that clung to her black jacket. But Orvadish men—like Oneahn men—were reserved.

"The people here will not have ears for your music, even less for your story," Raal said. "They are backward."

"Humankind is backward everywhere," Ayesh said bitterly.

He lowered his gaze.

"Mayhap not everywhere," she said, not wanting to insult him. But he couldn't know, as Ayesh had known, how bright had been the one true flower of civilization. Orvada might rise above the lands nearby, but Oneah had towered above all that Orvada might ever become. Even after weeks of hearing Ayesh tell the history and wonders of Oneah, the captain could not truly know what Oneah had been. He had never been there. The story of Oneah, no matter how many times she told it, no matter how careful the tellings, only faintly echoed the truth. Who could know the Roof of Lights, who had not stood beneath it?

"You lie," he said. "To me and to yourself, you lie about what you seek."

She turned to look again at the barren shore.

At the after railing, some of the men were fishing, and one shouted exultantly, "A butterfish! We eat well tonight!"

"Aye," shouted another, "if you don't snap the line. Careful! Careful!"

"If you will not think of yourself, what of your stories?" the captain said. "An honest captain does not endanger his cargo." Then he lowered his voice. "The hills are alive with goblins. They swarm here like ants."

Ayesh stood as tall as she might, which was not very tall. "Do you think I fear goblins?" she said over the water. When he rapped his pipe sharply on the rail, she flinched.

"No," he said. "I think you do not fear them *enough*."

"Hate fills my heart," she said, "and leaves no room for fear."

He seized her wrist. "Fear is what would keep you alive!"

"I have never died yet," she said.

"Ayesh! There are yet things to live for!"

She closed her eyes. He was wrong. She had not yet resolved to die. She only felt that if there were not soon something more to hope for, some promise of making Oneahn history outlive her, *then* she would have no reason to live.

"Put me ashore."

He shook his head.

She turned. "Did I not pay you in gold, Captain Raal?"

His eyes hardened, and the color drained from his face. He let go of her wrist, stung.

She looked out at the shore, as if she might there find a way to take the words back. The first league inland was barren rock. That ground was in reach of the moonswimmers. At night, they would come ashore and thrash their great white bodies, writhing their way to the forest's edge. She said, "The day grows late."

He did not respond.

Ayesh had never seen a moonswimmer, but the captain had. A ship like his, he had told her, would be a dainty morsel in those sea-foaming jaws.

"I mean you no disrespect," she said. Indeed, had her life been any different . . .

He took a step back, bowed to her, and said, "As you will." When he stood straight again, his gaze lingered on her for a moment. Then he turned and whistled for his mate to ready the boat.

"Gods protect you and keep you, Captain Raal."

"And you." She heard the heaviness in his voice. When the crew lowered the boat, he was not at the rail to see her off.

An hour later, Ayesh was ashore and beyond the barren limits of the moonswimmer grazing grounds. In the deep shadow of the mountains, she turned one last time to see the ship sailing east on the Voda Sea. The craft rode sparkling waters, and for a moment she longed to still be on it, sailing with its captain into light and life. Then she turned toward the mountain shadows and followed the river valley. Ahead, somewhere, was the town. How far? The mate who rowed her ashore would have told her had he known. The captain and crew, though, had always avoided this shore. "Up the Boiling River," was all the mate could say.

As she found her way along the rising valley, the slopes grew closer together and the river coursed in a steeper and steeper bed. The thin trail that followed the river grew harder to see as it led over bare stone. Here and there were the remnants of cairns, piles of stones meant to lead the way where the trail was hard to see. The cairns were neglected, the stones scattered into random heaps.

She had not gone much farther upriver when she began to sense that she was not alone. The signs weren't subtle—a rustling bush here, a moving shadow seen from the corner of her eye.

One thing she could count on with goblins was this lack of subtlety. Like children, they had no discipline, especially when there were many of them together. From the signs, she estimated that twenty or more goblins lurked among the nearby rocks and trees.

So soon? she thought. She had not really believed that coming ashore late in the day would immediately assure her of a fight. Ayesh had counted on arriving within the town walls before dark, for wasn't this a trading village? Surely it would be near the sea. But there was no stockade in sight. The one sign of human habitation that she had seen was a ruined wall, the remnants of a stone foundation near the limits of the moonswimmer grazing ground.

She heard a goblin in the shadows mutter with anticipation, and another answered it. Then came the clatter of scree tumbling from the rocky slope, and Ayesh turned to see small stones sliding over one another and a goblin dashing away, up the slope, no doubt to carry the news of her arrival to others in their caves. Twenty-to-one would not be odds that the goblins would like. They'd want something more like fifty-to-one.

She felt half resigned to the fight. Maybe Captain Raal was right. Maybe she *was* ready to die.

But no, no, even if she were ready to die, she would want time to prepare, to make her peace, somehow, with the memories of the honorable dead.

She picked up her pace, considering what she might do. Completely open ground was a problem. If she could fight with her back to a wall . . .

When she rounded the river bend and could see what terrain lay ahead, she uttered a soft curse. With the valley growing narrower, she had hoped to see a box canyon ahead with steep walls. Instead, the valley opened again. This was not good terrain for fighting a large company of frenzied goblins.

Ayesh looked up. The clouds were already tinged with orange. Before long, the light would fade, and as the sun sank, the courage of the goblins would rise. Unless she did something to make them think about it some more, she could expect the attack to come with the first glimmering star.

Ayesh slowed her pace. She stepped uncertainly, even slower now. She stopped, turned, and looked about as if she had lost the trail. "Damn," she muttered, retracing her steps, stopping again, turning.

She could feel the change in the goblins. A few of them muttered with barely contained excitement. The more lost she looked, the more eager they were. Did they stop to consider that it was impossible to lose this trail? All Ayesh had to do was keep following the river until she picked the trail up again. But they would not stop to reason it out, Ayesh knew. They would not see how they were being duped.

Ayesh turned and turned in place, looking about. Wherever her back was turned, goblins rushed forward to the next closest hiding place.

Now to bait the trap. Ayesh took off her pack, set it on

the ground, and massaged her shoulders through the black quilted jacket. She stepped away from the pack.

A goblin howled, and another hissed at it. Ayesh turned toward the howl, trying to look scared. But not too scared. If panic crossed her face, the goblins would rush her all at once. She must look weak, but not completely helpless.

She sidestepped several paces, and the pack lay on the open ground as if forgotten.

She could feel the anticipation in the air. Each goblin was measuring and remeasuring the distance between Ayesh and the pack. What treasures did she carry? Was she far enough yet?

Ayesh sidestepped still further.

From opposite directions, two goblins burst from the bushes that hid them and dashed toward the pack. They looked like gray-skinned children with pointed ears, except that the nearest one's black hair was streaked with white. "*Moinay!*" the elder goblin shrieked. *Mine.* This word, at least was the same here as it was for the goblins of the Red and Hurloon Mountains.

The goblin seemed aware only of the pack and his rival for it. Ayesh vaulted beside him and kicked his knee. He fell to the stony ground, shrieking this time in pain.

His rival grasped the pack, and other goblins, sensing easy booty, stood out from their hiding places. But they froze when they saw how quickly Ayesh covered the ground between the first goblin and the second. As Ayesh dove and grasped the goblin's ankle, his prize flew from his hands. Now a third goblin dashed from its hiding place and made for the pack.

Better finish this quickly, Ayesh thought, *before it gets out of hand.*

The second goblin had fumbled inside its leather vest for a dagger. As he slashed at her, Ayesh grabbed his wrist and bent it forward. It popped. The goblin yelped, dropped the blade, and went to his knees.

With her free hand, Ayesh punched him in the face. The goblin sprawled backwards, stunned. Ayesh sprang past him, sprinted to meet the third goblin, a female, as she lifted the pack from the ground.

By now, the goblins all around were shrieking and chattering. The racket could be a good sign or a bad one, Ayesh knew. Their emotions were at a fever pitch. They would be mastered by them—either by fear or jubilation. It all turned on how the struggle for the pack went.

Ayesh wasted no moves. This third goblin already had her dagger out, and she swung the blade in a wide arc, aiming for Ayesh's neck. Ayesh stepped into the swing, the last thing her foe expected, and ducked the blade. She clapped one hand on the goblin's shoulder to keep her spinning in the direction of her swing, then reached over the goblin's other shoulder to grasp her chin. With just the right leverage, Ayesh tugged hard.

The goblin's neck snapped.

From every side, the chattering goblins fell silent.

Ayesh went back to the second goblin, who sat dazed, blood streaming from his nose.

"I might show you mercy," Ayesh said, "if your kind knew what mercy was." And then she said in the goblin tongue she knew, "*Min kli moina tlit ekleyla jla.*" *None who cross me shall live to see the far dawn.*

She killed him as she had the first.

The goblins that had stepped out of hiding were hidden again, or were retreating up the valley slopes.

The third goblin was whimpering and limping away. Ayesh put on her pack and walked behind it.

"Not kill! Not kill!" it whined.

"And would you spare me, if I were wounded?"

"Not kill! Not kill!" Its hands trembled as it tried to outdistance her. It wore red, fingerless gloves, an odd article of clothing for a goblin, no doubt booty taken from some other traveler. "Not kill! *Oufyit!*" *Go away.*

Ayesh stepped closer, and the goblin shrieked and rolled onto its back. It stretched its open hands toward her. "Pity me! Pity me!"

She stopped. There was a saying among the elves of the Savaen Forest: *To know compassion, pity the goblin.*

"Pity me!" the goblin pleaded as it crabwalked away on its back. "Pity!"

It had to use the Voda-tongue word. There would be no word for *pity* in any goblin dialect.

The second half to that saying of the Savaen elves went: *To know prudence, fill the goblin with arrows.*

"Damn your hide," she said. "I should give you what you deserve. *Oufyit tee la!*" She spat on the ground, then turned away from the miserable creature and walked back toward the trail.

The clouds were a brighter orange now, and the sky behind them a darker blue. Ayesh had done little, she knew, except to buy herself time. Knowing that she was dangerous, the goblins would wait for their numbers to grow, and they would pace her from a distance all night, expecting weariness to at last make her easier prey. But now she might have a chance of getting to the town before the goblins' courage returned.

A stone the size of a fist clattered at her feet. Ayesh looked up at where it had come from, and there stood Red Gloves, far up the slope, waving his fist at her.

She picked up the stone and made ready to throw. He had the advantage in elevation. Even if she could throw the stone that high, it wouldn't land with any force. But Red Gloves yelped and scampered into the shadows.

Alone, goblins were slinking cowards. But one rarely found them alone.

She let the stone fall from her hand.

CHAPTER

2

WHEN TOWNSMAN OLF SQUINTED IN THE FIRE-
light and saw how many gaps showed in the stone wall,
he threw his cap down on the ground.

"No, blast you all!" He shouldered aside the young men
and women who were bringing stones to add to the wall.
"It's got to stand even after goblins try to knock it over!"

He planted his boot against the wall and, with a grunt,
rolled one of the stones free. Other stones tumbled after
it. "How long do you think that would stand against a
dozen goblins? And there's more than a dozen about
tonight." He sniffed the air. "Many more."

In truth, he could not know the number of lurking goblins by their smell, though there was a stench to them, as
of rotten meat and offal, and it was strong this night. But
what actually told him their number was the sound of
them moving in the darkness around the camp. One goblin might be stealthy, but never a pack of them. And certainly not a crowd such as this.

"Townsman Olf," said one of the young men who had
been working on the wall, "it's hard to make the wall
strong when we can hardly see what we're doing."

"Townsmen Rav and Tull are doing the job well enough," Olf growled. But the older townsmen were experienced in building defensive walls in a hurry. They had made this trading journey between town and the sea many times, and the youngsters who labored on this side of the defense were making the trip for the first time. He looked at the fire, which burned on a platform of stones so that it illuminated the area outside as well as inside the wall. But the fire was small. "All right. If you can't see, we'll build the fire brighter, then."

"But we haven't enough wood to last the night!" whined Ilif.

"Then you and I shall have to fetch more, shan't we?" He cuffed Ilif on the ear. "If you'd brought enough to begin with, we'd have all we needed. Lad, how is it that you shirk the simplest task?" In general, this was an earnest lot of youngsters making the trading trip, carrying goods down to where the ships would come tomorrow. But there were always exceptions, like this lazy Ilif and that girl, Juniper. She didn't get on Townsman Olf's nerves the way Ilif did, but Juniper was nearly as useless. She often had a dreamy look to her eyes, and she had to be told to do things twice.

Indeed, where was she?

"Juniper!" he barked.

A moment later, she stepped into the circle of light. She had a stone in her hands. A small one. "The goblins, they're all around," she said. "I can hear them. There must be forty or fifty of them nearby."

"Aye, I know," said Olf. "Let me worry about that, girl." He was impressed by her count—it matched his own. She had a head on her shoulders, if only she could keep it out of the clouds. "Come on, Juniper. We need larger stones than that for the wall, and a lot of them."

Olf threw several more branches on the fire, and soon the flames leapt high enough that he could spot, here and there, the glint of goblin eyes shining from the forest.

"All right, Ilif. Let's collect some wood."

"Out . . . out there?"

"Where else do you suggest?" Olf snatched up his

crossbow. "Come on, boy!" Then he turned to the men who were chinking their side of the wall. "Rav! Tull! Come here and show these children how to build a wall!" Olf climbed the wall and turned once, holding out his crossbow that all the goblins might see it. In truth, he would not dare to fire the bolt once he had stepped outside of the enclosure. The only thing that would keep him safe was the goblins' certain knowledge that the first to rush him would die. Once the first had been killed, the other goblins would be upon Olf before he could crank, cock, and reload the weapon.

Olf jumped down to the hard ground, then turned.

"You coming, boy?"

Ilif didn't answer. He crouched at the top of the wall, looking left and right into the dark woods.

"Sooner started, sooner done," Olf said. He walked into the shadows. Ilif jumped down from the wall and tried to stay close.

"There." Olf stopped at the edge of the forest. "There's deadwood aplenty here. Gather it up while I stand guard."

"But I can't see!"

"Do it by feel, then."

"What if there's a goblin there?"

"Then put the wood down and throttle the rotter!"

Ilif crept slowly forward, and Olf gave him a kick in the seat of his pants.

"Sooner started, sooner done!" Olf said again.

A raspy voice in the trees up slope said, "Sooner started, sooner done!"

"Say that again, you rotter," Olf said. "I can aim by the sound of your voice!"

The first goblin was silent, but another snickered.

By Xatta's icy breath, these goblins were in a feisty mood this night. He'd hoped that the prospect of storming a wall would hold them off, as it often did, but tonight, he wasn't sure. Of course, high spirits could make them turn and run as easily as attack. Agitation in goblins was a general sort of thing. Something might be making them confident, or it might be that something had them spooked. But what? There certainly wasn't anything out of the ordinary about this little group of traders from Bathtown—just three townsmen and the usual lot of youngsters nearly come of age.

"Sleep well," said another goblin voice. Then it added something else in its own tangled language.

Yet another goblin, closer than the first, echoed, "Sleep well," and chuckled.

"Ah, that one's close," Olf said, aiming the crossbow. The goblin, unnerved by the accuracy of his aim, scrambled noisily for deeper cover in the bush. Had Olf shot, he would have killed it. But he dared not shoot.

"I—I have the wood!" Ilif announced. He emerged from the brush carrying three pitiful sticks.

"Aye. That's wood enough to toast a raisin. Drop it at your feet and get some more!"

"But I'm afraid!"

"I'm afraid!" said a goblin voice, and others took up the refrain: "I'm afraid! I'm afraid!"

Olf ignored them and said to Ilif, "Think of how much more afraid you'll be when all our wood's gone, and you're waiting for these cold-skinned rotters to scale the wall in the dark! Come on! At this time of year, the night's not long! Just get us a good thick branch or two!"

Olf shook his head as the boy crept into the shadows again. This had been, from beginning to end, a miserable day. They'd gotten a late start on their journey, else the wall could have been built and the wood gathered in full light. And why were they late? Because of Elder Laik and Elder Alik. The two old brothers had their long instructions for the travelers. Elder Laik assigned each one an herb to collect on the journey, which was at least a task that would come to some purpose, since Laik used the plants for healing. But then Elder Alik had to assign each of the young travelers a question to ask the trading party from the ship.

"How was the world made?"

"If a man dreams of twins, what is the meaning?"

"What is the greatest treasure of the world?"

"Who was the greatest woman who ever lived?"

When the youngsters returned, Alik would write down

the answers they had received in his great book. What good had ever come of this? What had Elder Alik learned but that sailing men from all the world tell different tales? It was a ridiculous exercise: questions and tales. Stuff and nonsense.

Alik's obsession with these matters was harmless except when it delayed the start of a trading party. And then it made Olf mad.

"Come on, Ilif! If I were a tree, I could grow wood faster than you gather it!"

There was a change. Olf stiffened and drew his crossbow close to him before he knew what had shifted.

It was the sound of the goblins. Those nearby had fallen silent, and others downriver from the camp were chattering, whether in anticipation or dismay, it was impossible to say.

And then a female voice came from the darkness.

"Hullo the town!"

Olf aimed at the voice before it sank in—that was no raspy goblin voice, but a human one.

From within the wall, Townsman Rav took up his crossbow. He looked at Olf, who gave no sign, but only looked again into the darkness where the voice had come from.

Ilif emerged from the shadows holding firewood no better than his first load.

Rav turned toward the sound of the voice. "This is no town that you hail. Who are you?"

"Hello the camp, then," said the voice. "Will you shelter a stranger?"

Rav called out, "How many are you?"

"Myself alone." She stepped into the light. She was small—a woman the size of a goblin. "I am called Ayesh."

Rav looked again to Olf, who bit his lip. The voice certainly was human enough, and his first impulse was to welcome the traveler. But who would be walking this road alone and at night? Could this be a goblin with the trick of mimicking a human voice? Goblins could do that sometimes. At this distance, she looked human enough. But the light was too dim. Could he trust his eyes? And if she were human, did that settle things? Could the goblins have a human confederate?

But who would be stupid enough to work with goblins? They turned so readily on each other that no human mercenary could hope to survive among them.

Just as Olf got out the words, "Come, stranger, and—" there was a rustling in the brush beside him.

Ilif yelped and jumped to escape something. He fell against Olf, whose finger was still on the crossbow trigger. The bolt hissed through the air.

And the goblins heard it.

Olf grabbed Ilif by the wrist and yanked him to his feet.

"Rav! Tull! Crossbows! Cover us!"

Olf dashed toward the wall, where Townsmen Rav and Tull had taken up positions in clear sight of the goblins. Each man held a crossbow, cocked and readied.

The goblins would not rush the wall as long as there were crossbow bolts sure of hitting the boldest of them. Every goblin wanted to follow the charge, and none was willing to lead it.

Things were at a stalemate again, Olf thought. But as he reached the wall, he heard a shriek behind him. He turned.

Ilif had not taken three steps before he had tripped. Six goblins fell upon him, two holding down each of his legs and two more pinning his arms. A seventh was stepping out of the shadows.

"Olf!" the boy cried.

"Olf!" mimicked one of the goblins.

"I'm afraid!" said the seventh goblin, a female. She had unsheathed a dagger, which she waved before Ilif's face.

The other goblins holding Ilif took up the chorus. "I'm afraid! I'm afraid!" They chuckled as Ilif struggled.

"What shall we do?" said Rav.

"What can we?" asked Tull. The crossbow stalemate could work both ways. The goblins were sure the men would not fire. To do so would be to invite the entire host of surrounding goblins to attack the wall.

Olf started back for the boy.

"Olf, no!" said Tull. "You can't save him. You'll only draw out more goblins, and we'll lose the both of you."

Olf handed his crossbow up to the man. "Load. And give me yours."

But Tull hesitated to give up his loaded weapon.

There was another, louder shriek, and at first Olf thought that it was Ilif's death scream. But he turned to see that two goblins lay sprawled on their faces, and a third, in the arms of the stranger, was kicking its legs madly. Like a walnut shell, something went crack!

The goblin went limp.

The goblin with the dagger had backed up a step, and Ilif had enough of his wits back to kick the one goblin who still tried to hold his leg. Olf could see more goblins in the shadows, hesitating between rushing the stranger or fading back.

Right now, a little bravado could go a long way.

"Save some for me!" Olf cried. "I love to crack their heads like melons, I do!"

As he strode toward the goblins, who had him hopelessly outnumbered, Olf could see them draw back into their hiding places. He grinned.

"Ilif, grab that one for me! I want to see if I can pull his ears off!"

The last goblin holding Ilif's arm shrieked and ran off. The dagger-wielding goblin tucked her blade away and dashed for the shadows.

The stranger helped Ilif to his feet, and Olf met them halfway.

"All's not well and done," the stranger said under her breath. "Walk, don't run, for safety. Give them your back and swagger like you could take on the whole lot of them. And hope you awe them just long enough."

"That's a good trick," Olf said, "snapping its neck. How do you—"

"Shut up and walk," the stranger said.

Rav and Tull helped them scramble to the top of the wall. One of the youngsters had cocked and loaded Olf's crossbow. She offered it to Olf, but the stranger grabbed it out of her hands.

"You ought to have a pin on this trigger," she said. Then she frowned. "You do have one! Why did you not engage it?"

"I did not know if you were friend or foe," said Olf. In the firelight, he saw her clearly for the first time. Her hair was black, threaded here and there with silver. She had seen about as many summers as Olf himself—certainly not many more than forty. "Besides, the weapon's nothing if I can't fire it when I want to."

"And when you fired it, was it because you wanted to? Gods and gashes, but a man who wields a weapon should wield the discipline it demands!"

Olf felt his face getting hot. "Listen, you . . . "

"No, you listen. If you knew aught of goblins, you'd know that a crossbow protects you from a crowd of them only so long as it is not fired."

"I know that!"

"Then wherefore did you fire?"

"Heavens, lady, it was a mistake!"

"And why were you away and about? When I approached, I could see you had wall enough already to discourage assault. Once a wall is made, the place to be is inside of it!"

"Do you think me utterly ignorant?" Olf bellowed.

She answered him with silence.

CHAPTER

3

AYESH SUPPOSED THAT SHE HAD NOT MADE
the best possible start with these people. Well, there was
nothing new in that. Throughout the Domains, the traits
she most honored in civilized human beings were rare.
There had been but one civilization worthy of the name,
and Oneah was gone.

The leader of these townspeople—his name was Olf, and
she had to bite her tongue when she heard it—sat on the far
side of the fire from her, nursing his wounded pride. The
other two men stood looking out over the top of the wall,
crossbows in hand. The young travelers all sat with their
backs to the walls, clutching the sharpened sticks or knives
they would use if the goblins stormed the stone circle.

Ayesh could feel the heat of Olf's anger. Well, let him
stew. How would he feel if some undisciplined yokel had
fired a crossbow quarrel at *him*? Olf. The name suited him.

But it would serve no good end to simmer in her anger.
Ayesh closed her eyes and drew her attention inward. She
took a deep breath, and in her mind's eye, she saw a
point of red light between her eyes. She let the point
expand, filling her head, and then she let the light fill her
body until she was filled with its red brilliance.

She let her spirit linger for a time. Red was the color of anger. She must inhabit it first to move beyond it.

When Ayesh let the first color fade at last, she imagined another point of light—orange this time. It expanded, filled her head, her body.

She heard the movements within the encampment walls, and she could feel the eyes of the young townsfolk on her. She could hear the sounds of the goblins in the forest as well. Someone walked close to Ayesh and stopped, but there was no menace in his gait.

Awareness of these things passed over Ayesh like a brook's water passing over a stone. She heard, she felt, but her mind was still.

Color by color, she dwelt in the hues of the Rainbow Meditation, burning bright with yellow, green, blue, and indigo. By the time she reached violet, she felt as subtle as that color.

She finished the meditation with the color after violet, the color of the unknowable. Though she could not see what was invisible, awareness of the Color That Cannot Be Named filled her head and then her body.

Slowly, she opened her eyes.

The boy called Ilif was standing before her, waiting. He held a wooden bowl in his hands.

"It was my fault, twice over," he said. "I hadn't gathered enough wood for the fire. And when I felt a goblin reach out from the brush and touch me, I jumped and made Townsman Olf shoot his crossbow."

Ayesh looked him over. "You are young."

She saw his relief in the shift of his posture.

"I did not say that youth excuses you," she said. "I have known children half your age who had twice your mastery. Master yourself and make no further excuses. Is that for me?"

He looked at the bowl as if he had forgotten it, then held it out to her.

"It augurs well that you know your mistakes," Ayesh told him, taking the bowl. "Now let them pass. What is done is done. Resolve that ever after, you will be not a goblin, but a human being. Then be so. That's all there is to courage."

Uncertainly, the boy said, "Thank . . . thank you."

Ayesh ate from the bowl. The food was a cold paste of beans and cracked grain, but there was some spice to it that made it better than she'd expected. "Bring me water, will you, Ilif?"

When the boy had gone to the waterskins, a girl who'd been listening to the conversation dared to creep a little closer.

Ayesh faced the fire, burning atop its pillar of stones. "Tell me," she said, "how far is your town from here?"

"Half a day's march," the girl said. Her eyes were wide.

"That's far from the coast for a trading town."

"Once Bathtown was the second town from the sea," the girl said. "But the winterspice trade from Nul Divva is not so great as it once was. Half the towns are gone. These ruins . . . this used to be the first town. It was over-run by goblins. So say the elders."

Ilif returned with a bowl of water.

"This is always the resting place for trade journeys," the girl continued. "In summer, the townspeople come to meet the ships at the half moon."

"And are all the townspeople so young?"

"This is the journey of midsummer," said Ilif. "The first for most of us. But after we've done this, we may serve as apprentices. And later, when we have journeyed ten times, we'll be townsmen." He looked at the girl. "Or townswomen. And old enough to marry."

The girl shrugged. "What *I* care about," she said, "is meeting the sailors and traders from other lands. Elder Alik says that human beings come in every color. Did you know that some have black skin? Or blue?"

"I've been among them," Ayesh said. "Red and green and yellow. But those are not all natural hues for human beings. Some are painted. And some are such barbarians that they are as much goblin in their souls as human."

"Hsst! Pipe down!" said Townsman Tull from the wall. "I scarce can hear the doings of the goblins."

Ilif and the girl both crouched closer to Ayesh. In little more than a whisper, the girl asked, "Where are *you* from?"

"From the Court of a Thousand Thousands and the Roof of Lights."

"Never heard of it," said Ilif.

"I have," said the girl. "That's Oneah."

Ayesh stared at her. She was almost a woman, almost the age Ayesh had been when the last Oneahn city had fallen twenty years ago. "What do you know of Oneah, girl?"

"Only that there was a great tower that rose as high as the sky. That was the Roof of Lights. And two princes who wanted to be king would climb to the top and try to throw each other off. The one who got thrown off the tower and killed would be the king of the dead, and the one who lived would be the king of the living."

"That," said Ayesh, "is among the worst perversions I have ever heard."

"Does sound weird," said Ilif. "Who ever heard of a king of the dead?"

"I mean the story!" Ayesh felt her anger return. She took a breath and let the feeling melt away. "In truth, I have heard worse distortions. But listen. The Roof of Lights was nothing like that. It was more dome than tower, and no princes fought atop it. Wrestlers vied in the ring beneath the dome, under the gaze of kings. And this business about a king of the living and a king of the dead . . . Now, that's muddled. Each year, the two grand champions of the court would wrestle. The winner became the grand champion and Master of Victory. The other was grand champion and Master of Defeat. Both were accorded equal honor, and neither died. Nor ruled, either."

"Hsst!" warned Tull.

"I like Juniper's version better," said Ilif softly.

"It's not my version," Juniper said. "It's what Elder Alik told me. He keeps all the stories."

"Well, I shall have to meet Elder Alik and tell him he has it wrong."

"But it can't be *wrong*," said Juniper. "Elder Alik says that every story is its own truth."

"Indeed," said Ayesh through her teeth.

Juniper opened her mouth to say something, then seemed to think better of it. She looked around at the wall and hugged herself. "I hope the goblins leave us alone now."

Ayesh said, "Not likely."

"Someday," Juniper continued, "I want to live far away from goblins. And from trolls and stone giants and ogres and orcs."

"And minotaurs," said Ilif.

"Why would you fear minotaurs?" Ayesh asked. "I've played my flute for them and told my stories to them. They were a good audience. If only human beings listened as minotaurs do."

"You've really spoken to minotaurs?" said Juniper.

"Aye. In the Hurloon Mountains."

"And they didn't kill you?"

"Kill me? They taught me to speak their tongue. They are a gentle race."

"In the Hurloon, maybe," said Ilif. "Not *our* minotaurs."

Juniper said, "At least with minotaurs, if you leave them alone they'll leave you alone."

"So says Elder Alik," said Ilif, "but I wouldn't be so sure. If ever I see a minotaur coming, you can bet I won't stick around to test Elder Alik's word."

"Better to meet with minotaurs than with goblins," said Juniper.

"Well, everyone I know has survived an attack by goblins," argued Ilif, "but I never once spoke to anyone who had tangled with minotaurs and lived."

"Minotaurs are smart and shy," said Ayesh. "Not like goblins." And a bit mysterious, too, she thought. It was said that Hurloon minotaurs could read minds. But perhaps they were merely masters of subtle observation. Even among humans, a careful eye and quick reason could make it possible to pretend mind reading.

Ilif looked at the wall. "Townsman Olf says that one day the goblins will get smart and carry away all the rubble from these ruins. He says that one day a trading party will arrive here with no way to shelter themselves."

"Well that's one wise thing that Townsman Olf has said," Ayesh told Ilif. "Don't count on goblins not to figure things out. Ever seen goblins attacking on a rock sled? Well, no, you wouldn't. None but the Rundvelt goblins make them. Well, imagine a stone sled that comes down a mountain almost as fast as a stone falls. Two of those would make rubble of this wall we have here. A rock sled, that's a nasty invention. Not all goblins are stupid. But none of them are masters of their own thoughts. More than stupidity, their weakness is fear."

"Then why haven't they carted away the stones already?" Juniper asked, looking at the wall.

"One goblin could do it in fifty years," Ayesh said, "better than fifty goblins could in a year."

Juniper's expression made it clear that this was a riddle.

"Rare is the goblin that can cooperate," Ayesh explained.

Clearly, Ilif was not greatly interested in better understanding goblins. He was looking at Ayesh's pack. "What do you trade?"

"Nothing," she said. "I don't trade." She pulled the pack near, opened it, and drew out her tinderbox and flute.

"You're a minstrel, then!" said Juniper. "I've heard of them from Elder Alik. We've never had a minstrel in Bathtown!"

Ilif said, "What's a minstrel?"

"She trades her songs for gold."

Ilif snorted. "Well, there's precious little gold in Bathtown, and I can't think of anyone who'd trade it away for a song. Except Elder Alik, maybe, and he hasn't any gold that I ever heard of."

"Minstrels don't sing for common traders," Juniper said, "but for kings and queens."

"I've played for kings and queens," Ayesh said, "and for common folk. And I never did it for gold."

"Oh," Ilif said to Juniper. "She's a beggar who plays."

Ayesh laughed bitterly. "So some would call me."

"Play for us!" said Juniper.

Ayesh looked up at the wall where Olf paced. "Not now."

"One song," Juniper pleaded. "Only one!"

"Well . . ." said Ayesh. She opened her tinderbox and spoke a soft word into it. An orange flame of unsmoking fire burst to life with a low *whoomp*.

Surprised, both Ilif and Juniper jumped back.

Ayesh smiled. She spoke another word to the flame, and it shifted from orange to green. She put one end of the flute into the fire, and the green fire spiraled up the length of the instrument and disappeared.

"It glows!" said Juniper.

On the wall, Townsman Tull turned as if to demand quiet again, but he only stared silently at the flute, which was now glowing green from the inside. He stared, as did all the young traders within the wall.

Ayesh put away the tinderbox, then brought the flute to her lips. She played a brief tune—fifty notes of a rich, tight cadenza.

"It's out of tune," said Juniper sadly.

"Nay," said Ayesh. "You know only the common scale. I was playing the thirteen tones of the moon scale. Here's something in the common."

She twisted the ring on the end of the flute. The colored light inside the flute shifted hue. It was now as much blue as green.

Ayesh played a pastoral melody.

"Stop!" said Olf.

Ayesh kept playing.

"I said stop!" The big man hopped down from the wall and strode over to her. "How are we to hear what the goblins are up to while you're playing music!"

Ayesh stopped playing. "One goblin attacks by stealth. But a band of them can't manage that. One goblin will not brave your crossbows, and the lot of them will not attack without screeches and battle cries. You'll hear what needs hearing, music or no."

"Indeed. You know all about goblins, do you?"

"I have killed more goblins than you have seen."

"Have you indeed! Well, I have seen more of the rotters than I would care to number."

"Pity, then, that you did not make a better study of what you saw. I know them well enough to know when I might ignore them for the moment. But by thinking on them at every turn, you give yourself no peace. If truly you know goblins, then you know I speak the truth. To insist on silence only for the sake of being right would mark you an unmastered man." She held out the flute to Juniper. "Care to try?"

"Bah!" said Olf. He made as if to tear a cap from his head, but there was no cap there. He looked about and found that it was already on the ground. "Bah!" he said again, and stalked off.

Ayesh held the flute out again to Juniper.

"But I don't know how to play."

"There's a remedy for that," said Ayesh. She molded the girl's fingers around the keys. "Think of the tune you want to play," she said. "Beginning to end, let it play in your mind."

Juniper closed her eyes and seemed to be thinking a tune. When she opened her eyes, Ayesh said, "Blow here and play."

"But I—"

"Just *play*."

Juniper lifted the flute to her lips, hesitated, and blew a sour note.

"Think the tune!" Ayesh said. "Your mind's all a muddle, girl. Think the tune you mean to play."

Juniper paused, pursed her lips, and blew again.

This time, the first three bars of a song came out, not quite in perfect time, but close enough to make one of the other youths say, "That's 'Red Phlox of Mirtiin'!"

"It is!" said Juniper. "That's what I meant to play! The flute moved my fingers!"

"It's a teaching flute," Ayesh said. "In time, with practice, you'd learn to play on any flute tuned to any scale."

"It's a marvel!" said Ilif.

"It's Oneahn," said Ayesh. She put the flute in her lap. "I've some other things to show you."

As she opened her pack, half the youths inside the wall stood up and stepped close.

"All right!" said Townsman Olf. "The music was bad enough, but I'll not have you drawing these youngsters from their posts. Or do you mean to make it easy for the goblins to overrun us?"

The Bathtown youths slunk back toward their places at the wall. Ayesh went on digging through her pack as if Olf's protest had been nothing but a distant goblin yelp.

"Here," she said. She drew out something that glinted in the firelight.

"Diamond?" said Ilif, his eyes huge.

"As beautiful and as clear, aye, but no diamond was ever as big as this." She handed it to Juniper. "This is a crystal from the Roof of Lights. All the roof was made of such. When the sun shone through that roof, the chamber below was shot through with a million tiny rainbows. That's proof of the *true* Roof of Lights."

"Common glass," muttered Townsman Olf. "Coulda come from anywhere." He threw the last bit of wood onto the fire. "Blast you, Ilif. Next time I tell you to fetch wood, you'll bring me a forest! The rotters need only wait for the fire to die, and then they'll rush us."

"Likely they'll rush sometime, when they think we're weary," said Ayesh.

"Indeed, lady. But these charges of mine, as you see, are green lads and lasses. Some seasoned townsmen and townswomen might fight well in the utter dark, but not these lambs."

"Then there shall be light," said Ayesh, "or haven't you been watching?"

Ayesh blew into the end of the flute. The blue-green glow guttered and died like a candle flame. Then she took out the tinderbox again, spoke her word into it, and with a *whoomp* the air above the box burst into orange fire.

Ayesh said another word to the flame. It shifted to white.

"By Xatta's icy breath," said Olf, and he spoke for the others. None of them, to judge by their expressions, had ever seen white fire before.

Ayesh passed her hand through the flame. "It gives no heat," she said, "but that's light enough for any battle."

The Glittermoon was high overhead, and dawn would not be long in coming. Ayesh, head resting on her pack, had dozed lightly now and then. The campfire had long since died, but the white flame of unsmoking fire had replaced it on top of the piled stones. For all its brilliance, the white flame's light was hypnotic, and it was easy to drift in and out of sleep while watching it.

Suddenly she was awake.

Something had changed.

She listened.

Silence. Not even the flame of unsmoking fire made a sound.

Her body tensed. As she had first drifted off to sleep, she had been aware of the quiet chattering and occasional complaints of the goblins. Now, there was not a sound from them.

Ayesh was on her feet a moment before a twig snapped, a goblin yelped, and a dozen other goblins echoed his yelp as a war cry. More voices joined them.

Ayesh didn't have to look over the edge of the wall to know what was happening. She shook Ilif. Juniper, and those around her, had already been startled awake.

"Here they come!" shouted Olf.

Tull had been dozing inside the wall. He jumped to his feet and turned just in time to shoot a quarrel through the first goblin who vaulted to the top of the barrier.

Not all the youths were quite awake and alert enough to think straight.

"Get your pike up, lass!" Olf shouted.

"Stand away from the wall," Ayesh told another. "You don't want one dropping right on your head!"

Two goblins appeared atop the wall side by side. Olf shot one with his crossbow. The other dodged as a youth tried to spear it with his pike. Two more goblins appeared on either side of the one that dodged.

Ayesh grabbed the pike from the boy's hands and swept all four goblins from the wall.

"Don't worry about making a kill," she told the boy. "Just knock them down, or prick 'em lightly if you must."

"But if I don't kill—"

"Lad, if you spear one good, you'll be stuck with him. You can't do much good with a pike that's got a goblin wriggling on the end. Keep 'em busy and let the crossbows do the killing."

A few goblins spilled over one side of the wall and dashed for the center. The black blades of their daggers looked like long, dirty talons as they rushed the pikemen.

"Pikes up!" Ayesh commanded, but the inexperienced fighters backed away from this immediate threat.

"Those of you with knives," shouted Olf, cranking his crossbow, "get in front! Defend the pikes!"

But only one youth obeyed. It was Juniper. Though she held her knife awkwardly, the glitter of the blade was enough to slow the goblins a step. Another youth found his courage and advanced to stand beside Juniper.

Meanwhile, the pikes had fallen back so far that the wall now swarmed with goblins. They piled over the side like rats.

Ayesh grabbed a pike. She kicked her way through two goblins and stepped forward to sweep a dozen more from the wall.

From the corner of her eye, she saw a black blade sweep toward her. She sidestepped. The blade missed, but the goblin took another swipe at her as still another goblin charged.

Ayesh knocked more goblins from the wall, dodged the blade, and kicked its owner. But she stepped right into the second goblin's charge.

The black goblin blade sank into her leg.

Fire shot through her.

"Gods!" she shouted. She'd only felt such pain once before, when a marsh viper had bitten her.

And with the strength that comes from pain, she grabbed the throat of the goblin who had stabbed her. She crushed his windpipe.

"Their blades are poisoned!" she warned, and then regretted it, for these young fighters were timid enough to begin with.

But Olf shouted, "Of course the blades are poisoned. Goblins always poison their blades!"

Her leg was trembling as she kicked the life out of the next goblin. Goblins always poisoned their blades? Never, not in the years of Goblin Wars in Oneah, not in her years of traveling since, had Ayesh once encountered goblins who did so. Goblins poisoned each other's food in their warrens, and young goblins were even taught to hold food in their throats, awaiting the first tingles or swellings of poison before they swallowed. But poisoned blades required constant special care to keep them from rusting. What goblin had the patience?

But goblins were not the same in all places, no more than humans were.

How it burned! What poison was this?

If the fighters had been timid before, at least they were no more timid now. But then, they had already known that a mere scratch of the goblin daggers would bring pain.

And death? Would she die?

Three more goblins fell clutching at quarrels in their chests. Juniper and the boy beside her rushed the closest goblin, and with more luck than skill they wounded him. He shrieked and backed up.

The pikemen advanced enough to keep more goblins from coming over the wall.

Three more quarrels found their targets.

Ayesh felt her whole body begin to shake. She could hardly stand.

One more goblin came over the wall. He was wearing red, fingerless gloves.

Ayesh's head swam. She sat down. Hard.

The goblin with red gloves was grinning. It ran right for her. "*Min kli moina tlit ekleyla jla!*" It was what Ayesh had said when she had killed the two goblins at dusk. And spared this one.

The world grew foggy.

Let me master my strength before I die!

Ayesh bit her tongue. She tasted blood. The pain gave her something to focus on besides the fire of the poison. Her mind crystallized. She saw clearly enough to control the red-gloved hand that thrust a blade at her heart.

She turned the wrist. Just so.

There was a pop. A howl.

"A fool was I ever to suffer a goblin to live," she said. And the last thing Ayesh did before she passed out was break the goblin's neck.

CHAPTER

4

AYESH DREAMED OF PRINCES AND TALKING donkeys and peacocks with fire in their tails. She dreamed of islands that rose and fell and queens who were too beautiful to look upon and sailing ships that could fly. She dreamed the smell of sulfur, and all through her dreaming, a voice spoke to her.

"In the days when dwarves yet ruled in the Crimson Peaks and the cities of Icatia rose nearly as high as the clouds, there lived a dwarven captain who was very strict with his three sons. Of his first two sons not a slighting word was ever said, but his third son was known to all the other dwarves as 'Butter-Between,' for they said there was naught but butter between his ears. . . ."

Ayesh dreamed of a dwarf who won the hand of an Icatian princess. She dreamed of winged maidens, of a white knight trapped for a hundred years within a wall of ice. She dreamed of a river merman who fell in love with a farmgirl. Ayesh felt a great thirst. She longed to wake and drink, but she couldn't. She went on dreaming and dreaming, and the voice went on guiding her dreams.

"Pipi-ku was a slender stick of a boy whose master, a

carver, hardly fed him. The boy had a love for the air and
the light, and his eyes were so often raised to the sky that
his master was astounded whenever he could get any
work out of him. Now one day when he was gazing at the
heavens, what should Pipi-ku see but a mesa pegasus.
Pipi-ku had never seen so beautiful a creature, and in a
loud voice he called up to it. . . ."

Tapestry wolves leaped from the walls to devour evil
governors. A fisherman caught three great treasures in his
net: a jar, a needle, and a comb. A griffin tricked a fairy
queen and later paid the price.

"The sage Yerti-yertees, having said everything he
could think of to dissuade the young man without having
done so, went in secret to the old witch. . . ."

And always, through every story, the sulfurous smell of
rotten eggs pervaded. . . .

"Water," Ayesh croaked.

"Aha! Aha! She wakes!"

Ayesh opened her eyes, but they felt dry, and there was
a film over them. Her vision was blurry. She blinked. A
very large man was standing over her.

There was something in her mouth. She turned her
head and spit out a leaf.

"Laik, come! She wakes and asks for water! Bring some!"

"I'm coming," boomed another voice.

Ayesh blinked again. She sat up.

"No, no!" said the deeper voice. "Lie back, woman.
That's not sleep you wake from, but death."

"Laik, you exaggerate your skill!" said the first man,
laughing.

Ayesh rubbed her eyes. Tears came to them, reluc-
tantly, for she was dry as dust inside. Her vision cleared.
In front of her stood a roundish white-haired man, the
owner of the dream voice. Beside him, holding a waterskin, was another old man who was every bit as large as
the first. But while the first was all soft and white like
dough, the second's wrinkled face and hands were
tanned, and there was muscle in his big arms, not fat.

"Lie down! Lie down!" urged the muscular one.

Ayesh took the waterskin from him and took a swallow

before she tasted how bitter it was. Her mouth puckered. She coughed and shoved the waterskin away.

"I want water! What is that?"

"Tincture of beetlebalm and cindergrass tea. Have another swallow."

"I want water!"

"But this is—"

"Water! I'll drink nothing else!"

"All right. Very well. I'm only looking out for *you*," the old man said. He brought her a different waterskin. This time, Ayesh sniffed before drinking. The water smelled of sulfur. She wrinkled her nose but drank. She must be in a place with a hot spring.

Her arms were bare, she realized. She was wearing some sort of robe—a single piece of fabric, it seemed, with no sleeves. The sunburst tattoos on her arms trembled as she held the waterskin and drank some more.

"Enough." He took the water from her. "More than that, and you'll be sick. Now put this fresh leech leaf to your tongue and lie down."

Ayesh pushed away the offered leaf and remained sitting. She looked around the room. She could see her quilted jacket and leggings draped on a chair. And there on a table was her pack, open, with all its contents spread out. The tinderbox, the flute, the crystal from the Roof of Lights, the slender volumes of verse, and Master Hata's sash.

"My things!"

She swung herself from the cot and stood up, and her leg throbbed in protest. She looked down to see, among the tattooed reeds and grasses on her legs, a gash stitched closed with black thread.

"You ought not to stand so soon!"

"Yes, traveler. Lay you down and rest."

"You've been through my things!"

"You slept, traveler. We could not ask your permission."

"That is a fine excuse!"

"Forgive us our curiosity. Travelers come our way so rarely anymore. And as we expected you to die . . . "

Ayesh sat down on the cot. "The goblin," she said, remembering. "I took a poisoned blade."

"That you did," said the one who had given her water. "Now, take not so much upon yourself at once. Lie down. Let us introduce ourselves. I am Elder Laik, and this is my brother, Elder Alik."

"Good morrow to you," said Alik, jiggling as he bowed.

"The girl, Juniper," Ayesh said, remembering. "She spoke of you."

"Did she?" said Alik. "Well, she spoke of you as well. Did she remember your name aright? Are you Ash of Oneah?"

"Ayesh," she said.

Alik clapped his hands. "I'll have some stories from you, then! I have many stories of Oneah, but none yet to come from the lips of an Oneahn! Will you tell me some?" Alik gestured at the wall behind Ayesh. "I should like to write them down."

Ayesh turned, then blinked.

The wall was lined with books. *Shelved* and *stacked* and *packed* with books. "A library."

"I have a passion for recording stories, you see," said Alik. "They are the stuff of my profession."

Groggy as she still was, Ayesh felt her heart leap. Ah, to have her memories of Oneah recorded in books, in a library such as this! None had ever before made the offer to write down, to accurately preserve her words. Ayesh had sometimes thought to write her memories herself, but who would keep the book she made? Who would treasure it as it must be treasured?

Elder Alik, perhaps.

"Juniper, by the way, was quite interested in you," said Laik. "She's the sort of girl who ever dreams of foreign lands. If she could have, she'd have stayed to help nurse you. But she is gone with Olf, Tull, Rav, and the youngsters. They brought you to us for healing, then hurried to see if the ships would still be waiting."

"There are but two days of trading each month," said Alik. "Trade is slow. Not even when Nul Divva was in its prime were we on the great trade routes. Only bold sailors and venturers ever dared these shores."

"Were others wounded? Among the traders?"

"Not by poison, else you would see them here in a cot beside yours."

"Olf said you are quite a goblin fighter," said Alik. "From him, that's high praise indeed."

Ayesh remembered: she had upbraided Olf for not knowing goblins well. Yet she was the one who hadn't known to expect poison. She felt the blood rise in her face.

"Come," said Laik. "After a sleep of two days, I guess you'll have an appetite."

Only when she began to eat did she know how hungry she was. The bean soup they set before her in a copper bowl was richly spiced. The salad of greens she did not recognize was a welcome change from the hardtack and gruel of her ocean voyage.

"Good, is it not?" said round Alik. "Laik is a master herbalist, and his skills tend toward the kitchen as much as toward the infirmary."

"Healing is the easier skill," said Laik. "Inventing a good meal from the stocks one finds in Bathtown, now that's a challenge!"

"Have more, have more," said Alik, refilling Ayesh's bowl.

"I did not expect to find a library in Bathtown," Ayesh said.

"And you won't," said Alik. "That's no library in the other room. It's a few books salvaged from our flight. We couldn't bring much."

"From where?"

"From Nul Divva," Laik said. "Our exile was a hurried one. We were practitioners of the Twin Arts for the Merchant Lords in Nul Divva. Then came the revolutions. The Merchant Lords were dispossessed, and the trade in winterspice was all but ended. Those who meant to take over the mines managed, in their war, to cave them in. Hardly any winterspice comes along this trade route any longer."

"Twin Arts?" Ayesh asked.

"Why," said Laik, waving a meaty hand, "the very ones we practiced on you. Healing and distraction. My herbs healed you of the poison, and Alik kept dark thoughts from your mind."

"Not that some distraction mightn't be dark," said Alik. "It depends."

"Distraction?" Ayesh said. "Do you mean the stories you told while I was sleeping?"

"The Twin Arts are what people long for in their hearts," said Laik. "I heal the sick and wounded, that they may live a while longer."

"And I distract them from the knowledge," Alik said, "that healing will one day fail. If we dwell upon death, we shall succumb to despair. But my stories keep the sick or wounded from despairing. Aye, and not only the sick and wounded. The hale and hardy will die anon. I tell stories that they shall not think on it."

Ayesh's spoon hovered above her bowl. "Is that what you mean to make of the things I would tell you of Oneah?"

"I'll make nothing of them save what they are," said Alik. "Stories."

Ayesh shook her head. "I tell of Oneah, and play the music of her court, not that people might be distracted. I tell the story that Oneah might live. The Court of a Thousand Thousands was not the stuff of tales and fables. It was *real*. If you write down what I would tell you, you must preserve it as history."

"History, aye. I'll write it down as such, but it makes little difference, traveler. Histories and fantasies, prattlings and parables, religious visions and utter lies—I put them all in the same book. I tell them from memory and change them as I tell them. Thus are they improved."

"Improved!" Ayesh threw her spoon into the bowl. "Corrupted, you mean! I heard the story you told to Juniper about the Roof of Lights. It was a tower, you said, where princes contested on the ramparts."

"Aye, and she said you knew a different version. I want to hear what you say, traveler. I want to know your version."

"It's not a version! I wrestled beneath the Roof of Lights. It was a real place. I don't want you to record the truth of it so that you can alter it in your retelling. If you are to write down aught from me, you must preserve the truth!"

Softly, and with a gentle smile, Alik said, "Preserve it for how long?"

"Forever! Is that not what books are for?"

Alik set his own spoon aside. "Come. I'll show you something."

In the room with the cot and bookshelves Alik took down a heavy volume. The leather cover of the tome looked brittle. "Tell me, Ayesh. What do you know of the Lord Cedric Camman, the prime minister who served Emperor Henry Joseph in the lands of Icatia?"

"What all know. It's a story known in all countries."

"Why is it so widely known?"

"It is instructive."

"Tell me."

"Lord Camman sought to serve his own ends, rather than those of the crown, when Henry Joseph was wounded in the Battle of Bright Plain. His desire to extend the powers of parliament so concentrated his attentions that he did not prepare well to prosecute the war with the orcs. In the end, the general who could best have aided him, Lord Silvermane, was executed by Camman's command. He said Silvermane was a royalist, which no doubt he was. But the opponent Camman killed was the best defender against the orcs. Icatia fell."

"And the lesson learned thereby?"

"That the lust for power brings blindness."

"Much the same version was told in Nul Divva, but there the lesson was 'Greed for the copper today loses the silver tomorrow.' Well, that was before the revolution. The rebels cast the lesson as, 'Let the scorpion sting the asp.' That is, kill not your enemies, but turn them against each other. From Orvadish sailors, I have heard the story summed as defending the divine right of kings."

"Different ears hear a different story," said Ayesh. Indeed, she knew this too well, for she had often heard distorted tales of Oneah. "But however people take the meaning, the history remains the same."

"Indeed." The spine of the book crackled as Elder Alik opened to the middle pages. Bits of brown paper, like tiny leaves, fell to the floor. "This is a history of Sarpadia. It is, as you see, a very old volume, a book that crumbles each time I open it. It was written by a scribe in Windenby, who lived to see the fall of the Five Empires."

Carefully, Alik turned the brown pages. "Here," he said. His white finger rested on the middle of the page. "What name do you read here?"

Ayesh squinted. The ink was faded, and the brown paper so dark that she scarcely could see the letters shaped in an archaic hand. "Lady . . . Lady Margaret Ellsworth, Prime Minister."

"Lady Margaret Ellsworth, the Prime Minister of Icatia. As these pages make clear, Henry Joseph was served most ably and loyally by *her*, not by Camman. What is more, power was well balanced between crown and parliament. There was no great dissension betwixt them."

"But the history I was taught—"

"Is invention. Lord Cedric Camman and Silvermane are both the creations of fancy. Yet is it not a good story, to be told again and again as if it were truth?"

Ayesh stared at the page. "So even written history is betrayed."

Alik smiled. "And how not? Look upon this brittle page. Breathe upon it, and it turns to dust. Books burn, and whole libraries are lost to time. Where, in the chaotic lands that are the Sarpadian continent, where would you go to find the library that contains the sister volumes to this tome? No, true history passes. But people believe the history that makes the better story. No story can be wrong, only more memorable or less."

"No!" Ayesh limped to the table where her pack and possessions were laid out. "The Five Empires of Sarpadia are dust and sand, but look you here!" She held up her crystal. "This is a piece of the Roof of Lights!" She showed him the book of verse. "Rhymes and aphorisms by honored poets of the Court of a Thousand Thousands!" She held up the sash. "This was worn by the master of my school! And what would you say of the flute, of the tunes I play? All of this is Oneah. All of this is real! Can no one preserve these things? Can no one write a true history that will endure?"

"These things are props more than evidence. They can support a good tale, be it truth or fancy. The truth has no lasting home."

"Then what of *me*?" Ayesh said. She cast aside the robe they had dressed her in. She stood naked before him and indicated the reed and grass tattoos on her legs. "Here dwells the truth of Oneah!" She grabbed her clothes. "The tattoos on my body are more than prop. I lived there. I was of Oneah!"

"Do I say I doubt you?"

"But you deny the importance of history, of truth!"

"I say only that it does not last. No more shall your tattoos last forever. But let us not dwell on that. I mark such reeds upon your legs that I wonder, have you ever heard the story of the reed and the oak?"

Ayesh covered the reeds and grasses with her quilted leggings, then hid the sunbursts on her arms, the stars and moon on her torso, beneath her jacket. "Oneah *was*! I was a wrestler of the Court of a Thousand Thousands! I contested beneath the Roof of Lights!" She put on her soft-soled shoes. "I fought goblins with the Dance That Breaks Bones! I am Istini Ayesh ni Hata Kan. But if you will not tell my story only as it truly was, then I shall not tell it to you. What does it matter? You are right. All comes to dust, even the stories themselves."

And I have nothing left to live for.

The realization sank into her belly like ice.

The old man gestured gently with his hands. "Soft, soft, Oneahn. I do not doubt you. I say that details do not matter, only the essence of stories."

"You would turn Oneah into a fairy tale!"

"As a fairy tale, it might somewise endure."

"No! Oneah was no fairy tale, nor shall it be! If it may not be preserved, *as it was*, then let it die!" Ayesh began stuffing her belongings into her pack.

"All that lives changes in time. . . ."

"I know," she said bitterly. "Year by year have I come to know it more certainly. Memory dies. Even books die."

Ayesh checked the pouch that contained her coins. They were few, but all were there.

Laik appeared in the doorway. "Alik, see how you have alarmed her! She must rest!"

Ayesh slung her pack onto her back and, limping, slipped through the narrow gap between Laik's crossed arms and the doorway. "Laik, what do I owe you for the healing?"

"Nothing," said Alik behind her. "We thought you might repay us with your tales. Your *history*."

There was one silver among the coppers. Ayesh put it on the table. "Oneah is not for sale. Let the honorable dead have their rest."

By the front door, a crossbow rested, cranked and cocked. She stepped over it carefully, then opened the door of their house.

"The poison still corrupts your blood," said Laik. "Stay and rest. Let me tend to you until you are—"

Ayesh closed the heavy door behind her, so she did not hear the last of his words. The front of the door, she noticed, was painted with two hands—one black, one white, for the Twin Arts, she guessed.

She stood looking at the narrow street, at the large houses that badly needed whitewash. The shutters on some of the houses were crooked, and a third of the windows were broken and boarded up. From the cobblestone street, some stones were missing. In the bright noonday sun, these details stood out all the more. This once had been a great trading town. Now it was crumbling.

Alik was right, damn him. Things decay. All things come at last to dust. Even Oneah, the Seven Cities with their thousands of sun shrines, the solar observatories, grand court, and the Roof of Lights . . . all of that was in ruins, and even the traditions of the Oneahn wrestlers would vanish with time. She had been a fool, pledging to keeping it alive in memory.

To keep the memories alive, that was the lie she had lived. And it still had the power to trick her, to seduce her.

The truth was this: She must die. She owed that to the wrestlers who had died defending the Roof of Lights.

There are yet things to live for! cried an inner voice.

No, she thought. *Be silent. It's time to die.*
Live to keep the memories alive!
No, she thought again. *That's a lie. I will not live a lie.*
And if the voice of the lie would not shut up, she knew a way to drown it.

CHAPTER
5

AYESH FELT THE STARES OF THE PEOPLE ON THE street. Bathtown, which once had seen many strangers and summer caravans coming through to trade, was now a town unaccustomed to outsiders.

She walked up and down the streets looking for a sign that would indicate a tavern. At last she stopped to ask directions and found that she had passed the tavern three times. If there had ever been a sign, there was none now.

When she entered, the three men talking at a table fell silent. It took Ayesh a moment to adjust her eyes to the darkness.

"Yes?" said a woman's voice from the shadows.

"Who is the master of this tavern?"

"No master," said the woman. "But I am mistress."

Ayesh said, "I want some wine and a wineskin."

"Seven copper, that would be."

Ayesh checked her pouch again. Five coppers. She shook her head. "That's high." Actually, it wasn't a bad price. The woman must be out of practice when it came to fleecing travelers.

"Wineskins come dear," the tavern mistress said. "I can

give you a jar instead. Holds more wine, anyway. That would be five copper."

There might be a better bargain to strike, but there was no point to saving coppers now. Ayesh agreed to the price.

The spherical jar was awkward to carry. The neck was too short to hold with one hand. Ayesh trudged up the mountainside cradling the jar in her arms. Snow lingered here and there, and twisted trees grew only in the crevices where they were sheltered from the wind.

After a while, she stopped and surveyed the town below. Some said that Nul Divva, on the other side of the mountains, was the end of the earth, the most remote human outpost in the world. Ayesh had never seen Nul Divva and now would never see it.

But Bathtown might stand as well for the last human habitation in the world. It looked appropriately forlorn. Ayesh could see that the roofs needed repair. A few were so bare of thatch that they must have been abandoned years ago. Only the town's stockade, an outer defense of sharpened poles, was well maintained. All but the most necessary defenses were falling to ruins.

The town lay at the edge of Boiling Lake. One side of the lake was still locked in ice. From the shore nearest the town, great clouds of steam rose from the hot springs.

Fire and ice and the end of the world. Fire and ice and decay.

Ayesh unstopped the jar and took a drink. The Prophet Eziir was not Oneahn, but Ayesh had heard his aphorisms so often in her travels that she sometimes confused them with the teachings of her Master Hata. They thought alike, in many ways.

Wine is the bane of reason. Those were the words of the Prophet Eziir. And Master Hata had taught that the first of the Seven Virtues was reason.

Well, there was no purpose to honoring the Seven Virtues any longer. All that was virtuous had crumbled with Oneah. Ayesh herself should have died with it, twenty years ago, when she was hardly more than a girl.

She drank deeply. The wine was tart, and like all things of Bathtown, it tasted of both spice and sulfur. Such flavors did not mingle well. But she kept drinking.

Drink until you can drink no more, she told herself. Ayesh would soon be dust, as all the grandeur she remembered was dust already.

All these years of telling Oneah's story, she had lived a lie. She had wanted to keep Oneah alive in memory. Why? Because she had failed Oneah, failed the traditions of the wrestlers, failed herself.

Keeping the memory alive had been a reason to live, she'd told herself. But now she saw truly. She had no right to life. She had lived twenty years too long.

No fruit is so bitter or so sweet as truth. Master Hata had said that. She knew the bitterness well enough. But she tasted nothing sweet.

She looked one last time at the town. Then she stopped the jar and stood. The inner voice was muted now. Soon the wine would drown it altogether. Her leg throbbed, but the wine was good for that, too. The pain was growing distant.

She continued up the trackless mountainside. Somewhere in these mountains she would find goblin caves aplenty. She would break necks and drink wine until there was no more wine to drink. And she would keep breaking necks, one after another, until the gray-skinned skulkers over-numbered her at last.

That would bring things full circle. That would bring everything to its proper end.

The day was long. The sun curved north as well as west. Summer days in these northern latitudes seemed to go on forever.

Ayesh, still cradling the wine jar, covered a lot of ground. There was no trail to follow up and down the steep slopes, but nor were there obstacles, save for the fields of boulders. As she walked, she crossed more and more such fields of fallen rock.

And as she walked, she sometimes caught the scent of

goblin caves—the stench of carrion and offal. The smell grew stronger, and she could feel her heart pounding in her chest.

Ayesh, you may yet turn back.

Be still! she answered herself. *Turn back to what? This has long been my destiny.*

At last she descended into a ravine where the stench was almost overwhelming.

"All right, you skulkers, you rot-mouthed murderers," she said under her breath. "I'm coming for you."

She followed the ravine to where the ground leveled off and opened to a shallow lake. Goblin stench fouled the black water. A few trees fringed the lake, sheltered in part by the steep slopes on all sides and protected from the wind even more by the enormous boulders that had come to rest there.

Stopping to listen, Ayesh heard only the wind in the trees. Goblins lived very close by. Why didn't she sense any lurking behind the boulders or among the trees? The lake shore should be acrawl with them, from the smell of it.

She walked to the edge of the lake. The stink made her gag. But where were the goblins?

When she had gone a little further around the lake, she looked up. The mountain slope here was almost vertical, and from bottom to top it was riddled with goblin-sized holes.

The sight made her heart sink. For all her determination to face her old enemy, the thought of them pouring out of those holes, a gray flood of smelly leather-skinned bodies, made her breath catch in her throat.

See? You want to live!

She unstopped the jar and took a drink. Then she wet her fingers with the wine and smeared it under her nose. The wine's scent was not pleasant, but it was much better than the stifling slaughterhouse smell of the caves.

Why weren't they coming for her? They must know she was here. Even from inside the caves, surely they had spotted her by now.

She took another drink, then set the jar down. She took off her pack and set it next to the jar. She'd have no more need for her things. Better to fight completely unencumbered.

Something moved beneath the trees to one side.

Ayesh spun.

She squinted into the shadows. She could see nothing there. She waited a long time, and there was no more movement.

She looked again at the caves. If they would not come to her, she would go to them. She picked up the jar for one more swallow of wine.

"If I must come to you, then I'll show you who it is who comes!" she said. She took the first stance, closed her eyes, and rooted herself in the earth. Then, with perfect balance on the uneven ground, she began to step and turn and strike and punch the air, advancing toward the caves, dancing the Dance That Breaks Bones.

"*Eehey! Ayeen Istini Ayesh ni Hata Kan, e na aihana mey aililla nawli e aifoi li nassa ni kraleen!*" she shouted in Oneahn. "I am Istini Ayesh ni Hata Kan, and I come to snap necks and crush the breath from throats! I come to stop hearts with a punch!" She punched the air. "I am death! Come to me, ye goblins who would die! Come, that I may open the maw of never ending emptiness and cast ye in! Come, that ye may die and die and die!"

She repeated her death invitation in the goblin dialect she knew. "*Ounyit, da teyey ekmigyla kofk ke kofk ke kofk!*" *Come out, that you all shall die and die and die!*

There was a chatter of goblin voices from inside the caves, but still no goblins poured out of the holes.

But they would come, Ayesh's stammering heart told her. At any moment, they would come.

Closer and closer, she danced.

When she stopped, she was close enough to see black eyes glittering inside the nearest caves.

She clenched her fists. Her arms were rigid with fear and righteous anger. She tried to focus her mind. She must master her feelings if she were to fight well, to fight with quickness and surprise, as she had always done.

Her heart hammered. The wine made it hard to center herself.

"Come out!" she shouted. *"Ounyit!"*

In the shadows, the goblins muttered. Then one said, *"Mi. Ounyahk."* No. You come in.

Goblin laughter followed. It was like the sound of someone choking. Other goblins took up the invitation. *"Ounyahk! Ounyahk!"*

The mouths of the caves were smoke blackened. Just a few feet from the entrance, the shadows were as deep as the emptiness between stars.

"No," said Ayesh. "I'll murder you in daylight, thanks. Come out. Oh, you rot eaters, come out!"

Something big moved in the forest behind Ayesh. She whirled.

Nothing there.

Behind her, the goblins were laughing. "Come in, come in," one invited in the Voda tongue. "Come be safe with us. Yes, it be safe in here. Come!"

Ayesh picked up a rock, turned toward the caves, and flung it with all her strength. A goblin inside yelped, and the others laughed. *"Ounyahk!"*

"You'll come to me." She looked down at her pack and wine jar. Ordinarily, goblins would have darted out to make off with these by now. "You'll come to me, because I have treasures. Lots of pretties. But some of you, many of you, will have to die to get them." She repeated it all in their language.

She turned her back and walked back to her belongings. The goblins chattered, and some kept calling, *"Ounyahk!"* but none pursued her. None tried to dash from the caves to snatch her pack before she got to it.

"Stones from Heaven!" she said. She sat down. Never before had she found goblins so shy. Something had them badly spooked.

She looked into the trees again. A bear? But surely so many goblins would not cower from a bear. More likely they would swarm and kill it. Besides, would a bear stay concealed like this?

Not a bear. A stone giant, perhaps.

She squinted into the shadows. She was prepared to die, but if she died fighting aught but goblins, then even her final gesture would be without meaning.

"Go away," she mumbled. "Whatever you are, clear out. This is between me and them."

As the sun skimmed the southwestern horizon, Ayesh ventured into the trees to gather firewood. She heard nothing, and she saw no obvious tracks on the carpet of pine needles.

Whatever had been here was apparently gone.

In a ring of stones, she built a fire. She piled on the wood so that the flames leapt high. This was more than a campfire. It was a taunt aimed at the goblins. Here she was, at their very door. *Come and get me,* she thought. *Come and die, you maggot-eating rotters.*

She opened her tinderbox, kindled the unsmoking fire, and charged the flute. She turned to watch the caves, though as the sky darkened, she could soon see nothing beyond the light of her fire.

It didn't matter. She'd know they were coming by the sound of them, by the smell of them.

She played a song, one that had words to it. She wished she could sing as she played. Wondrous though it was, the flute was not quite so wondrous as to let her both play and sing.

It was a wrestler's song that she played, a song that called for strength, for grace, for beauty in the ring. Victory or defeat were not what mattered, but the struggle of Powers, the flow of moments, the endurance of the Now.

She stopped playing.

Outside of the ring, it did matter who won and who lost. For Oneah, in spite of its beauty, in spite of the strength and grace of its defenders, had drowned under the goblin tide. The unity of victory and defeat, that was not a lie. One was necessary for the other. But there had been no beauty in the defeat of Oneah. There was no beauty in the victory of goblins.

What was true beneath the Roof of Lights, what was true within Oneah, was not true in the wider world.

More than a civilization had fallen in the Goblin War. A reality had been tested and destroyed.

Ayesh extinguished the flute, but she didn't bother to

rekindle the flame of unsmoking fire. Instead, she drank wine and watched the flames die in her ordinary fire. Then, eyelids growing heavy, she watched the embers fade as she drank the last of her wine.

She slept.

She woke suddenly, her heart hammering, though she did not know what had awakened her. A sound?

The stars over her head were brilliant. The Glittermoon was right overhead, but the Mistmoon had not yet risen. All around her was blackness.

And five or six large silhouettes blotted out the stars. The creatures were too big to be goblins. Much too big.

One leaned close to her. It said, *"Maynoonzhanrax."* And it moved closer still. Fingers closed on her wrist.

"Eeyeh!" Ayesh cried. Her shout made the creature flinch. Ayesh sprang, tucked, and rolled. She somersaulted backwards from the ring of creatures.

"Maynoonnaen," rumbled another voice. Low laughter.

She stood. Her wounded leg throbbed, and her muscles were stiff with sleep. And with wine, she thought ruefully.

The creatures were harder to see now that they were not silhouetted against the stars. Black shapes against the black mountains were all but invisible. Ayesh would have to rely on hearing, on the *feel* of their approach.

There was no sound from near the fire pit. They had not moved. They all still stood before her. She might back quietly away . . .

From behind her came a booming laugh. *"Qurraxpoylannaen-payanayeennartoonstasee!"* The accent was strange, and her sleep and wine-addled brain took a moment to catch up to the sounds and sort them out. *"Qurrax, poylan naen payanayeen nartoon stasee!"* She knew this language. *Qurrax, I've not seen you jump like that before!*

That told her three things: these were minotaurs; there were more of them than the ones near the fire pit; and they could all see in mere starlight. She had suspected, in Hurloon, that minotaurs saw in the dark. Now she was sure.

"Well, she's slippery as an otter," said another in their booming language. "For all I know she has an otter's teeth!"

The laugh came again.

"Be not so amused that she escapes you," said a very low voice. "Tiaraya, put down your trident. I mean for her to be caught, not killed."

"I'm minded of what Qurrax said. She may have teeth."

From the first voice came laughter again.

Ayesh almost spoke in their own tongue, but thought better of it. In Voda, she said, "Who are you? What do you want with me?"

"A good question," said the one who laughed. He spoke in Voda. "Zhanrax, what do we want with her?"

"My interests," said the low voice in the minotaur language, "are scientific."

Laughter again. "That one word says much, Zhanrax. I never knew you to harbor such interests!"

Two of the minotaurs snorted. With humor? Derision?

Ayesh felt hot breath on the back of her neck. The breath had the scent of wet grass, the perfume of flowers.

She ducked, then sprang forward. Her shoulder slammed against a boulder she couldn't see. She stood, aching.

"Almost had her," said a new voice.

How could minotaurs, thick-hoofed creatures that they were, move so silently?

A hand closed on Ayesh's shoulder. "Got her."

That's what you think, Ayesh thought. She put her hands on the massive wrist, turned the hand just so . . .

There wasn't the *pop* and the howl of pain Ayesh expected. The minotaur's wrist bent, but the grip only tightened.

Well, she had never made a study of minotaur anatomy. She'd never planned on having to wrestle one.

With two hands, now, the creature pulled Ayesh close. Ayesh let her opponent pull her close, and then . . .

"Eeyeh!" Ayesh shouted. She slammed her heel down hard, trying to aim at the delicate bones above the hoof.

She missed.

The grip did not lessen, and Ayesh felt pain shooting

up her leg. She had bruised her heel. The hoof was as hard as stone.

She aimed another kick at the minotaur's knee.

Her captor grunted and relaxed its grip. But the knee had given too easily. Minotaur knees were jointed backwards like an animal's. The minotaur didn't fall, but Ayesh nonetheless wriggled free.

Again, laughter from the one who had spoken first.

"Phyrrax, be you sober," rumbled the deep voice. "I can scarce hear my thoughts for all your laughter." Then it said, "Wellyraya, use the net."

Ayesh didn't like the sound of that.

She put her hands before her, and she sprinted.

She tripped. She got up again.

She ran right into a pair of woolly arms, but she pulled free and ran on.

She tripped a second time in the darkness.

The net descended as she tried to stand.

Many hands held her. She tried to kick, to punch. But they had her. And with stout ropes, they tied her. They hobbled her feet. Strong arms pulled her up.

She could walk, but not kick. She was led by three ropes: one ahead and one on either side.

"To the halls," said the deep voice. "And mind that she doesn't fall. I don't think she can see in the dark."

They began to march her through the blackness.

CHAPTER
6

HER CAPTORS MARCHED AYESH OUT OF THE valley and along a ridge. There, with the sky turning from black to deep purple, she could clearly see a sharp enough silhouette to know that these minotaurs were not like the ones she had known in the Hurloon. For one thing, they were bigger.

Her heel was badly bruised and tender. That's what came of bad aim. She had stamped with all her strength on a hoof as hard and senseless as stone.

As the sky grayed toward dawn, Ayesh could see the great clouds of breath that steamed from the minotaurs' massive heads.

Thinking about the hardness of their hooves, Ayesh couldn't understand how these minotaurs moved so quietly. When she had been among the minotaurs of the Hurloons, their stone chambers within the mountain had echoed with the clatter of hooves. And outside, on the mountain trails, the minotaurs had clomped along as noisily as any horse. No, *louder* than any horse, for the feet of minotaurs were the size of helmets. How could a minotaur be stealthy?

Before long, it was light enough for Ayesh to see the answer to this question. The minotaurs wore shoes.

Or, one might say, they wore grain sacks upon their feet, for that's how the shoes appeared to Ayesh. They were made of a course-woven fabric, like burlap, and tied with leather thongs. The soles were trimmed with fur, which muffled sound.

In the dark, she hadn't known how many minotaurs there were. Now she could see that she was marched in the middle of a large column. There were a dozen minotaurs before her and a dozen more behind, plus the two that flanked her, holding the ropes.

The more she could see of them, the more she could tell that they were distinct from Hurloon minotaurs. Their clothes were finer and more varied than the red woolen kilts of the Hurloon. Some did wear kilts and shirts in the Hurloon style, but of fabrics that might have been cotton or silk. So these were minotaurs who traded, since neither silk nor cotton could be cultivated in these far northern climes. But what did they trade? And with whom? Not with the people of Bathtown, and presumably not with Nul Divva.

Hurloon minotaurs armed themselves with great axes. There were some of those in the hands of these minotaurs as well—with axe heads as big as shovels. But some held tridents instead. At each minotaur's hip hung a leather strap. A sling. And the leather bags fastened next to these must carry stones. If she was guessing aright, then these minotaurs were precise soldiers. Any barbarian could carry a sling and use whatever stones were handy as missiles. But a soldier who wanted precision would carry stones all of one size, so that every throw was like every other.

The Hurloon minotaurs were great fighters, but their traditions placed more weight on singing and storytelling than on military campaigns and tactics. Clearly, these minotaurs were unlike the Hurloon.

Yet in other ways, these were no different from the minotaurs Ayesh knew. Ritual scarring had tattooed the creatures' faces and horns in labyrinthine patterns. Capping the horns were metal ornaments—some silver, some gold.

There was something odd about the hands of these minotaurs—it took Ayesh a little while to see what it was. Like the Hurloon, these minotaurs had short, black-tipped fingers and no thumbs. Or, rather, they had many thumbs and no fingers. The digits were all opposed. Was it any wonder that Ayesh had struggled to control the grip of such hands? The arrangement of bones was a mystery to her. Human and goblin wrists would snap when turned too far inward. Not so, the flexible wrists of minotaurs.

Their wrists were not their only anatomical advantage in a fight. Like birds or cattle, minotaurs had backward-bending knees. Kick, and the knees would give, not break.

But what was it about their hands? At last, she realized what was strange. These minotaurs had just four digits. There were four-fingered minotaurs among the Hurloon as well, but they were the exception. Most Hurloon had five fingers.

With a jerk, Ayesh came to the end of her rope.

Without any signal she had seen, the column had halted.

"What—"

The minotaur with the lead rope turned and signaled her to be silent. For a long time, the column stood unmoving.

Their nostrils were flared, Ayesh noticed.

Ayesh sniffed. She smelled nothing but the damp scent of tundra and a faint whiff of pine.

The broad-shouldered minotaur in the lead was a head taller than the others. She guessed it was a male, but with minotaurs it was always hard to know until they addressed each other. To speak a sentence in their language, you had to reveal the gender of both subject and object.

The big minotaur walked silently back down the column, signaling with his hands to each minotaur in turn. He pointed now and then at features of the landscape ahead. Then he made a peculiar sign, making a circle in the air and jerking his hand down. The motion reminded Ayesh of casting a snare and pulling it closed.

Without a sound, the column melted away, fanning out around the ridge line ahead. Only Ayesh and the three minotaurs holding her ropes remained behind.

Some of the minotaurs disappeared over the ridge, but

Ayesh could still see some of the others where they crouched and readied their slings.

For the space of a few breaths, they all awaited a signal.

Ayesh could not see the leader, but she knew when he had given his silent signal. All the minotaurs stood, and they whirled the slings.

The stones took flight.

There was no sound. The minotaurs along the ridge advanced, still silent.

If I'm going to run, Ayesh thought, *this will be my best chance.* She looked at the minotaur to her right, who returned her gaze. She wondered, *Can you read my mind?* Because if it could, there was no chance of surprise.

But hadn't she surprised them in the night, when they had thought she was sleeping? If they could read minds, wouldn't they have known that she was awake before the first one had reached for her? *Maynoon,* one had said. *She sleeps.*

Trying to escape would at least tell her whether they could read her intentions.

The leader reappeared on the ridge line. He signaled, then turned his back.

The minotaur with the lead rope tugged once to urge Ayesh forward. Ayesh relaxed. Let there be no tension in her, no shift in her weight that would signal to them that she was about to spring.

The gaze of all three captors was straight ahead. The ropes were slack in their hands.

She sprang to the right.

It was an awkward leap, for her feet were still hobbled together. She planted both feet against the right minotaur's knee.

It bellowed. The rope slipped from its fingers.

The other two minotaurs tugged their ropes. They did Ayesh a favor, actually, for with her arms tied she had no way to catch herself as she fell.

She got her feet beneath her, but she had done all she could. The two remaining ropes were taut in her handlers' hands. She could advance toward neither one.

"Oomaam mayinoyaa maya naryaal?" came a voice

from behind. *Still some fight in her?* Ayesh recognized it as the voice she had heard laughing during her struggles in the dark. She looked over her shoulder. The minotaur who stood watching wore a green tunic with gold trim. It was hard to read minotaur expressions. They curled their lips up the same way for a smile or a grimace. But the minotaur's eyes were wide. Ayesh had no doubt that this one was smiling.

"Why don't you come hold her tether if you think she's so amusing, Phyrrax," said the minotaur Ayesh had kicked. He limped to where the rope lay.

"A generous invitation, Qurrax," said Phyrrax. "I thank you. Later, perhaps."

I thank you. Poystiiliin payd. Both speakers were male.

Qurrax snorted. Phyrrax laughed, which was also a sort of snort. The other two minotaurs said nothing, but jerked Ayesh into motion.

Well, at least Ayesh now knew one thing for certain. Whatever the powers of Hurloon minotaurs, *these* minotaurs did not read minds.

They stopped again at the top of the ridge. In the shallow vale below, Ayesh could see a copse of scrubby pines. Minotaurs walked among the stunted trees, stepping over the sprawled bodies of goblins. Aside from the bodies, there was no sign of struggle. The goblins had apparently died before they knew the minotaurs were near.

The minotaurs bent to retrieve the stones from their slings. The sling stones were easy to pick out from the ordinary ones nearby. The missiles were polished and as bright as metal.

"Steelstone," said Ayesh in Voda.

"What did she say?" said Qurrax.

"Steelstone," Phyrrax repeated in Voda. Then he bared his teeth and widened his eyes—another smile. If Ayesh hadn't know the gesture for a smile, it would have been intimidating. *"Boondaloonseylaan,"* he said in his own tongue. *Sling stones.*

Qurrax tugged the rope. "That's right," he grumbled in his own language. "Try to escape again, and I'll split your head with one."

"Would you really?" said Phyrrax, walking alongside. "What has she done to merit that?"

Aye, thought Ayesh. *What indeed?*

Qurrax shrugged. "Humans are *flakkach.*"

The word was unknown to Ayesh, but she could guess what it meant by Qurrax's tone. Humans were *unclean.*

"And you would kill her for that?"

"We kill goblins for it."

"But humans aren't to be killed unless they violate *purrah.*"

"Such is the tradition," said Qurrax. "But the traditions crumble around us every day. I don't know what's right. We suffer Iron-in-Granite's experiments within the Halls of Mirtiin." Qurrax shook his head.

"Best to err on the side of killing her then, eh?" said Phyrrax. "Killing a sentient being, a creature with the powers of speech, for doing nothing but escaping capture?"

"I said I don't know what's right anymore," Qurrax said angrily. "Don't make light of it, Phyrrax. These are difficult days."

"The times *are* difficult," Phyrrax said, brushing the sleeve of his green tunic. "No, I don't make light of that."

One by one, the minotaurs were reforming the column, half ahead of Ayesh and half behind. The leader came to stride beside the limping Qurrax. He lowered his massive head and said, *"Paydsaen ma?" Are you well?*

"She kicks like a troll," said Qurrax.

Ayesh smiled, then lost the smile when she noticed Phyrrax looking at her.

Phyrrax said, "There may be more to this creature than you guess, Zhanrax." He spoke the sentence in the male-to-male form.

Zhanrax snorted. Ayesh couldn't guess what that meant.

"Zhanrax," Phyrrax continued, "you should consider what you do here. To bring this human into the halls—"

"I have considered."

"You have considered your own interests. But consider hers. She is *flakkach,* but she is without guilt. To bring her into the halls . . . Well, things are uncertain. It could mean her death."

"What are you talking about?" said Ayesh in Voda. She stopped, but the minotaurs dragged her forward. With her hobble, it was hard to get back on her own feet. "What are you planning on doing with me?"

Zhanrax spoke over her head. "She is of interest," he said.

"You've taken sides," Phyrrax observed. "You've done this to curry favor. Ah, Zhanrax, your mother won't be pleased." Phyrrax laughed. "I want to see her face when you bring a human to her!"

Big Zhanrax was silent.

"In truth," Phyrrax continued, "you've done this to curry favor twice." He chuckled. "What, do you suppose, will Myrrax's daughter make of this human? An interesting substitute for flowers, my friend."

In dangerous tones, Zhanrax said, "Do not speak imprudently."

"That's the only way Phyrrax knows to talk," observed Qurrax.

Phyrrax laughed, but then said seriously, "I speak plain truth. Zhanrax, you play with fire. You will not settle the political struggle this way."

"I expect to settle nothing. My aims are personal."

"But you *will* stir up trouble. Once we bring this human into the halls, we slip down a river that flows one way only. What you do can't be undone."

Zhanrax kept his gaze straight ahead. In the full light of day, Ayesh could see that his tunic, which had first looked black, was actually a subtle pattern of black on midnight blue.

"Myrrax may favor you. But what about Betalem?" said Phyrrax. "The priestess will urge her followers to kill this human. And you'll have new enemies."

Ayesh tried hard to absorb these strange names. What was she being pulled into?

"Betalem is Stahaan," said Zhanrax. "She has no followers in Mirtiin. We are our own."

Stahaan, Ayesh thought, grateful for a hint. That was the next mountain range north and west. And *Mirtiin* were the mountains they now were crossing.

"Zhanrax," said Phyrrax, "if you will not see the wall into which you run, what aid can your friends give you?"

"My friends," Zhanrax said very softly, "can give me their axes and tridents when the time comes."

Phyrrax's eyes were wide, then he shook his shaggy head. "Again," he said, "you surprise me. Oh, your mother will not like this at all."

"My mother guides the clan," said Zhanrax. "But she may not rule my heart. And why do you show this concern? You are the one who pointed out the human to me. You are the one who mentioned what use Scaraya might make of such a creature."

Make use of such a creature? Ayesh wanted to shout at them in their own language, *insist* that they tell her what they were talking about. But tied up and hobbled, the only small advantage she had lay in mock ignorance. She would not speak their tongue until she saw some advantage to it.

"I?" said Phyrrax. "I pointed out the human to you? Ah, you misremember."

"Indeed," said Zhanrax. "It seems I often misremember in matters that concern you."

"But this concerns *me* not at all!" Phyrrax said. Then he looked at Ayesh. "Human," he said, "you are in more trouble than you can know." He watched her expression carefully. Ayesh gave him a blank stare.

Then Phyrrax and Zhanrax both walked to the head of the column.

"What were they talking about?" Ayesh asked in Voda. But the minotaur on her left would not meet her gaze, and the one ahead of her did not turn.

Qurrax, however, tugged on her rope. "Your words sound just like goblin chatter. Trouble me no more, or so help me . . ." He let the words trail off. Ayesh limped along beside him, wondering. Did they intend to enslave her? Make her someone's pet? Or was there some darker design?

They came at last to a cliff face. A narrow ledge sliced up the cliff for a great distance. They ascended slowly, hugging the face as the pine trees dwindled below. Where the ledge ended was a dark opening just broad enough for Zhanrax's massive head and shoulders. One by one, the minotaurs filed in.

Phyrrax waited at the ledge by the entrance. He caught one of the ropes as Ayesh's handlers passed. "Wait," he said to Ayesh in Voda.

She stopped, and when the other minotaurs released the ropes and entered the mountain, she didn't try to kick Phyrrax. He seemed to be the only one who had any concern for her.

Besides, it was a long way down from the ledge.

Hours ago, Ayesh had not planned to live through the night. Now she wanted to find a way to live long enough to at least decide her own fate. To die in battle against goblins, that was a worthy end for her. To die a prisoner was another matter.

"Zhanrax!" Phyrrax called.

The big minotaur filled the entryway again.

"What do you wait for? Bring her!"

"Wait. Look at her," Phyrrax said. "Look into her eyes. It matters what happens to her."

Zhanrax looked at Ayesh, but his words were for the other minotaur. "What would you have me see?"

"Look into her eyes. She's half minotaur."

"Don't blaspheme."

"You know what I mean."

Zhanrax's black eyes narrowed. He took Ayesh's rope and seemed to contemplate it meditatively.

"I have considered," Zhanrax said.

He tugged on the rope, pulling Ayesh inside.

It was dark, but not pitch black. Low flames burned in torches set into the polished walls, and the ceiling sloped away from the door, rising higher and higher, beyond the light of the torches. The other minotaurs were taking off their shoes.

The floor, Ayesh realized, was carpeted, not like the Hurloon labyrinths at all.

Zhanrax unhobbled Ayesh's feet, though he left her arms tied.

"Zhanrax!" said a minotaur wearing a red robe. Another minotaur, in similar garb, stood behind the first. Both brandished tridents. "This creature is *flakkach*! What do you mean by bringing it within the Halls of Mirtiin?"

Zhanrax raised himself to his full height. He was a head taller than the guards. "This is Mirtiin business, and no affair of the temple. Let us pass. Or is it true that Betalem craves war?"

The guards looked at each other. "Zhanrax," said one, "it shall be known in the temple what you have done."

"Be it so," Zhanrax said, and he shouldered past them, pulling Ayesh by her rope.

CHAPTER
7

DEORAYA STOOD IN THE CORRIDOR BEFORE THE
tapestry and clutched the phial that hung from her neck.

The tapestry depicted the goddess Lemeya giving birth
to the world. Upon the Goddess's horns were balanced a
bolt of lightning and a black stone: the active powers and
the still ones.

Inside Deoraya's phial were the mingled ashes of her
ancestors, countless generations of minotaur females who
had guided the clan.

Help me, Mothers, Deoraya prayed. *Now that my son
has done this thing, show me a safe path. Give me wise
words.*

But the dead whispered nothing in Deoraya's ear. She
did not feel the presence of her foremothers, as if even
the dead were baffled by what Zhanrax had done. They
could offer her no wisdom.

Betalem was expecting her, but Deoraya couldn't bring
herself to lift the tapestry and enter the temple. Deoraya
had accomplished so much for the Rock-in-Water clan
with silence. To delay speaking, and then to delay a little
longer in order not to take sides . . . that had been the

strength of Rock-in-Water under her leadership. But now, silence was impossible.

"My son," she said under her breath, "you were ever a trial." But it wasn't truly Zhanrax who tried her. It was the priestess, Betalem, and the chieftain, Myrrax. Deoraya was trapped between their powerful gazes. Betalem's eyes were sharp stones. Myrrax's gaze was a storm that does not quite break . . . yet.

Deoraya lifted the curtain.

"Blessed are the Mothers," said the temple guards, two enormous males armed with axes.

"May the Mothers be blessed," said Deoraya. "I come to have speech with Mother Betalem."

"She awaits you in the afterchamber, Rock-in-Water," said one guard.

Deoraya nodded, and the guard held aside a second tapestry. As she passed through the temple, Deoraya paused at the edge of the Well of Ashes. She peered into the black shaft that carried the ashes of Mirtiin minotaurs back to the heart of the earth, that they might dwell forever in stone. *Help me, Mothers,* she thought again. Then she kissed the lip of the Well.

Then she bowed to the Lamp of Passing Flames. She watched the clockwork assembly of metal disks. As the disks turned, the lamp wicks they were studded with were kindled by other wicks, or were extinguished. No wick burned throughout the entire cycle, but at least three wicks were aflame at any time.

Behold. The flame is passed. It is extinguished, yet it never goes out. Manifestations change. The fire burns forever.

Deoraya closed her eyes before the lamp and repeated the names of her mothers and grandmothers for nine generations.

Inside the afterchamber, Betalem sat reading from a scroll that rested on a stone lectern. Seeing Deoraya, Betalem rose to light a braid of sweetgrass from the lamp set into the wall. The priestess blew out the flame, and the end of the braid continued to glow red. Without a word, Betalem waved the braid in circles around Deoraya's horns, then purified herself in the same manner. She indicated a stone bench. Deoraya sat.

"A thing has happened," said Betalem.

"Yes," Deoraya said, grateful for the absence of judgment in the pronouncement. Betalem had not said, "Your son has done a thing," or even, as she might have said, "Your son has done a foolish thing."

"You are troubled," said Betalem. Lamp flame danced in her eyes.

"I am," said Deoraya. She clutched at the phial again. "I mean to do the temple no offense."

"Did you kiss the mouth of the Well of Ashes?"

"Yes, Mother."

"Did you honor your Mothers at the flame, three times three?"

"Of course, Mother."

"Then the temple takes no offense, Deoraya. You know the prescriptions, and you have followed them." She waved her hand. "You may go."

"Go? But I—"

"For any question you have of me in this matter, you have an answer already," Betalem said.

Deoraya shook her head. "I do not see—"

Betalem snorted impatiently. Immediately, Deoraya saw her error. She should have let Betalem dismiss her. Deoraya could puzzle out the subtleties later, on her own. So much for avoiding judgment.

"Your son has brought a creature into the Halls of Mirtiin," Betalem said slowly, as if to a child. "A *flakkach* creature. Would you spit into the Well of Ashes?"

"No, Mother."

"No more shall you suffer this *flakkach* human to shelter in the walls of your clan."

"Mother Betalem, the circumstances are unusual, are they not? For the human did not venture into the halls. It was brought against its will. How can I then say that it violated *purrah*? And the goblins—"

Betalem pointed at the scrolls. "Where is it written? Show me where the scrolls say, 'Here are the words of the ancestors. Honor them unless the circumstances are unusual.'" Betalem folded her arms. "As for the goblins, I would expect you to kill them if they were in your keeping. Do you not honor the Mothers? Do you harbor some soft feeling for this human?"

Should Deoraya tell her what the human had done? No. Of course not. Betalem was Stahaan. The honor of a Mirtiin clan meant little to her compared to the forms of Stahaan orthodoxy. Deoraya held her tongue, except to say, "I regret that this human has come."

"In Stahaan, it would not have drawn three breaths within the halls." She looked hard into Deoraya's eyes. "You must kill it at once. Your son has strayed from the path. Set him aright."

Deoraya said, "I will speak my heart to you, Mother Betalem. I honor my ancestors, and I honor Stahaan. Bones of my ancestors lie in both Mirtiin and Stahaan. But to embrace either faction—"

"Faction?" Betalem rose to her feet. "Are the voices of our ancestors only that to you? A *faction*?"

"Of course not, Mother Betalem. But as the world began in Stahaan, so does it continue in Mirtiin. My loyalties lie with both. I do not say this to offend. It is simple truth—it is hard for me to know what to do."

Betalem closed her eyes. "I do not compel you," she said. "I advise, and I hold the true forms of the temple, as only Stahaan may do." She opened her eyes, and her gaze was more intense than ever. "But if you suffer this human to live, you choose, Deoraya. And the Mothers see you choose." There was menace in her voice when she said, "The Mothers see you, yes, and *more* than the Mothers."

Myrrax watched from his granite throne as the guards escorted Deoraya into his audience chamber. The guards bowed, and Myrrax waved them away.

The throne was an odd piece of furniture, with its unangled seat. It was made for crouching more than sitting, and Myrrax perched upon it like a varicolored bird. Behind him hung the banners of the eleven clans, and he wore a cloak of the eleven colors.

Deoraya touched a hand to her forehead.

"I see thee, Rock-in-Water," Myrrax said. "What wouldst thou say?" His voice was even deeper than the voice of her son Zhanrax.

"You know why I have come, Myrrax-who-is-Mirtiin," said Deoraya.

Myrrax said nothing. He simply stared at her while the storm clouds in his eyes grew quietly darker.

Finally, he leaned forward, and his hooves scraped the stone shelf of the throne. "Zhanrax has done me no favor."

"My son means well," Deoraya said.

Myrrax was again silent for a time. "Means well," he said.

After a time, Deoraya said, "I don't know what he was thinking."

"I can't imagine," Myrrax said.

"The human is *flakkach*."

"That is so." Myrrax nodded.

"Betalem has instructed me to kill it."

"Soon enough," said Myrrax, "she will *command* thee to do so. What wilt thou do then, Deoraya? Thou wert ever looking both ways."

"Both ways?" Deoraya nervously clutched her phial.

"In Stahaan, they turn their eyes to the past, Deoraya. And Mirtiin's eyes are upon the future." He breathed deeply. "If thou killest this human, Rock-in-Water is declared for Stahaan. Dost know how close we tread to war within our halls, Deoraya?"

"If I suffer the human to live," said Deoraya, "then Betalem has one more grievance."

"Zhanrax brings us a step closer to war. This is the gift from thy son." Myrrax shook his head. "Do not kill it, Deoraya. While it lives, we may yet decide. If it dies, the stone is hurled, and we cannot unthrow it."

"I will not kill it," she said. She did not reveal to him that there were other reasons, further complications, that made it nearly impossible for her to kill the human.

Myrrax sat looking at her for a long time. The lamps along the walls hissed gently. Deoraya could hear her heart beating. And Myrrax continued to gaze at her in silence. Then he leaned forward, rising from the throne, and in the dark storm of his eyes, there was a hint of light.

He stepped down to the floor.

"Tell me," he said. "What is the human like?"

"Not young. Not yet old. Her face is not tattooed, but the skin of her body . . . "

"So I have heard. But what is she *like*?"

What is the human like?

One word leapt to Deoraya's mind.

Sly. The human was sly. But Deoraya had not said so to Myrrax. She did not care for anyone outside of her household to know the details of the human's arrival within the walls of her clan. But she thought of it again now, as she returned home from her audiences with the priestess and the chieftain.

She had been cleaning the wick of the clan's hearth lamp when Zhanrax had come home. That smirking Phyrrax had come in with him, for she had heard his laughter in the first chamber.

"I am in the hearth room!" she had called to Zhanrax. She hoped that Phyrrax would stay in the outer room. She did not approve of Phyrrax. He made a mockery of all things.

She had finished with the lamp, and she called to her younger son, who tended the hearth flame in the innermost room. "Tana! Bring the flame!"

Then she had turned to greet Zhanrax. "My son, how fared—"

She fell silent. In her son's hand was a rope, and at the end of the rope . . .

"Merciful Goddess!" said Deoraya. "Zhanrax, in the names of your Mothers, what have you done?"

"I have brought a prize," Zhanrax said. He bowed toward the hearth lamp, though no flame burned in it. Phyrrax bowed slightly, too, though the smirk on his muzzle made the gesture a parody.

"It's *flakkach*!" Deoraya said. "You bring ruin on this house, Zhanrax! Ruin and shame! And who knows what it's been stepping in? I have just cleaned the carpets!"

"It is no goblin," Zhanrax said. "It is human."

"It is an animal!" Deoraya cried. "And in the hearth room!"

The human bowed and said an astonishing thing, then. "I am Istini Ayesh ni Hata Kan. My mother was Istini Oriah, and her mother before her was Istini Elicia. For the line of my Mothers, I greet you."

Deoraya's hand went to the phial at her throat, but she only stared at the creature and said nothing.

Zhanrax looked no less stunned by the creature's words. This human animal spoke the tongue of minotaurs!

Deoraya felt as if she were frozen to the floor. She closed her mouth only after she felt her tongue against her lip.

Phyrrax laughed. "It is an animal with manners. Better manners than the clan of Rock-in-Water has, it would seem."

"I—I am Deoraya, and I speak for Rock-in-Water," she said. "My mother was Cleyaraya, and my mother before her was . . ." She dropped her hand. "What am I doing, greeting such a creature?"

Tana had come in then, bearing the flame for the hearth lamp, but not watching where he was going. No, his eyes were wide as he stared at the human. There was such wonder in his gaze that you'd think that some dream creature stood there, not an animal. So it was that he tripped on a seam in the carpet, and a drop of burning oil spilled onto the floor. Tana stamped it out with his hoof, but as he did so, he only spilled another burning drop.

"Tana!" Deoraya scolded. "Pay attention to what you're doing!"

The young minotaur bowed his head. He was, alas, at that age where his body seemed too large for him to manage. He proceeded to light the hearth lamp, glancing once over his shoulder at the human. Then he extinguished the smaller lamp and went to the corner of the room to close his eyes. "May the Mothers of this hearth hear me," he said. Then he cast an apology for his clumsiness into the clan's Well of Ashes. It was a smaller well than the one in the temple, but its stones were no less ornately carved. When he was done, he backed away, bowed to the hearth lamp, and backed out of the room, watching the human.

Deoraya put her fingers to her temple. "Zhanrax, you have done foolish things before. But this is a disgrace like no other. This is the hearth of your ancestors, and you bring in this, this—"

The human did not wait to see how it would be characterized. It sprang to the corner, agile as a goblin. It peered into the Well of Ashes.

Lady of Stones! Was it going to defile the holy shrine of the clan?

Zhanrax seemed frozen by surprise. The rope had slipped from his fingers. Deoraya looked about for a weapon. She hated to spill blood in this room, but things were getting out of hand. She seized the iron shears that she'd been using to clean the lamp.

"May the Mothers of this hearth hear me," the human said.

This was sacrilege! Deoraya stepped toward the human and raised the iron shears.

"I beg the shelter of this hearth, by the honor of all Mothers, and in the name of She Who Was First."

Deoraya stopped.

"Is it not said," asked the human, looking up from the Well, "that minotaurs and humans have a common Mother?"

Deoraya blinked.

"In Her Name," said the human, "I ask the shelter of this hearth. I ask in the name of our kinship. Though it be ancient, is there not a common strand to our lineage?"

Phyrrax laughed. "She knows the Hurloon heresy!"

Zhanrax said, "Human, have you been among the Hurloon?"

"I have."

Deoraya frowned. "Then she is twice unclean! Once for being human, and once for dwelling among the five-fingered heretics!"

"But that aspect of the heresy was never resolved here in Mirtiin," said Phyrrax. "If humans and minotaurs do indeed have a common Mother, then perhaps humans are not truly *flakkach*. And in any case, she takes refuge in the names of your Mothers. Would you deny her?"

Deoraya looked at her son. He was as surprised at this development as she.

She shook the shears in her hand. "Would that the scrolls could be read one way! Would that the gods spoke plainly!"

"Then would our lives be far too peaceful," said Phyrrax with a laugh, "and the gods would not find us so amusing."

Deoraya turned toward the human. "You shame this clan even by asking such a thing!" she said. Imagine! A *human* taking refuge in the Mothers of Rock-in-Water!

She wrapped both hands around the iron shears. "You will not wear the colors of this house," she said. "None will know of your refuge."

"I will serve," the human said, bowing.

"Indeed not. Unclean hands will not sully the treasures of this clan, or even handle its night soil." She felt the muscles in her jaw grow tense. "Zhanrax, untie her."

"But—"

"Untie her! She invokes a common ancestor and takes refuge in the clan!"

Her son, looking a little dazed by this turn of events, cut the cords that bound the human's arms.

"Upon the honor of my Mothers," said the human, "I will obey you, Mother of Zhanrax."

"There is safety in this," observed Phyrrax. "Betalem and Myrrax cannot contest for your loyalty where you have no choices, Deoraya."

Deoraya looked at him and narrowed her eyes. "And for that reason, I cannot tell them what has happened. For when Rock-in-Water has no choices, neither do we have power. By the breath of your Mothers, Phyrrax, you will not speak of this to anyone!"

"By the breath of my Mothers," Phyrrax said, "it shall remain my private amusement."

Deoraya threw the shears at him. Phyrrax dodged and laughed.

CHAPTER
8

"WHERE ARE YOU TAKING ME?"

Zhanrax just grunted and urged Ayesh forward through the stone passages, but Phyrrax smiled. "Nowhere in particular, I think. We're just making sure you're seen often enough to become irresistible."

They passed a cluster of young minotaurs who stopped playing their game with polished stones and a wooden game board. The youngsters stared at Ayesh.

"Irresistible to whom?"

"Be quiet," Zhanrax said. He took a sudden turn and pulled Ayesh behind him. At least he hadn't led her with a rope since she had taken sanctuary in Deoraya's hearth.

Phyrrax said, "If you walk her around long enough, Zhanrax, she'll soon know the halls as well as we do!"

Ayesh had some faint hope that Phyrrax was right. Her best chance for getting out of here was to know the mazes well. But the mazes were a chaos of twisting corridors, angled pillars, and dark-colored curtains that covered long stretches of stone walls. Passages rarely met at right angles, so it was hard to create a mental map of the corridors she passed through. Somewhere behind the long curtains were doors, but Ayesh couldn't see how the minotaurs knew where to part the curtains to find the entrances they sought. Here and there, stelae rose from the floor, and they were etched with the labyrinthine minotaur script. Perhaps these were maps, but Ayesh could not read them. Not only was the script unknown to her, but the oil-fed lamps in the halls were placed far apart. There was light enough for minotaurs to read by, but not enough for Ayesh.

If the stone mazes were confusing and subtle, the invisible webs of power within Mirtiin were even more so. Even the powers within the household were mysterious. Deoraya was the leader of her clan. Her husband, Teorax, lived in the household but seemed to have no power in it. In fact, he wasn't Rock-in-Water but of the Grass-Above clan, like Phyrrax. Zhanrax was a commander when he was outside of the halls, but his position in his mother's household seemed ambiguous—Deoraya ruled the household, but Zhanrax seemed above her when it came to most decisions about Ayesh. This wasn't, as Ayesh first supposed, because he somehow owned her after taking her captive. It had to do with Ayesh's usefulness to some unspoken ambitions of Zhanrax that took priority over his mother's wishes.

If household politics were unclear, the whole of Mirtiin was a much greater puzzle. Eavesdropping in her first days of captivity, Ayesh understood that two factions vied under the Mirtiin Mountains. One faction was favored by the chieftain, Myrrax, and the other sided with the priestess from Stahaan, Betalem. There were other names, too, of clan leaders and their hearths: Dzeanaraya of Stones-Afalling, Ceoloraya of Flame-in-Void, Neshiearaya of Grass-Above. Deoraya sometimes spoke of the Eleven, so Ayesh guessed that there were eleven clans. But just who was loyal to whom, and to what end, was hard to figure out. Zhanrax and his mother would answer none of Ayesh's direct questions.

But one name evoked strong emotions always: *Scaraya*. In Deoraya's household, and in the general Halls of Mirtiin, it was a name sometimes said with disdain, sometimes with admiration, sometimes with fear, but never with neutrality.

"Come on," Zhanrax said. "This way." They turned down

a corridor that was hung with ochre-and-white curtains. Again, the only minotaurs in sight were youngsters, who stopped playing and stared. Zhanrax nodded at them, baring his teeth and widening his eyes in a smile.

"Right under her nose, eh?" Phyrrax laughed. "It's risky, Zhanrax. If she happens to step into the corridor while you're here, you spoil your gambit."

"If I've been so close and didn't bring the human to her," Zhanrax said, "then she'll know that I'm not making the first move. She'll have to come and ask." He pulled on Ayesh's arm. "Step lively!"

Ayesh stopped and tried to dig her heels into the carpet. Zhanrax easily lifted her from her feet.

"If you want my cooperation, Zhanrax, then you can at least tell me what's going on!"

"Keep your voice down!" Zhanrax said, setting her down. "We pass her door!"

"Whose door?" Ayesh said.

"Quiet, I said!" Then, in a low voice, as if anyone but Phyrrax were there to overhear, Zhanrax said, "Do as I say. Are you not a guest in our household?"

"I'm hardly treated as such!" Ayesh said loudly.

There was a noise nearby, the lifting of a latch. Ayesh saw panic in Zhanrax's eyes. He lifted her by her wrist, turned as if to race down the corridor with her. But door hinges creaked. It was too late. Zhanrax set her down, stood erect, and calmly turned toward the sound.

Bright light, white as sunshine, emerged from behind the curtain, and a minotaur in ochre robes stepped into the hallway.

"Iron-in-Granite!" said Zhanrax, blinking. "What a surprise!"

The ochre-robed minotaur widened her eyes and showed her teeth. She was like no minotaur Ayesh had ever seen, for her eyes were as blue as a summer sky. She wore golden spectacles.

"A surprise?" she said. She stroked her tattooed muzzle with her fingers. "A surprise to find the matriarch of Iron-in-Granite here in her own corridor? A surprise to discover my interest when I hear a human voice outside my door? But surely, Zhanrax, this is no accident. Do you not bring this creature to meet me?"

"I was only . . . That is, I wasn't deliberately . . . "

"Son of Deoraya, you didn't mean to bring her so close and not ask me the favor of examining her?"

Another door opened in the corridor, and another ochre-robed minotaur peered out to see what was going on.

Ayesh could see some recognition pass between Zhanrax and the Iron-in-Granite matriarch. Zhanrax had been playing for some sort of one-upsmanship. And he'd just lost. He bowed his head. "I know of your interest in such *flakkach* creatures as have speech. This is such a one."

"You are wise to consult me." The minotaur looked down at Ayesh and asked in Voda, "Human, how are you called?"

Ayesh considered her for a moment, then bowed as she had done before Deoraya. "*Moysaen cassadalaam* Istini Ayesh ni Hata Kan," she answered.

The minotaur blinked with astonishment.

"*Moyin maamaan saenyi* Istini Oriah, *eyen mayin maamaan nartoon may saenyi* Istini Elicia," Ayesh continued. "For the line of my Mothers, I greet you."

The blue-eyed minotaur smiled. "And I am Scaraya. I speak for Iron-in-Granite," she said. "My mother was . . . "

But Ayesh did not hear the rest of the introduction. She was thinking, *Scaraya!* Here was the minotaur whose name seemed to be at the heart of all that happened in Mirtiin.

"I've no time for her *today*," Scaraya said to Zhanrax. "But bring her again tomorrow, won't you?" And she retreated into the brilliance of her chambers and closed the door.

Phyrrax held his sleeve over his mouth.

"Oh, shut up!" said Zhanrax. He stamped down the corridor and tugged Ayesh behind him.

"Did I say anything?" Phyrrax said, showing his teeth but squinting to disguise his grin. "But Zhanrax, it makes little difference whether she comes to you or you to her. Why, it's only a matter of stature."

Zhanrax halted. "Stature is everything!"

"But you'll still have what you want!"

Zhanrax showed his teeth, half closing his eyes. This was a grimace. "I may. And I may not. If Scaraya had come to me . . . It's not the same, Phyrrax! Now she gives to me, not I to her!" He grabbed Ayesh by her wrist and lifted her.

"Put me down!"

He held her at arm's length, looking into her eyes. "You'd have done me more good by keeping your mouth shut!"

"If only you'd answer some of my questions—"

"Minotaur matters are not for you to understand," Zhanrax said. "Ours are great doings. There isn't room enough in your little head for them."

Ayesh drew her legs up and answered him with a kick in the muzzle. Zhanrax flinched and dropped her. She sprang away from him and down the hall. As she turned down a dark side corridor, she could feel the heavy pounding of hooves behind her.

She turned at another intersection, dodged when she felt fingers on her shoulder. She rounded another sharp corner and found herself in a corridor hung with purple curtains. In the center of the corridor stood two purple-clad minotaurs armed with glittering axes. They turned toward Ayesh as she dashed toward them, and one bared its teeth, hefting its blade.

"Stop!" said the voice of her pursuer. It wasn't Zhanrax chasing her, Ayesh realized, but Phyrrax.

She halted. The axe-wielding minotaurs were now loping down the hall toward her.

"Come on!" Phyrrax tugged at her wrist. "They'll kill you if they get the chance!"

Ayesh hesitated.

"Ayesh, come! I'm not welcome here either, and I don't want to answer for a fight between their clan and mine. Come!"

The floor shook with the approach of the minotaur guards.

"Ayesh!" Phyrrax pleaded.

"All right, all right." She turned and followed Phyrrax as he sprinted back in the direction they had come. Ayesh looked over her shoulder. Their pursuers followed only as far as the purple curtains reached. Phyrrax half-guided, half-herded Ayesh back into the ochre-and-white corridor of Iron-in-Granite. Zhanrax was still standing there, wiping the blood from his massive nose.

"Purple is Shade-in-Ice," Phyrrax said to Ayesh, panting. He held his hand over his chest. "They could scarce be more orthodox. In their corridors, they may act as they see fit, and never mind what Myrrax says." He sat on the carpet and leaned against the curtained wall. "I've not had reason to run like that for many winters!"

"Aye," marveled Zhanrax. "Such an interest you take in this *flakkach*, Phyrrax! Dashing into the halls of your enemy . . . "

"I have no enemies," Phyrrax said. "I'm very careful about that."

Zhanrax shook his great head. "And yet what house is glad to see you?"

"I could have dodged them," Ayesh said. "I could get by two guards."

"Not when they bellowed the clan's alarm and the corridor filled with Shade-in-Ice," said Phyrrax. "Zhanrax has risked much to bring you here. You might be so polite as to stay alive."

"Whether I live or die is my business," Ayesh said.

Phyrrax laughed. "Do you hear, Zhanrax?" he said. "I risk an axe in my head, and thus does she sing her gratitude!"

"She may mimic manners," Zhanrax said, "but don't expect fellow feeling from such a creature."

"Ah, gentle, Zhanrax. Gentle. She is a prisoner here."

"Would that she were. Would that I could tie you up again, human," Zhanrax said. He snorted, and blood flecked his muzzle. "You think you are clever."

"She *is* clever, Zhanrax. She reasoned how to ask sanctuary of your hearth, and with few clues."

Zhanrax frowned and said to Ayesh, "Be as clever as you will, human, but do not bring my hopes to ruin. Without hopes, I would be without honor, and without honor, I would not care whether your sanctuary were observed or not." Then he seized her wrist and dragged her back to the corridors of his clan.

CHAPTER
9

LIGHT, SO WHITE AND DAZZLING, SO STARTLING
after days underground, days without seeing the sun;
what startled Ayesh was the aliveness of it, and the aliveness of the room where she beheld it. Aye, the room was
alive, and so were the corridors that stretched beyond.
Rooms deep underground, but bright with sunlight and
astir with birdsong and the buzzing of insects.

She blinked, and the minotaur Scaraya leaned close to
her, exhaling her flower-scented breath. "Did you think
that all the Halls of Mirtiin were dark and dead?" Scaraya
asked. "But how then would we dine upon fresh grass in
winter, or blossoms in autumn?"

Scaraya smiled gently. The light glittered on the lenses
of her glasses and in her blue eyes. Behind her, expanding
from this room like the rays of a sunburst, there stretched
corridor after corridor of blossoming trees, flowering
shrubs, and just-sprouting rows of sweetgrass and beebalm. Closer at hand, ivy clung to the stone bookshelves,
purple blossoms alternating with the titles that Ayesh
could not read. The ivy rustled as sparrows flew in and
out of leafy hiding places. From somewhere came the

gentle sounds of flowing water. Ayesh heard even the buzzing of the bees.

All Ayesh could think to say was, "How? By wizardry?"

Scaraya shook her head. "Wizards are rare among minotaurs, and among all races they are unreliable. No, these gardens are not made by magic, but by science. Do you know the difference?"

"Oneah, too, was built upon reason," Ayesh said. "I know what science is." Then she squinted as she peered down one of the tree-lined corridors. "Are those mulberries?" She had to use the Voda word. There had been no mulberry trees in the Hurloons.

"How else would we keep our silkworms fed?"

"Silk? You make your own?"

"All that we use, we make or grow ourselves. Hidden among the ice and boulders far above are mirrors. They conduct the light inward, bend the light, and concentrate it. And so the sun shines even here, deep beneath the jagged peaks. Minotaurs have long done this. In Stahaan, our ancestral home, minotaurs once lived above the ground and made labyrinths only to store winter hay. But with the first Coming of Ice, we learned to bring the sun underground, else we would have starved."

The other minotaur, Scaraya's assistant, spoke up to ask, "Shall I tie the human to the chair, Scaraya?" *Moysayenya . . . Shall I . . .* The grammar revealed that the assistant was female. She held a rope.

"You shall not!" said Scaraya.

"We always tied the other ones," said the young female. She wore a silken tunic—turquoise and pink with four black circles in the front.

"Other ones?" said Ayesh.

But Scaraya ignored her question. "This is not at all the same, Cimmaraya. Ayesh is a human being, and our guest. And please know that she is a daughter of Mothers and knows it. Therefore, afford her the respect she merits." Then she indicated a chair. "Won't you sit down?"

It was the first piece of furniture Ayesh had seen in the halls that was scaled to her size. Was it intended for minotaur children? But no, that couldn't be the answer.

Because of their backward-bending knees, minotaurs could not sit comfortably in a chair made for humans. All the minotaur furniture Ayesh had seen was limited to stools for sitting and stone benches for lying down.

She sat. Scaraya poured tea into two enormous mugs. She offered one to Ayesh and brought the other to her own lips. Ayesh sniffed the brew. It was flowery and sweet, a little like the Oneahn harvest wine made of spring nectars. She tasted it, and the warmth of it spread from her mouth and throat.

The younger minotaur, Cimmaraya, sat at a table and opened an enormous book. "If you do not object," Scaraya said, "I'd like to ask you some questions and let Cimmaraya record our conversation."

"For the sake of argument," Ayesh said, "what if I do object? I do not greatly own my destiny within the Halls of Mirtiin. I am a prisoner here."

"Within Mirtiin, true," said Scaraya. "But not here at my hearth, in my gardens. You are my guest, and free as long as you are sheltered by the walls of Iron-in-Granite."

"If that's so," said Ayesh, sitting up, "then when Zhanrax returns for me, I don't want to go with him."

"Zhanrax?" said Cimmaraya. "What has he to do with this human? Rock-in-Water was ever a neutral clan."

Scaraya said, "Young Zhanrax brought this human to the halls and delivered her to us today. I thought surely your father would have told you."

"He never bores me with politics," said Cimmaraya.

"But do you not love science, Cimmaraya?"

"You know that I do!"

"Politics, my dear, is more science than it is mere formalities and gossip. It may be mathematical in its calculations. You might learn by what your father does." Scaraya turned back to Ayesh. "You ask more than I can offer, asking me to keep you from Zhanrax. He thinks he profits by bringing you to me, and so you must be returned to him. For now."

The last words gave Ayesh hope. Her life in Deoraya's household was no higher than a dog's would be, if minotaurs kept dogs.

"Zhanrax profits?" Cimmaraya said. "I never saw that Zhanrax cared for science. How does he profit?"

"You are so young," Scaraya said, smiling. "The answer is closer than your nose." Then she turned to Ayesh. "What of answering my questions?" She sipped her tea.

Ayesh drank, then nodded. What point was there to resistance for its own sake? Besides, she could use an ally. Phyrrax showed concern for her, but not enough to help her escape the halls. Perhaps Scaraya would prove more helpful, eventually.

"What can I tell you?"

"Tell me first," said Scaraya, "of the land of your birth."

"Oneah," Ayesh said. She took a breath and let it out slowly. "Once I could not speak enough of Oneah," she said. "But it is fallen, now. Seven great cities turned to dust."

"But memory endures."

"Not forever. Year after year of telling the history taught me that. People distort what they hear, or lose the truths even where they desire to keep them. Nothing lasts, and wherefore should I then dwell on fallen glory?"

"Ah," said Scaraya, "but it *was* glorious, you say."

Cimmaraya snorted. Ayesh had been among the Mirtiin minotaurs long enough now to recognize this as a snort of disdain.

"Human glories," Cimmaraya said. "Would those be like goblin glories? For what are humans but goblins that live aboveground?"

Ayesh clenched her fists.

"Peace, Ayesh," said Scaraya. "Sip your tea, and if you would correct Cimmaraya, do so by enlightenment. She knows only of the humans she has seen in the towns hereabout."

"Humans," Ayesh said, "have built civilizations as grand as anything seen beneath Mirtiin! Do you know . . ." She thought of launching into the history of Oneah, but then decided to save the best for last. "Do you know of old Icatia, the empire that flowered in the far southern lands?"

Ayesh began to tell them the story of the kingdom on the plains. She told of the birth of the alliances, the ebb and flow of the long wars, and she ignored the fact that

much of the Sarpadian history she knew had been pronounced wrong by Bathtown's Elder Alik. These minotaurs, especially this Cimmaraya, needed to know what a
human being was, and that, at the heart of things, was
what the stories were about. As Ayesh spoke, she warmed
to the telling. Long she spoke, uninterrupted.

"They might have stood alone to resist the tide of orcs,"
Ayesh said, winding up her tale. "They might have drawn
into themselves and saved their lands. But to the end,
though it sapped their strength, they were faithful to their
allies—the mountain dwarves, the merfolk of Vodalia, the
elves of Havenwood. Even unto their ancient rivals, the
human Order of the Ebon Hand, even there did they offer
succor. It was for loyalty that they suffered. It was for
nobility that they died." She glowered at Cimmaraya.
"Think of their greatness as folly, if that is the minotaur
way. But do not mistake them for an instant as like unto
goblins. What goblin ever thought of aught but itself?"

Cimmaraya had stopped writing. "Is this truly the way
of humans?" she said.

"Of some," said Scaraya. "They are no more the same
in all places than we are identical to the Stahaan or the
Hurloon. Doubt not that humans can be noble."

"Then I see the hope of this enterprise," said Cimmaraya,
beginning to write again.

"What's she talking about?"

Scaraya waved the question away. "Tell me more," she
said, "about the other civilizations you have known."

Ayesh found that her tongue was loose. She rattled off
histories with ease: the island empire of Orvada, the
rumored wars of the red and blue barbarians, the long
peace in the farmlands of Varnalca and the elven alliance
that extended it. . . .

Her eyelids and limbs grew heavy as she spoke, yet still
she continued, telling of the eastern lands where only
women own property, the Tivan Desert where only men
do and women *are* property, the islands where every
human has a touch of wizard in him.

And then it seemed that she left off talking. It seemed that she only dreamed, now, of wars among humans and between humans and other sentient creatures. There were wars of wizardry, but more common were the wars of arrow and blade, of sieges and great machines of war: catapults and battering rams, juggernauts and mines, underwater ships and fortresses by the sea. These were the histories she had traded for throughout the Domains. Dominaria, earth, the world that was, seemed, as she dreamed of it, one great everlasting war.

Her thoughts turned to Oneah. She dreamed of the history of the kings and queens, and how the cities came to elect them. She dreamed of the Great Library in Onirrah, the Solar Observatory at Onlish, the palace of artisans at Onmarakhent, the School of the Sun in Onnilla, where they loved wisdom for its own sake. She gazed on the Galleries of the Sun at Onvia, where they loved beauty even more than the other cities. And at Xa-On, the city of her birth, she saw again the Roof of Lights and the wrestling school. Every city had its greatest school or museum, yet there were students of all subjects. And the finest wrestler in Xa-On was expected to paint well . . . *and the most entertaining juggler in Onmarakhent could name the constellations and their stars. . . . e llefawli keskedi jungudeen ni Onmarakhent ved lemen brillinef e tend brilli. . . .*

"Speak the Mother Tongue," said Scaraya's voice amidst the dream. "Or Voda. You keep drifting into a language I do not know."

There, upon the Plains of Oneah, arose the greatest civilization that had ever been. And Ayesh had been first among the young wrestlers of her class. She was lithe and quick. She could bend when she must, hence the reed tattoos upon her legs. Yet there among the reeds, the green snake waited. That was her style, to dodge, to flex, to escape until the moment was right and her opponent too confident.

Then would she strike, like her snake tattoo. Then would she win.

She had stood beneath the Roof of Lights, all aglitter

with scattered sunshine. She had stood before the thrones, a champion. Because she was small yet dangerous, her nickname was Goblin. She actually cherished the name before the wars, before the fall of the cities.

Oneahns had ever kept the goblins at bay. Though the plains were ringed with mountains, the gray-skinned hordes had kept their distance. But in that one dark year there flowed from the caves such a tide of teeth and daggers, such a chattering and howling foul-smelling tide . . .

She recalled standing with Master Hata outside the Roof of Lights. The city was in flames, and the gray tide of goblins swept forward along the avenues, looting and killing.

"We stand as wrestlers of the court!" Hata reminded them. "We are the grace of the Thousand Thousands. Goblins do not master us. We know fear, and we are not mastered. We stand! Upon these very stones, we stand!"

And the goblins, seeing the tattooed wrestlers ringing the Roof of Lights halted their advance. For a moment. For just a moment they froze at the sight of the wrestlers, men and women too pure to fight with weapons, too sure in the eternal moment to fear the next. Victory and defeat were one to them. There was only the fight, and no matter the odds, it was clear that the goblins who attacked them would die and die and die.

"*Oun*," challenged Grand Champion Khairt in the goblin tongue, "*da teyey ekmigyla kofk ke kofk ke kofk!*"

For a moment, the goblin tide hesitated. Ayesh, eyes open, mastered herself with a meditation. She was ready. She turned both fear and fury aside. Then was she the perfect warrior.

And then . . .

No. That she would not remember. What happened next, in the confusion, in the howling of the goblins and the momentarily triumphant shouts of wrestlers . . . what happened next, Ayesh would not remember.

The Roof of Lights was . . . No. Stop thinking of it. Blackness. Unmemory. She would *not* recall what followed in the Roof of Lights.

There were other things to remember. There were

better things. There was Onyikhairt with its School of
Solar Music. There were the songs in the moon scale,
the heart scale, the glitter scale, and the grand sounds of
the sun scale. There was the "Hymn of the Sun," the
renewal song that could stir Ayesh's heart in the darkest
of times. She recalled it now. She and the others had
sung it as the goblin flood rushed toward them. It had
made them stand taller, stronger. In that song were
hints of all that made Oneah great: sun mind, reason,
mastery.

She had not sung the tune for years.

She heard it now, in her own voice.

Hot tears were on her cheeks. Her voice cracked.

Ayesh blinked. Blue eyes stared into hers. Blue eyes,
magnified by polished lenses.

She swallowed, wiped at her face with her hands. She
realized that all this time, she had been speaking these
thoughts aloud. She had even been singing. She said,
"You drugged me."

"Only as I drugged myself," said Scaraya. "The tea is
made of herbs that make easier both the telling and the
listening." She gently took Ayesh's hand. "What dwells
inside that shadow in the Roof of Lights? What happened
there that you cannot face?"

Ayesh pulled her hand away and glowered. "You
drugged me. You *stole* my thoughts."

"You did not tell me anything you would not willingly
tell with time," said Scaraya. "And yet the Roof of Lights
holds a secret. It's something that you carry deep within."

Sparrows chattered in a corner of the room. It was
strange to wake from a trance far underground and hear
sparrows.

"First I was made a captive. Now you campaign to steal
my secrets," Ayesh said, turning her face away.

"It is said among the patrollers who caught you that
you courted death outside the goblin caves. You invited
the goblins to come out and kill you, as if you no longer
wished to live. Was that madness, I wonder, or bravery?"

"What does this matter to you?" Ayesh said. "What do
you *want* with me?"

"From what the patrollers told," said Scaraya, "I observe this: Even as you stood before the goblin caves, taunting, you did not enter the caves. You did not take the last step to sure destruction. You waited for them to come to you. You remained outside, where there might still be hope."

Ayesh cried out at that last word. "Hope! Gods protect me from hope!"

Scaraya took Ayesh's chin and gently turned her face. The minotaur's blue gaze met Ayesh's glower. "Life holds on," Scaraya said. "Look about you in the light of this room. The ivy climbs toward the sun. There is a saying: *The birds sing not because they have an answer. They sing because they have a song.*"

Ayesh's lip quivered. "That saying is Oneahn."

"It is Mirtiin, also," said Scaraya. "Howsoever you are wounded, human, so also do you crave life. Do not surrender. You sprang from a people who loved knowledge and art and all things of the sun. While you live, all of that lives in you."

"I am a lie," Ayesh said. "I have lived twenty years too long. Only let me die killing goblins. That is all I ask."

"I will not grant you death," Scaraya said. "I would offer you instead a reason to live."

And then she asked, "What if Oneah might not be dead? What if there were a way to make the music live, to keep the poetry, to teach the science of mind to new generations who would hold it in holy trust? If I could make some of Oneah last throughout the generations, as it might have lasted without the Goblin War, would you accept the offer?"

"Oneah lies in ashes."

"But if it might live, truly live by your teaching, would you agree to teach?"

Ayesh said nothing.

"Say you will," said Scaraya. "Say that you want a reason to live."

CHAPTER

10

"STAND TALL," PHYRRAX ADVISED. "YOU MUST look confident on the way there, and all through the proceedings."

"No one sees us," Ayesh said. The Halls of Mirtiin were empty, more empty than she'd ever seen them. No children played in the common corridors, and she saw no guards in the corridors of color.

"We're early, and most are busy with preparations," said Zhanrax. He cradled an oilcloth bundle in his arms. "But there are peepholes. Be not lulled by the emptiness of the hallways. We are observed as we pass. Be sure of that."

Zhanrax halted before a narrow side passage, then looked up and down the corridor. "Only let no one see us just now," he whispered. He entered the passage and motioned Ayesh to follow.

There was no light. Phyrrax guided Ayesh from behind, then whispered for her to wait.

With a sharp *clack* each time, sparks flashed once, twice, three times. In the flashes, Ayesh could see that the minotaurs were trying to kindle a torch.

"Zhanrax," she said, "someone will hear. Give me my things."

"Why?"

"For better light than torchlight," Ayesh said. "And quieter kindling."

"No tricks?" the big minotaur said. "You won't run?"

"As if I could find my way out of here alone."

Zhanrax grunted. Ayesh felt him press her pack into her hands. By feel, she found the tinderbox of unsmoking fire. She opened it, spoke two words, and an orange flame sprang to life and shifted to white.

"So bright!" Zhanrax said, blinking.

"For once I can *see*," Ayesh said.

The two minotaurs led Ayesh through a passage she had never seen before. The floor here was not carpeted, and Phyrrax and Zhanrax raised dust with their hooves. The farther they walked, the more rubble there was on the floor. The walls and ceiling of this passage were reinforced with large timbers. There were cracks in the walls and puddles on the floor.

"Does anyone live here?"

"None but starving spiders and skinny rats," said Phyrrax. "This rock is too soft. These passages were cut in search of firmer stone. No one comes here, but we may pass to the Assembly Chamber by this route."

"Aye," said Zhanrax. "It spoils all if you are killed along the way to Assembly, human."

They stepped over piles of rubble. Eventually the crumbling walls gave way to more solid ones.

"Put out the light," Zhanrax said. Ayesh did so, and the minotaurs guided her, blind, until she saw the flicker of lamplight again.

The room they entered was a jumble of jagged pillars. It was as if someone had broken the insides of the mountain and shaken the pieces.

"Wipe your feet," Phyrrax advised. The floor, for all the apparent disorder of the walls and ceiling, was carpeted. The three of them set out across the maze of jumbled stones.

"How do you know where you're going?" Ayesh asked.

"Silence!" Zhanrax whispered. He held his axe before him as he stepped carefully around each sharp-edged pillar, looking this way and that.

Pillar by pillar, they advanced, or Ayesh *guessed* they advanced. For all she could tell, they walked in circles until, suddenly, Zhanrax seized her hand and pulled her into an opening in one of the pillars. They descended dark stairs that opened onto a circular corridor. Ahead, between orange torches, was an open doorway.

"The Assembly Chamber," Phyrrax said.

It was as grand a room as any in the Seven Cities. Indeed, the Assembly Chamber's circular rows of stone stools descending to a stage in the center of the room, reminded Ayesh of the Roof of Lights.

Along the curving wall of the Assembly Chamber hung the curtains of the Eleven Clans—green and gold for Grass-Above, purple for Shade-in-Ice, gray and sky blue for Stones-Afalling, red on black for Flame-in-Void . . . Phyrrax named them for Ayesh.

Zhanrax guided Ayesh to a row of stools before the dark blue-and-black curtain of his clan. They were high above the stage here, but would be able to see all of the room. Zhanrax straddled one of the stools and sat down.

"Why is no one else here?"

"We arrive first so that none can fight to keep you out," Zhanrax said. "We present them with a deed accomplished."

As Zhanrax said this, the first purple-clad minotaurs and a few wearing white and ochre entered. The purple minotaurs of Shade-in-Ice pulled up short when they saw Ayesh. Two of them felt in their belts for their axes.

But the minotaurs in white and ochre smiled, and one said, "I remind you, Shade-in-Ice, that you stand in Assembly."

"You knew of this outrage?" said one in purple. He drew his axe in spite of the warning. "This creature violates *purrah*, and in Assembly! To kill her in Assembly is lesser sacrilege than to bring her here!"

Zhanrax pulled a strip of black-and-blue cloth from his

belt, and he draped it across Ayesh's shoulders. "Istini Ayesh ni Hata Kan, this human, asked and was granted the sanctuary of my mother's house," he said. "Whosoever would harm her feuds with Rock-in-Water."

Phyrrax curled his left lip in a minotaur grin. "I thought that was to be a secret."

Zhanrax made no answer. The gesture had its result: the minotaur of Shade-in-Ice returned his axe to his belt, saying, "Dark days, when holy law is flouted."

Phyrrax went to sit with his own clan. Ayesh watched as the clans trickled in and took seats before the curtains of their own colors. By the expressions of the minotaurs who watched her, she could guess which clans were allied with Scaraya's and which opposed her. It seemed three supported Scaraya, three opposed her, and the other five were mixed or neutral. The room soon buzzed with dozens of soft conversations, and many gazes were turned to Ayesh. Row by row, the benches filled. Ayesh had never seen so many minotaurs in one place.

When Deoraya entered with Teorax, young Tana, and the rest of the household in tow, her eyes narrowed at the sight of the cloth draped over Ayesh. Then she made her face impassive.

Practiced politician, Ayesh thought.

"She'll have my hide, or yours, for this," Zhanrax said.

Teorax, Ayesh noted, went to sit not with his wife's clan but with the red and black of Flame-in-Void. Males kept their own colors, it seemed, even after they married and moved to the households of their in-laws.

Flame-in-Void appeared to be neutral. None of the minotaurs on those benches were fingering their axes the way so many minotaurs of Shade-in-Ice, Ants-Below, or Cups-Ashattered were.

A female in red-and-white robes entered. There were no curtains in her colors on the walls, and from the glare she fixed on Ayesh it was clear who she was even before Zhanrax whispered, "Betalem."

I am ringed with enemies, Ayesh thought. *What do I think I'm doing?*

Of course, she didn't really *know* what she was doing.

She had put her faith in Scaraya, who had said, "You want to live, but you don't know if you have anything to live for. Trust that I shall give you a reason. Oneah shall rise. You must do as I say."

Next entered Myrrax. He stood so tall, strode with such assurance, that Ayesh would have guessed who he was even if he did not wear all the colors of the Eleven Clans in his robe. At the very center of the stage, he climbed onto a great throne facing the doorway.

Scaraya was one of the last to enter. Behind her walked four minotaurs who carried enormous, oddly shaped boxes. They brought these into the center of the great room and set them down as Scaraya crossed to her seat at the head of her clan.

Myrrax held up his hand, and his throne began to revolve slowly on a turntable. As his gaze fell upon this clan, then that one, conversations fell silent. Shade-in-Ice, to the left of the door, was the last clan to quiet. Ayesh could see in their faces that many of the purple-clad mino-taurs wanted to leap to their feet and challenge her right to be present, but they held their tongues. Zhanrax nudged her as if to say, *See? It worked to sneak you in first.*

Myrrax said, "We are assembled in council."

Every minotaur voice in the room rumbled in unison: "We are assembled."

"There is," Myrrax said, "a visitor in our midst."

There was some grumbling.

The throne revolved to face Ayesh. She found herself looking into gray eyes, stern as storm clouds. "Who art thou?" Myrrax rumbled.

He was an imposing figure, but Ayesh looked at him through the eyes of the Cool Ray Meditation. She felt union with the moment and whatever passed in it. What would pass would pass, as the cool rays of moonlight pass through water. What anxiety she felt, she mastered.

"I am called Istini Ayesh ni Hata Kan of Oneah," she said, and she told him the name of her mother and her mother's mother.

Myrrax said nothing for a long time, then observed, "Thou wearest the color of Rock-in-Water."

"I asked sanctuary of that house."

There were murmurs of disapproval, and Myrrax raised his hand. The room fell silent.

"In the name of what Mother, human, didst thou ask sanctuary of a house of Mirtiin? For I see five fingers upon thy hand, not the four of the First Mother. I see thee tread upon fleshy feet, not the hooves of She Who Was First."

Ayesh, drew herself up. "I asked shelter in the name of our First Mother." More murmurs. "I asked it, asked honor of the lineage that all assembled here do share with me."

Betalem sprang to her feet. "Heresy!"

"I speak as I was taught in Hurloon," Ayesh said, "where the names of the Mothers are remembered, even to She Who Was First. It is from your cousins in those distant mountains that I learned who I am: cousin to minotaurs, daughter to Lemeya, who the Hurloon know as Light-Mother—"

"We who honor her," said Betalem, shaking with anger, "do not speak her name aloud! As for the Hurloon, they are outcast! Far better that such as they had died those many generations ago! They would not yet spread their lies in the world!"

"I speak as I was taught," Ayesh said, bowing slightly. *And as I was coached,* she thought, for the precise formula of what she should say was given to her by Scaraya.

"Do you deny," said Betalem, "that such as you are *flakkach*?"

Ayesh bowed with more respect this time. "No, Mother. For it is written in the first chapter of Knowing Purity: 'By this shall you know the division: The fifth finger is *flakkach*.'"

Betalem opened her mouth, then closed it. She was clearly surprised at having minotaur scripture quoted by a human. Her eyes narrowed, and she looked at Scaraya, who smiled.

Betalem recovered her composure. "Hurloon lies hold no sway here," she said.

"The Hurloon heresy was never decided for Mirtiin," Myrrax said quietly.

"There was no need," Betalem answered. "The heretics were driven from Stahaan, not from here! All that I need do for a letter of suppression is send a message to the Holy Library—"

"Mirtiin asks no judgment on the question, and by my word, none shall come," Myrrax said. "The heresy, so-called, does not stand in question."

"The Hurloon were driven out for their suggestion that minotaurs were cousins to humans," Betalem said. "Be careful, Myrrax. You tread a thin floor over a deep crevasse."

Myrrax said, "Mirtiin goes its own way . . . "

There were some murmurs at this, approving and disapproving.

". . . while yet we honor our First Mother. The issue of right action in the matter of this human is undecided. The human, though *flakkach*, was brought to Mirtiin against her will. Thus she did not violate *purrah*. She is under the protection of a house. Thus she may sit with that house in council. We proceed."

"But—"

"Betalem, our sister from Stahaan," Myrrax said with studied patience, "thou art not Mirtiin. Speak as thou wilt in temple, but in this chamber, thou art our guest."

Betalem frowned and sat down.

Myrrax waved his hand, and the minotaurs who had brought in the four strange boxes stepped forward and undid the latches on the lids.

Ayesh leaned forward. What could be inside? One box was shaped like a great bell. Another was like two triangles intersecting. The last two were tall cylinders.

A minotaur lifted each lid.

Betalem leapt to her feet. "Stop!"

Slowly, Myrrax's throne turned to face her.

The priestess bowed low. "I beg your indulgence, Mirtiin. I could not hold my tongue while this was done." She raised her head to meet Myrrax's gaze. Ayesh saw fire in her eyes. "I ask again, Mirtiin, and of all who are yours beneath this mountain. I have asked it here before, and I must ask it now in this final moment, before it is too late.

Is the sight of our holy instruments for *flakkach* eyes? Are the holy sounds of our music for *flakkach* ears?" She turned toward Scaraya. "Would you defile the very ways that come to us from the First Dawning?"

Scaraya rose and gestured, arms wide, to Myrrax.

"Mirtiin, may I speak?"

The chieftain nodded.

"Betalem," said Scaraya, "you are right. Minotaur music is not for *flakkach* hearing, and it is not to be made by *flakkach* hands."

There was much murmuring at this, and Betalem looked stunned. Whatever the history of this debate, Scaraya had apparently just changed tactics. "You agree?" Betalem said. She raised her gaze to the ceiling. "Have the Mothers touched your resisting heart? Are you ready now to slit such throats as must be slit?"

Scaraya squinted. "No argument for murder has touched me," she said. "Reason, and only reason, convinces me. There has been much dissent over this question of music. Very well. It stands resolved. We shall all agree that Mirtiin music is forbidden to *flakkach* creatures."

Betalem said, "And will you then forget the whole of your sacrilegious scheme?"

"Nay. I will not forget to do what seems wise to do."

Betalem smiled. "But Scaraya, how many times have we heard you argue that music is the tool that matters most, that it is both means and test?" She folded her arms. "You must abandon your ambitions."

"Indeed, not," said Scaraya. She turned again to Myrrax. "By your leave, Mirtiin, I would give a demonstration."

The chieftain nodded.

"Now," Zhanrax told Ayesh.

Ayesh gathered up her tinderbox of unsmoking flame and the Oneahn flute. Holding her head high, ignoring the murmurs that grew in the room, she walked down the aisle that separated her reluctant Rock-in-Water allies from her glaring Ants-Below enemies.

Scaraya brought a wooden footstool to the center of the stage and set it among the still unopened boxes of sacred musical instruments.

The air in the room had grown stale and hot. Ayesh pushed up her quilted sleeves.

Minotaurs, seeing her tattoos for the first time, murmured again. Though their own faces were scarred with intricate tattoos, it seemed they had never seen a human decorated in kind.

Ayesh kindled the flame. She charged the flute and brought it to her lips.

Something soothing, Scaraya had told her earlier.

In the heart scale, Ayesh began to play the "Lullaby of Serra Wings." After the first bars, the murmuring ceased. Ayesh closed her eyes and concentrated or playing with all the heart, all the gentleness, that she had ever heard in the tune. *Soothing,* she reminded herself often. *Play them to sleep.*

When she had finished and opened her eyes, only Betalem still looked angry. The rest of the minotaurs, as far as she could tell, wore softened expressions. A few smiled at her.

"*Flakkach* shall teach *flakkach*," Scaraya said. "What is sacred and secret among us shall remain so. This human knows music, and more. Science of mind. Meditations. There is much that this human might teach."

Zhanrax came down the aisle to collect Ayesh. They left the chamber as Scaraya was launching into a history of Oneahns and their ways.

"You did well," Zhanrax told her as they walked the empty corridors back to Rock-in-Water.

"What, exactly, did I do?"

Zhanrax smiled. "Soon enough, human," he said, "it will all be clear. After you meet Gur."

It was a child's name, Ayesh guessed, for all the Mirtiin names for adults ended in -aya for females or -rax for males. But why would a child hold the key to understanding the web in which Ayesh was tangled?

CHAPTER

11

ZHANRAX TAPPED THE DOORPLATE WITH HIS hoof, and his little brother, Tana, opened the door for them.

"You did so well," Zhanrax told Ayesh, "that you may stay here in the outer chamber until Deoraya returns." He tried to take Ayesh's pack from her, but she held on.

"If I've done so well, let me keep my things."

Zhanrax only tugged harder and pulled the pack from her hands. "Would I leave a captive goblin with her dagger? No more would I let you keep your magic."

"What magic there is in my possessions can do you no harm, Zhanrax. And you just demonstrated to all of Mirtiin that I'm no captive, but a guest."

"In the common halls, yes," Zhanrax said. "Here within Rock-in-Water, you remain a captive." He tossed the pack to Tana, who dropped it.

"Careful!" Ayesh shouted.

Tana shrugged meekly. "Sorry."

Zhanrax shook his fist at his brother. "Don't apologize! You are Rock-in-Water, and Ayesh is *flakkach*! Would you apologize to a beast?"

"There are times, Zhanrax," Ayesh said, "when I find you almost civilized. And then you open your mouth."

"I offer you a privilege for service well done. You did as Scaraya instructed you and deserve reward. But if you argue with me, you will go to the bare stones that are reserved for you!"

Ayesh folded her arms and stalked to the wall where the room's lamp burned. She did prefer this carpeted room over the corner of the kitchen that Deoraya had consigned her to. Carpet was more comfortable to sit or lie upon than polished stone. But she was Zhanrax's dog in either case. Pampered dog or chastened, she wasn't happy with her place.

Someone tapped at the door.

"Tana!" Zhanrax bellowed. "The door!" Tana hurried from the room where he had hidden Ayesh's pack.

The visitor was Cimmaraya, Scaraya's assistant.

"Greetings, Gems-in-Hand," said Tana, bowing. Then he stood awkwardly, unsure of what to say next.

"Will you not bid me enter?" asked Cimmaraya.

"Well," said Tana, "there is none here but myself and my brother. . . ."

Zhanrax strode to the door. "Cimmaraya, honored daughter of Gems-in-Hand! Greetings!" He gestured uncertainly. "I am very happy to see you here! But, ah, what my little brother says is true. My mother and my aunts remain in Assembly, else I would gladly bid you—"

Cimmaraya made a face. "I don't come courting, Zhanrax."

His face lost its animation as if he'd just been clubbed.

"I come to see the human."

Zhanrax brightened again. "The human! Of course!"

Ayesh put her hand over her mouth. Sun and stars, was *this* what Zhanrax had captured her for? As a lure for the scientifically minded female whom he fancied?

"Yes, the human," Zhanrax continued. "If you'll only return after my mother has come—"

Cimmaraya stepped past Tana. "I don't care for the old forms and the niceties."

"Yes, yes," Zhanrax said, so obviously flustered that

Ayesh was actually embarrassed for him. "But if my mother returns and finds you here, she might conclude . . . that is, if another time you were to come because I . . . that is, if you *were* to later think me worthy—"

"Gods and gashes, Zhanrax, cease your stammering," Ayesh said. "I may be *flakkach*, but I'm old enough to serve as chaperone." She bowed to Cimmaraya. "In the name of Rock-in-Water, whose protection I enjoy, I welcome you, Gems-in-Hand. Tana, close the door."

Tana looked at his brother, who shrugged. Tana closed the door.

Ayesh gestured to one of the upholstered stools. "Won't you sit?"

"Ah, yes, sit, please, Cimmaraya!" said Zhanrax.

"Will you have some refreshment?" Ayesh asked. "Tea?"

"Please, and I thank you." Cimmaraya straddled a stool and sat down.

"Tana," Ayesh said, "see to it."

The young minotaur looked at Zhanrax, who impatiently gestured toward the kitchen.

"Your presence has changed things here in Mirtiin," Cimmaraya said to Ayesh. Then she frowned as Ayesh sat back down on the floor. "But come," she said, gesturing to another stool. "Come where I can see you as I speak to you."

Ayesh looked at Zhanrax. "I'm not allowed on the furniture."

"Not allowed?" Cimmaraya's tone was incredulous.

"Are you not the same minotaur who offered to tie me up before Scaraya began to question me?"

"But this is different!" Cimmaraya looked at Zhanrax. "Your mother accepts her as a sheltered guest of the house, yet does not allow her to sit?"

"Oh, I don't have to stand all the time. I can lounge on the floor all I want. With the rats."

Zhanrax waved his hands and laughed nervously. "It's my mother, you see. Deoraya is not entirely pleased to have this human under our protection." He forced another laugh. "Well, you know my mother. Not orthodox entirely, but, *conservative*, shall we say?" Then, through his teeth, he said, "Sit on the stool, Ayesh."

Ayesh smiled and climbed onto the oversized seat.

Cimmaraya said, "In the chambers of Gems-in-Hand, you would be afforded high honor, Ayesh of Oneah. Your presence has turned the tide."

"Tell me," Ayesh said, "for much remains a mystery."

"Tomorrow," Cimmaraya said.

"When I meet Gur?"

Cimmaraya glared at Zhanrax. "How much did you tell her?"

"Nothing. Next to nothing."

"I can vouch for that," Ayesh grumbled.

"Soon, soon indeed, all will be clear," said Cimmaraya. "But what I can tell you now is that there was a struggle afoot in Mirtiin when you came. A controversy."

"It seems to me I *am* the controversy."

"No," Cimmaraya said. "You are only a new development. Ere now, I feared there might be mutiny between those who support Betalem on one side and my father on the other."

"Your father?"

"Cimmaraya is daughter to Myrrax," Zhanrax said. "He who speaks for Mirtiin lives in Gems-in-Hand, the house of Cimmaraya's mother."

"But he is not *of* our clan," said Cimmaraya.

"I've figured that much out," Ayesh said. "Teorax is husband to Deoraya, but he wears the red and black of Flame-in-Void, and he sat today with his birth clan in Assembly." She looked at Cimmaraya. "What clan is your father?"

"He was born Shade-in-Ice . . . "

That got Ayesh's attention. Shade-in-Ice had clearly demonstrated an eagerness to see her dead. But she'd been figuring that Myrrax was on her side.

"Shade-in-Ice?" Ayesh asked to be certain. "Purple?"

Cimmaraya nodded. "My father was born to purple, and so he would remain if he had not been elevated to speak for the Eleven."

"Elevated?"

"Two males are chosen by our matriarchs in a council that can last days. Those two, between them, must decide which shall rule."

"If they do not decide by peaceful means," said Zhanrax, "then they do so by combat."

"Now, of all the minotaurs of Mirtiin, my father and his personal guards are the only ones without clan. He *is* the Eleven. He is Mirtiin. But if he did not still claim some loyalty from purple, we'd have come to war long ago in these halls. No chieftain but one of the orthodox houses could have supported Scaraya and lived so long."

"So why is Scaraya reviled?"

"Reviled by some, admired by others," said Cimmaraya. "You already know she is a scientist, Ayesh. She would have us be ruled by reason, not merely by tradition."

"And?"

Cimmaraya smiled. "Tomorrow, you will learn more. For now, I would ask a question of you. About the beliefs of humans."

"Why not ask Scaraya? She pretends to know as much as I do now. Did you hear how she told the history of Oneah? As if she had been there!"

"She knows only what you told her. And the drug does not compel you to tell what you would not willingly say. You answered her questions, Ayesh, many questions, and I wrote down your answers. But there is still much left unasked."

Tana brought the tea, then, one cup only, for Cimmaraya.

Zhanrax rubbed his forehead. "Brother, will you prove as stupid as you are clumsy?"

Tana gave him a blank look.

"You brought no tea for me!" Zhanrax thundered.

"Nor for Ayesh," said Cimmaraya.

Zhanrax looked at her, mouth open slightly, then said, "Yes, yes! Tea for everyone!"

"Make a cup for yourself," Ayesh said. "You can drink it in the kitchen, Tana, where no one will yell at you."

"Since you will no doubt spill it!" Zhanrax added.

"Were you not clumsy at his age?" Ayesh said. "Human males are so when they reach fourteen or fifteen years."

"*About* humans," Cimmaraya said. "Is it truly a human belief that humans and minotaurs share a common ancestor?"

Ayesh bit her lip. "That I am granted shelter, both in this house, and within Mirtiin, assumes such an ancestor, does it not?" She gave Cimmaraya a narrow look.

"I know what you've said, and I understand your reasons for saying it," said Cimmaraya. "But what do humans truly believe?"

"Beliefs vary," Ayesh said. "Yet some claim that the first minotaur was born of a human queen and a white bull. The bull was a gift of the sea god, given as a sign to the king, her husband, when he was but a princeling. When he attained the throne, the god expected return of the bull in sacrifice. But the bull was beautiful. The king so prized it that he sacrificed another in its place. His queen thought the bull so beautiful that . . . Well, it is said that the race of minotaurs was born of this union between queen and bull."

"As punishment," concluded Cimmaraya, "for a promise of sacrifice, unfulfilled."

Ayesh nodded.

Cimmaraya bared her teeth and said with irony, "We are the monsters born of human sin, Zhanrax. Or so humans would have it."

"What a vile lie!" said Zhanrax. "Even the Hurloon say only that humans and cattle are the offspring of minotaurs made degenerate! They did not honor their ancestors, and thus did they fall from grace! That I might believe, but this other perversion . . . "

"The true beginnings," said Cimmaraya, "are lost in time, Zhanrax. The world is ancient. The generations we remember may not be all the generations that have been. And is it not rumored that the Hurloon were outcast not for their heresies but for having five fingers? Perhaps their heresy grew from the fact of the fifth finger. That some of our cousins are born with five fingers, is that not perhaps a sign that humans and minotaurs had a common Mother in the distant past?"

"Take care," Zhanrax said. "I think well of you, Gems-in-Hand. But what you speak now is blasphemy."

"You are not sure where to stand, are you, Zhanrax?"

"I know that in Stahaan, if you uttered the theory that the human just described, it would mean death. To suggest that there are generations not remembered is also heresy there."

"We are not Stahaan," Cimmaraya said. "That, once and for all, is the thing that we decide in these days. If I were Stahaan, Betalem would have ordered you to kill me, Zhanrax, for daring to think my own thoughts. And if you were Stahaan, you would have obeyed her."

"Betalem seems to want a lot of people dead," Ayesh said.

Cimmaraya said, "None more than you, human."

Tana came in, bearing the tea for his brother and for Ayesh. He brought a cup for himself, too, and bravely drank it over the carpet. And at first, he did not spill it.

Deoraya arrived.

As she stood in the doorway, she opened her mouth, unable to speak at first.

"To me, my sisters!" she bellowed.

Zhanrax's aunts, also returning from Assembly, crowded the doorway to see what the trouble was. No doubt they expected murder.

"I return from Assembly," Deoraya said, "and what do I find?" Her hands shook. "My eldest son, with an eligible daughter of another house, unsupervised in the privacy of my hearth!"

"Mother," said Zhanrax, "Cimmaraya was only—"

"While an animal, wearing the colors of this house, colors that I forbade my son to let it wear, looks on . . . "

"My apologies, Rock-in-Water," said Cimmaraya, "I meant no—"

". . . and the *animal*," Deoraya bellowed, "sits on the *furniture*!"

That last word she roared so angrily that all in the room flinched.

Then did Tana drop his tea.

CHAPTER
12

DARKNESS. THE TORCH FLAME DANCED BEFORE
Scaraya, but in the minotaur's shadow, where Ayesh
walked, it was dark. The stone steps curved and
descended. Down, down, down, corkscrewing deeper and
deeper into the mountain.

The spiraling passage grew narrower as they descended,
and air rushed by as in a continuously in-drawn breath.
Chill breath. Lonely breath.

Scaraya and Cimmaraya could not have made the
descent any worse for Ayesh if they had tried. For the
narrowing passage, the rushing air, the threatening darkness all reminded her of . . .

But she would not think of it.

Ayesh's legs trembled. How far had they already come?
Bad enough that she should be unnerved this way, but the
long descent made her knees feel rubbery. The steps, cut
to accommodate the backward-bending knees of minotaurs, were shallow. But they were also spaced for creatures with much longer legs, and Ayesh could not find a
comfortable rhythm for her strides.

The rock pressed in on her from all sides. The air was
thick.

Be reasonable, she told herself. *This passage was built for minotaurs.* It would never narrow enough to trap Ayesh. Even so, she could not help but notice how Scaraya hunched her shoulders and ducked lower and lower, crowded by the walls and ceiling.

She felt her throat tighten, her breathing quicken. *Relax! This is not then! I am not trapped and alone.*

But she was a prisoner, and she was alone among the race of minotaurs.

The air, it seemed, rushed faster as they continued down.

For a moment, Ayesh halted. She could not take another step. Cimmaraya bumped her from behind.

"What is it?" said the minotaur.

Ayesh closed her eyes and focused on her breathing.

"Is something wrong?"

Ayesh opened her eyes. "It is nothing." She continued down the stairs, but her heart still hammered. "This is a ventilation shaft," she said, trying to sound casual.

"One of many," said Scaraya from in front. "The air is drawn by convection. There are smelting furnaces deep in these passages. Their fires draw the air."

"It was the same in Oneah," Ayesh said. "In the . . . in some buildings." She swallowed hard, trying to banish memories.

"Your people were engineers, the same as us," said Cimmaraya.

"Engineers, philosophers, scientists, wrestlers, artists," Ayesh said. "We studied to be ruled by light and reason. We studied mastery." *And one time in my life, mastery truly failed me.*

Ayesh could feel the stone steps vibrating beneath her feet, and she heard a low, continuous rumble. It had been going on for some time, she realized, but she had only just now become aware of it. They soon passed an opening in the wall, a doorway leading into a small room where the rumble was louder. Ayesh caught a glimpse, in the passing light from Scaraya's torch, of a great stone shaft revolving between floor and ceiling.

"Mill shaft," Cimmaraya explained. "We harness the powers of the rivers that pass beneath the mountain."

Ayesh nodded, tried to be interested. "Is that how Myrrax's throne turns in the Assembly Chamber?"

"Aye," said Cimmaraya. "That, and more important things. The shafts turn the rollers that stamp our ore."

"You mine?" But of course, hadn't Scaraya just mentioned smelting furnaces? Still, it was strange. Ayesh had always thought of dwarves and humans as miners, never minotaurs. As far as she knew, the minotaurs of Hurloon dug their labyrinths only for shelter. They did not trade in anything but stories.

"Yes, we mine," said Scaraya. "We are born of stone, and from stone we nurse our riches."

They came to another doorway. The spiral continued downward without them. How far? Ayesh imagined it going deeper, narrowing forever until it *would* be tight enough to trap her.

Scaraya led the way to an annular passage with many doorways. They took one that looked like any other, and then they were making turns this way and that, as in the labyrinths above, until at last Ayesh saw the light of another torch.

They entered a passageway guarded by axe- and trident-wielding minotaurs. They wore the white and ochre of Scaraya's clan, as well as the green and gold or pink and turquoise of her allies.

"These do not look much like miners," Ayesh said.

"But we are," said one of the guards.

"Indeed?" said Cimmaraya. "What do you mine, Cianarax?"

"Of old," said the minotaur, looking up and down the passage, "we mined gold and silver here. But now . . ." He smiled. "Now we mine the future."

When Scaraya brought her into the long, narrow room, Ayesh still felt shaken, both from the long descent and the memories she wished no longer to have.

"Sit," said Scaraya. She indicated a stone stool.

Ayesh sat. She closed her eyes and tried to compose herself.

"Are you not well?" asked Scaraya.

"I am fine," Ayesh said. "It is nothing. Bring me to Gur. I want to know, finally, what this is all about."

"Gur is here already," said Scaraya.

Ayesh looked about. "Where?" There was no one within the reach of the torchlight, though the far end of the room was cloaked in blackness.

"She is here," Scaraya. She mounted her torch on the wall. "And I leave you to get acquainted."

Scaraya left. Ayesh heard a door close behind her.

Ayesh squinted into the darkness. "Hello?" she said.

No answer came.

She rose and went to the torch.

"No," said a voice. "Leave it. It is best this way." The words were in the minotaur tongue, but the accent was strange.

Ayesh hesitated. "I see you not."

"I would not have you see me," said the voice. "Sit and be still. Wait. Wait."

Ayesh shook her head. "Everything must be cloaked and guarded and secret in Mirtiin. This is madness!"

"As you will. But sit, I tell you. Wait."

Ayesh considered disobeying. Instead, she took a breath. *Patience. Let this play out, and* then *decide what to do.* She sat on the stone stool. She waited, and she used the time to calm herself from the long, dark descent into the mountain.

"So you are Oneah," said Gur at last. "You are the salvation they promise. 'If you can build this Oneah, if you can live as these vanished people lived, then you shall realize your dream. Our dream. All hope lies in Oneah.'"

Ayesh did not know whereof Gur spoke, but she noticed two things. The first was that the voice was not a minotaur voice. It was not deep or resonant enough. The second thing she noticed was the effect of these words on her. *If you build this Oneah . . .*

It had not died, the hope she had harbored these twenty years, the hope that somehow, Oneah might rise. She had labored these many years to see that Oneah would not vanish from memory. That was her duty, and her penance.

But memory was a melting thing, and the more she told the world the story of the Seven Cities of the Sun, the more the world forgot. She had hoped that her memories might somehow be made more than mere memories.

If you build this Oneah . . . But it was impossible. Oneah was dust. Whole cities could not be raised, no matter what she had hoped.

But the small voice inside of her, the part of her that had never wanted to die, the part she'd tried to drown in wine, that part sang out, *Oneah can rise from the ashes!*

That easily, Ayesh's hopes were revived.

"I must say," said Gur, "you disappoint me."

"Disappoint you how?" Ayesh said. "You know naught of me."

"I know the things Scaraya told me," said the voice of Gur. "Yours was a great race with subtle music, delicate arts, and . . . a science of the mind."

"That and more," said Ayesh.

"But even as I watch you now, how do I see that science of mind play out on your body? For when you entered, did your hand not shake? Fear was writ upon your face. And when I bade you wait, were you not nervous? Waiting is the hardest art. What I would learn is to calm myself when emotion rages, and yet you are not the master of emotion, I see. Emotion masters you."

"Not so," Ayesh said. "For I am calm now." And she marshaled her resources that she might be so. She watched her breathing, and she emptied her mind. She made a meditation of the room. The pulse of the torch flame, the hardness of her stone seat, the black shadows from which came Gur's voice—all of this became her meditation. She saw, and she let it pass through her, just as her breathing passed through.

"Aye," Gur admitted, "there is some art to that, I see. But your mind was all a jumble when you entered. That was plain."

"Mastery does not mean ceasing to feel," said Ayesh. "It means feeling, but choosing right action in spite of feeling. Mastery is not the absence of fear. One masters fear by turning it aside."

"And yet, for me, the struggle at every turn is the flame of fear. If I may not extinguish it, I fear it will grow at any moment, by any cause. And mistake me not, Ayesh of Oneah, there was terror writ upon your face when you entered. Am I so terrible that you should fear me so?"

"I do not know you," said Ayesh. "But what you saw in my face and hands had naught to do with you."

"What, then, did you fear?"

Ayesh did not answer at first. She stared into the darkness. "Over many years, I have mastered myself. But there was a moment, long ago, when my skills failed me."

"You see? Skills that fail, that I cannot have. Mine must be the mastery that endures."

"And so it may be, for with time, I have overcome my weakness."

"With time? Slow solutions do not serve."

"And you asked me to wait. You thought to measure *my* patience." Ayesh peered into the dark. "Coming to see you, I was made to recall that time when I failed myself. It is my greatest weakness. But am I mastered by it? You saw fear in my face, in the tremor of my hands, but you did not see me falter in my will. I fell but once, Gur, though it was a great fall."

"Tell me of your mastery. Tell me what you feared, or else it all seems to me the mastery of a child who fears only the wind and falls finally asleep. That is no mastery. What I must master is terror so deep that you cannot have known it."

Oh no? Ayesh thought. But what she said was, "Why need I convince you?"

"You need not do it. I will only say to the minotaurs, 'You are wrong. Oneah knew no great skill of mind. All the teachings that Ayesh promised, they are a lie. Oneah rose from common dust, was common while it stood, and to common dust returned.' As I *shall* tell them, without some proof that you have some mind gold, some brilliance of thought to teach me."

"And if I do," said Ayesh, "what hope is there that you can give me what I want? If I teach you the ways of Oneah, all the lore I remember of my people, will you rebuild the Seven Cities? Will another Roof of Lights arise? Will wrestlers again train in mind and body to know perfection?" Even as she said it, Ayesh knew it was a vain hope. And yet . . .

"If you can do as Scaraya says, if you can teach what she promises, you will have your cities. It will take time. But all that you convey will be kept and cherished. One day, a second Oneah will rise. Here in the Mirtiin Mountains, it will rise."

Ayesh shook her head sadly. "It can be but an echo."

"An echo that endures, generation after generation. *If* you teach true mastery."

Ayesh squinted into the darkness. "Come, Gur. Show yourself to me."

"Soon," said Gur. "For now, be content to know this. We are much alike, you and I. The Mirtiin brought each of us here against our will. To each of us, they offer something we crave."

"I would have Oneah in some wise restored," said Ayesh, "but I do not understand what it is that you want."

Gur was silent, then said, "We have another thing in common. Each of us hates the ways of goblins."

Ayesh balled her fists. "And I do hate them."

"They are parasites," Gur agreed. "And so doomed."

Ayesh laughed. "Doomed? They swarm the world!"

"And as they swarm, they threaten all. Goblins grow so numerous, the balance is threatened. When the parasite overwhelms the host, all are brought to ruin. All die." Then, very softly, Gur said, "Tell me of the one great fear that mastered you. Tell me how you have come at last to master *it*. And if you convince me, then shall we raise your Seven Cities."

Some time it took Ayesh to find her way into the telling. She had told the history of her cities, but never had she told all the truth about herself. Not to anyone.

Yet she had been ready to die mere days ago. Had Zhanrax not been there, had the minotaurs not taken her captive, she *would* have died. And thus, she thought, she might be free to tell the tale. For it was as if this were her second life. All she had been, before she was saved against her will, that was the life of another Ayesh.

So she took in breath, and she let out words. And in the words were the truth of Istini Ayesh ni Hata Kan, a young wrestler for the Court of a Thousand Thousands. In Oneah. In once upon a time. Long ago.

One by one, the cities had fallen. At last, only Xa-On, with the Roof of Lights and the Court of a Thousand Thousands, remained unplundered. There was hope that the wrestlers, more numerous in Xa-On than the other cities, were enough to keep the goblins away. But the gray hordes were so numerous, there was little, together, that they feared.

One goblin is ever a coward. But many thousands of them, crowded together by previous plunder . . . that many goblins could not help but be fearless. Such numbers stirred them to frenzy.

And so it came to pass that the walls of Xa-On were breached. The city was in flames. Goblins poured along the wide avenues, a filthy flood. Good people, wise people, gentle people died under the rush of biting goblin teeth and slashing goblin daggers.

Goblins did not wait for the wounded to die before they chopped off fingers for the rings. They did not heed any pleas for mercy. They did not heed the promise that they could have everything, only please spare the children.

They were senseless, chattering, unfeeling death. On and on they came.

Ayesh and all the wrestlers of Master Hata's school ringed the Roof of Lights. "We stand as wrestlers of the court!" Hata reminded them. "We are the grace of the Thousand Thousands. Goblins do not master us. We know fear, and we are not mastered. We stand! Upon these very stones, we stand!"

"How we fought them," Ayesh said, staring into the darkness that obscured Gur. "I snapped so many of their necks that my arms ached with the labor. We waded through their gray bodies as we fought, and still they charged. And with my brother and sister wrestlers at my side, I mastered all my fear. Aye, I might die, but not alone. Not alone. From time to time, the goblins surged, and one wrestler or another would fall under a dagger, or sink into the general sea of flailing gray limbs. Our circle around the Roof of Lights grew smaller as wrestler after wrestler fell. I saw Yusha fall, and Raikha. Mashala died, and Khairt, grand champion, was felled with a blow to the head."

She could see, in memory, the great doors of the Roof of Lights, standing open.

"And Master Hata called to me, 'Ayesh! Bring out the pennant of our school, and hold it high, that they may know who slays them!'"

Ayesh stood and turned in the torch-lit room, seeing it all again. "I went in. There stood the banner on its pole, among the banners of the other schools. In other parts of the city, the students of other masters were fighting as we were. They were dying, as we were."

Ayesh bit her lip. Tears welled now as they had welled then. She let them come.

"Inside, alone, I failed. I heard the goblin screams, and I did not want to die. I did not master the fear, but looked around the room, wild like an animal, asking myself how I might live. And there, in the wall behind the throne, I saw the metal grate."

She blinked her tears away. "We were, as are the minotaurs, fine engineers. The Roof of Lights would have been unbearably hot in summer if not for the cool air that coursed in through long corridors beneath the ground.

"I am small. I unfastened the grate. I went in feet first, that I might secure it behind me. And then I cowered as my brother and sister wrestlers died, as Master Hata fell, and the goblins stormed the Roof of Lights. I could hear them, gleeful in their victory, quarreling amongst themselves for spoils, breaking and defiling all that they did not think was treasure.

"In my fear, I backed deeper into the passage, though it narrowed, though my shoulders ached with the tightness.

And when they had gone, when the chattering had ceased, I could not move. I was trapped."

She looked into the darkness where Gur listened.

"Long days and nights, I was trapped. And then I was mastered by many emotions. By shame that I would die of thirst where I might have died a hero. By the heartache of betrayal for whichever wrestler died last had died alone."

She stopped.

"Yes?" said Gur. "And?"

"You see that I did not die. After days of thirst, I shrank as leather does. I crawled out and found the vultures, the reeking dead, the remains of a great city. I stayed long enough to salvage some remnants, a hidden treasure or two that I knew of. And then I became Oneah's minstrel, singing over her grave in any land where people would hear me."

"As punishment," said Gur.

Ayesh shrugged. "Before now, none heard this tale. Before now, I had no reason to tell it. But if it's true that some of Oneah might be restored, if some of her traditions could be made to live . . . "

"I do not think you were mastered by fear," said Gur, "but by *life*. What creature, given sure death or sure life, would not choose to live?"

"The other wrestlers chose mastery," Ayesh said bitterly.

"And died."

Ayesh bowed her head. "It were meet that I had died with them. I have lived twenty years too long." She raised her gaze. "Only give me hope that I lived for a reason. Tell me that you will learn what I teach, and that others will learn it. Tell me that Oneah will endure."

Gur stirred with the sound of leather on stone. "I shall be your student," Gur said. "I, and the young ones with me. We will learn this mastery of your wrestlers. And your music, as well, for Scaraya tells me there is soothing in it."

Gur stepped closer to the light.

Close enough for Ayesh to see what she was.

Pointed ears.

Gray skin.

This was betrayal, this trick of Scaraya's, this masquerade. And Ayesh had unburdened herself, told the secret of the dark corner of her soul, to this Gur.

This goblin.

Ayesh did not stop to consider how strange were Gur's ways, how ungoblinish the reason of her speech. She scarcely noticed the odd tremulant twitching of Gur's hands and head.

Pointed ears.

Gray skin.

Ayesh, leaping, cried, "Die!"

Gur, instead of standing to fight, turned and ran into the room's deep shadows. Ayesh heard a *smack!* Then silence.

The goblin moaned. Ayesh closed in on the sound.

"*Kofk, geglack,*" she said. *Die, goblin.*

The door opened. Torchlight filled the room.

"Stop, Ayesh!" said Scaraya.

Ayesh whirled. "Betrayer! You tricked me! I unburdened my heart into the hearing of a *goblin*!" She turned to keep hunting the shadows. "Where are you, Gur? Are you hurt? I bring an end to all pain, you rotter. *Ekmigyla kofk!*"

Scaraya crossed the room and seized Ayesh's arm. Two more minotaurs entered the room, torches raised high.

In the new light, Ayesh could see Gur lying on the floor, cradling her face in her hands. She had run headlong into the bare stone wall.

"Let me go!" Ayesh shouted. She kicked Scaraya, who let go of her. Ayesh crossed the room and pulled Gur up by her hair.

The goblin was dazed. Her eyes seemed to not focus. Ayesh put her hand on the goblin's throat, but hesitated. And in that moment, the guards caught up with her and pulled her away.

CHAPTER
13

"MIRTIIN," SAID THE YOUNG MINOTAUR, A Grass-Above named Journaraya. She bowed, and so did the other three. "We thank you for granting audience."

As if I ever did anything else, Myrrax thought, *but listen and judge.* But he nodded in return—not so respectful a nod as these four youngsters might expect. Myrrax had no desire to encourage them, for he knew before they spoke what they were here to say. They'd been granted audience before. "Say what thou wouldst say," Myrrax said, perched on his throne. "Mirtiin listens."

They looked among themselves, unsure which should speak first. Finally, Keerax, who was Shade-in-Ice, stepped forward. "Mirtiin must take a stand," he said, "for *Mirtiin.* We are sick of the ways of Stahaan. We have our own history, and our own hearts, yet Stahaan would pretend to rule us in all things but name."

Myrrax stared in silence long enough to unnerve the youth. "And thou dost speak for Shade-in-Ice, aye?" he said at last.

The youth bowed his white-maned head. "You know I do not, Mirtiin. But nor is Shade-in-Ice all of one mind."

He raised his gaze. "You rose from Shade-in-Ice to believe in more than Stahaan orthodoxy. You are not unlike us, Mirtiin. Yet you do not act! Why? Why do you not cast out Betalem?"

"Cast . . . her . . . out," Myrrax said, as if chewing the words. "What dost thou mean by that? How indirect a motion, to cast Stahaan's priestess out of Mirtiin. If I had a mind to do that, why not, more simply, invite Gynnalem to raise a Stahaan army against us? Dost read history, Shade-in-Ice? Dost know that four times before Mirtiin has fallen to the might of Stahaan?"

"But we might prepare to meet them!" said Robaraya. She was Iron-in-Granite, a niece of Scaraya's, but without her aunt's circumspection. "We might lay in a store of food against siege. We might build great walls to defend the peaks where the mirrors are hid! Aye, we might gather sunlight for our crops and live in comfort for years while Stahaan tires of laying siege."

Myrrax shook his head. "Wouldst have war when peace is in hand?"

Vedayrax, Gems-in-Hand, said, "We would have peace, but the peace of Mirtiin. We would have peace with the freedom to think our own thoughts and choose our own ways. In Stahaan, they take the fruits of Mirtiin science while ever distrusting Mirtiin thought. They fetter us, Mirtiin. Let Mirtiin, with this generation, at last stand free!"

"I mean no insult," said Myrrax, "when I say that youth speaks here more than reason. It has ever been thus in Mirtiin. It has ever been the young who called for Mirtiin to be itself and not a mere shadow to Stahaan." He turned to the Shade-in-Ice youth. "Keerax, thy mother's mother before thee was such as thee. She even came before the Mirtiin of her day and asked as thou dost ask. 'Throw off Stahaan,' said she. Now see how strict she is in honor of the hearth and Well, and in the Stahaan manner."

Keerax smirked. "The mind softens with age, Mirtiin."

"Mayhap, Shade-in-Ice. Or mayhap the answer is thus: To each generation that craves to be free, there comes the discovery that Mirtiin *is* free."

All four youngsters snorted.

"Howso free?" said Journaraya. "Betalem sits in judgment of all that we do. Scaraya's experiments, which seem the very height of wisdom, are ever schemed against."

Myrrax bit his tongue at the thought of Scaraya's experiments. Ah, what a blind corridor he and Scaraya were running to there! Blast this human that at one turn seemed a solution and at the next proved only a complication.

He said, "And yet what Mirtiin chooses to do, Mirtiin does. Consider it another way, Journaraya. Mirtiin is free to choose war or peace. Is that not a manner of freedom?" He leaned forward on the throne, an eagle about to take flight. "Do not mistake the enthusiasms of youth for a change in the heart of Mirtiin," he warned. "The orthodox dwell in each of your houses. Think not that the split of Mirtiin and Stahaan divides only Stahaan from Mirtiin. It divides Mirtiin from itself."

Myrrax pointed at the axe at Vedayrax's belt. "Wouldst draw thine axe, Gems-in-Hand—" Myrrax gestured at his forehead "—and cleave my head in two?"

"Mothers forfend that I should think it!"

"As thou wouldst not cleave one body of Mirtiin, cleave not the other." In a lowered voice, he added, "Politics is an art that comes with age. Be thee each patient. Watch how unfolds the unfolding and force not the hands of thine elders." With that, he dismissed them.

He could but doubt that they took his advice to heart, for such was youth. Mother of Mothers, he thought after they had gone, let these four at least remain rebels in word only. Aye, these four and the many like them who were too cautious to ask audience. Rebellions by Mirtiin youth were common in the histories, but let this generation pass without one. There were enough matters of import to keep Myrrax busy.

Indeed, the next matter of import awaited the next audience.

"Well?" Myrrax asked.

Lamplight danced on the lenses of Scaraya's spectacles

as she walked about the chamber. There was something odd about her gait, Myrrax noted, as if she would have a limp were she not trying to disguise it. "Not good, I fear. Not the worst, but not good."

"Tell me of Gur."

"Resting. She'll be all right, I think."

"And the human?"

"Furious. She likens me to beasts I'd never heard of ere she said I was one. What, I still wonder, is an orgg?"

"It was unwise to surprise her."

"And it would have been no wiser to tell her everything from the beginning. She'd have refused once we told her goblins were concerned."

"Hast told her everything? All of our intentions, thy methods? Hast made her understand how we labor to civilize goblins?"

"As best I might, Myrrax. To explain to her now is like speaking gently to a storm. Her thunder crashes so that I scarce hear what I say myself."

Myrrax got down from the throne and began to pace. "All this because she so hates goblins?"

Scaraya's lip twitched in a way that might have become an indrawn breath that might have become a sigh, except that Scaraya checked herself.

"Thou art transparent, Iron-in-Granite," Myrrax said. "So tell me what thou dost hesitate to tell."

"Her anger . . ." She stopped to look at the lamp flame, though there was nothing extraordinary about it.

"Tell all. I must know all."

"Her anger is threefold. First, that she should find that we ask her to teach goblins infuriates her. Yet she is a creature of reason and might be persuaded. Not easily, but this is what I expected."

"Go on."

"Second, she did unburden her heart about matters she had told no one ere now. She spoke her secrets to a goblin."

Scaraya took to studying the flame again.

"And the third cause of her anger?" said Myrrax.

Scaraya turned away from the flame. Yes, she *did* favor her left leg. "My greatest fault," Scaraya said, "has ever been my curiosity. It has been my strength as well. I make no apology."

"How didst thou anger her, Scaraya?"

"By so swiftly coming to rescue Gur," Scaraya said, "that she must know I had not withdrawn, as I pretended, to grant them privacy. I was listening, and I heard all that Ayesh unburdened herself of. Ere now, I think she trusted me."

"Didst always walk with a limp?"

Scaraya snorted. "She kicked me. For so small a thing, she kicks like a troll."

"For so small a thing, much rides on her shoulders. A mountain. Will she not help us, much is lost to Mirtiin." He looked into Scaraya's eyes. "Thou didst advise me that she was the passage to fresh air. Now we have caved in the tunnel behind us, and I do not see light ahead."

"With time—"

"With time, mountains are windblown to dust. But too much patience ill serves us. Dost not feel the currents flowing under Mirtiin, Scaraya? I mean not the rivers. I mean the tides of hope and fear. If Ayesh can aid us soon enough, if thine experiment shows promise of fruit, hope shall win out and Mirtiin be united in support for thee. But in delay, fear grows. And Betalem, she tends the shoots of fear where'er she may. Ayesh must be made to serve and quickly."

Myrrax put his hand on Scaraya's shoulder and stood muzzle-to-muzzle with her. "Bring me Ayesh," he said.

"Here? No, Myrrax! She will be seen! Come you into the mines, disguised—"

"I am Mirtiin," Myrrax said, "and what Mirtiin does is seen by all. Indeed, it is dangerous to our future hopes to bring Ayesh here to meet me, alone, in the Assembly Chamber. It signals much that I would fain not signal. Yet how much worse that Mirtiin should skulk and sneak and wear disguises? No, by that would Mirtiin be shamed. The path behind, as I have said, is blocked with fallen rock. We have but the forward passage. Let us act as if it were the path we chose from many."

He stroked his chin whiskers. "Tell me what it was, this secret that she held so close. Then bring her."

The guards half-carried her in. Myrrax dismissed them.

The human's eyes burned like embers. The red anger in them might at any moment burst into flame. Her jaw was set, and she held her shoulders rigid. Whatever Myrrax would say, he could see that she was already resolved to refuse. Bid her sit, and she would stand. Tell her stand, and she would sit . . . or somersault, whate'er she found would please him least.

And so he said nothing, but only watched her.

She seemed to sense the game before it had begun. She faced him and watched in return. If he meant to be patient, then she would be more patient still.

He watched. She watched. He watched her watching.

At last, it was a meditation, this watching, this letting pass whatever should pass. Myrrax noticed that the anger in her eyes was now more an anger that she wore than an anger that she *was*. She possessed it, not the other way around, for she settled easily to waiting in its presence.

"Thy mastery is a visible thing," Myrrax said at last. "I see thee wear it in thine eyes."

She did not answer.

"I am aggrieved thou wert betrayed. And Scaraya, she grieves, too. She meant thee no dishonor."

The light in Ayesh's eyes burned a little hotter, if anything.

"I risk much to bring thee here, Ayesh. Before, thou wert the experiment of Scaraya. But now Mirtiin speaks with thee, and there can be no doubt that I do more than tolerate Scaraya. I support her."

Ayesh only stared.

"Before, I left room for doubt. I might maneuver as I must. But to bring thee here leaves me no retreat. I shall tell thee true, though, that the patrols Scaraya sent out to capture young goblins went with my assent. Ere now, I strove to keep that secret, to let all appear to be Scaraya's doing alone."

Was she even listening? There was no glaze of entrancement over her eyes. She listened, aye.

"Ere thou camest, had we a plan for these goblins. Scaraya herself was teaching them discipline, as best she could. Once we had them sufficiently . . . settled, we would use our music and other such sacred serenities to finish the work Scaraya's herbs had begun. Now we have renounced that path. We cannot return to it. Thou art our only hope."

She scarce blinked. The embers still glared in her pupils.

"If we must abandon all we have done, we lose more than thou might guess. And we could do naught but sacrifice the goblins. It seems a pity, after all that has been done, to murder them."

Her gaze shifted. "You would change my mind by telling me that only thus may goblin lives be spared? Pray give me a million chances to refuse, that all the goblins in the world might die!"

"Thusly did I think, once," said Myrrax. "But this path I would have thee take for us leads to an end not much different. If we accomplish what we hope, it shall be as if all the goblins in Mirtiin had died. And then, perhaps, all the goblins in the world."

"It is folly, what Scaraya attempts. Goblins cannot be made as rational as human beings."

"Folly. But ere thou sawest, didst not think Gur a human being? Was she not rational in speech and seeming?"

"One goblin, alone, with the trick of sounding human. That is not a howling tribe of gray-skinned murderers transformed. One goblin alone may do what ten cannot together."

"I would show you ten such goblins. Scaraya's charges, under the influence of the herbs, are most unlike goblins thou hast ever known."

Ayesh held up her hands. "I would break goblin necks with these hands, not teach the skulkers to mimic the Oneahns whose cities they destroyed. Kill me sooner than make me a teacher of goblins."

Myrrax watched her in silence for a time. The hardness did not leave her face. "Thou art without pity," he said.

"Pity goblins?" She snorted. As far as he could tell, it was not a meaningful snort, such as a minotaur would make, but a mere animal sound. "'Pity and arrows,' so goes a saying among the Savaen elves."

"They deserve pity more than arrows, human." How might he teach her this? "What dost thou know of goblin history?"

"History?" Ayesh shook her head. "What history could goblins have? They reproduce, they overrun, they steal things they know not the meaning of, and they reproduce some more. What changes but the history of those they steal from? They have no history of their own. They have nothing of their own. All is stolen."

"That *is* the history of goblins," Myrrax said. "To be without history, to live always in the teeth of chaos. Fear rides them. They attack because they are afraid they will starve. They thump each other for they fear the other is about to do the same. They make nothing of their own because, in the midst of their fear, they have no time for any thoughts but paranoia. With Scaraya's herbs, their fears diminish from bonfire to mere spark. With music, with the sort of mastery thou knowest, they might learn enough calm to extinguish the spark."

"Experiment as you will," Ayesh said, "only rely not on me. All that I loved in Oneah was brought to ruin by these creatures. Let me go, Myrrax. Let me leave, Mirtiin, to live or die as I choose."

"I thought thou didst love Oneah."

"You make a mockery of what I love."

"Then the kings of Oneah, they loved war?"

"No! Oneah was built upon reason. It was the goblins that made war on us!"

"And so would I prefer peace and reason to war. The goblins that infest our country foul the waters and the air with their stench. When they extend their caves, they sometimes dig into our labyrinths. Then hundreds of them pour into the halls for mischief. Since the coming of the First Great Ice, long generations ago, when minotaurs first dug deep homes in the earth, our kind has warred with theirs. Minotaurs who might be mining, or learning poetry, or studying the stars must devote themselves to hunting our enemy. Were it not better to be able to reason with goblins, rather than kill them? Would it not serve better to make of them creatures who would also care to make poetry or study the heavens?"

"Oneah was bright sun and reason. As you say, Myrrax, goblins are dark caves and fear. It is too great a leap."

Myrrax studied her. What might he say that would change her mind? For if she did *not* change her mind . . .

"Mirtiin shall fall as Oneah fell," he said. "For if all this struggle is in vain, if all this work is for naught, then the factions that are most Mirtiin are greatly weakened, and those that are Stahaan grow strong. Ere long, there shall be only orthodoxy: in Stahaan, Stahaan, and in Mirtiin, Stahaan."

"What should I care for the fate of Mirtiin?"

"You and I shall be alike then."

Ayesh smiled and mocked, "Thou hast forgot to speak in lordly manner."

"When I speak to you as *thou*, I speak for Mirtiin. But now I tell you, as Myrrax to Ayesh, that all that is like Oneah in Mirtiin will fall. Science and reason are not the ways of Stahaan."

Ayesh shrugged.

"We will both have lost all. But consider, if you tried what Scaraya asks, and if you succeeded, what then?"

"Mirtiin would endure," Ayesh said disinterestedly.

"And the last Oneahn wrestler of Xa-On," said Myrrax, "would have unmade all that was ever goblinish in goblins. She would have built Oneah upon the bones of what once was goblin. And the Seven Cities of the Sun would be victorious, after long delay, in their Goblin War."

"It could not be done," Ayesh said. But even as she declared it impossible, she considered it. There was a subtle shift in her gaze, a new focus for her anger.

Now was the moment to draw her in by pushing her away.

"Go, then," Myrrax said. "Be gone from my sight, Ayesh of Oneah. Leave the Halls of Mirtiin and never know what might have been."

CHAPTER

14

COOL THOUGHT. CALM THOUGHT. REASON.

On this tenth day of the teaching, Gur sat in the midst of the young goblins. She watched as human Ayesh opened the box of fire magic that made her flute work. And as Gur watched, she let her mind be as still as a leaf floating upon a windless lake.

But at the door stood the four minotaurs that ever observed while Ayesh taught.

Gur was learning. She sat, legs folded beneath her, hands in her lap, in the manner Ayesh had instructed. The ten young goblins around her sat in the same position, and in their shoulders and heads, Gur saw the same tremorless calm that she felt in herself. Gur's breath entered and left. She was almost at peace.

Almost, for even as calm as she felt, she knew that she stood always on the edge of fear. Like a wind that blew up from a bottomless pit beneath her feet, fear reminded her of where she might fall if she did not learn all that she needed to learn.

And even then, she thought, *will the fear of fear ever leave me?*

Be still, she reminded herself. Ayesh had begun to play

the flute, and the sounds were so sweet that even the black wind might cease to blow for now. Gur closed her eyes.

So much could change in ten days, she thought. She was learning. The young goblins were learning . . .

The music ceased. Gur opened her eyes and saw Tlik, one of the boys, raise his hand. He trembled not at all as he did so, and Gur marveled at this. In ten days, they had come so far.

Ayesh's face was impassive. "What wouldst thou know, Student Tlik?"

"Teacher Ayesh, will you tell me how the flute works? And how one may be made?"

"Approach, Student Tlik."

The youngster bowed twice as he'd been taught, rose gracefully, and bowed twice more. There was only the slightest tremor in his motions. He approached his teacher, bowed again, and knelt to receive instruction. The rest of the goblins looked on as human Ayesh, *Teacher* Ayesh, explained the nature of the flute.

"As to the manner of this one's making," said Teacher Ayesh, "I can tell thee little. It is a magical flute for teaching, and I know not how such things are created. But as to what makes the sound of an *ordinary* flute . . . "

She went on to explain how the air must flow, how alterations in the dimensions and finger holes changed the sound. Ayesh even let Tlik hold the flute to examine it.

Explanation at an end, Ayesh bowed. She extended her hands for return of the flute. Tlik also bowed. He held the flute out to express his willingness to return it, but said, "Teacher Ayesh, may I borrow it to study?"

And human Ayesh's shoulders stiffened.

So much could *change in ten days,* Gur thought, *but how much* has *changed?*

"May I borrow it?" Tlik asked again. And Gur knew that there would be much revealed in the answer.

The human Ayesh had not truly chosen, with all her heart, to do what she did for Gur and the youngsters. In all that she did, there was a wooden quality, a resistance.

"This is Mok," Gur had said on the first day, "and Tlik, and Murl, and Rip, and Kraw."

Human Ayesh had repeated the names of the boys as if they left a bad taste in her mouth. It was the same with the girls: *Bler, Nuwr, Kler, Styr, Wlur.* The human's mouth twisted as she said them, as if there could be no beauty to the name or the one it named.

In her teaching, too, was the human Ayesh hard and wooden. She kept strict order in this class, as if this were her mask and armor. Or perhaps this was the way of Oneahn teaching. Gur could not separate the teacher from the tradition. Certainly, though, Ayesh seemed content to teach in a manner that kept her distant from the students. She even spoke in the lordly manner. "As thou wouldst learn, so must thou release thy will," she instructed on the first day. "The head and heart that are overfull with willfulness can have no room for learning."

Hard though she was, human Ayesh seemed to hold nothing back in her teaching. From that first day, she taught them things they might make good use of.

"The name of the stance," said Ayesh, standing with her legs a little more than a shoulder-width apart, "is the Stone Bench." She bent her knees. "When thou standest Stone Bench—" she bent her knees still further, sinking "—if 'tis properly done, a slipper may rest atop thy thigh and not fall. See how the arms are held. Notice that forearms parallel thy legs." To the goblin nearest her, she said, "Canst do it, Student Murl?"

Murl grinned. "Of course. It's easy."

Trembling from the effect of the minotaur herbs, but still grinning, he took what *looked* like the position, but Ayesh pushed him over easily. "Done right, Stone Bench stands thee firm. Thou needst bend deeper."

"I *did* bend deep!" Murl complained. "I didn't know you were going to push me."

Ayesh made him try again. Again he fell when pushed.

"Canst argue when I correct thee, Student Murl," Ayesh said, "or canst learn. Choose as thou wilt." She had Tlik try. When he fell over, he didn't argue, but only followed her instructions and corrected his stance on the next try. He fell again, but only after Ayesh spent effort in the pushing.

"Well started," she said, and she had them all stand the stance. When all had begun the stance, she placed slippers on their legs. She went back to the front of the room and assumed the stance herself.

"Stand as long as thy legs will hold thee," she commanded. "If thy slippers drop, thou must sit down and watch those who have learnt the lesson better."

At first the stance had felt almost comfortable. Soon, though, Gur's legs had begun to burn with the effort. She trembled already from the minotaur drugs that calmed her mind, but soon she shook with fatigue as well.

Her slippers fell. One by one, the other goblins failed the test. Nuwr sat down, then Rip and Styr. Then Murl. Mok groaned and sat, rubbing his legs.

At last, only Ayesh and Tlik stood. The young goblin's body swayed slightly as the aching of his legs compelled him to subtly shift his weight. Ayesh stood unmoving as the stone wall behind her.

Then Tlik's slippers fell.

"Again," said human Ayesh, "stand the stance, and put the slippers on thy thighs. Show thy teacher how much goblins may endure."

It was with pride, then, that the goblins stood and resumed the stance, bending their knees, holding their arms rigid. Ayesh, meanwhile, had not yet broken the stance, nor had her expression changed. She appeared to concentrate, but in no wise to strain.

"Stand without falling," Gur commanded, for she wanted the human to see proof that goblins, as well as humans, could stand a test of will. Ordinary goblins, wracked with fear and suspicion, might not stand such a test. But Gur could. Gur's young goblins could.

Gur made her mind as calm as she might, and she fought to deny the pain that returned to her legs. Soon, though, her breath came in gusts. She gritted her teeth. The tension in her legs spread to her face. She felt sweat roll down her face.

"Arms up, Student Gur," commanded Ayesh. She did

not look Gur full in the face, as if the sight of Gur's bandaged head angered her. Did the human regret that she had not succeeded in killing Gur?

Gur gritted her teeth and raised her arms to the right level. The human would see what a goblin *could* be!

Kraw's slipper dropped. Then Nuwr's.

Bler and Wlur sank to the floor.

"Keep standing, the rest of you!" barked Gur. Even as she said this, Rip dropped out.

Before long, only Gur and Tlik still stood facing Teacher Ayesh. Tlik was shaking so hard that his slippers fairly leapt from his legs.

Gur was shaking, too. *Stop it!* she thought. *If this is her test of our resolve, let us pass it! Let this human know that we are worthy!*

Her legs burned. *Do not think of the pain!*

She fought to think of something else, anything but the fire in her thighs. She need only fall to quench it.

No! She must keep the slipper resting on her legs! No matter how much she wanted to rest.

Gur's jaw was clenched so tightly that her teeth hurt.

She must endure this! If she were to fail . . .

At that thought, she felt the black wind of fear blow up from beneath her. Her slipper fell.

"Again," said Ayesh, still standing the stance herself.

The goblins all stood, all tried again. When they had fallen for the third time, Ayesh said, "Now will I teach thee a step in mastery."

A fourth time, the goblins stood the Stone Bench. Immediately, now, their legs burned.

"Notice well the pain in thy legs, Styr. Mok, dost feel how it burns? Kraw, canst feel it? Gur?"

They all nodded.

"There is a color to the pain. See it."

"There is no color to pain!" whined Wlur. "It just *hurts*!"

"Tlik," said Ayesh, "dost see the color of thy pain?"

The boy hesitated, then nodded.

"What color?"

"Orange."

"It has a shape as well," said Ayesh. "Nod when thou seest it, Tlik."

In a moment, he nodded.

Rip's slipper fell. He sat down. So did Nuwr.

"Canst see the size of thy pain, Tlik? Styr?"

They nodded. Gur could see it, too, the orange fire the shape and size of her thighs.

"Change the shape," said Ayesh. "In thy mind's eye, Gur, alter it."

Gur found that she could do it. The pain in each leg was shaped like a hedge badger now, all round and bristly. As Ayesh told her to, Gur found that she could change the color of her pain, move it down to her knees or up to her shoulders, rotate it, make it brighter, dimmer, larger, smaller.

"Now move it from thy body," Ayesh said. "Hold thy pain in the air between they hands. It is yet pain. It is yet thine. But now it is in the air before thee."

No other slippers fell. No other goblins dropped out. Gur felt the muscles of her face relax. Indeed, only the muscles that held her in the stance were rigid.

"Guard!" Ayesh said, and one of the minotaurs by the door was startled to attention.

"Aye," said one. "Is there something amiss?"

"Nay," said the human, "but I would have my flute and tinder box. Bring them for me, that I might not move from my stance."

And when the flute was lit within by its magical flame, Ayesh played music for the goblins as they stood attending to their pain.

The song ended, Ayesh said, "Do ye as ye would, goblins. The lesson is ended."

Gur and the others collapsed and fell to massaging their legs. Ayesh, however, rose smoothly to her full height. She put away her flute and flame box and said, "This is already more than I thought the goblin mind could hold. Thus I will pour in no more this day."

Gur knew well enough not to take that as a compliment. But she was proud, even so. And grateful. This was the very sort of teaching she had hoped for.

The second day brought a lesson in gracefulness. The goblins learned to walk so slowly across the room that a single step was the labor of a hundred heartbeats. This was the day when the minotaur Zhanrax came to watch the teaching, along with a young minotaur Gur had not seen before.

"There are roots that grow from the bottoms of thy feet, Gur," Ayesh instructed. "They hold thee fast. Then, they grow tall and support thy foot when it is raised. Thou need never tremble or waiver."

"'Tis the herb that makes me tremble," said Gur.

"Nay. 'Tis thy mind."

Gur looked hard at the human. How much did Ayesh understand? For it was the mind, in some wise, that caused the goblins to tremble, though the minotaur Scaraya thought it was caused by "ill humors of the herbs." Not so. Scaraya's herbs calmed the goblins by cutting them off from their own fear, but fear still jittered and scampered in their minds, still howled up from the pit in their deep-below thoughts. The fear that the herbs made distant was yet the thing that made the goblins' heads and limbs shake.

"Do not think to move," said Ayesh. "Only see the roots grow and shift. See only how the roots beneath thy feet shift thee across the floor. When the roots do move thee, then wilt thou cease to tremble."

And 'twas so! Before long, each goblin could cross the room, fast or slow, with the grace of a swan aswimming, and none trembled. Aye, they might shake like leaves in the wind in the next moment, but while they walked with the roots beneath them, they trembled not.

So impressed was the young minotaur who watched that he pleaded to study alongside the goblins.

"Tana!" said Zhanrax. "Think what you ask, little brother! To be enrolled with these . . . "

"What I'm not dropping I'm always tripping over, and what I'm not tripping over I am breaking." The minotaur then said to Ayesh, "Will you not teach me to be less clumsy?"

The human smiled. "If I take you on as student, Tana, I

must speak to you in the lordly manner, and you must answer with respect here, in the classroom, and also at your home."

The young minotaur nodded, and Zhanrax rolled his great eyes. "Mother will skin us both, Tana!"

"Where would you have me stand?" Tana asked.

"Student Tana," said Ayesh, "thou must ask me, 'Where would you have me stand, *Teacher Ayesh*?' And I will answer thee this time even so. Stand thou behind Nuwr. As thou art the newest student, thou dost begin to learn from the back row and the bottom rung."

Zhanrax groaned. "My own brother, least among goblins!"

"I don't care!" said Tana as he made his way to the back row. "I won't be so clumsy!" And in his enthusiasm, he tripped and went sprawling.

But he, too, learned to walk the Rooted Walk, and his motions were fluid and confident.

Day by day did the lessons progress. There was always music at the end of them, and that was the finest moment in Gur's view.

Before she had been captured in a fight, long years before she had ever set eyes on the minotaur Scaraya, Gur had heard the throb of goblin war drums. That, too, Scaraya told her, was music. But Ayesh's music was the opposite of drumming. Drums made fear all the greater. The black winds of doubt and paranoia that ever blew across a goblin's heart were made to blow harder and colder by the drums. But the flute could almost still that wind.

It was the fifth or sixth day when Ayesh, a mixture of scorn and curiosity in her voice, asked, "What dost thou hear, Student Gur, when I play? I see a change in your face, but tell me true: How moves thy heart to the music?"

"My heart stirs scarce at all," said Gur. How to explain to the human what it was like to be a goblin, drugged with herbs, who heard this human music? "Before Scaraya bade me drink her herbs, I was ever falling into the well of fear," she said. "With the herbs, I found myself standing on a ledge in the well. The ledge was narrow. I stood upon my heels. My toes yet hung over the void, and I might go falling again. But your teachings extend the ledge, Teacher Ayesh. And your music so grows the ledge that I wonder if one day it will not close off and cover the well, that I may walk in safety, without fear of falling."

Ayesh looked surprised, as if the answer gave more meaning than she expected.

Now, on the tenth day, Tlik gently held out the flute, but asked for a third time, "May I borrow it, Teacher Ayesh?"

The human looked at Gur, who looked back.

So much could *change in ten days, but how much has* really *changed?*

Ayesh bowed. "It is a precious thing," she told Tlik. "Take good care of it until the morrow, when thou must return it to me."

So ended the day's lessons.

CHAPTER
15

THE STONE ROD WAS THE LENGTH OF AYESH'S forearm and as intricately marked. A red-garbed guard brought it to Deoraya's household, announced at the door that it was for Ayesh, and was admitted to deliver it to her in the kitchen.

"What is it?" Ayesh said. She rotated the rod in her hands as if she could read the labyrinthine script that wound about its carved surface.

Both Deoraya and Zhanrax looked stern. "Summons," said Zhanrax. "Betalem summons you to the temple for an audience with her."

Tana came into the kitchen and stood a little distance away, looking wide-eyed at the stone rod.

"What happens when I fail to appear?"

Deoraya said, "Fail to appear? The priestess of the temple, surrogate of She Who Rules in Stahaan, summons you and you fail to appear? I think not, human! Not while you enjoy the protection of this house!"

"No," said Zhanrax. "Ayesh is right. She must not answer the summons. Or do you forget, Mother, that the floor of the temple is laid with flagstone from Stahaan? It is, by long tradition, as much Stahaan as it is Mirtiin. Betalem might do as she wished with Ayesh there, and neither this house nor Mirtiin himself could have aught to protest."

Deoraya said, "But to ignore a summons!"

"Well, we'll not ignore it," said Zhanrax. "We'll return it with reason. Children are not made to answer summons, for they are without name. Ayesh, like a child, is not of name. If Betalem will name her—"

"Name me?" said Ayesh.

"Call you Ayeshaya," Zhanrax said, "or even Ayeshalem, in the Stahaan manner." He laughed.

"She would never do that!" said Deoraya. "Naming confers rights of Assembly! Rights of courtship! Would you have such given to this creature?"

"Of course not!" Zhanrax said. "But as Betalem would not name her, Ayesh need not answer the summons."

"You toy with Betalem, my son," said Deoraya. "As you mock the temple, you diminish my room to maneuver. Betalem will think this house lost to her and sided with Myrrax as firmly as Iron-in-Granite or Grass-Above. As firmly as Gems-in-Hand."

"I do what I must for reasons you know," said Zhanrax.

Deoraya rolled her eyes. "Oh, the courtship rights of sons! What a trial to mothers! Yet did I hope you would be wise, Zhanrax. Had I known that your loins would rule your brain—"

"Not my loins, but my heart rules me," said Zhanrax in a low voice.

Tana had crept a little closer. He said to Ayesh, "May I hold the summons?"

"Wouldst hold it in full mindfulness, Student Tana?"

He bowed. "In full mindfulness, Teacher Ayesh."

"Mother of Stones," said Deoraya, "would you look upon my sons and weep? One of them thinks only on dangerous courtships, and the other speaks to a human as if she were Mirtiin himself! How have I failed as a mother? What great wrong did I do that I deserve this?"

While Deoraya ranted and pleaded with She Who Hears All, Ayesh and Tana bowed again, and Ayesh handed him the rod. Tana was clearly in awe of the object as he examined it.

"'Tis cut from Stahaan stone," Zhanrax said, "from near the Well of Beginnings. It is a holy thing, from a holy place."

"Would Tana bear any blame if he brought the summons back to Betalem?" Ayesh asked. "Would she hold it against him?"

"Tana is without name, and thus too young for serious blame," said Zhanrax.

"Let Tana carry it?" said Deoraya. "Zhanrax, are you mad? He'll drop it!"

"No, he won't," said Ayesh, and then she added to Tana, "For thou shalt carry it in full mind, and with thy feet rooted at each step, and in mindfulness of all that is about thee. Is that so, Student Tana?"

Tana nodded at her, then looked at his mother. "I won't drop it. I'm not clumsy anymore. I'm not full of goblin mind anymore."

"Goblin mind?" said Deoraya. "What heresies does the human teach?"

"'Tis a manner of speaking only," said Ayesh. "The mind that is full of fears and distractions is goblin mind. But Tana, when he wills it, has the power of diamond mind. He will guard the summons better than Betalem's guard did in bringing it here."

"Go," Zhanrax said to his little brother. "Take the summons to Mother Betalem and tell her that Ayesh may not answer, for Ayesh is without name."

Tana bared his teeth in the lopsided manner of a minotaur grin and was gone before his mother could take the job away from him.

No reply came from Betalem in the days that followed, and the summons was not repeated.

The lessons of the goblins progressed apace. Ayesh began to teach them—and Tana, too—some of the first moves of an Oneahn wrestler.

"When dost fight with a weapon," Ayesh taught them,

"canst ever be disarmed or caught unprepared. But when thy weapon is thy body, as thou dost breathe, thou canst fight."

But, as she also taught them, learning to wrestle was a matter of learning much more than how to fight. The objective that mattered most was mastery. Body, mind, ego, all must be guided and mastered. "More important than winning or losing," she said, "is being present."

Including Tana in the instruction was both curse and blessing. Along with Gur and the young goblin Tlik, Tana was among the most eager of students. He took instruction well. What caused the complications was not his attitude, but his anatomy.

Ayesh had to rethink wrestling from the ground up. When it came to striking techniques—kicking and punching—Tana couldn't do things the way Ayesh and the goblins did. His knee was hinged backwards, so that his snap kicks in front had to be taught like hammer kicks behind, but then all the balance technique had to change, for one kick was more *up*ward and the other more *out*ward. Moreover, Tana's four fingers, all curled to the center of his hand, made a useless fist. It absorbed shock better than it delivered. Ayesh settled on teaching him to strike with open hands.

The blessing of Tana was the other side of rethinking wrestling. As Ayesh had learned, a minotaur could not be controlled with the usual holds, so oddly jointed were they. Tana would let her experiment on him during a demonstration.

"We have learned to turn the hand inward to control a goblin," Ayesh would say. "Now, for the like move against a minotaur . . ." She took Tana's black-fingered hand, turned it this way, that way, splayed the fingers, pressed them together, pulled the hand to one side, asking all the while, "Does this hurt? This? How about—"

"Ow!" Tana dropped to his knees. "Ah! Stop!" he cried as Ayesh figured out how to force him all the way down.

"I thank thee, Student Tana. Please stand." And she would teach the move. Then, to make sure they had it, the goblins all had to practice what they had learned on Tana, for neither Zhanrax nor Cimmaraya nor any of the guards would be subjected to such humiliation.

He never complained. "Young Tana, thou art on the path of true mastery," she told him. If Tana resented his treatment, he gave no sign at all. Ayesh did have an oft-repeating dream, though, that the young minotaur twisted her this way and that way, pulled her hair, stepped on her feet, calmly asking all the while, "Does this hurt, Teacher Ayesh? This? How about—"

One morning, as Ayesh, Zhanrax, and Tana prepared to leave the halls of Rock-in-Water, Deoraya headed them off in the front room. Her sisters were with her—half a dozen female minotaurs in all. They quite effectively blocked the door.

Zhanrax put his hands on his hips. "My mother," he said, "I go courting this morrow, and I see my way is blocked. Is this the way of Rock-in-Water, to deny the rights of its sons?"

"I would only delay you for a short time," said Deoraya. "But if you would pass, then pass. I only insist that the human remain."

"Why?"

"A visitor approaches."

"Who?"

Deoraya smiled. "But I would not keep you from your courting," she said. "Does it matter so who visits the human? Pass without. I would not bar your way."

She stood aside, but Zhanrax stayed where he was.

"What are you up to, Mother?"

"Trying to save Rock-in-Water from further embarrassments, if I may," said Deoraya.

"Student Tana," said Ayesh, "get thee to Scaraya and tell her what happens here."

But Deoraya grabbed Tana as he passed. "*You* are not of that impossible courting age yet, so I may still command you. You will *not* do as the human tells you, upon the honor of your Mothers. Understood?"

Tana looked from his mother to Ayesh and back again. "I understand," he said.

"Swear."

"Upon the honor of my Mothers, I will not do as Teacher Ayesh has commanded me." It was a solemn vow.

So much for help from Scaraya, thought Ayesh.

There came the tap of hooves against the doorplate.

"I'll answer," Tana said, and his mother let go of him.

Tana opened the door, and there stood the temple guard—all ten of them. In their midst stood Betalem. She glared at Ayesh.

"Mother Betalem! Do come in," said Deoraya. "And bring your escort."

Tana had to step into the hallway to let the broad-shouldered, axe-wielding guards enter. When the five guards ahead, Betalem herself, and the five guards behind had all crowded into the front room, the door closed behind them.

All eyes were on Betalem. If anyone besides Ayesh had noticed that Tana was gone, none gave sign of it.

"You would not come when summoned," said Betalem, glaring.

"With good reason, Mother Betalem," Ayesh said, bowing deeply, "as you were given to know."

"Do not call me Mother!" said Betalem. "There is no link in my lineage and yours!"

"In Hurloon was I taught otherwise," said Ayesh.

Betalem snorted. "Hurloon! But we have heard this from you already. Let us not mine a barren shaft. I would make you an offer, human. Accept it, and you live. Otherwise, I cannot promise your safety."

"Is that a threat?" said Ayesh. "I asked and was given the protection of this house."

"Much against my will," grumbled Deoraya. "But she knew the right forms of asking. Learned from the Hurloon, no doubt."

"This is a strong house, and an important one," said Betalem. "To kill you would stain the honor of Rock-in-Water. I am priestess to all of Mirtiin. I would not gladly make an enemy of this house. Times are troubled in Mirtiin, but I would have peace if it is possible."

"Mother Betalem, I owe all respect to the temple," said Zhanrax. "All that is done with the human, I do for the purpose of courtship. Do the scriptures not say, 'Unmarried and with name, he seeks alliance with another clan. Deny him in no wise as you would honor the whole of thy lineage'? Therefore, stand aside and let us pass. I am courting, and Ayesh is the gift I bring to the one I would woo. Like flowers."

Even among humans, Ayesh thought, *that would be demeaning. But minotaurs eat flowers!* Still, she held her face impassive.

"The temple matters more than your desires," said Betalem.

Deoraya said, "Cimmaraya is a bad match, my son. Her clan is small, and their lineage is not as full of heroes as ours. You should court in Cups-Ashattered or Stones-Afalling. Even Flame-in-Void can offer you a better marriage."

"If you court her for her father's favor," said Betalem, "know that Myrrax will not speak for Mirtiin forever."

Zhanrax drew himself up indignantly. "I do not court to gain favor with Mirtiin. And do you threaten him, Betalem? He who speaks for these very stones?" He stamped his foot on the floor. It would have been a more meaningful gesture if not for the carpet.

"It's true," said one of Zhanrax's aunts. "Myrrax shall not long stand as Mirtiin."

"It *is* a threat," said Zhanrax.

"Only wisdom," said Betalem. "Mirtiin is small next to Stahaan. Whenever heresies have sprouted in Mirtiin, there has been disaster for him who speaks for Mirtiin." She pointed at Ayesh. "The thoughts that let *flakkach* live in Mirtiin, those are heresies. War looms."

"You spoke of an offer," said Ayesh. "I would hear it."

"She'll dangle nothing but tricks," said Zhanrax.

"Not so," said Betalem. "Ayesh, you are captive here. But my guards and I would give you escort to the limits of Mirtiin patrols. To the very sea we would take you and set you free."

"You can't trust her," said Zhanrax. "What does she mean exactly? Would she take you to the border of Stahaan to release you? She could arrange to have Stahaan guards there to kill you."

"To the shores of the Voda Sea, if you will it, Ayesh," said Betalem.

"Still you may not trust her. Does she promise not to kill you? But you are *flakkach*. Her word to such is nothing."

"True," said Betalem, "and thus would I make my pledge to you, Zhanrax, and to your mother and aunts. Ayesh is in your protection. If she agrees to come with me, I will give her the shelter of the temple. Not that she may enter the temple to receive it. But it is my word that she shall not be put to death. If she agrees."

"You mustn't go!" said Zhanrax. "Cimmaraya needs you!"

"You stand opposed to the temple, Zhanrax," Betalem warned.

Zhanrax bowed to her again. "I ask only the right given me by scripture."

"We will get you married," said Betalem. "Well married. Into Shade-in-Ice, perhaps? There are many pious young females in that house."

"I am within my rights!" bellowed Zhanrax.

Betalem's guards stiffened, hands on their axes.

"And I am within mine," said Betalem. "I will guide Mirtiin down the true and sacred path. By any means. I would prefer the bloodless path, Zhanrax. But if you would oppose me, know that your Cimmaraya treads so treacherous a path that even if you court her as you would, she may not live long enough to marry."

"Outrage!" Zhanrax bellowed. He gripped the axe at his belt.

"Simple truth," said Betalem. "Human, how say you?"

Ayesh looked long and hard at the priestess. At last she said, "You fear me because I may succeed."

"I oppose you because you are the tool of heretics," Betalem said. "I neither fear nor hate *flakkach*. I would only do as scripture commands. Yet would I once make an exception and suffer you to live, even after you have violated *purrah* and seen the inner Halls of Mirtiin."

"No," said Ayesh, shaking her head. "I know you. I have met your kind among humans and among all races.

Once you have found your way, the one narrow way, you will cling to it and force others to do the same. But what if a better way opens before you? Then will you put out your eyes rather than see it." She smiled. "I make progress, Betalem. The goblins learn. Soon there will be a new race in Dominaria—the goblins of diamond mind! And there will be peace in Mirtiin while goblins and minotaurs in Stahaan are doomed to war."

"Goblins are *flakkach*! We *must* war with them! We *shall* war with them! All Mirtiin does by improving its goblins is make for itself a more dangerous enemy!" Betalem turned to Deoraya. "Withdraw the shelter of your house! Let me seize this human and deal with it as I will!"

Deoraya looked at her sisters and at her son. "The form was correct," she said.

"But based on Hurloon heresies!"

"If you would show me in scripture, Mother Betalem, where it says clearly—"

"Idiots!" cried Betalem. "I speak for Stahaan! *That* is as firm a proof as scripture." Then she said to her guards, "Kill the human."

"By our honor, you will not!" shouted Zhanrax, stepping in front of Ayesh. He freed his axe as the ten guards freed theirs.

Uncertainly, his outnumbered aunts hefted their own axes.

"In the name of She Who Was First," said Deoraya, "would you war with this house, Betalem? We can but resist you. It is our honor!"

Betalem only said again, "Kill the human."

CHAPTER

16

FOR LONG MOMENTS, NO ONE IN ROCK-IN-
Water moved. Ayesh half expected one of Zhanrax's aunts
to drop her axe, turn, and grab Ayesh to surrender her to
Betalem's guards. Rock-in-Water had no love for her.

But the outnumbered matriarchs stood poised for battle, axes at the ready. Honor was at stake.

Honor would be at stake for Tana, too. What was he
doing out there in the hall of Mirtiin? Honor-bound by a
promise to his mother, he surely could not fulfill Ayesh's
instructions to tell Scaraya what was happening. Even to
obey the letter of his mother's command but skirt her
intention would bring dishonor. So he couldn't tell
Cimmaraya and hope that she would tell Scaraya, or tell
Cimmaraya so loudly that Scaraya would overhear.

Even if Tana shamed himself and went to Scaraya,
what help could the near-sighted scientist provide now as
things threatened to turn ugly?

So Ayesh worried about whether Tana could find a way
to bring help, while in the front room of Rock-in-Water,
Betalem's guards moved forward with a cry of, "Stahaan!"
Axes clashed.

The matriarchs of Rock-in-Water were twice disadvantaged. Ayesh could see it in their eyes: They could hardly believe they were fighting to protect a human. And they were outnumbered. So they fought half-heartedly, only to show that they would resist. They expected Betalem to back down.

"Surrender the human!" Betalem cried. Her guards pressed their attack full force. Axe heads rang again and again. One Rock-in-Water fighter bellowed in pain as an axe was buried in her shoulder. Two other guards closed on her, chopping, as Ayesh tried to melt to the back of the room.

"Djenaraya!" Zhanrax cried to his aunt. She sank to her knees, dying. Zhanrax roared. His axe found the neck of the nearest guard. His mother and aunts were stunned for a moment longer as if they could not believe that the temple guard would murder their sister. Their hesitation created more openings. Another guard's axe found its victim.

"Kheshiraya!" bellowed Zhanrax, anguished. Then, with fury, he cried, "Mother! *Fight!*" His shout kindled flames in his mother's eyes.

"Betalem!" cried Deoraya, "for this outrage, you die!"

"The survivor makes history," said Betalem. "It will be remembered that Rock-in-Water, accursed house, lured a priestess of the temple and attacked her there."

Now Rock-in-Water had its own reasons to fight, and they fought with fury. At last Ayesh could enter the fray without fearing that *both* sides would swing at her. But Rock-in-Water was down to Zhanrax, Deoraya, and three of Deoraya's sisters, opposed by eight guards. Only the close quarters of the room gave the defenders some hope of holding out a little longer.

Ayesh darted through into the forest of furry legs. She kicked as she passed, aiming where Tana, by his wounded grunts, had taught her to aim. But now she kicked full force.

One guard grunted. Another toppled.

From the corner of her eye, Ayesh saw Zhanrax hack at the leg of the fallen guard. There were more bellows. Ayesh kept moving as one sharp hoof flew at her head.

She ducked. Now another. She rolled, kicked again, rolled Band somersaulted out of the fray, in reach of Betalem.

"Do you think I can't deal with you myself?" Betalem sneered. She reached for Ayesh.

It happened as if in slow motion. Betalem could not have bent forward more awkwardly, more invitingly.

Ayesh grabbed the hand that meant to seize her. She turned the wrist not forward or back, but *outward*.

Pop.

Betalem howled in pain and rage. Ayesh kept pulling her arm so that she toppled in a heap onto the floor. Turning the arm, leveraging with her shoulder, Ayesh pushed until she heard a louder, deeper *POP*. She aimed a kick at Betalem's muzzle. On a smaller creature, it would have been a killing blow, but Betalem would have only a bloody nose.

The priestess bellowed again. She could not get up. Ayesh still held the dislocated arm.

Enraged, Betalem cried, "The human! Kill the human first!"

The guards were unlikely to all turn their backs at once upon Rock-in-Water's survivors. But one guard did turn and aim an axe blow at Ayesh's head. She ducked and rolled away.

Betalem struggled, with one arm, to sit up.

"Kill her!"

The guard started one way with the axe, then changed directions. Gods and gashes, but these minotaurs were strong! The move took Ayesh by surprise. The blade grazed her hand as she fell backwards, toward Betalem.

Her hand had been laid open. It gushed blood.

The guard advanced.

Ayesh rolled. From the corner of her eye, she saw something black descending. She moved, but not in time. Betalem's hoof fell with bone-shattering force. Ayesh winced.

"There!" said Betalem. Still sitting, she shifted all the weight she could onto the hoof that held Ayesh's ruined finger. "She's pinned! Finish her!"

The axe began its descent. Ayesh did not think. She yanked. She felt pain, resistance. She yanked again. Flesh and sinew tore, and she rolled away.

The axe split carpet and cracked open the stones beneath.

The front door opened. A deep minotaur voice cried, "Stop! In the name of Mirtiin and all her clans, whoever strikes the next blow shall die!"

The fight stopped.

The room was full of the sound of panting and the smell of blood.

The guard whose axe had just missed Ayesh glanced at his mistress. Ayesh saw Betalem give him the slightest nod.

He yanked his axe out of the floor and raised it to swing at Ayesh. She was ready to spring away.

The blow never fell. A lance transfixed the guard so suddenly that it seemed to have materialized in him.

The axe fell from his fingers. He knelt, clutched at the thick shaft, then fell to his side.

The minotaur with the deep voice strode into the room. He wore a gray tunic and a sash of the Eleven. He surveyed the situation, then shook his head. "Blood between clan and temple! Mothers save me, now I've seen all!"

"We were attacked, Captain Tekrax," said one of Deoraya's sisters.

The captain only shook his head.

More guards followed him in. Outside stood Tana, eyes wide with fear. From other Rock-in-Water doorways, other minotaurs were peering into the black-and-blue curtained hallway.

Ayesh went to the dazed youngster. "Tana," she said. She raised her hand to him, seized his wrist. "That was wise, going to Myrrax!"

He stared. She followed his gaze into the room.

Two of his aunts lay dead. His mother and older brother were covered with blood. Three temple guards lay dead. A third aunt held the stump of her severed hand.

Ayesh looked at Tana again. Now his gaze was on

Ayesh's ruined hand. Bright blood pumped onto his fur where she held his wrist. Her least finger was gone, and there were shreds of torn flesh all around the wound.

"Diamond mind," she said. "Now is the time to know whether you have it or not."

"Diamond mind," he repeated.

"Follow your breathing."

He closed his eyes, nodded.

"Feel what you feel," she told him. "But don't be mastered by it. Feelings pass, like breath."

He opened his eyes and followed her in. As they entered the room, Deoraya cried, "Do you see what you have done, Zhanrax? Your aunts, who did love you when you were in the cradle and did love you still this morning, they have died for you! They have died for you and for this fruitless courtship you make!" Then she sobbed, "My sisters, my sisters!"

Zhanrax knelt over his Aunt Kheshiraya. He closed her eyes with his black-tipped fingers. Then he raised his head and made a sound that was half bellow, half moan.

Tana knelt beside his brother and wept.

Ayesh expected the minotaur cries and keening to give way to the low, vibrating hymns she'd heard the Hurloon sing to the battle-fallen. But no minotaurs sang in Rock-in-Water.

Indeed, Ayesh recalled, the minotaurs in Zhanrax's patrol had not sung for the goblins Ayesh had seen them kill. So here was another way that the traditions of Mirtiin differed from those of Hurloon minotaurs.

An hour later, while Scaraya cut away the useless flesh and sewed Ayesh's wounds closed, Tana led the class of goblins. Ayesh had told him to stay behind with his grieving family, but Tana had wiped away his tears and said in a cracked voice, "Someone must lead the class. Diamond mind, Teacher Ayesh."

"You must grieve," Ayesh said.

Tana had pursed his lips and given her as hard a look

as he could manage. "I do grieve. I feel what I feel," he said, "but I won't be mastered by it."

She opened her mouth to argue, but thought of a saying of Master Hata's: *Like birds in autumn, the wounded heart knows where it must fly.* So she nodded and let Tana go lead the goblins.

"I hope he doesn't set them back," Scaraya said as she worked on Ayesh's hand.

"He'll make a fine teacher."

Scaraya mistook her sincerity for irony. "Well, it will be fun for him and can't do much harm. Children must have their adventures!"

"He's hardly a child, Scaraya. He's my best student."

Bees buzzed in the mirrored sunlight above Scaraya's head. All along the subterranean corridors of Iron-in-Granite, birds sang. Fruit hung heavy on some of the trees.

"Children must have their adventures," Scaraya said again as she dabbed blood from Ayesh's wound. "Just as long as he doesn't set the goblins back. They're making progress, don't you think? Will they be ready soon for Assembly? I think so. Yes."

As much as Scaraya underestimated Tana, she overestimated the goblins if she thought them ready for public performances and demonstrations. No matter how much self-mastery the goblins managed, Ayesh was sure that the less they were seen, the better. Minotaurs of some clans still muttered whenever they saw a thoroughly self-controlled human. Would they be any happier seeing goblins who could reason? And showing off the martial skills of the goblins, now that would be madness! To wrestle took self-control, but all the assembled minotaurs would see, Ayesh was sure, was a dangerous enemy made more dangerous still.

And was this not perhaps what they *were* creating? Yet Scaraya had lately kept asking, "What demonstration? What can we show? Something soon, yes?"

Scaraya took up a scalpel from her tray.

And if there were a demonstration, what would it demonstrate? Oneahn virtues?

Ayesh had long since given up the illusion that she was

teaching Oneahn culture, whole cloth, to the goblins. The truth was, she contributed to a mélange. What she taught, her students heard with goblin ears. Tana, when he repeated the lessons to the goblins, altered things in subtle ways that made them minotaur. When Ayesh spoke of the Invisible, Tana repeated it as the Hidden. It was, Ayesh mused, the difference between a culture of the open plains and a culture of the labyrinth.

Scaraya's scalpel struck a nerve. Ayesh flinched.

"Almost done," Scaraya said.

Ayesh looked at the tray of instruments, the clean blades and needles shining in the subterranean sunlight.

"There's the other one to do," she said. She held out her left hand.

Scaraya blinked uncomprehendingly.

"Take the least finger of my left hand," she said. "Then I won't be *flakkach*."

Scaraya's blue gaze met hers. "No. You're wrong."

"You haven't great political sense, Scaraya," Ayesh said frankly. She had learned from Tana, days earlier, that not all matriarchs were chosen for their political prowess. Each clan selected its leader by consensus. Election meetings, Tana had said, could go on for days. If any adult female of the clan objected to a particular nominee, the selection was invalid. There would be debate and withdrawal of either the nominee or the objection. The meeting would be reconvened, day after day, until a nominee was named and no one spoke up to object.

Scaraya had been elected for her scientific knowledge more than her political wisdom. She knew her herbs and their powers. Her gardens were miracles of optics and horticulture. Yet Scaraya simply could not see the true state of things in the goblin classroom.

First, she dismissed Tana, Ayesh's best student, as a mere class mascot. Tana knew more than the goblins knew, for he lived in the same household with his teacher. There were times when he asked so many questions that Ayesh would ask him to leave the kitchen for a time so that she could have a moment's solitude. But if he were gone long, she would miss him. He alone, in the halls of Rock-in-Water, treated her with real respect.

If Scaraya were oblivious to Tana's real place in the classroom, how could she navigate the far subtler matters of Mirtiin politics?

"Cut the finger," Ayesh said again. "Cut it, and we cut the ground from beneath Betalem's feet."

The minotaur shook her shaggy head.

"If you won't do it, I'll ask Zhanrax to. He'll understand why it's useful, Scaraya. He just won't know how to cut cleanly."

Scaraya squinted at her.

"First chapter of Knowing Purity. 'By this shall you know the division: The fifth finger is *flakkach*.'"

"Only an extreme fundamentalist would agree that cutting off the fifth finger—"

"Do it," Ayesh said. "Do it well, or I will have Zhanrax do it poorly."

Scaraya met her gaze in silence for a long time, then turned to look at the tray of glittering blades. She selected one that looked like a miniature cleaver.

CHAPTER
17

CIMMARAYA SAT BETWEEN THE GUARDS, UNDER
the lamp, watching the lesson begin. The news of the
Rock-in-Water skirmish had stunned her. And she was
even more surprised to see that Tana would come and
lead the class while his family grieved above. Aye, lead
the class, and lead it well. With confidence beyond his
years, Tana led the stretching exercises and the heartbeat
drills, and then he led the class through questions about
the Seven Virtues. Ayesh had taught five of the virtues so
far. That was as many as Tana could test the goblins on.
He knew no more.

Cimmaraya's heart was four-times troubled. First, she
worried that Tana, knowing little more than the goblins,
could make but a poor teacher. Second, she was concerned
for Ayesh, who Scaraya said had lost a great deal of blood.

Third, she was worried about Zhanrax.

In one corner, Zhanrax stood in the shadows. With
eyes that seemed not to see, he stared at the proceedings.
He did not blink. Sometimes his hands closed on the
empty air as though to crush the life from his enemies.
Sometimes his whole body sagged with sorrow.

Big Zhanrax, leader of patrols, eldest son of a clan Mother, was half-mastered by an anger he dared not act upon, and with grief he was not properly observing. But it seemed that if his little brother would come to class as if nothing had happened, then so would Zhanrax.

Cimmaraya had always found Zhanrax terribly full of himself. When Scaraya had made plain that he'd brought them Ayesh only that he might thus court Cimmaraya, Cimmaraya had counted him a fool. A useful fool. She was grateful that he had brought Ayesh. But a fool all the same. And so she had treated him.

Now though, to see him so disconsolate softened her heart. Aye, still a fool was he. But he was a fool who suffered in the wake of death. He was a fool she might be gentle with. At least she could cease to ignore his suit, as she had done so far. She ached with the thought that her indifference was but one grief, now added to others. She did not think him a likely mate for her—his family was so conventional! Yet she might ease his heart rather than break it.

Tana began to teach something called the Rainbow Meditation. Cimmaraya had not seen it taught before and supposed it something Ayesh had taught Tana alone in the halls of Rock-in-Water. "With eyes closed," said Tana, "you will first see the color red. . . ."

The goblins all seemed a little restless, which was not surprising under the circumstances. Yet Cimmaraya expected to see signs of even greater restlessness in two or three goblins. And that was the fourth thing that troubled her.

The guards by the doorway stirred. Scaraya had entered, and with her was Ayesh. The human's face looked pale and drawn. She leaned against Scaraya.

"Human Ayesh!" said Rip, and Nuwr said, "Teacher Ayesh!" Half the goblins turned their heads.

"Are you animals that you stir at the least distraction?" Ayesh said sternly. "Tana teaches, and while he does, you must give him as much attention as you would to me!"

The goblins turned their heads forward and closed their eyes again. Cimmaraya thought she saw the slightest of smiles on some gray faces. By her outburst, Ayesh proved that she was herself.

"How goes the lesson?" asked Scaraya.

"Passing well," said Cimmaraya. Then, quietly, she added, "But there is a problem."

Ayesh was looking into the shadowy corner of the room. "Poor Zhanrax," she said.

"Aye, he suffers," said Cimmaraya. "But wounds of the heart do heal. At the moment, we have a problem of willful disobedience. I fear . . ." She let her voice drop to a whisper. "I fear rebellion stirs among the goblins."

Scaraya looked surprised. "What makes you—"

"It were best we spoke in the corridor," said Cimmaraya. She rose and cautioned the guards to watch the goblins carefully while she and Scaraya were away.

Ayesh came, too, leaning against Scaraya.

"Now," said Scaraya, "what makes you think rebellion is afoot? Should the goblins not be agitated by what passed and what nearly came to pass today?"

"You know that I give them free rein after they've had the herbs," said Cimmaraya, continuing down the corridor. "As long as they do not stray far, and once the guards have determined that our enemies have laid no ambush, I let the goblins have the freedom of the mine."

"The less our charges feel fettered, the better. They will have their freedom altogether one day."

"So you say, and thus is my practice. Today, I bade them drink the infusion. I watched as they did so. After some minutes, I let them have the run of the mine. Later, when Ayesh did not come, I called them back to the chamber. Then happened all that happened today—a fair riot of events, in the midst of which I happened to walk this corridor to gather my thoughts." She pulled a torch from the wall.

"Yes," said Scaraya, "but you haven't said—"

"Here," said Cimmaraya. She lowered the torch that its light might shine on the dusty floor. There was a dark spot.

"Can you stand on your own a moment?" Scaraya said to Ayesh. Then the elder minotaur crouched beside the spot. Reflected torchlight danced on her spectacles.

"Mud?" said Ayesh.

Scaraya sniffed. "Aye, but not ordinary mud. I smell the tang of carlinall and the bitterness of witchbalm. There is the sweet of tinderblossom . . ." She stood. "It is the infusion we give the goblins to still their minds."

"Now you know why I allege rebellion."

"How?" said Scaraya. "Vomit has its distinct odor, yet there is no stench of chyme."

"You mean you don't know?" said the human. "Goblins, in their warrens, are practiced poisoners. Young goblins learn early to hold food and drink in their throats, unswallowed."

"But they ran about in their exercise!" Cimmaraya told her. "They talked!"

"That is their talent," said Ayesh. "Amongst themselves, they would await the first signs of poisoning and only swallow when they are sure 'tis safe."

"How then did they swallow the first draughts of herb that we gave them?"

"They were watched, were they not? They might not spit unseen. Besides, for a goblin in its natural state, 'tis easy to make it forget itself and swallow. They've no mastery, as we know. And among themselves, I think poisoners often startle their victims by design, to make them swallow. If the poisons did not often have their effect, wherefore would they be so commonly employed?"

Scaraya said, "How many, Cimmaraya?"

"I found three such places. I cannot but guess if there are more."

"Grave developments," said Scaraya. "These are days for grave developments." She looked at Ayesh's bandaged hands.

"I have watched the teaching," said Cimmaraya, "waiting for the moment when three or more goblins should shout their defiance and attack the guards. And so I have advised double caution. The guards' hands rest upon their axe hafts."

"As if we haven't had enough of axes today," said Ayesh. She let herself slide down the wall of the corridor to sit. "We must find the rebels out before they rise up.

Any advantage they manage to acquire might give the wrong sort of encouragement to the others, no matter how severely we punish the insurgency." She shook her head. "They had almost convinced me that they *wanted* to change."

"Perhaps some do," said Cimmaraya.

Ayesh shook her head. "Perhaps," she said, "but a goblin will ever be a goblin." She closed her eyes. "I see the manner by which we may smoke our quarry. There are a few things I will need." She opened her eyes. There were dark shadows beneath them, a detail Cimmaraya had not marked before. Was that a sign of stress, of weariness in humans?

"Cimmaraya, who's the best axe-handler among the guards?"

"Zhanrax," answered Scaraya.

"But he won't do, not after what he's been through. No. Someone else. I want control more than sheer power."

"Yaharaya?" suggested Cimmaraya, and Scaraya nodded her assent.

"All right," said Ayesh. "Here's what we do."

By the time Scaraya had found the things that Ayesh needed and Ayesh had instructed Yaharaya in what she was to do, Cimmaraya had decided on at least one suspect among the goblins. "Kraw," she reported, "is restless. His gaze wanders as Tana instructs, and he wiggles his foot all the while he is kneeling."

"Good," said Ayesh. "We will test Kraw first. When he fails, that will help to unnerve his compatriots." She tied the ribbons Cimmaraya gave her to the shank of Yaharaya's axe. They were made of slitherskin, a material as airy as thin parchment, yet with the strength of thick leather. The minotaurs traded for it with the merfolk, and Cimmaraya did not know how it was made. Ayesh, waving a strand of it through the air, had pronounced it perfect for her need.

In the classroom, while Scaraya positioned the wooden

block and set a melon on top, Ayesh thanked Tana for filling in and took control of the class. Tana bowed to her, then took his place among the other students.

Zhanrax, Cimmaraya noticed, had at some time slipped out of the room. She resolved that when this matter with the renegade goblins was finished, she would go to him and offer her condolences.

"All along, have I tested," said Ayesh. "All along have I been well impressed with what self-control might be found in goblins. Murl, thou hast learnt well the Dance of the Spinning Pins. Bler, thou art mistress of attentive concentration and dost repeat thy lessons in detail. Indeed, I do think thou dost take them to heart. True?"

"I do, Teacher Ayesh," said Bler. "'Tis true."

"But these are easy tests," said Ayesh. "True mastery is shown in the calm reason of one who faces death. Thus does death come to test us this day in the guise of the minotaur Yaharaya."

"Teacher Ayesh," said Gur, "are you well? Your hands—"

"Student Gur, did I give thee leave to speak?"

"No," said Gur. "I am only concerned that—"

"Death stalks thee, Student Gur," said Ayesh. "Have room in thy mind for no distractions. Master thy curiosity. Be still and watch."

At Ayesh's signal, Yaharaya strode to the wooden block.

"One," said Ayesh, and Yaharaya brought her axe down on a diagonal stroke, chipping one end from the melon.

"Two," said Ayesh, and a like stroke chopped off the melon's other end.

"Three," said Ayesh, and the third stroke came straight down and cleaved the remaining melon in two. The pieces tumbled from the block. Cimmaraya felt a little stab of envy. Though she had always thought science more important than the warrior's arts, still she wished that she might handle an axe with Yaharaya's precision. Such skills, though, had never been hers.

"'Tis a sharp blade," said Ayesh as Yaharaya wiped red juice from the blade. Yaharaya nodded.

Ayesh knelt, resting her bandaged hands on her lap. Yaharaya stood behind her, axe at the ready.

"Though she assures me of her loyalty to Scaraya," said Ayesh, "Yaharaya is of Grass-Above. As I do not know all the intricacies of Mirtiin politics, how do I know that it does not serve Yaharaya in some wise for me to die? May I trust her with my life?"

Cimmaraya read disquiet in the faces of the goblins, but Kraw was more agitated than the rest.

"What's more, may I trust Yaharaya's expertise? Yaharaya, have you ever erred in handling your axe?"

"Not in a long time," said Yaharaya.

"But it is not impossible?"

"Even minotaurs," said Yaharaya, "are not perfect."

"And your axe . . ." said Ayesh. "Are you sure that the head is bound firmly to the hasp?"

"Sure as may be. I must rely on it in battle."

"Yet there ever lingers some doubt."

"Aye. Head and haft may separate when I would least desire it."

"There is much to be doubted," said Ayesh, "for the world is somewise ruled by happenstance. Yet Scaraya says that you handle an axe with skill, and thus will I lay my doubts aside. What comes to pass shall pass." She closed her eyes. "Ready?"

Yaharaya hefted her axe and grunted.

"One," said Ayesh, and Yaharaya swung the axe. Aimed at the human's shoulder, the blade swooped, ribbons shishing behind. Every goblin and even Cimmaraya flinched.

The blade stopped. The ribbons fluttered against Ayesh's cheek, and she moved no more than a stone would.

Yaharaya readied the axe.

"Two," said Ayesh. The blade swooped. Ribbons shished and kissed Ayesh's cheek. This time, the blade nicked the curve where the human's neck and shoulder joined. Blood welled in the thin red line. Ayesh gave no sign that she felt it.

That was not intended, thought Cimmaraya. Yet it was to good effect. The goblins scarcely dared to breathe.

Yaharaya readied again.

"Three." The blade dropped from straight above. A goblin yelped—Cimmaraya didn't see who it was. The blade stopped, and the ribbons settled over Ayesh's face.

"The essence of this test," said Ayesh, "is concentration. Be still. Do not ignore what is happening, but do not be moved by it. Breathe."

She stood. "Now line up, facing this way. Kraw . . . "

The goblin started at the sound of his name.

"Art nervous, Kraw?" said Ayesh. "No minotaur has killed thee yet. Is that not a hopeful sign? Kraw, thou art at this end, then Styr, Murl, Wlur, Bler . . . "

She assigned them places, leaving Gur for the last position. Yaharaya took her place behind Kraw, and she turned her axe so that it would fall blunt end first. Ayesh had said that she did not doubt Grass-Above's skill, but that an axe head *might* truly separate from shaft. It were better, in an accident, to do the least possible damage.

"Ready, Kraw?" said Ayesh.

The goblin was trembling.

"Ready, Yaharaya? One."

Yaharaya brought the axe down. At the touch of the ribbons, Kraw almost jumped out of his skin. He shook all the more, balled his fists, and tried to sit still.

"Are your hands sweaty, Yaharaya? Yes, do wipe them dry. Ready? Two . . . "

"No!" screeched Kraw. He launched himself onto Ayesh, bowling her backward. "Not kill! You die before you kill Kraw this way!"

Ayesh looked a little awkward as she somersaulted to her feet. She swayed a moment, as if dizzy. No surprise. Tana had reported that the front room of Rock-in-Water was slick with blood, and some of that blood was Ayesh's.

Kraw swung his fists furiously, and Ayesh blocked, wincing when Kraw's blow struck a bandaged hand.

"Kraw!" cried Gur. "Stop this at once!"

"Guards," said Cimmaraya. Two minotaurs seized the struggling goblin and hauled him out the door.

"Leave the door open," said Ayesh. Cimmaraya nodded to the guards.

"Styr, art ready for thy test?" Ayesh asked. The goblin nodded, and Ayesh said, "One . . . "

"They mean to murder us!" cried Kraw from the hallway.

The axe fell. The ribbons fluttered against Styr's cheek. She did not flinch. Nor did she stir for the second or third stroke, though Kraw was shrieking in the hallway.

Ayesh smiled and said, "Diamond mind, Styr. Thou art found worthy."

On down the line went the test to Murl, Wlur, and Bler.

Nuwr jumped to her feet, shrieking, before Yaharaya had even come to her. Guards seized her and took her from the room. Now two goblins shrilled in the corridor.

Ayesh smiled to Scaraya and mouthed the words, "Two found."

Cimmaraya suspected Tlik. He kept his face passive as the axe came closer to his place in line, but he fidgeted and seemed to labor to keep his composure. Sweat glittered on his brow.

At last only Tlik and Gur had not been tested.

Yaharaya's breaths came in great gusts. The fur about her neck and shoulders was wet and matted. It was greater labor, Cimmaraya guessed, to stop the axe than it would be to follow through.

"Tlik," said Cimmaraya from across the room, "what end comes to traitors?"

"A bad end, usually," he said. His voice was high.

"Kraw and Nuwr did not drink their elixir," said Cimmaraya. "They intended to deceive us all."

"Three did not drink," said Ayesh.

"Test me," said Tlik. There was a quaver in his voice.

"Your manner betrays you already," said Cimmaraya.

"Teacher Ayesh, test me."

"It is as well," said Cimmaraya. "I think beheading might fit so dangerous a crime. Yaharaya grows tired, and she might slip. Therefore, Yaharaya, turn the blade to his neck. And test."

There was fire in Ayesh's eyes. She made no protest when Yaharaya turned the axe so that the blade would descend edge first.

"One," said Ayesh.

The axe fell. Stopped. The ribbons landed.

Tlik did not stir from his pose.

"Two," said Ayesh.

Again the blade fell.

If anything, Tlik looked *more* peaceful.

"Three," said Ayesh.

The axe descended. The ribbons shushed and fluttered against Tlik's face.

Ayesh blinked, then began to stare at Gur.

"You doubt me," said Gur. "Even me."

Ayesh looked uncertain, and Cimmaraya felt some of that uncertainty herself. Gur had been their very first subject. She was eager for her elixir and reveled in the quiet liberation it brought to her mind. Surely, not Gur. . . .

"Test me," Gur said.

"Gur, there is no need," said Tlik. "I—"

"Be silent, Tlik. I am a student, as are the others. I would not have Teacher Ayesh ever doubting me. Therefore, hold your tongue." She bowed to Ayesh. "Test me, just as Tlik was tested."

Ayesh looked uncertainly to Scaraya, then to Cimmaraya, who did not know what to counsel. "Very well," Ayesh said.

Each count was counted. Each axe stroke fell.

Gur sat impassively.

Tlik bowed his head. He had begun to tremble in earnest. "Do not kill us," he said.

"So!" said Cimmaraya.

Ayesh held up her hand, then said quietly, "Tell us, Tlik."

"We meant no rebellion. 'Tis true, 'tis true, Kraw, Nuwr, and I conspired to spit out the drink. But it was not rebellion!"

"Then what was it?" said Cimmaraya. "Do we not caution you often that you must drink? And yet—"

"Soft, Cimmaraya," said Ayesh, and she said to Tlik, "If not rebellion, then what?"

"The third virtue," said the quivering goblin. He held his shoulders as if shivering with cold. "Self-reliance. We would practice what you teach. We would depend not on the drugs of the minotaurs but on ourselves. If the herbal gives us diamond mind, that what have we achieved?"

All of a sudden, Cimmaraya saw a great weariness or despair descend upon Ayesh. The human sat down in the dust before Tlik and lowered her head. "And thou didst pass the test," said Ayesh softly.

"Yet do I now feel shadows overpowering me!" wailed Tlik. "I fear what will become of me, and of Kraw and Nuwr. They are blameless! It was my idea!"

Ayesh put her hand on the shivering goblin's neck. "Possess thy fear, Tlik. Let it not possess thee."

"I try!" he cried. "But my head is filled with horrors!"

"They pass," said Ayesh, "as dust blown on the wind. Only breathe. Only be aware that thou art. Diamond mind wells up in thee, Tlik. Only be patient. Do not ask that all may change at once."

"There is more elixir," said Scaraya. "I will bring it."

Ayesh nodded and said, "No punishment, Scaraya. They suffer enough."

Scaraya said, "Aye. I see."

The day's class, Ayesh concluded, must finish as always. There must be a round of sparring, and then music. Ayesh herself did not spar. Indeed, she left the goblins to referee themselves.

Tlik was given elixir, and it was poured down the throats of Kraw and Nuwr as well. When all were calm enough, they rejoined the class.

"My flute?" said Ayesh when the sparring was done.

Tlik was in the habit of borrowing the flute each night and bringing it each day to class. He brought it to Ayesh, who stood looking at the flute and at her bandaged hands.

The human took a deep breath and sighed a great sigh.

"Tlik," she said, "canst play the tunes I have taught thee?"

Meekly, he nodded.

"Well, come, then, and play."

Tlik looked around, as if not quite sure he could have such good fortune on so difficult a day. He was still trembling a little as he came to take the flute from her.

After a while, Ayesh said, "Well, wilt thou not play?"

"I am not ready," said Tlik, "as I was not ready to do without the elixir."

"Thou art more ready than knowest."

"Teacher Ayesh, please, *you* must play."

She shook her head. "Never again," she said. "It is an instrument for ten fingers, and I have but eight."

The goblins stared at her. None dared to ask how this had come to pass.

In the days that followed, a new routine emerged. Every day, Zhanrax brought Ayesh and Tana to their classroom in the mines. Once the class had begun, Zhanrax would melt into the shadows to nurse his anger. Cimmaraya each day tried to think of something she might say to console him, but what words could help?

At the end of each day, Scaraya would say to Ayesh, "Well, are they ready for a demonstration? What can we show in Assembly, eh?" Ayesh would say something about how much farther there was yet for them to go, but Scaraya seemed blind to any but promising observations. Cimmaraya worried that Scaraya was losing her objectivity.

Cimmaraya would try again to say something comforting to Zhanrax. Words would fail her, and she would finally just bid him farewell.

Then they would all go home—all except the goblins, for whom the dirt-floored classroom was all the home they had. At night, they weren't even permitted to roam the nearby passages, partly for their own protection. Partly.

There was, in these dark days, one bright moment.

At the end of class one day, Tlik brought Ayesh a present.

"A wooden box?" she said, turning it in her still-bandaged hands. It was about the length and thickness of her forearm.

"The gift is *inside* the box," said Tlik, almost beside himself with glee. He grinned conspiratorially at Cimmaraya.

The other goblins were grinning, too. So was Tana.

And Scaraya. Zhanrax, if unsmiling, at least appeared interested.

Ayesh pried off the lid.

The flute was copper. The keys were mounted on silvery springs, as on the Oneahn flute. Writing wound from one end to the other in minotaur script.

"I designed it," said Tlik, "but Cimmaraya's clan mined the metal and made it."

"Gems-in-Hand ever excelled in metallurgy," Cimmaraya explained, hoping she did not sound boastful.

Tlik drew the second flute from behind his back. "They made two! I need not borrow yours, Teacher Ayesh!"

"There are but eight keys and holes," said Ayesh, inspecting the flute.

"That an eight-fingered human may play it," said Tlik.

Ayesh froze for a moment. So did Tlik, uncertain. Then she smiled, and Tlik smiled, too.

"That a minotaur might play it, too," Tlik added. He laughed. "If a minotaur can ever learn to blow."

Ayesh brought the instrument to her lips and played, with stiff fingers, an ascending scale.

"That is very like the heart scale," she said, "but not quite right."

Tlik smiled. "It is the goblin scale. And I shall play for you the first goblin song, if you like."

Cimmaraya could almost guess Ayesh's thoughts as the human studied the flute: Minotaur construction of a goblin-scaled version of an Oneahn design. Ayesh marveled at it.

This was what they were making in the class, Cimmaraya thought. Something human and goblin and minotaur all at once.

Was it a good thing?

"I would be honored to hear thee play, Tlik," said Ayesh.

"Aye, Tlik," said Cimmaraya. "Give us a tune."

The goblin bowed. The tune he played was almost hauntingly beautiful. *Almost,* because there was something a little off about it. It had an edge. A fearful edge.

Goblins, Cimmaraya was reminded, will ever be goblins.

At the end of the song, Scaraya applauded and cried,

"That is our demonstration! That is how we shall show to the Assembly that our efforts bear fruit!"

Ayesh closed her eyes. "Please, Scaraya," she said. "It's still too soon!"

"She's right," Cimmaraya said.

But Scaraya waved them off. "You'd delay forever!"

In the end, Scaraya would not forget the idea. In the end, Tlik, with his human teacher beside him, played two of his new goblin tunes before the Assembly. Cimmaraya was there to hear, and to see.

The goblin played with confidence and poise. He was down to one-quarter rations of Scaraya's herb infusions, and he nonetheless acquitted himself expertly beneath the stern gazes of the eleven houses. Cimmaraya could see how proud Ayesh was of him. Diamond mind, indeed.

And in truth, the demonstration itself probably did not do the harm Cimmaraya feared it might. The real problem, she could see, studying the faces, was the Assembly itself.

Zhanrax, Deoraya, and all the rest of Rock-in-Water glared at Betalem, who glared back.

So much for Deoraya's devotion to neutrality.

There was tension between the orthodox houses and the liberal ones, a more chaotic, hotter tension. The divisions were internal now. Cimmaraya heard the whisperings all the time lately. The fallout from Betalem's attack was splitting the houses from within. Half the orthodox were furious that Betalem would go so far, and half were furious that any doubted the necessity. Meanwhile, half the liberals were furious with what Betalem had done, and half were wondering if all this fuss with goblins was worth blood feud. Or war.

The human had sacrificed her fingers to force things to a head. Not being orthodox herself, Cimmaraya was not sure how to judge the reactions of her own kind to the human's gesture. Many minotaurs in Stones-Afalling stared at the human, but they had stared before.

Only her father and Scaraya were unperturbed by these recent turns. Myrrax seemed above it all, though

Cimmaraya knew that might be only the mask of leadership he sometimes wore. As for Scaraya, the tension
seemed to pass over her head without a ripple. Dear
Scaraya could be so oblivious. When Tlik had finished
playing, she smiled.

Scaraya might politic one-on-one, but the bigger pic-
ture was generally beyond her.

Cimmaraya could feel how loyalties were shifting in the
room. She was no political adept herself, but she understood better than Scaraya, at least.

Tlik's performance ended with silence. Heated silence.
Aside from Scaraya's proud smile, Tlik might have received
as much approval had he skittered across the floor like a
rabid rat, snapping his teeth and waving a dagger.

Ayesh seemed to sense this. It seemed to Cimmaraya
that the human was becoming sensitive to minotaur politics. Tlik, too. Ayesh bowed to her student. He returned
the gesture and then they both looked about, wary. But
they needn't have feared, at least for the moment.

The minotaurs were hardly paying attention to the
experiment any longer. Ayesh and Tlik were, in a way,
becoming irrelevant. What mattered to the minotaurs of
Mirtiin now was the bad blood between them.

CHAPTER

18

THE ASSEMBLY CHAMBER COULD BE THE QUI-
etest room in Mirtiin, Myrrax mused. Throughout the
halls, axes might clash with tridents, fighters might bellow with rage or injury. Yet here, deep in stone, at the
ends of the Great Maze, the curtained walls of the Eleven
were still and silent.

Myrrax did not perch upon his throne but walked
around it. If there were many such days during his rule,
the carpet would be worn through to stone. That it was
thick was testimony to the success of his rule. There had
been few occasions for him to truly fret and worry.

Captain Tekrax entered.

"What news?" said Myrrax.

"We were not surprised," said the captain. "Skirmishes
began where and when you predicted, and houses that
you named to me do seem to stand as faithful allies. Only
Shade-in-Ice, Ants-Below, and Horns-of-Gold are proved
firm in opposition, and Horns-of-Gold may be wavering."

"Cups-Ashattered?"

"We are cut off from their hall. Whether they fight
with or against Betalem, or if they stand firm on neither

side, I cannot say. But you know what is whispered of Moyaraya. From the start, she considered the human's tattoos as a possible sign of holy kinship. Then she was much affected by the human's gesture."

"I'd not have guessed that what lay between Moyaraya and loyalty to Mirtiin was a finger."

"As I say, our access to Cups-Ashattered is blocked. I cannot say for certain whether she fights, or on what side."

This was ever the problem of fighting in a labyrinth. As the enemy controlled key points, so did she limit communication. Messengers could not say what happened beyond certain hallways.

"What intersections does Betalem control?"

"Root and branch of Ants-Below, root of Shade-in-Ice, root and branch of Cups-Ashattered, root at least of Horns-of-Gold, and branch of Rock-in-Water," said the captain.

"She shall not stand long in Rock-in-Water. Deoraya and her sisters fight blood feud. And they have Zhanrax. I would not care to stand against him when he is in blood rage."

"He does not stand with his mother, from what I know. The guard I sent into the mines reports that Zhanrax fights there."

"How fares it? Are the goblins protected? Is the human safe?"

"I know only what I said. The way was blocked by battle. My guard saw Zhanrax fighting and your daughter with him."

"Cimmaraya is well?"

"She *fights* well, or with fury. So reports my guard."

"She was never handy with an axe."

"Mayhap Zhanrax has an influence."

Myrrax snorted and paced.

"Betalem also controls the branch of Sun-on-Forelocks, though that house opposes her. And she has blocked off the Great Way."

Myrrax spun about to face his captain. "She controls the Great Way? Why didst not tell me that first?"

"'Tis of little value, Mirtiin. She saps her strength to hold it."

"It means retreat! Tekrax, she must not escape!"

"We are secure," said Tekrax. "We shall have her."

"Nothing is certain while axes yet ring, Captain. We cannot know that we will win this fight. Much less canst assure me that Betalem shall be caught. Controls the Great Way! That is everything, Tekrax!"

"I'll pass the word."

"Thou shalt do more, Captain! I want the guard, *all* the guard, dispatched through Gems-in-Hand. We must cut off her retreat. If she dies, we can plead our own case before Stahaan. But if Betalem lives and runs, she will have Gynnalem's ear ere we have had a word to say. Then is all lost, my captain."

Tekrax bowed. "With respect, Mirtiin, I remind you that this is not your fight. It is a struggle of the houses."

"Then avoid engagement where necessary, but appearances matter less and less. Strike where thou must. Bring her to me, Captain, or see her dead. Betalem does not leave Mirtiin alive, or else war, true war, and not this small rebellion, shall crash upon our heads!"

"Would you have me leave you unguarded, Mirtiin? If Ants-Below should break out, they are near enough to—"

Myrrax drew his axe from where it leaned beside the throne. "I can protect myself."

"Against the whole of a house?"

"Take the full guard, Tekrax. *Go!* This matters more."

The captain turned to go. As he did, a figure clad in green and gold appeared in the doorway. Phyrrax.

"What dost thou want here, Grass-Above?" Tekrax asked him.

"Audience of Mirtiin. I have a problem."

"*Thou* hast a problem?" roared Myrrax. "By Lemeya's horns, Mirtiin cuts herself and bleeds as we speak! And thou hast a problem?"

"This is an inconvenient moment, I gather," said Phyrrax.

"Shall I see this buffoon out?" said the captain.

"No, no," said Myrrax. "Leave him. If this is a matter of no import, I will crack his skull myself."

As he passed Phyrrax, Tekrax said, "I see that your axe is not yet blooded, Grass-Above."

"Captain," said Phyrrax, "I offer you an insight: a minotaur is often *hurt* by fighting."

Tekrax snorted. In the hallway, he bellowed to the other guards, "To me! We'll not await the fight to come to us. We go to it!"

There was the sound of hooves tramping the hall, then the deep silence of the Assembly Chamber.

"Well?" said Myrrax.

"Do you think Tekrax suspects my nature?"

"If he does, it is not from any sign I gave him, though I dislike to practice deceiving him. He is both brave and loyal."

"How goes the fight?"

"Thou art to bring *me* intelligence."

"Not of the battle once it heats," said Phyrrax, shaking his head. "I stand aside as best I may."

"It goes well, mostly," said Myrrax. "All was as thou didst say it would be, down to Rock-in-Water's loyalty."

"That was the easiest thing to guess. There's blood between them and Betalem. It was harder to say where Horns-of-Gold and Sun-on-Forelocks would fall."

"How is it that thou hast the trust of so many houses, Phyrrax?"

"'Tis not a matter of trust, Mirtiin. They dismiss me as a gad."

"What dost think of our chances?"

"Passing good. I think Cups-Ashattered fights with us. I've heard that Moyaraya was last night quoting scripture at Betalem to prove that the human was not *flakkach*. Aye, our odds are passing good, if Betalem does not escape."

"She controls the Great Way."

"Dark tidings, those."

"Aye. I have sent the guard to stop her."

"And if they fail, Mirtiin?"

Myrrax laid his axe aside and leaned against his throne. He stared into the dark doorway as though he might glimpse the undetermined future.

"If they fail," he said, "then darker tidings still. Far darker."

CHAPTER
19

THE AXE FLASHING DOWN TOWARD SCARAYA'S
head was the first warning Ayesh had of the ambush.

It happened on their way to the goblins' class. They
had just come out of the spiral passage and entered the
annular corridor. Scaraya was in front, Cimmaraya and
Zhanrax just behind, and Ayesh and Tana taking up the
rear.

There were several doorways in the ring-shaped corridor, and the axe came flashing out of one.

"Scaraya!" Ayesh shouted. The minotaur's name was
long, and the axe had but a short way to fall.

"No!" screamed Cimmaraya. The attacking minotaur,
wearing the orange and gray of Ants-Below, emerged
from the doorway.

Scaraya's skull was thick. She still stood, but looked
wide-eyed at her attacker, as if the blow had knocked out
of her the sense to know what was happening.

"She's not armed!" Cimmaraya screamed. But the
attacker raised the axe again.

Zhanrax had his axe free and raised it as well.

Two other attackers, both Ants-Below and both with

axes, emerged from side passages ahead. Ayesh turned. From behind her and Tana, two more Ants-Below had emerged. They hefted tridents. "Tana!" she warned. "Look here!"

Ayesh could hear Zhanrax and another minotaur grunt. She heard the wet sounds of axes meeting flesh, but she couldn't turn to see. She and Tana had their own troubles.

"Their thoughts are on the trident blades," Ayesh reminded Tana. He nodded that he understood.

The advantage in fighting someone who used a weapon, Ayesh had taught, was that such a fighter attended mostly to the weapon. The field of battle, as far as these trident bearers were used to thinking, was everything in the reach of their tridents. They thought of attacking and they thought of blocking entirely as matters of where to move their weapons.

A hard thing for a wrestler to learn was this: Fight not the weapon, but the one who bears the weapon. Tana knew the words, but could he practice the strategy? He had sparred against goblins armed with wooden weapons, never minotaurs, armed or not.

Behind Ayesh there was another outraged bellow: Cimmaraya. Was she wounded? Joining the fight? But, like Scaraya, she didn't even carry an axe, and Ayesh had heard her say she was no good with one.

The attention of the trident-bearers was only half on Ayesh and Tana, who were, after all, unarmed and easy prey. Zhanrax was the warrior here. They were looking to see that he was still occupied.

Axe head rang on axe head.

Ayesh saw her moment and sprang toward the tridents, ducking beneath the metal teeth. She aimed a kick—not at the unfeeling hoof, but at the delicate bones above it.

The minotaur bellowed and tried to raise its trident to spear her at close quarters. But the shaft butted the low ceiling. There wasn't room enough for the minotaur to attack as it wanted.

Ayesh grasped and twisted the sensitive fur inside the thigh. Again, the minotaur bellowed. Ayesh kicked, damaging the other foot.

Meanwhile, the second trident-bearer was distracted. Tana made his move, grabbing the trident shaft so suddenly that Ants-Below almost lost hold of the weapon. Pulled forward, off balance, Tana's foe was unprotected for the kick Tana aimed between the legs.

Tana's kick was masterful. With the strength of his whole body, his hoof slammed home.

The Ants-Below was too hurt to bellow. Clearly a male, as Tana must have known, he was in too much pain to breathe. He dropped his trident. Tana seized his finger and twisted to force him to his knees, then to his belly.

Ayesh's minotaur tried to line up its trident to spear Tana, but Ayesh slammed her elbow into its kidneys. It gasped.

Ayesh grinned. It was only thanks to Tana that she knew where a minotaur's kidneys *were*.

She aimed a punch between the legs. Only then, as the minotaur merely grunted, did she know for certain that she fought a female.

It was a female who learned from her mistakes. The weapon was a liability. She dropped her trident and seized Ayesh's neck with her hands.

They were powerful hands.

Ayesh's vision went red as she felt for the finger she knew she could twist. Somehow, it wasn't where it should be, where it *had* to be.

The edges of her vision were going black.

She tried to kick, but the minotaur only lifted her out of reach. Ayesh dangled by her neck. It was like being hanged. She felt for the finger on the other hand, found it.

The black edges grew inward. Her hands felt numb.

Ayesh weakly tugged the finger. It wouldn't budge.

The floor rose up to meet her. The grip relaxed, and her vision returned.

The minotaur's knees had collapsed beneath her. Tana was kicking her head once, twice . . .

The third kick missed. The minotaur had collapsed after the second blow.

The head of the first minotaur was a red mess. Tana's hooves were bloody. His breathing came in great snorts.

He strode a little unsteadily to the fallen female and readied himself to kick again.

"Diamond mind," Ayesh choked out. "She fights no more. Enough. Enough."

He was still poised to kick.

"You're angry," Ayesh said hoarsely. "You should be. Anger can be diamond. But if you kill her now, it's for hate, and hatred is goblin mind."

He stood, considering his fallen foe. Then he lowered his foot gently to the floor.

"Little brother?" cried Zhanrax. "Are you all right?"

Tana nodded.

The fallen female stirred. Her eye opened.

"Attack in ambush, will they? Attack in ambush, when there is but one axe between us? Would you do such as that, Ants-Below, and *dare* to go on living? Would you attack my little brother and live to tell of it?" With two hands, he raised his axe.

"Zhanrax," pleaded Tana. "No!"

But the axe was already falling. The blow cleaved the great neck with a sound Ayesh hoped never to hear again. She shut tight her eyes.

Cimmaraya was sobbing.

Ayesh went to her where she knelt next to Scaraya's savaged body. Cimmaraya held a bloody axe, decorated with the orange-and-gray ribbons of Ants-Below. Cimmaraya had taken it, Ayesh guessed, from the first attacker, after Zhanrax cut him down.

"'As I do not arm myself, who will harm me?' That's what she always said." Cimmaraya's grip tightened on the axe as her other hand clutched Scaraya's bloody fur. "Fool, fool, fool, Scaraya! Oh, you wise and gentle fool!"

"Even armed," said Ayesh, "what could she have done? There was no time. There was no opportunity."

Cimmaraya shook Scaraya's body. "Ants-Below will pay! To the last, I swear, they shall die!"

"Is it not better," Ayesh said gently, "to carry on what Scaraya has done?"

"How?" Cimmaraya asked bitterly. "Don't you know

that with her dies everything? Everything that mattered, she kept in her head!"

"Are you not her student?"

"Quiet!" Zhanrax demanded.

They fell silent.

Distantly, they heard an echo of clashing metal and the throaty bellows of minotaurs in battle.

"The guards are assaulted," Zhanrax said.

Cimmaraya said, "The goblins . . . "

Tana dashed toward the sound of the fighting, his hooves raising dust in the dark and twisting corridors. Ayesh followed him.

The battle was for the broad corridor outside the goblin classroom. The six Shade-in-Ice and Horns-of-Gold fighters didn't even turn when they heard Tana's hoofbeats. One of them shouted to the evenly matched Gems-in-Hand and Grass-Above defenders, "*Now* will you yield!"

They think we're reinforcements, Ayesh thought, and she looked over her shoulder to make sure that the hooves she heard behind here were truly Zhanrax and Cimmaraya, rather than more fighters of the enemy houses.

When Ayesh turned again toward the fighting, Tana was airborne. He landed a winged side kick into the small of a Shade-in-Ice's back. He was up and kicking again, taking down another attacker before it knew that he wasn't on its side.

Ayesh cried "Eeyeh!" for Tana's victory and hurried to join him. The odds had now turned. The minotaur defenders pressed the attackers back and kept them so busy that none could turn away to hack at Tana.

Ayesh flew at a minotaur's back and landed a kick like Tana's. The effect wasn't the same. The minotaur only grunted, and Ayesh thought, *Hooves and a bull's weight would come in handy sometimes.*

Zhanrax and Cimmaraya thundered up. One defender looked back, again expecting reinforcements. At the sight of Zhanrax, the Shade-in-Ice dropped his axe. "We yield!

We yield!" he cried. The other fighters glanced over their shoulders, then dropped their weapons as well.

Had the surrendering minotaurs been Ants-Below, Ayesh was sure Zhanrax would have murdered them. As it was, it seemed to take all the big minotaur's strength of will to slowly lower his axe.

"Find rope and tie them tight!" he said. One guard went off for rope.

"The goblins?" said Cimmaraya.

"Are well," said a Grass-Above. "They sit in their room. We told them to stay put."

"Did they have their elixir this morrow?"

"Aye," said the guard. "We gave it them before we were attacked." He looked down the broad corridor. "We must expect another wave. Their allies in Ants-Below tried to come in at the other end, but the corridor was too narrow. They've gone the long way around."

"Ants-Below?" said Zhanrax, hefting his axe. "Let them come in great numbers. I am eager for slaughter."

"Be not so eager, Rock-in-Water," said the guard. "They are twenty or more."

"They will be fewer than that before I cease to swing my axe." Zhanrax looked at the narrow end of the corridor. Fighting still went on there, though even now a leader of Shade-in-Ice, seeing his side surrendered in the broad part of the corridor, was calling for retreat.

"Would that we could press our advantage as they retreat," said another guard. "But there are side passages, narrowings, and many opportunities to isolate, flank, and ambush."

"They pull back to await the assault of Ants-Below," the first guard observed.

"How many are we?" asked Cimmaraya as a guard returned with rope and began to tie the prisoners.

"You aren't enough," said one prisoner, a Shade-in-Ice. "Take care to tie gently. Soon enough, the same rope shall bind you, if you yet breathe."

"Tie him tight," Zhanrax ordered the guard. "I don't care if his hands fall off." He stood muzzle to muzzle with the Shade-in-Ice. "Your allies set ambush and murdered the first of us when we had but one axe among six. No quarter were we offered."

"Murdered?" said the guard. "Who . . . ?" But he looked from Cimmaraya to Zhanrax and said softly, "Scaraya."

"It is well she died," said Shade-in-Ice. "She was the cause of all that we suffer."

Ayesh saw Cimmaraya's jaw tighten. "Whatever you are too dense to understand, Shade-in-Ice," she said, "that also do you hate. You hate much, I think. Perhaps you hate all."

"We must tell Iron-in-Granite how she died," said Zhanrax, looking at the narrow end of the corridor. "They will crave the blood of Ants-Below as I crave it."

"I come to crave the blood of Shade-in-Ice," said Cimmaraya.

"Cimmaraya!" said Ayesh.

"You do not understand the call of blood feud, human," said Cimmaraya.

"I do," said Ayesh. "With shame, I tell you I know it too well."

The last prisoner was bound and led to the center of the corridor, where all were tied together and their feet hobbled.

"Again I ask," Zhanrax said, "how many are we?"

"Six at this end, six at that," said the guard, "plus you yourselves, that's fourteen—fifteen if you count the youngster."

"The youngster has acquitted himself as a soldier," said Ayesh.

"He bears no axe."

"He needs none. And you leave me out of your count. I make us sixteen."

"Fifteen and a third," said the guard. "Still, the attack will come from two sides. At the narrow end, they can come three abreast. Here, all twenty of them have room to swing."

"We have the goblins," said Ayesh. "They'll guard the narrow end."

The guard snorted. "With all respect, human, and

agreeing that you've taught them manners, goblins weigh not a third what we do. I'll not fight when none but goblins guard my back."

"Even if the goblins are mowed like hay," said Zhanrax, "that gives us time. 'Tis the best way. Go get them, Ayesh. You and the goblins will guard the narrow, minotaurs, the broad."

The guard snorted again. "Thus do we purchase a few seconds. Three minotaurs can hold the narrow, ere the first falls. I would sooner trust—"

"On patrols am I captain," said Zhanrax, "and I claim captaincy here. We'll do it my way."

The sound of hoofbeats echoing from a distant corridor cut off further debate.

At first, no attack came at the narrow end.

Some of the goblins were nervous, Ayesh could see. They glanced over their shoulders at the broad corridor behind, where all the clashing of axes and bellowing came from.

"Eyes ahead, Styr," Ayesh said.

"But if they break through behind . . ."

"That's a matter that we'll deal with if it happens. Eyes ahead. We guard the rear. Unless I alert thee otherwise, that is thy single task. Guard the rear."

The goblins holding the free end of the hidden rope nodded.

Before Ayesh could see movement in the shadows, Gur said, "They come!"

"Wait for the moment," Ayesh reminded them. "Remember how Tana yells when you twist his nostrils?"

Kler snickered.

"You know where to strike, and knowledge is power. But it takes mastery, too. Wait for the moment."

As the minotaurs charged into the light, Ayesh could see the expected six—and three more. "They've picked up some helpers," Ayesh said. "There are still more of us."

Mok whimpered.

"Diamond mind," Ayesh reminded them all. "Fight like what you are becoming, not like what you once were."

As they saw who opposed them, the first rank of minotaurs broke into lopsided grins. They bellowed and
charged as if they might simply run right through the
cluster of goblins.

And they might have, had they kept charging. Three
hundred sprinting pounds on the hoof would be hard to
grab. But the goblins held their ground and the minotaur
leader, expecting a trap, slowed and held out his arms to
caution the others. He looked warily at the walls and
floor, though still he pressed forward.

When the front three minotaurs were close enough,
three goblins sprang at their faces. The minotaurs all
raised their axes at once, but the goblins were quick.
They tightly grasped the tender spot between the minotaurs' nostrils, then hung there with all their weight.

And the first three minotaurs, for an instant, forgot
about everything but the pain in this tender spot. They did
what Tana had always done, and like Tana, they did it as
reflex. They dropped down close to the floor to relieve the
strain of goblin weight. That's when other goblins threw
dust in their eyes and still more twisted back the fingers
that held axes. Three axes fell to the floor. That quickly, a
third of the attackers were blinded and disarmed.

Flailing their hooves, the downed minotaurs were still
dangerous. One clouted Murl with a kick that almost
took his head off. An axe from the second rank of minotaurs fell with a great chop to finish Murl off.

Ayesh felt sickened at the sight of the goblin's blood.
Once she'd have cheered.

The minotaurs still standing held their free hands up to
guard their muzzles as they waded forward. The goblins
flew against their delicate ankles and kicked their vulner-
able knees.

Mok and Nuwr twisted the fingers of a blinded minotaur to make it hold still. Gur struggled to lift an axe and
bring it down on the massive neck.

Dust flew.

Two more minotaurs hit the floor, damaged knees
unable to support them. Gur hefted the axe and let it fall
again and again. Minotaurs stumbled, blinked against the

grit in their eyes. They swung their axes blindly. One chopped its companion's arm. Ayesh blinked to keep her own vision clear. She kicked ankles here, knees there . . .

The minotaurs now bellowed with frustration and pain. All nine minotaurs were on the floor. Gur had axed the necks of four. One or two goblins restrained each of the others with some painful hold that threatened to break a wrist or dislocate an arm.

Ayesh could not see through the cloud of dust they had made to know how the battle for the other end of the corridor went. Were the goblins needed there? Would the enemy break through?

Gur stood over another minotaur, struggling again to lift the axe.

"Wait," Ayesh said. To the minotaur, she said, "Do you yield?"

"To *flakkach*? Never!"

"Yield or die."

"I die then!"

There's no other way, Ayesh thought. The other fight still raged. If they would not yield, then these minotaurs would be a threat again as soon as they were allowed to stand.

"His foot," she said to Gur. "He can't attack if he can't stand."

The goblin obediently moved from neck to ankle and chopped at it enough to assure that the minotaur could not stand. Ayesh felt sickened. If there were but another way . . .

"Will you yield?" she asked the next minotaur.

That minotaur refused. She, too, was crippled.

No more of this, Ayesh thought, *though their refusal sap our strength, no more.* "Tlik . . ." She could see enough of Tlik in the dust and gloom to tell his head was bleeding. "Tlik and Bler, Wlur and Kraw . . . Who else is hurt?"

"Murl is dead," said Gur.

"I know," Ayesh said. "Who else lives and is hurt?"

If any other goblins were injured, none would say so. "All right. The four I just named, plus Gur and Nuwr, stay behind and keep these stubborn louts from going anywhere. The rest of you, follow me. We join the other battle."

Zhanrax and the others were just holding their own. Four goblins, plus Ayesh, were enough to turn the tide in their favor.

Reduced to half his fighters, the Ants-Below captain dropped his axe to ask for surrender.

Zhanrax cut him down. The fight did not cease until the last Ants-Below fighter was dead.

"Your gray-skinned *flakkach* fought well," Zhanrax said. "Those that survived."

"All but one survived," Ayesh said. "Six guard the Shade-in-Ice and Horns-of-Gold who would not yield. We were met by nine, not the six expected."

Zhanrax looked surprised. Then he wiped the blade of his axe and said, "Never did I think to see a day when I would count goblins as my allies. Aye, but there may be more good to them than I had guessed."

The sash he used was so bloody that it did not clean the axe but only spread the blood around.

"Ants-Below tried to surrender," Ayesh said.

"I would not have them do so."

"There are goblins that are goblins," Ayesh said, "and there are goblins that are not."

He gave her a blank stare, still wiping.

"Dark day," said a Gems-in-Hand, "when unarmed goblins best minotaurs with axes. What have we wrought?"

Ayesh realized her legs were shaking. She was tired. Tired, and sick of blood. In the corridor, there was so much blood.

"Go where the goblins are," Ayesh told the Gems-in-Hand, "and accept the surrender of the minotaurs who will not accept mercy from a goblin."

Who will not understand, she thought, *the miracle of mercy granted by a goblin.*

CHAPTER
20

CIMMARAYA COULD SEE, AS SHE POURED THE hot water over the pastes, leaves, and blossoms, that the water running out from the other end of the strainer was not quite the right tint of green. She sniffed the steam.

Zhanrax watched over her shoulder.

From her other side, Phyrrax said, "Well?"

Rillaraya, the new matriarch of Iron-in-Granite, asked, "Have you made it aright?"

Cimmaraya looked at the brightly lit gardens beyond the concocting table. Bees hovered above the blossoms. Birds sang just as sweetly as they would in the world above. Though the gardens grew deep under the mountain, all was well in their ordered rows radiating from Scaraya's front room, as far as the birds were concerned.

All was not well. Scaraya was dead. This was not her front room any longer, but Rillaraya's. Cimmaraya and Zhanrax used Scaraya's rooms only thanks to the good will of Iron-in-Granite's new matriarch, who wanted the gardens maintained and the goblin project continued. But so much was going wrong. Greater dangers loomed. And Cimmaraya couldn't get the elixir properly mixed.

Cimmaraya shook her head. "This isn't right either," she said. In some step involving the bubbling alembics, the heavy mortar and pestle, the curing racks for the leaves and flowers . . . in some obscure step, something was going wrong.

"Maybe it will work anyway," Phyrrax said. Then, "Are you sure you did everything as it says in the book?"

Cimmaraya shook her head irritably. "No! What notes Scaraya bade me write are scattered through the pages of this and other books. I am not sure I have found every notation. And it would not matter anyway, Phyrrax. The first instruction is 'begin with equal portions of red paste and green.'" She waved at the remnants of dissolving paste on the strainer. "These pastes she had concocted long before I came to study with her. I always thought I understood how she made them, but now I see how little I knew. Something may be missing from the very base materials. From the first step, we go awry."

"Would it not be wise to write down what you *are* sure of, all in one place?" Phyrrax said.

Cimmaraya glared at him. "As if you cared for science!"

"Right enough, Cimmaraya," Phyrrax said, opening his hands. "Accuse me of no interests, please! I only spoke my mind. As an observer, shall we say."

"He's right," said Rillaraya. "Mark the notes in the great books, and I will make a copy."

"When there is time, when there is time!" Cimmaraya said.

"Well," said Zhanrax, transferring the off-colored liquid into a flask, "you can try again tomorrow."

He made it sound so easy. "Scaraya was *years* in finding the formula! She poisoned three goblins ere she found the mixture that stilled Gur's mind. We don't have years, and we don't have the luxury of poisoning the goblins with our mistakes!"

He looked at her evenly. A great calm had settled over him in the last few days. It was as if, before the fight, all his rage had been dammed up. In the battle, he had released a flood of fury, a flood that had made Ants-Below a broken and shamed house, along with her allies in Horns-of-Gold and Shade-in-Ice. Now, in victory, Zhanrax was quiet, almost somnolent.

He was furious with his enemies and gentle to her. There was much to credit him with.

"What will be, will be," Rillaraya said. "I've faith in you, Mirtiin's daughter. You will discover the formula now and succeed with these goblins. Or it will be later, with different goblins."

"I am grateful for your faith, Iron-in-Granite," Cimmaraya said, "though I cannot but think that time runs out, that there will be no second chance."

"Second chances abound," said Phyrrax. "The universe is made of them. Were not the first worlds Lemeya gave birth to dead and barren? Yet here do we live in a world alive!"

"Come," said Zhanrax, raising the flask. "The goblins must break their fast."

"It tastes oily," said Mok. Today, his voice had more of the raspy sound of a wild goblin.

Bler and Nuwr nodded in agreement.

"Is that amiss?" said Ayesh.

"I *like* oily!" said Mok.

"But it's not how it tasted before," said Tlik, handing his wooden bowl back to Cimmaraya. "And I don't feel the warmth in my throat I used to feel at first."

Warmth in the throat, Cimmaraya thought. *What caused that?* She thought it might be the carlinall. Too much witchbalm might counter that effect. Should she leave witchbalm out of the base?

"It's better," said Kler.

Kraw grinned. "Tastes better."

"It doesn't work the same," said Gur.

"It hardly works at all," said Tlik.

Kraw pushed him. "Who cares?"

"Kraw," said Gur, "stop that."

All of the goblins' voices sounded more raspy today, even Tlik's and Gur's.

"Yeah, Kraw!" said Rip. "Don't *shove*!" With the last

word, he gave Kraw a push that knocked him over. Kraw rolled with the fall and sprang to his feet in fighting stance.

"No one spars without permission," said Ayesh.

"I won't spar," said Kraw. "Gonna kick his head off for real!"

"You can try!" taunted Rip.

The other goblins started to take up sides, some taunting Rip, some taunting Kraw, and a few following Gur's lead and telling everyone to shut up.

The voices grew louder. And raspier.

Ayesh strode to her place at the front of the room and clapped three times. That was the signal to come to attention. Only Tlik and Tana went immediately to their places, bowed, and knelt down. Tlik looked straight ahead as he should, but even Tana couldn't keep his gaze from wandering to the goblins.

Bler walked to her position, but remained standing, watching the squabble.

The human clapped again. The voices only grew louder.

Gur cuffed Rip on the back of his head. "I'm chieftess here! I tell you what to do, and you do it!"

Rip crouched submissively, but kept glaring at Kraw.

"All of you get to your places!" Gur demanded.

They went. Gur did not take her usual place in the two rows of students, but knelt at one end of the room, with Ayesh to her left and the young goblins to her right.

"Wilt thou not take thy place?" said Ayesh.

"I need to watch 'em!" Gur rasped.

Ayesh looked at Cimmaraya, who could do naught but raise her empty hands. The formula was at least slowing the deterioration. Perhaps by the end of the day she'd have discovered the missing ingredient, the missing step, the mistaken proportion.

"Rainbow Meditation," said Ayesh.

The goblins were twitching as they tried to sit still. All but Tlik. At the name of the meditation, he closed his eyes and began without guidance. To the others, Ayesh said, "Red first. See a point of red before thee. Bright red. Now it grows. Red all around thee . . . "

"Rip's blood," muttered Kraw.

Goblins giggled.

"Begin again," said Ayesh. "Red. Before thine eyes, see a point of red . . . "

"A hole in Kraw's head," said Rip.

More raspy giggles.

With cool patience in her voice, the human said, "We begin again . . . "

It took half a dozen tries to get the goblins to focus on the meditation. At last they were still. After Ayesh had guided them through the colors of the rainbow and the color of the unseen, they were calm. When they stood and began to count off their exercises, there was more control to their voices. Gur went to stand in her usual place.

All was not lost, Cimmaraya reminded herself. If the goblins could still be controlled enough to *start* their morning routine, that routine had a powerful effect on them. They would not soon lose all that Ayesh had taught them.

"Let's go back and try again," she told Zhanrax. "I'll mix a new red paste from the beginning."

When she returned to Iron-in-Granite, she found Phyrrax and Rillaraya searching through the great books for notes that related to the elixir. Cimmaraya had written most of those notes herself, dictated by Scaraya. No one else but she and Scaraya had turned those pages. Now strange hands were upon them. Rillaraya had the right, Cimmaraya reminded herself, for all that was Scaraya's was hers now. Still . . .

"Grass-Above," Cimmaraya said, not trying to disguise her irritation, "how come you to be so interested in science?"

"Curiosity and passing fancy," Phyrrax said, shrugging. "Rillaraya would look. I hold the page."

"Aye," said Rillaraya, curling her lip in a grin. "He said I should look, and I said I would. He opened the page and holds it."

"He pokes his muzzle everywhere it fits," said Zhanrax.

"Everywhere it fits and is made welcome, my friend."

Zhanrax snorted. "Deoraya would rather you never entered Rock-in-Water."

"Ah," said Phyrrax, "but do I not bring cheer to all I visit? A gentle jest to lift the heart?"

"She'd like to lift *your* heart," said Zhanrax. "Or I should say, rather, she'd like to tear it out."

"Alas that I am not appreciated," Phyrrax said.

"Alas that your tongue wags."

"Shut you up, the both of you!" said Cimmaraya.

Rillaraya, Zhanrax, and Phyrrax all looked a little stunned.

"I've work to do," Cimmaraya said. That was all the apology she made. Then she busied herself.

The elixir of the next day was no more effective. Nor that of the next, though Cimmaraya stayed all the night in Iron-in-Granite, sleeping briefly on a bench only when she must. Four times she made a new red paste. Four times she was disappointed.

She stopped visiting the classroom. She sent Zhanrax with the elixirs and went back to work before he returned with the next disappointing report.

"They are goblins as goblins ever were," he said one day. "The human began the class only by making threats. They did not sit still for her until I summoned a guard to stand behind each. Axes they obey, more than her."

Cimmaraya rubbed the fur between her eyes. "What can I do? What have I not tried?"

"The music will ofttimes calm them, when Tlik plays."

"If we could but make Tlik ten times over." She snorted. "One success in eleven tries." She shook her head.

Cimmaraya was alone, grinding tinderseed in the mortar, when two guards, a Gems-in-Hand and Grass-Above, carried Ayesh in from the hallway.

"I can walk just fine!" the human protested, and the guard said, "Aye, and track blood with every step."

The human's calf streamed scarlet.

"Put her here." Cimmaraya cleared a place on her bench.

"It's not as bad as it looks," Ayesh said.

Cimmaraya wet a rag and wiped blood from the wound. Ayesh winced. There were two jagged semicircles:

a bite wound. "Though it bleeds much, 'tis not deep. What happened?"

"Gur got a bit testy."

Cimmaraya stopped wiping. "Gur did? Gur?"

"The goblins got wild during sparring, and she was dealing with it by thumping heads. I tried to reason with them *and* her."

"They change," said one guard. She hefted her axe. "This is the reason they understand best, now."

"No!" Ayesh said. "It's just a matter of keeping them calm. They haven't completely reverted. And look at Tlik. He at least has mastered himself, even without an elixir that's more than flavored water."

Cimmaraya felt her shoulders stiffen.

"Sorry," Ayesh said. "I know you're trying."

Cimmaraya set some water to boil on the worktable. "I'll make you a poultice," she said. "It will keep the gangrene from setting in."

"I am sorry," Ayesh said.

Cimmaraya said, "You can go, you know."

The guards took her words for dismissal. They snorted at her apparent ingratitude. She didn't explain herself. Let them think what they would; it was as well that they left the room.

"I meant you, actually," Cimmaraya said when the guards had gone. "You could leave Mirtiin."

Ayesh snorted. It was a fairly expressive snort from so unimpressive a nose. "You forget. I'm Zhanrax's pet."

Cimmaraya opened a drawer that held dried witchbalm. "I can persuade Zhanrax."

Ayesh snorted again. There was actually some expression to the sound—did she intend the derision? Or was she only expressing humor? She said, "I bet you can."

"You don't understand how things have been developing," Cimmaraya said.

"Oh, I understand," said Ayesh. "I was a courtship gift to you. Among humans, flowers would serve the same."

"Flowers serve among minotaurs."

"Well, humans don't *eat* them."

"What I mean," Cimmaraya said with studied patience,

"is that you don't understand what has developed in Mirtiin. There will be war soon."

"Again?"

Now Cimmaraya snorted. "That was no war those few days ago. That was a contest of wills within Mirtiin, a political skirmish. It shamed those who would divide Mirtiin. We're stronger than we were ere we fought."

"Well," said Ayesh, "we're certainly better off without Betalem. I'll give you that."

"It matters much *how* we are free of her. If she'd been killed, things would stand in better stead. But by now, she has made her way to Stahaan and made her pleas before Gynnalem." Cimmaraya poured hot water over the leaves and sprinkled on wanderseed ashes.

"Who is?"

"What my father is in Mirtiin, Gynnalem is in Stahaan. And more. She is also high priestess. Betalem served here as her representative."

"She won't be pleased by what Betalem says."

"No, she won't. Whenever Mirtiin tries to find its own path, a path that is not Stahaan, Stahaan brings war. Gynnalem will raise her army for siege."

"But why?"

"Stahaan wants Mirtiin ever to bow before it. Stahaan was the first hall. They would ever be the hall that rules in matters of belief. If Hurloon were near enough to war against, Stahaan would war there, too."

"And is Stahaan so great a power?"

"Four times since Mirtiin was spawned in these mountains, four times in the long span of generations, Stahaan has warred. Four times has Mirtiin fallen." Cimmaraya spread the steaming mixture over a dry cloth, then slapped it against Ayesh's wound.

"Ow!"

"But Mirtiin has always fallen," Cimmaraya said, "because she was divided from within. Now the houses that would side with Stahaan are weakened and ashamed. The houses that ever vacillate are decided for Mirtiin. We may this once stand against Stahaan. Or . . ." She poured hot water over the cloth.

Ayesh flinched.

"Or things may yet take a bad turn," Cimmaraya continued. "As they have always turned before. If Stahaan should again be victorious, you would die. And I would die. All who Betalem should name as an enemy of the temple would die." She wrapped a bandage around the human's leg. "Can you stand?"

Ayesh swung her legs over the bench and tested her weight.

"You've trust in your father's skills to hold Mirtiin together?" Ayesh said.

"These have been dark and turbulent rivers he has brought us through ere now," Cimmaraya said. "But Mirtiin has ever before fallen."

"I know," said Ayesh, "but *this* time . . . "

"He is my father," said Cimmaraya. "Judge as you will."

Ayesh looked at her long and hard. "Like daughter, like father. As I trust that you'll soon rediscover the elixir, so will I trust your father to hold the Halls of Mirtiin united."

"You risk much," Cimmaraya said.

"I am a teacher now," said the human. "With that comes responsibilities to my students."

"Such as they are."

"Tlik holds his own. And Tana—Tana could have stood beneath the Roof of Lights and demanded the right to wrestle. None could say him nay." She looked at the alembics. "Find that elixir again, and we can have the others back. They could even stand among the defenders of Mirtiin and bloody Stahaan's nose for her. That would give her a turn, aye?"

Cimmaraya widened her eyes and bared her teeth in a minotaur smile. "It would."

"You'll find it," said the human. "I know you will."

CHAPTER
21

OUTSIDE THE TEMPLE DOORWAY, MYRRAX bent to pick up the tapestry from the floor. Sharp blades had shredded the goddess Lemeya. Then strong hands had ripped the whole tapestry out of the bolts that had fastened it to the wall. "Among the first memories of my childhood," Myrrax said, "is the memory of standing before this tapestry with my mother. We waited for audience with the priestess. My mother said, 'Here is the beginning of beginnings.'"

He lowered his head and held the shredded tapestry over his eyes. He thought, but he would not say, *What have we wrought?*

"There are worse crimes within," said Captain Tekrax. He held aside half the red curtain—an unnecessary gesture since the other half had been torn down. "Blessed are the Mothers."

"May the Mothers be blessed," said Myrrax.

The second tapestry also lay on the floor. Tekrax was right, though. There were far worse crimes than that.

Myrrax stared at what was left of the Well of Ashes. The broken stones bore the scars of pickaxes. All the stones that had once formed the lip of the Well were missing.

"Where?" said Myrrax. "Don't tell me . . . "

Tekrax looked into the depths of the Well, into the blackness where generation after generation of Mirtiin ashes had drifted down, down, down to the heart of the mountain, to the core of the earth. "We have not found the stones," he said. "We can only guess that they threw them in."

Myrrax knelt beside the rough, violated ring of remaining stones. He kissed a jagged edge. *My mother kissed this stone,* he thought, *and her Mothers before her, to the beginning of Shade-in-Ice, to the dawn of Mirtiin.* And yet it was not true. His Mothers had kissed not this stone, but the stone that was missing, that was cast down, beyond recovery.

Myrrax knelt long, gazing into the blackness.

He had not noticed the sound at first, the grinding of stone on stone. He had not noticed the absence of light in the far end of the room.

He rose and strode into the shadows where the Lamp of Passing Flames once burned. The delicate metal disks had been pried apart, warped, and dented. The shaft that turned the greatest disk now rasped and shuddered in its stone bearing. The copper tubes meant to feed oil to the rotating wicks were twisted in all directions and crimped.

Myrrax tried to bend one of the tubes back into place. It broke off in his hand. He stood looking at it, feeling the muscles grow tight around his eyes and lips.

"Bring them to me!" he said. "Bring them *here*!"

"With all respect, Mirtiin," said Tekrax, "is it meet to bring them ever again into this holy place? Are your pronouncements as Mirtiin not better issued from the Assembly Chamber?"

"They will answer for their crimes in the place where they committed them!" Myrrax said, fingering the broken tubing. "Here! Bring them here!"

*   *   *

The four young minotaurs' hands were bound before them, and their feet were hobbled so that they had to shuffle into the temple slowly behind their guards.

Myrrax stood by the shattered Well of Ashes. He glared at each youngster as he or she entered. Three held their heads high. Journaraya alone seemed to sense what she had truly done. She would not meet his gaze.

"Do I see pride in thy mien, Keerax? Robaraya? Tell me, Vedayrax, is Gems-in-Hand renowned for its long generations of criminals? Is that why thine aspect is so lofty?"

"If we are proud," said Keerax, "it is for finally finishing what began when Betalem was cast out of Mirtiin. All that remained of Stahaan was this temple, and we have cleansed it."

"Cleansed," Myrrax whispered. "Cleansed." He ran his fingertips along the broken edge of the Well of Ashes. "Cleansed!" He clenched his teeth. "Wouldst wipe away the ashes of thine own mother and call that cleansing? Wouldst smear with spit the name of thy house and call it improvement?"

Journaraya turned her head away. The other three yet looked defiant.

"Who gave thee birth, Robaraya?"

"You know who, Mirtiin."

"I do not. I thought it was thy mother, an Iron-in-Granite. That is a liberal house, but not one to despise the very stones of Mirtiin!"

"Stones of Mirtiin?" said Keerax. "The stones of this temple are Stahaan. What we have done, we have done *for* Mirtiin!"

"Indeed?" said Mirtiin. "It seems to me that Shade-in-Ice has of late wanted to do much for Mirtiin. Thy house sided with Betalem, who set cousin to murdering cousin, and this in Mirtiin's name."

"I fought *against* my own house," said Keerax. "I swung my axe for Mirtiin, not Stahaan and its cursed priestess!"

"Yet hast fought for Stahaan this day," Myrrax said. "Thou hast struck hard a blow for Gynnalem. Scouts say that Stahaan labors to bring its harvests in early. She raises an army, does Gynnalem. I might send thee to meet her with the news of what thou hast done. She would be wise to crown thee with mulberry leaves and give thee a captaincy for thy loyal service."

"We hate Stahaan!" said Robaraya. "We hate all that is Stahaan!"

"And the tapestry that was chopped like an enemy . . . dost hate the Mother of All?"

"I honor Lemeya," said Robaraya, "but the tapestry was made in Stahaan."

"Aye, in ancient times," said Myrrax.

"By Stahaan weavers! Stones for the Well of Ashes came not from our own mines but from the black deep of Stahaan. Whose hands made the Lamp of Passing Flames? Not Mirtiin hands! It was all done long ago in Stahaan!"

"If we are to be free," said Vedayrax, "then let us be fully free! Let us make the temple anew!"

Myrrax strode to Journaraya and took her muzzle in his hand. She turned her face to his. "Hast not spoken, Grass-Above. Hast thou not the same fire that burns in the blood of thy conspirators? Dost not long to see all that is Stahaan cast out?"

Journaraya looked miserably at the Well of Ashes. "My mother . . ." she said.

"Ah," said Myrrax. "Thy mother. Yes. She was killed by Ants-Below in the halls of thine own house. She is not many days dead." He grasped the thin chain around Journaraya's neck and drew from her tunic the phial of ashes. "Thou dost yet keep her close to thy heart. Thy mother, and thy Mothers' Mothers."

Myrrax tugged to snap the chain. Journaraya winced.

"Unworthy," said Myrrax. "Thou art unworthy of them." He strode to the Well of Ashes and held the phial above it. "Dost cherish thy mother in one breath, yet despise her in the next, Journaraya?"

"Leave her alone!" said Robaraya.

"It doesn't matter!" said Keerax. "Let him throw in the ashes. They are the past. What's done is done. We'll write our own scriptures! Mirtiin belongs to the *future*!"

"The future," said Myrrax. He snorted. "Ere thy crimes were done, Keerax, the houses were united. The cracks were for once healed. We were for once ready to stand before Stahaan and make of Mirtiin *Mirtiin*!"

"Half measures," sneered Keerax.

"The houses will unite behind us when they understand," said Vedayrax. "You are the one who is behind the times, Myrrax. Mark my words, you will not long rule!"

Very quietly, still dangling Journaraya's phial, Myrrax said, "There may be truth in thy words." His hand closed around the phial. He strode from the Well.

"I would not wound thee as thou hast wounded others, Journaraya." Myrrax placed the phial in her tied hands and closed her fingers around it. Journaraya bent her head and sobbed.

"Did I not tell thee to be patient?" Myrrax asked her. He looked at the others. "Did I not ask it of all four of you?"

"We're going to fight Stahaan on our own terms," said Keerax. "Mirtiin will stand on its own feet! Why fight for half a victory? If we cast out Stahaan, let us cast out every *stone* of Stahaan."

"Stahaan gave us birth," said Myrrax.

"Long ago," said the young Shade-in-Ice. "Now we are grown. Now we stand free!"

Wearily, Myrrax rubbed the fur between his eyes. "For a brief moment, aye," he said. "For a span of days shall we stand."

The audiences Myrrax had later that day were as he knew they would be. The first to see him was Iron-in-Granite.

"I do not doubt," said Rillaraya, "that you judge this a serious crime.

"Serious is hardly the word," said Myrrax. "The temple stands defiled. Even if this were not a crime against Mirtiin, it is a crime against our ancestors. *Our* ancestors, thine and mine. The ashes of every house mingle in the Well."

"And yet," said Rillaraya, "may this not be seen as a gesture well intended?"

Myrrax snorted.

"Hear me, Mirtiin. I, too, am grieved by the injury to our Mothers. But are not Robaraya and her friends right in judging Mirtiin reborn? Now may we rebuild the temple as Mirtiin, not as an echo of Stahaan."

"This is not what weighs most upon thy mind," Myrrax said. "What dost thou plead for her?"

"Pardon, full and complete. Only make them rebuild what they have destroyed. Make them labor to quarry new stones, Mirtiin stones, for the lip of the Well."

"*Pardon?*" Myrrax said. "Dost know what some other houses will ask?"

"The other houses," said Rillaraya, "have been in error before, have they not?"

"I speak for Mirtiin," said Myrrax. "I do not force her down corridors she would not travel by her choice. Indeed, I cannot force her down corridors I would not travel myself. Pardon them? After such injury, pardon them?"

"You must, Mirtiin. It is justice. Though they have injured all of us, yet did they mean to make Mirtiin look to itself and turn once and for all from Stahaan. Yes, pardon them."

"Other houses will demand death."

"These are our children, Myrrax. We have stood beside you. Iron-in-Granite, Grass-Above, Gems-in-Hand ... have we ever faltered? Have we ever failed to stand with you? Let us deal with our children in our own way."

"Injury demands recompense."

"If you must spill blood to slake vengeful thirst, let them have Keerax."

"Spare your niece," Myrrax said, heat rising in his face. "Let the Grass-Above and the Gems-in-Hand live, but sacrifice the Shade-in-Ice. Dost forget what blood runs in me?"

"Then spare them all," said Rillaraya. "That is what I first asked." She reminded him again, "These are our sons and daughters. Spare them, Mirtiin, for we have ever stood beside you."

"And if I spare them not?"

"I meant no threat. Yet if our own children should die in a cause that many do not find unjust—"

"To defile the temple is justice?"

"To make the temple anew," said Rillaraya, "is to make Mirtiin anew."

Myrrax blew out a long breath. At last he said, "I will consider."

Next came Dzeanaraya and Aanaraya to speak for Stones-Afalling and Ants-Below.

"It is well that thou art come with Dzeanaraya," Myrrax said to the Ants-Below. "It speaks of wounds made whole."

"Nay," said Aanaraya, "we come because we are wounded in common. In a matter so grave, we will put aside past injury to speak with one voice."

"It is an injury common to all," said Mirtiin.

"Is it?" said Dzeanaraya. "Was Iron-in-Granite not here, pleading for the lives of these four desecrators? Will her house show no respect to our Mothers?"

"Iron-in-Granite would bless the Mothers."

"As they blessed the Mothers with an invasion of *flakkach*?"

"That was fought and considered," said Myrrax. "Peace."

"It was fought and considered before we knew where next it would lead," said Dzeanaraya. "All that is holy is fouled by these four. I fought for Mirtiin to be Mirtiin and proud, not Mirtiin and desecrated. If none but Stahaan can keep us pure and ruled by scripture, then must we bow to Stahaan."

"But a Mirtiin that is pure might be a Mirtiin we could stand behind," said Aanaraya. "Thus do we say, Mirtiin: purify. Sacrifice these four. Let them die in Assembly that all may see we have not turned our faces from She Who Was First."

"Would this satisfy thee, Ants-Below?" asked Myrrax.

Aanaraya said, "It might, Mirtiin. It would be a step."

Myrrax snorted. "Give us blood, Mirtiin, and we *might*

stand together with the other houses. Thou art asking much, Aanaraya, considering the state of thy house."

"She is not alone in asking," said Dzeanaraya.

Myrrax said, "I will consider."

"Consider well, Mirtiin," said Aanaraya. "Much hangs in the balance."

Myrrax glared at her. "Mirtiin hangs in the balance," he said. "Do not imagine that I am unaware."

His last audience was one that he called. His daughter bowed to him.

"I did not bid thee bring the human."

"Mirtiin, much is afoot this day. You must make grave decisions, and as they are likely to involve the human, I thought to bring her."

"Thou hast brought her," said Mirtiin, "that she may help thee to change my mind."

"I know not what you will bid me do," said Cimmaraya. "I know not that I will want to change your mind."

"But I know thee, daughter. With thy mother, it was ever the same. Thou wouldst have a friend by your side to plead thy case whenever thou wert chastened." He squinted at the human. "Why art thou bandaged so?"

The human looked self-consciously at her bandages. There were two on one leg, one on her left hand, and another on her right arm. She said, "The goblins have taken to biting."

Myrrax snorted. "What I must tell thee to do was the better choice, even had the temple not been degraded. The potions that Scaraya made, they cannot be mixed aright."

"I need more time," Cimmaraya said.

"Wouldst have me kill thine age-mates?" Myrrax said. "Eight of the Eleven bid me kill Robaraya, Keerax, Journaraya, and Vedayrax. Eight of the Eleven would have me heal Mirtiin with blood."

"Spare them!" said Cimmaraya. "Father, Vedayrax is my cousin!"

"All with blood in common would have them pardoned, save Shade-in-Ice. Keerax wins no love in any house. Even his own aunts plead death for him."

Cimmaraya said softly, "What will you do?"

"They inherit the sky," said Myrrax.

Cimmaraya shuddered.

"What?" asked the human. "What does it mean?"

"They are cast out," said Cimmaraya. "They may not shelter nor ask succor in the halls."

"When they die," said Myrrax, "their ashes shall not know the heart of Mirtiin. They are cut off."

"It is mercy," observed the human.

"Cold mercy," said Cimmaraya.

"It satisfies no one," said Myrrax, "yet I can think of no course that fractures less the unity of our halls. But it is not enough. I must give more to those who clamor for death and cleansing."

Cimmaraya shook her head. "No."

"It is the only way, daughter. The human will I release. She has violated *purrah*, but not of her own will. This is compromise enough. Do not ask me for more."

"They will fight for you!" said Cimmaraya. "The goblins are so close to becoming what Scaraya dreamed they could be!"

"They deteriorate. So do the human's bandages tell me."

"What's he saying?" asked the human. "What does he plan?"

"The goblins," said Myrrax, "must be sacrificed. It will heal the wound that fractures Mirtiin."

"No, it won't," said Ayesh. "You'll lose the loyalty of your strongest allies! The houses that have worked so hard for this—"

"I am decided."

"Father, give us a little more time. Give us a week, at least! I am close to the formula."

"I am decided."

"This is madness!" said Ayesh. "You throw away your best opportunity, Mirtiin! If we succeed, if the goblins stand by Mirtiin when she is attacked from without, will that not unite the houses? Will that not prove that by this experiment Mirtiin is strengthened?"

He blinked and looked at her. It was a possibility he had not seen. It was true that to kill the goblins would alienate his firmest supporters, yet . . .

"I see thy bandages, human. What hope is there? I think there is, in truth, risk that the goblins will become a greater liability with each day that passes."

"They are your best hope," said Ayesh. "We can do it. We can give you goblins that fight as allies. Can't we, Cimmaraya?"

His daughter hesitated, then nodded. "A week," she said. "I am close."

"Gynnalem assembles her army," said Myrrax.

"Five days," said Ayesh.

"Three," said Myrrax. "In three days, I must announce sentence for the temple desecration. All news must come at once, that it may balance. Ten civil goblins, or ten dead ones. Give me one or the other in three days."

CHAPTER
22

ALL OR NOTHING IN THREE DAYS. IT WAS, AYESH soon realized, too much to ask of Cimmaraya. She stopped sleeping altogether, and the strain showed in her decisions of the second day.

"I want you to tell the goblins what is at stake," Cimmaraya said in the corridor outside the classroom. She held a tray of small phials rather than the usual flask.

"What? Tell them?"

"If they know, they can concentrate more."

Ayesh shook her head. "They barely concentrate as it is. Cimmaraya, goblin mind is shadowed by *fear*. Should we fail, then must the goblins die. Telling what's at stake—"

"I insist," Cimmaraya said. "I change tactics this day. I'll give them small tastes of elixir, two or three batches at a time. But they must be of a mind to help."

"No," Ayesh said. "Cimmaraya, uncontrolled though they may be, yet do they *want* the elixir to work. As long as they remember what it is like to know mastery, they will long for that state."

"Tell them."

"I'll not."

So Cimmaraya told the goblins herself, striding into the classroom with her phials. All the goblins but Tlik were cavorting like gray apes when Cimmaraya and Ayesh entered. They jumped on each other's backs, argued noisily, pulled ears, shrieked. Through all of this, Tlik sat in his place and meditated, though he flinched now and then when one of the others threw a pebble at him.

"Listen to me," said Cimmaraya.

Tlik opened his eyes and looked at her. The others kept up their nervous games until Gur stopped tussling with Bler and said, "Pay attention!" When Bler relaxed, Gur tripped her, then grinned. "*Always* pay attention!"

Cimmaraya said, "I have three elixirs for you to taste. I want you to try each one and concentrate first on how it tastes. There's not enough in each sample to change how it makes you feel. That comes later."

"Stop it, Nuwr!" cried Rip, wiping dust out of his hair. Nuwr snickered. Ayesh glared at them both to no effect.

"At the end of tomorrow," Cimmaraya said casually, "if the elixir is not found that will calm you—"

"Cimmaraya!" Ayesh said. "This is unwise!"

"—then will you each and all be put to the axe," Cimmaraya finished. "Now who will be first to taste?"

There was no rush of volunteers. The goblins muttered, looking at Cimmaraya or at the axes hanging from the minotaur guards' belts.

Tlik stood up.

"Yes," sneered Wlur. "Tlik will try. *He's* not afraid. They *like* him. He's good at pretending not to be goblin."

"I can bash you, Tlik," said Rip. "Sometime gonna show you. Gonna make Tlik scream." He grinned and snapped his teeth.

Cimmaraya seemed to notice only that she had her first taster. Tlik tried each phial Cimmaraya offered, and she nodded as he reported how they tasted to him. One was too bitter. Another smelled about right, but missed some sharpness in taste. The last tasted too much of witch-balm.

"Next?" asked Cimmaraya.

"Do what she says," Gur growled, "or I'm gonna bash you all. Taste it and tell her."

One by one, the goblins tasted. "Yech," said Kraw to the first, and "It stinks!" to the second. Most of the other reports were similar, even though Cimmaraya tried to coax out more information.

Ayesh told Tana to get the class started. In the corridor, Cimmaraya said, "Well, Tlik gave me good information. The second one smells aright, but tastes bitter."

"Tlik would have been that helpful in any case," Ayesh said. "And he said the second lacked some tang. Bitter was the first."

Cimmaraya scratched her head for a moment, then said, "Are you sure?"

"Are you taking down notes? What about the notes Phyrrax made? Are you making use of those?"

"He made copies of notes I already have."

"He *organized* them."

"He didn't work with Scaraya. What he has is only partial. He doesn't know how she thought!" The tray of empty phials shook in Cimmaraya's hands. "I *knew* her manner of thought."

"You must sleep," Ayesh said gently.

"No time! No time! I hold a thread of thought that leads to the answer. If I sleep, perhaps I lose that thread."

"Or perhaps you dream the solution."

"A vain hope, that. No, by application, by trials—"

"I was no scientist," said Ayesh, "but to not even write down your results—"

"No time! No time!" Cimmaraya said, starting down the corridor. "Keep them calm, Ayesh. I return anon with more samples."

Ayesh folded her arms and blew out a long breath. Then she returned to the classroom and took over from Tana, who had managed to get half the class doing warm-up exercises in synch with him. Half was good, these days. The rest muttered in pairs as if passing secrets.

When Cimmaraya returned, Zhanrax was following her, carrying a second tray. "Six tries, this time," Cimmaraya said. Again the goblins tasted the samples, and again, Tlik's responses were the most useful. *All* the goblins agreed that these samples smelled and tasted much like the original, but they disagreed about which was the closest.

"Gur's hands tremored as she drank the third," said Cimmaraya, "as they trembled with the elixir, ere Ayesh began to teach. Mayhap the first or second sample caused that?"

"First and second both smell right," said Gur. "*Taste* right."

"I was thinking fourth and sixth were best," said Tlik.

Gur whirled. "What do *you* know? You don't even need it! If the rest of us are chop-chop-chopped, you won't be!"

Tlik looked at Ayesh.

"I don't know if that's true," Ayesh said. She looked from Tlik to Gur. "Myrrax said nothing about sparing Tlik."

"They likes him," said Mok.

Styr said, "They thinks he's a minotaur! *He* thinks he's a minotaur."

Tlik said to Ayesh, "Teacher, may I play the flute?"

Ayesh noticed the others grinning at this. The flute music was the one thing they all still seemed to like about Tlik. "Play," she said.

Even as Tlik fetched the flute from its corner, Mok and Nuwr tossed pebbles at him.

"Wait!" said Gur. She held up her hand and looked at the guards next to the doorway. "Can't stop thinking about axes. Minotaurs say they gonna chop with axes. Don't want music if we gotta look at axes."

Cimmaraya said to the guards, "Wait in the corridor."

Gur grinned, but Zhanrax said, "No!"

The guards waited.

"Cimmaraya, you can't be serious. Dismissing the guards?"

"They'll be right outside," Cimmaraya said, "and if it helps the goblins concentrate . . . "

"Gur," said Ayesh, "you never had a problem with the guards before."

"Before," said Gur, "they wasn't gonna chop!" The others nodded and echoed, "Wasn't gonna chop!"

"We're running out of time," Cimmaraya said, touching Zhanrax's arm. "We have to try everything." She ordered the guards into the corridor. This time, Zhanrax let them go.

After Cimmaraya had gone, Zhanrax stayed behind to watch the class. The goblins did not seem to mind *his* axe, at least not after Tlik began to play. Music was the one thing that reliably calmed all of them, at least temporarily.

After the flute music, the class went smoothly for a while. Ayesh wondered if perhaps one or more of the elixir samples might be working. No goblin threw dust or pebbles at another. The muttering had ceased. They all sat and tried to meditate when she told them to, though only Tlik did so without fidgeting.

At the end of the class, the goblins seemed almost subdued.

"She makes progress," said Zhanrax in the corridor after class. The guards had returned to the classroom, and the goblins had not protested. "Do you not think she makes progress?"

Ayesh shrugged, and the big minotaur snorted.

Tana said, "I worry for Tlik. I would not want to sleep in that room with the others."

"I worry for all ten," said Ayesh. The three of them started down the mining corridor toward the spiral shaft. "Tomorrow is their last day, unless—"

"Cimmaraya works, even now," said Zhanrax.

"She should sleep," Ayesh said, "even if only for an hour or two. She must clear her thoughts." She stopped walking. "Send me to her, Zhanrax. Let me sleep this night in Iron-in-Granite. I'll watch over her. I'll take notes, be Cimmaraya to her Scaraya."

"No. You belong to Rock-in-Water."

"Zhanrax, whatever you hoped to gain by my capture, now you have it. Do you not? Does Cimmaraya not look upon you gently?"

He shook his shoulders, a gesture Ayesh had never

seen before. She took it for embarrassment. "Let me go to
Iron-in-Granite," she said.

He considered, then said, "For a time. For this night, at
least. As for later . . . "

"And let me take my things. My pack, my possessions."

"No." Zhanrax smiled. "All that is yours stays with me.
In that wise do I guarantee your return, if I demand it."

"Zhanrax," said Tana, "do you not owe her—"

Zhanrax silenced his brother with a short snort. "Do
not say, Tana, that I am beholden to *flakkach*!"

They were silent the rest of the way home.

Watching for long hours how Cimmaraya would stare
into the flame of her alembic, head nodding in time with
her breathing, made even Ayesh feel exhausted.

"You must sleep," Ayesh said for the hundredth time.

"You said you would help me work," said Cimmaraya,
"yet all you do is sing the same ceaseless song."

"All *you* do for long minutes at a time is stare.
Cimmaraya, sleep for but an hour! Clear your thoughts!
Tomorrow, you must have the solution!"

"No time," Cimmaraya said, closing her eyes. "No time
for sleep."

The alembic had ceased to boil some time ago, but now
the bubbles started in the glass again.

"Ah! What have I done! There will be water in the
fraction!" Cimmaraya grabbed the hot tubing, then
dropped it. Glass shattered, and steaming fluid ran across
the table.

Cimmaraya turned to the cabinets.

"What are you doing?"

"Replacing what I broke. I must start the distillation
anew."

"No," Ayesh said. "I'll do it. I've watched you. You
wait until the mixture ceases to boil, then draw off the
liquid here." She pointed at the smaller glass vial. "Then
empty the first glass, pour in the fraction, and do the
same again."

Cimmaraya squinted. "Aye, that's right."

"Lie down," Ayesh said, gesturing toward the bench.

"I won't sleep."

"Even if you don't sleep, lie down. I will wake you in an hour."

"Twice distilled," Cimmaraya said.

"Isn't that what I just said I would do?"

Cimmaraya nodded. She lay down on the bench. In the space of a hundred heartbeats, her half-open eyes glazed with sleep.

Ayesh watched the alembic, yawning now and then. These Iron-in-Granite garden rooms were the brightest place in Mirtiin during the day. At night, they somehow seemed the darkest. The lamp on the table cast a dim orange circle.

She opened some of the labeled jars of herbs while she waited for the alembic to boil. She peered inside this jar, then that one. She sniffed at trefolia and bearsbane. The smell of peppermint helped her feel more awake, so she sniffed that several times. The witchbalm smelled odd. She brought the jar to the light and found that several leaves of beebalm were mixed in. She plucked them out, but wasn't sure she got all the pieces.

Would Scaraya have let her ingredients get mixed up? Ayesh doubted it. She doubted, too, that Cimmaraya could stumble onto the true formula, or a working substitute, in time. She had Scaraya's enthusiasms but little of her method.

I won't let them kill the goblins, Ayesh thought. *Not without a fight.* Then she paused for a moment, thinking on the novelty of this. Mok, Rip, Kraw. Bler, Nuwr, Kler, Styr, Wlur, and Gur. Some she still hardly knew from the others, for they could be so alike—goblins practicing diamond mind or goblins lost in goblin mind, there was a sort of sameness to them. Tlik stood out, of course. And Gur was a leader, whether a rational or goblinish one.

They were *her* goblins. And she would fight to keep them alive, to give them one more chance.

She felt a twinge in her leg and looked again at her bandages. Goblin bites here, and here, and there. And even so, she would fight to give them opportunity to prove the diamond mind was there within them, waiting to be rediscovered.

So much could change in so short a time.

Cimmaraya woke with a snort. Then she bellowed.

"Tinsalt!" she cried. "Tinsalt!"

She jumped to her feet, knocking over the bench.

"Tinsalt! Tinsalt!"

She tore open cabinet doors, searching.

Rillaraya and one of her sisters clomped into the room hefting axes. "What? What is it?"

"Tinsalt!" Cimmaraya crowed, scattering wooden boxes until she found the one she wanted. She held it up triumphantly. "The red paste always started with tinsalt! I had forgot!"

She started to work, and Ayesh opened the great book. Ayesh wrote, "First ingredient for red paste: tinsalt." She said, "Tell me all the rest, Cimmaraya. Tell it to me step by step, all we need to know."

"No time!" Cimmaraya said.

But Ayesh insisted, so as Cimmaraya worked, she recounted all the steps she was sure of and all the likely guesses she had made. She explained the action of tinsalt as Scaraya had explained it to her. And Ayesh tried to miss no important detail.

"Tinsalt!" Cimmaraya sang. "It slows the action of the herbs, but regulates them."

"Slows them?"

"If the goblins have not drunk of it for some days, the elixir will not work immediately," Cimmaraya said, tapping her head. "I had forgot the action of the tinsalt."

"How long will it take to work?" Ayesh said, quill pausing above the page.

"If they haven't had the proper mixture in a while, the full effect won't come on them for two days," Cimmaraya said.

"Two days!"

"But we'll know that it works! In hours, they'll be calm enough to give a good account of themselves. After two doses, over two days, you will have your students back, Teacher Ayesh!"

Ayesh smiled an uncertain smile.

Two days.

The goblins seemed strangely subdued. They were not tussling or squawking when Cimmaraya, Tana, Ayesh, and Zhanrax entered the classroom. They sat or stood, more or less in their places.

All except Tlik. He was waiting by the guards near the door. To Ayesh he whispered, "Something's wrong."

"We have the elixir!" Cimmaraya announced. "It will work! I know it's going to work!"

"Good," said Gur evenly. "Good, good, good."

To Tlik, Ayesh said softly, "What's wrong?"

"I don't know," Tlik told her. "They're just acting . . . strange. Like they have a secret. No one will talk to me."

"You're the black sheep," Ayesh said. "Tlik, we really may have the elixir."

"And if you don't?" Tlik said, eyeing the guards' axes.

"If we don't, then you and I will have a fight on our hands. I'm not going to give you up."

Some of the shadow passed from Tlik's expression. Only some.

"Stay up front with me and Tana in class today," Ayesh told him. "Things will be back to normal soon. Count on it."

He nodded.

Zhanrax and Tana, meanwhile, were passing out bowls of elixir. Each goblin drank, and Ayesh watched them carefully.

Zhanrax brought a bowl to Tlik.

"Doesn't need it," Gur sneered. "He's special."

"It's true," Ayesh said. "There's no reason for him to have it, is there?"

"It's all right, Zhanrax," said Cimmaraya. "Tlik has demonstrated he can do without."

"Are they swallowing?" Ayesh asked.

Tlik nodded.

Let this work, Ayesh thought.

Soon, every goblin but Tlik was trembling violently.

"A good sign?" said Zhanrax. "Or are they poisoned?"

"A good sign," said Ayesh. "For they often trembled so before I taught them."

"But not so soon as this," said Cimmaraya. "It used to take days."

"Meditation!" said Gur. "Teacher Ayesh, help us stop shaking! Lead a meditation!"

Ayesh nodded, then clapped three times to began the class. The shaking goblins knelt in their places.

"It works!" said Mok. "I feel the potion working!"

"Yes!" agreed Bler. "Better! It's better!"

"Teach us!" cried Rip.

"Wait!" said Gur. "The axes! Still make me nervous, all the axes! Take the axes away!"

Cimmaraya turned to the guards. "Get out," she said.

"Him too!" Gur said, pointing at Zhanrax.

"Go," Cimmaraya said.

Zhanrax shook his head. "No, I—"

"Zhanrax, go! We'll be all right!"

"Far away!" cried Gur, shaking violently now. "Don't want to *ssss-see* them!"

"All the way down the corridor!" Cimmaraya said.

"But if there's trouble—"

"They're scared. There won't be trouble. Go!"

The guards left. Zhanrax backed out of the room.

"All the way down the corridor. *Leave* if you like. The elixir is working. We'll be fine."

The goblins put their hands in their laps.

"Close your eyes," Ayesh told them.

They closed them. So did Ayesh, but she opened them when she heard a goblin stir. It was Kraw. He had gone to the doorway and peered into the corridor.

"Axes gone?" said Gur.

"They're gone," Cimmaraya said. "Pay attention to your teacher."

"Axes gone," Kraw said, grinning. He wasn't trembling any longer. Nor was Gur, Ayesh realized. None of the goblins trembled. One by one, they began to stand.

"Axes gone," Gur repeated. "That good." She held something that glinted in the lamplight.

Other goblins produced similar objects—short blades

that protruded from beneath their thumbs. "Spoons," said Tlik, backing closer to Ayesh.

"Sharp spoons," said Mok.

"Gonna cut and slice," said Gur. "Minotaurs not gonna chop us. No. Goblins gonna cut cut cut!"

"Guards!" shouted Ayesh.

Cimmaraya cried, "Zhanrax!"

Nine goblins shrilled and attacked.

"Fight the goblin!" Ayesh shouted. "Not the weapon!"

Tana's hoof met Styr in midair. She shrieked. The makeshift knife went flying from her hand.

Nuwr and Bler sliced at Tlik. He sidled and backed away. In sparring, Ayesh would have told him to stand his ground. For the moment, she didn't care. He could do whatever kept him alive.

Mok and Gur split up, trying to flank Ayesh. Ayesh advanced, kicking, to drive Gur back. She felt Mok rush her, but she stopped short when Ayesh began to turn.

"Stop this!" Ayesh shouted. "Give the elixir time to work! You'll be all right!"

"Minotaurs gonna chop," said Gur. "We say *no*!"

Tana bellowed. From the corner of her eye, Ayesh could see that Rip clung to Tana's sensitive nose. Tana was fighting the reflex to kneel. Styr, holding her injured side, stabbed and sliced at his knees.

Cimmaraya was down. Wlur held her nose, while Kraw and Kler sliced at her. Their hands were bloody.

"Cimmaraya!" Ayesh shouted. "Fight!"

Cimmaraya bellowed once in pain.

Hooves thundered in the corridor outside. Ayesh rushed Gur, kicked her head *hard*, then spun to dodge Mok's blade. Mok jumped back.

Tana bellowed again. He was punching Rip, who still clung to his nose. Every punch must have hurt Tana more than it hurt Rip, but still Tana wouldn't yield to the pain. He kicked Styr again. She howled and rolled away.

As the guards rushed into the room, the three goblins paused in their bloody work on Cimmaraya. They stood. When the guards and Zhanrax were well inside the room, they shouted, "Run!"

Rip dropped from Tana's nose. Mok dropped his sharpened spoon. Nuwr and Bler threw their weapons at Tlik. Seven goblins sprinted between the guards' legs and out into the corridor. Now they were all shouting, "Run! Run!"

Two guards spun to pursue them. A third raised her axe above Tlik.

"No!" Ayesh shouted.

The axe fell.

Tlik dodged, rolling away.

"No!" Ayesh sprinted to Tlik and stood between the goblin and the guard. The minotaur hesitated.

"He fought with us!"

"Cimmaraya!"

The minotaur lowered her axe. She and Ayesh both turned toward Zhanrax where he knelt. Cimmaraya's white fur was bloody. Tana, too, knelt beside her. His legs were also streaked with blood. He hung his head.

"Mother of Mothers!" Zhanrax pleaded. "No!"

He shut his eyes, and his fists pounded his flanks.

The mines of Mirtiin echoed with his anguished bellow.

CHAPTER
23

THEY WERE BOUND, THE THREE OF THEM,
hand and foot, and the ropes were cinched so that they
could scarce do aught but kneel. Even had she been free
to stand, Ayesh would have knelt at the foot of Mirtiin's
throne. Even after being so tied for two days and aching
to stand, now would she have knelt.

Myrrax had been silent since the guards had carried
them in. Ayesh strained her neck to see him. She noticed
that Tlik would not raise his gaze from the floor. Kler,
too, kept her face down. Her body shook now and then as
she wept quiet tears.

"Hast naught to say?" said Myrrax at last.

"What might I say?" said Ayesh. "She was your daughter. Like you, I grieve."

Myrrax snorted. It sounded angry. "Tell me, Ayesh of
Oneah. Is it true, as I have heard, that humans bleed cattle from their necks?"

Ayesh bowed her head and shut her eyes tight.

"Is it true?"

"Some humans," Ayesh said.

"Wherefore is this done?"

"To mix the blood with milk, for food."

"Is there not another reason?"

"Mirtiin, why would you ask me this?"

Very quietly, his voice deeper than before, he said, "Is there not another reason, Ayesh of the humans?"

"By this means," Ayesh said, "cattle are sometimes slaughtered."

"I thought it so," said Myrrax. "Such bleeding is the practice of the goblins when they steal cattle from humans. I wondered at the origin, whereat the goblins did learn it."

"Mirtiin . . ."

"Hast eaten the flesh of cattle, Ayesh of the humans?"

She did not answer him. In the silence, she could hear the distant rumble of machinery below the Assembly Chamber. Below them were the great waterwheels and shafts. Deeper still were the mines. Somewhere down below, three goblins yet dodged from shadow to shadow, uncaptured. Ayesh didn't know which ones. The captain of the guard, Tekrax, had only told her that she had killed Gur, that Bler died from the kicking Tana had given her, that three more goblins had been hunted down and killed.

What dreadful things would the three survivors find to eat? How long could they stay alive beneath the minotaur halls?

"Goblin and human alike are meat eaters," Myrrax observed. "Hast eaten meat?"

Ayesh gritted her teeth. "Why do you do this, Mirtiin?"

"Tell me, hast eaten flesh?"

"Not since I came to the Halls of Mirtiin!" Ayesh said.

Mirtiin snorted. "It was not offered thee here."

"I despise what was done!" Ayesh said. "Blame me not for it! If you must kill us to sate some faction's vengeful thirst, then kill us! But know what you do! I'd have risked all to save Cimmaraya, had I the means!"

"No faction thirsts for vengeance more than I," said the minotaur chieftain. "There are not goblins enough in the world for me to kill."

"Well," said a familiar voice, "there are two less, now.

Tekrax, before he let me enter, told me two more were killed in the mines. Only one free goblin lives."

"Phyrrax?" said Ayesh.

"Thou ought not have come," said Myrrax. "Hast revealed much to Captain Tekrax by bidding entry at such a time."

"Tekrax reveals as much by allowing me to pass. Did I not tell you that he likely guessed my nature?" He carried something in his hand. Ayesh squinted in the low light.

Tlik spoke for the first time. "My flute!"

"An artifact at once goblin, human, and minotaur," said Phyrrax. "Oh, the promise in this object. The promise lost."

Myrrax's throne grated as it turned. The chieftain faced Phyrrax. "What wouldst *thou* have me do, Phyrrax?"

"Release the human. She has no blame in this."

"And Tlik!" Ayesh said. "He fought at my side!"

So softly that she was sure only she heard him, Tlik whispered, "And Kler." Kler went on crying wordlessly.

Myrrax was silent a long time. "Now, as power slips from me, do I come to know what power *is*. I might have them live, or have them die. Yet in how few days will it no more be mine to say?"

"You are Mirtiin," said Phyrrax.

"And Mirtiin lives forever, though Myrrax dies."

"There is yet hope. . . ."

Myrrax silenced him with a wave. "Gynnalem's scouts grow ever more numerous in our mountains. My own scouts do not always return. Her warriors near. Canst not feel their hoofbeats, Grass-Above? The very stones of Mirtiin shake with them."

Very quietly, looking at the floor, Phyrrax said, "It is as you say, Myrrax. Mirtiin endures forever."

"But I am Mirtiin for a short time. I feel the houses crumble beneath my feet, Phyrrax. What do they say but that my rule has come to nothing but ruin? And are they wrong?"

Phyrrax nodded at the captives. "Be merciful."

"While I have yet mercy to exercise, aye. That is how I know I yet have power. Ayesh, thou wilt be freed. Thou knowest too much of the mazes to be let free, yet will I trust that thou shalt return no threat. I grant thee life."

"And Tlik," said Ayesh.

"He is goblin."

"No," Ayesh said. "Not any longer."

"Is his skin not gray? If not goblin, then what is he?"

Tlik said, "I am what you made me. What all of you made me."

Myrrax was silent for a time.

"Tlik shall live."

"And Kler," said Tlik.

Myrrax thumped his throne. "Shall I prove infinitely merciful? My daughter lies dead. Thou knowest, goblin Tlik, that she herself, this Kler, did cut the chords of Cimmaraya's throat! Kler dies!"

"Be merciful!" Tlik pleaded.

"I *have* shown mercy," said Myrrax. "I will have justice as well!"

Kler wailed. "Why? If you meant to kill me, minotaur, why did you not leave me as I was when I was caught? Why did you not kill me *then*?" She wept loudly.

"It is not just!" Tlik said. "You made her rational again! You made her into a creature that could not do the crime she dies for. And *now* you kill her!"

Softly, Phyrrax said, "We had to know that the elixir was found again. We had to know that it would work."

"Then save her!" Ayesh pleaded. "Tlik is right! There is no justice in this! She killed out of fear!"

Slowly, Myrrax said, "If I forgave all crimes that were begun in fear, what crimes would I punish?"

"This is vile! It is vile to restore her to reason that she might suffer for a crime that now repels her!"

"We cannot keep her," said Myrrax. "To hold power even for a few days longer I must see that no *flakkach* yet lives in Mirtiin." He sighed. "If she were as thou art, goblin Tlik, then might I spare her. But without the elixir, she will be what she was when she murdered my daughter. Worse, she will know Mirtiin, its mines, some of its halls. That is dangerous knowledge to let spread among *flakkach*. I risk too much for you and Ayesh. I should kill you as well. I should."

"I'm sorry!" Kler cried. "I'm sorry!"

Softly, Myrrax said. "Goblin Kler, thou shalt not suffer painful death. Thou must die, but I will not have thee killed in vengeance. For what hast done to ... to Cimmaraya, I do ... "

The words were heavy.

"I do ... forgive thee."

"Yet is it murder that you do now!" Tlik cried.

"Even so," said Myrrax. "I can do no better." He summoned Tekrax. Ayesh and Tlik were cut loose.

"At least untie her!" said Tlik.

Myrrax nodded. Kler's ropes, too, were undone.

For a moment, as Kler stood, Ayesh saw Tlik glance to take in the guards, the placement of the door, Kler's readiness ...

"No," said Ayesh. "Don't try, Tlik."

Kler looked at Tlik, who still hadn't decided. She knelt again before the throne. "For the mercy you have granted, Mirtiin, I am grateful."

Tlik bit his lip.

"This is yours," said Phyrrax, holding out the flute.

Tlik did not take it from him. Ayesh accepted it.

"Take them from the halls," Mirtiin said to his captain, "and set them beneath the sky."

Tekrax pulled Kler to her feet.

"Not that one," Myrrax said.

"Come on, Tlik," Ayesh said.

"Diamond mind," Tlik whispered to Kler. "To the last."

Kler nodded one sharp nod. "Diamond mind."

"Take us by way of Rock-in-Water," Ayesh told Tekrax. "In that house are some things that belong to me."

"No," Myrrax said. "No detours. No complications."

"But my flutes!" said Ayesh. "My pack!"

"Take them the shortest way," said Myrrax, "and get them gone!"

Cold mist and gentle rain. Ayesh had almost forgotten about weather after so many days in Mirtiin. And though the mist turned all but the nearest ridges into shadows, and though the light was gray and muted, even so, the world seemed wide and brilliant.

Atop a ridge, under trees, she lay on her belly. The pine needles were soft, and the air smelled fresh with balsam and rain. But her gaze was not on the wider world and freedom. She was looking back toward Mirtiin.

"It would be madness to return," said Tlik.

"Zhanrax has things that belong to me," Ayesh said. "Precious things."

"If a patrol finds us in the open . . . Have you ever seen how they use their slings? How accurate they are over distance?"

Ayesh thought of the Mirtiin minotaurs on the first day she had met them, picking up steelstone missiles from beside goblin corpses. "Aye, I have seen. And it's not only Mirtiin's patrols we'd have to worry about, but scouts from Stahaan. Reason points me away from Mirtiin. And yet . . . "

"If you would have a flute, Teacher Ayesh," said Tlik, "then take mine." He held it out to her.

"That one is yours," she said.

"And who shall I play for? All who had the ears to hear are dead, save for you, Teacher."

"Call me Ayesh," she said. "Only Ayesh." She looked again toward the rock face where Mirtiin's doorway was carved. "I have a flute of my own, Tlik. Two flutes. I want them back. Come with me if you will. Wait if you prefer. Or wait not. As you will."

"Where you go," Tlik said, "there will I go." Softly, he added, "I must."

"The question," said Ayesh, "is how we get in."

"That is the first of many questions," said the goblin. "After we enter, we must find our way."

"I know the way."

"Any minotaur who sees us may try to kill us. Do you not think that the word has been spread in Mirtiin by now? The halls are swept clean of *flakkach*, save for one that hides in the mines. If I am seen, I am dead. As for what they would make of your return . . . can you be sure that even the minotaurs that once guarded our classroom would not attack you now?"

"There has to be a way," Ayesh said. "There *has* to be."

She was still puzzling it out when the net descended. The first she knew that others were near was the thud of the net's weights against the ground. The weave was thick and strong. As she and Tlik tried to struggle out from beneath the net, strong hands seized them.

Gods and gashes, she thought. *I had forgotten how silently these minotaurs can move.*

Their robes were red, and for a wild moment she thought, *Hurloon!* But the red was silk, not wool, and most of these minotaurs bore tridents, not axes. On their feet they wore fur-lined shoes like the Mirtiin patrols. But they weren't Mirtiin.

Ayesh said, "Stahaan."

CHAPTER
24

GYNNALEM, FIRST PRIESTESS AND ARCH- matriarch of Stahaan, Speaker of Stone, Most Revered Living Mother, stood atop a ridge overlooking the entrance to the Halls of Mirtiin. The entryway was a narrow slit high up in the cliff face, and the ledge leading to it would force attackers to approach in a single file. No frontal assault could take Mirtiin. The only hope was in laying siege, though siege was not without its own problems. To starve minotaurs into submission would harden their hearts, even the hearts of those who would willingly support Stahaan.

This was the sort of problem that Gynnalem's predecessors had craved. They had each worn the arch-matriarch's robes with ease, all the way back to the dawn of time. So said the scriptures.

If any Speaker of Stone before Gynnalem had harbored any but holy thoughts, it was not recorded in scripture.

Gynnalem stamped the ground nervously, and the very earth seemed soft beneath her hooves. Not even the earth could be relied upon. Things shifted, and in the shifting there was danger. All depended on decisions that she would make, decisions that she would far rather leave to someone else.

General Eltarekst cleared his throat. Gynnalem had not forgotten that he and General Finnarekst stood behind her, awaiting orders. She had never ceased to feel their expectant gazes upon her back.

She clutched her robes close. There were words that strained to escape her lips, words of her heart. *Find me the safe path,* she thought. *Find the way that leads us through the maze without danger. Find me the answer to the irregularities of Mirtiin, the answer that makes the ground solid and firm. Get it over with. Let it be done.*

In the depths of Stahaan, in the full dark of the heart of the heart of stone, she would lie awake, dreading moments such as this. When they came, they were always even worse than she feared.

Finnarekst said, "We await thy command, Most Revered Mother."

If she gave them the wrong orders, they would smile, nod, seem to go along, and then ask if she had considered another course of action, one more in keeping with their expectations, with tradition.

The robes of the Most Revered Living Mother were soft, silky, and quite as constraining as iron chains.

Get it over with, once and for all, she wanted to say. *Bring me a fire more hot and pure than fire has ever been. Bring me flames that consume carpet and tapestry. Show me fire that will consume flesh and eat away stone. Give me a holocaust that consumes mountains, that will burn Mirtiin down to nothing but memory. Then give me fire that will burn the memory as well. Light me a fire that will burn from here to Hurloon and consume those mountains, too. Spark me flames that will hunt down all who are not Stahaan and scour them from the earth. Then shall the earth beneath my feet ever be firm.*

Not because she hated Mirtiin or Hurloon, but because she hated problems. She hated these grand moments that her tutor, Pyhrralem, had so loved, standing before generals and deciding the fates of others—warriors of Stahaan, and warriors of those who opposed Stahaan. Gynnalem would far rather stand on this ridge alone and feel the sun on her shoulders, the wind in her fur.

But she was Stahaan. She had to act the part because . . . because . . .

Because there was nothing else for her. Because no most revered Mother had ever abdicated her title and gone to stand, as Gynnalem longed to stand, alone in the open air, eyes wide to the world, ears hearing only the wind, grazing on the common grass and following the sun to southern lands. Instead, Gynnalem's ears every day must hear the droning of scripture readers and the yammering of most beloved Mothers who asked her to judge between fine distinctions of meaning.

All this, the trap of title and power, had come because she had loved words, had loved their history and sound. She had been too fine a student for her own good. Pyhrralem, ere she died, had anointed her, had trapped her for life in the cage of scripture and tradition.

She had heard so many words for so long that she no longer believed in them. Wind, sun, stones, and silence. These were the things she could believe in. These were the true signs of She Who Was First.

Gynnalem snorted with frustration and pounded the butt of her golden trident against the ground.

Both generals advanced and nodded sharply. "We stand ready, Most Revered Mother," said Eltarekst, and Finnarekst added, "How shall we bring them down?"

"Gently," said Gynnalem. "As gently as we may. These who threaten our power are our sisters, also. So commands the chapter of Knowing Sanctity."

Oh, to be able to simply walk away. Those were the twin urges: on one hand, to bring down Mirtiin with blood and fury, to destroy their air tunnels, to smash their great mirrors, to starve and suffocate them into the pledge that they would never again stray from the narrow path dictated by Stahaan. On the other hand, she longed to walk away, to leave Mirtiin to be Mirtiin.

"They make dangerous experiments with goblins," Betalem had said. "They flout scripture and suffer *flakkach* within their sacred halls." Gynnalem wanted to say, "What of it?" But her Holy Sisters rose up at Betalem's words to call for war, and they were like a sudden flood loosed in the underground rivers. Gynnalem could only ride the rising waters, or be drowned.

"Eltarekst."

He nodded his salute.

"Post thy force in full view near the openings of the air shafts, but not so close that thou needst engage their guards. Make a show of cutting trees in preparation to stop the vents." It was the command he expected, the command of long tradition.

"By Her Most Revered command."

"Finnarekst, position thy cohort near enough to strike their mirrored peaks. But only show thy strength. Do not advance. Command thy soldiers to gather stones, as if in preparation to assault and break the mirrors. Then wait. Attack not, unless harried. Even then, destroy only those who harass thee."

General Finnarekst nodded. "Most wise, Revered Mother."

Not wise. This was as it had always been done since the first war against rebellious Mirtiin.

"Both of you shall do all that might be done to increase their fear. But threaten only." She dismissed them and watched them walk back toward their ranks of red-clad troops. The red-and-white pennants of Stahaan waved in the breeze.

Powerful as her assembled forces appeared, Gynnalem knew, the siege would be a long one if Mirtiin did not yield at once. There was no way to force a quick solution. If she stopped the air shafts, Mirtiin would grow hot and stale, but not suffocate. If she smashed the mirrors, long months would pass before Mirtiin starved. The best chance for surrender came in the interval *before* such destruction, when the Mirtiin minotaurs, fearing that she would soon destroy their great mirrors and plunge their gardens into night, might prefer parlay to battle, surrender to struggle.

Let all be done with threat, she hoped. *Let all be over quickly.* She did not think such an outcome likely.

Someone was climbing the slope toward Gynnalem, bowing and nodding like a courtesan as she came.

Betalem.

Here, clothed in flesh, was the orthodoxy that hemmed Gynnalem in, that decided all questions for her.

While Mirtiin asked questions that the orthodox would rather leave unasked, Betalem and her ilk asked no questions at all. No, that was not true. They asked whether the ablutions of the chapter of Knowing Purity were countermanded twice a year by the practice of repose from the chapter of Knowing Sanctity. They asked whether *nartoon* must always have only a temporal meaning, or if it might sometimes be the same as the word, *nirteyan*. Scripture, read in the narrowest manner, was all the truth she sought.

Damn her. Were Betalem more flexible, there might be peace. Unfortunately, she was beloved among the Sisters for her very rigidity.

"They are caught!" Betalem crowed. "They are seized!"

"Mirtiin?" said Gynnalem. Could it be over so soon? "Scaraya? Captured?"

"No, not them," Betalem said, panting. "The human! The goblin! They are the ones that saw the Assembly Chamber in Mirtiin, yet were suffered to live!" She curled her lip in a grin. "Suffered by Mirtiin, but not by Stahaan!"

"Bring me to them."

The cages were meant to hold a minotaur in so little space that she might neither stand nor lie down in comfort. For a human or a goblin alone, however, it was spacious. Betalem sought to remedy that at once.

"Put the human in with the goblin," she told the guard. Then she glanced to make sure Gynnalem would approve the order.

Gynnalem did not intervene, though she didn't see much point in adding to the prisoners' discomfort. Eventually, the goblin and the human would have to be killed. It was expected. But they weren't going to be tortured. What could they know that would be worth the effort?

The goblin faced away from her and did not stir. It was unusually subdued for one of its kind. Perhaps it had been injured.

"Be careful as you move the human," Betalem cautioned the guards. "She has some tricks."

The guards snorted, and one gestured at the encamped minotaurs who polished weapons or sat waiting all around. "What trick would get her out of here alive?"

As the guard unlocked her cage, the human looked at Gynnalem. Her eyes were dark, but alive with reason. She did not look like she was contemplating an escape attempt. Nor did she look utterly defeated.

"All right, you," said the guard. She leaned her trident on the outside of the cage, then reached in to seize the human by her hair. The human grabbed the guard's wrist and did something that made her bellow and let go.

The other guard leveled his trident at the human.

"Only tell me what I must do," the human said, her gaze never leaving Gynnalem. She spoke the Mother Tongue. And spoke it well, considering that her mouth was of the wrong shape. "Do not treat me like an animal."

"But animal you are!" said Betalem. "You fouled the very Halls of Mirtiin with your stink, and now it will take an army of Stahaan to cleanse the place."

The first guard had recovered her trident. She aimed it at the human.

"I am no animal," the human said. She glared at Betalem, an impressive gesture for a creature facing two tridents.

Gynnalem said, "Thou art not as I expected a human to be." But she had never spoken to one before. "Art not shaken to know thy death is at hand?"

"Thus you may know her for an animal," said Betalem. "A minotaur has wit enough to gather her thoughts as she prepares to die. This human, I do not doubt, still harbors thoughts of escape, unreasonable as such are."

"I know I shall die," said the human, "but the question of when I shall die is yet undecided."

"Your fate is cast," said Betalem. "You will die the death of *flakkach* that violated *purrah*."

"I am not *flakkach*," said the human, holding out her hands. There were but four fingers on each hand. "First chapter of Knowing Purity, 'By this shall you know the division: The fifth finger is *flakkach*.'"

Gynnalem blinked. "How didst thou come to lose two fingers?"

"I relieved her of one," said Betalem, "and she had Scaraya take the other."

"Didst know the scripture then?"

"Of course. I would not be *flakkach*, when I could choose."

Gynnalem opened her eyes wide. There was much more to this human than Betalem had suggested.

"If we grant that your hands are no longer *flakkach*," Betalem told the human, "then perhaps the Most Revered Mother will spare your hands and put the rest of you to death." She looked out of the corner of her eye to see if Gynnalem smiled.

The human snorted its derision. Gynnalem did not know humans could do such a thing.

"Put it in the other cage," Betalem told the guards. "What do you wait for?"

One of the guards opened the goblin's cage while the other prodded the human with his trident. The human stepped out of the cage and hesitated a moment, as if she might try to escape after all. A steelstone would find her skull before she had run fifty paces. She must have known that. She got into the other cage with the goblin.

To make room for the human, the goblin stood. It did not appear to be injured after all. How then to explain its seeming calm? Caged goblins usually chattered and dashed their bodies against the bars.

"*This* creature," said Betalem, "is the one that played music in the Assembly. Goblin music, can my Most Revered Mother imagine it. In the inmost chamber!"

"Drums?"

"Not drums, but a flute. A flute made by Mirtiin hands.

That is one of the crimes I enumerated to you, Most Revered Living Mother. I told you."

She probably had, but once Betalem launched into her denunciations of Mirtiin's various crimes, it was hard to pay her full attention for long. "Tell me again. I thought goblins played naught but drums."

"I have the flute!" Betalem produced it from her robes: a copper flute.

Gynnalem took it from her. The maze writing on the cylinder said it was the product of Gems-in-Hand. That house, along with Grass-Above, had a long history of heresy and disobedience. The flute's pieces had been fitted with precision, and the characters cut into the cylinder were sharp and proud. Gynnalem felt admiration for these minotaurs who proclaimed their complicity in a great spiritual crime. They had to have known how it would all end—as these rebellions always ended. Yet they signed their house name to the work.

She extended the flute to the goblin. "Play for me."

The goblin looked at the flute but did not take it.

"Come," said Betalem. "The Speaker of Stone would know the extent and manner of your crime."

"Tlik's music is no crime," said the human, taking the flute. "He plays as no goblin before him has played music. He is the first of a new race." She handed the flute to the goblin, who only looked at it in his hands.

"Play!" said Betalem. "Gynnalem has commanded it!"

Still, the goblin only looked at the flute.

"Guards!"

At Betalem's word, they raised their tridents, ready to pierce the goblin for its disobedience.

"No," said Gynnalem. "Do not kill it."

"No," agreed Betalem, "but it must learn obedience!" She told one guard to jab the goblin's legs. Gynnalem did not bother to counter the order. This was a goblin, after all.

The creature scarcely flinched. He made no sound.

"Did you pierce him?" Betalem asked. "Strike again!"

"No!" said the human. "They wounded him! You have made your point!"

Gynnalem saw blood on the trident and said, "He was

struck and punished. No more." She looked closely at the goblin's face. He'd been looking down at the flute all this time, but now he met her gaze.

Such calm. Such intelligence, and in the eyes of a goblin. What had been happening here in Mirtiin? Was it perhaps as dangerous as Betalem feared?

Or was it a wonder?

Betalem would not be moved. "But he refuses to play, Most Revered Mother. I would have *some* music out of him. If he will not play the flute, let him sing out!" She grabbed a trident from one of the guards and jabbed the goblin. It was silent. Gynnalem saw blood soaking through its leggings.

"Tlik!" said the human, shaking the goblin's shoulder. "Cry out! Howl! Give her what she wants."

Betalem jabbed again.

"Stop," said Gynnalem. When Betalem readied the trident again, Gynnalem said, "By my command, stop! Or die!"

The second guard pointed her trident at Betalem.

"Revered Mother, I, I serve your interests!"

Would that all who strove to serve her so would drop dead. Then could Gynnalem know what her interests truly were.

The goblin's gray face was an impassive mask. Ordinarily, a goblin would be shrieking and chattering after such treatment. This one stood stiffly, bleeding and clutching the copper flute, gaze still fixed on Gynnalem.

"It is Mirtiin that plagues us. These creatures matter only as they serve to bring Mirtiin low."

She turned to walk away.

Betalem dropped the trident and tagged at her hooves. "You see? You see how they changed this goblin?"

"I saw."

"A goblin that does not gibber and shriek, a goblin that withstands pain. . . . That is a dangerous thing, Most Revered Living Mother. Think of mountains populated with such creatures."

"Scripture says that goblins must be ruled by fear," said Gynnalem. "Dost mean to tell me that this goblin is not so ruled?"

Betalem stopped short. "I— Certainly, I did not mean to ... Reverend Mother, do not think that I spoke heresy!"

"Where lies the heresy, then?" said Gynnalem. "Scripture and the goblin seem not to meet upon the same ground." That was as far as even Gynnalem dared to take the argument out loud, though in her heart, she had long known that not all things in the creation were bound up in the words of the scrolls, however much all of Stahaan might say they were.

"The heresy lies in Iron-in-Granite, Most Revered Mother. With Scaraya."

"Then Scaraya dies," Gynnalem said, because it was what she must say.

"I hope she is dead already. But there are others who must also die. I shall name them for you, when the hour comes. So many, Most Revered Mother, who must die that Stahaan shall be honored and the commandments of scripture shall be kept. And there are books that must be burned. Mirtiin's daughter wrote down all the doings of Scaraya. These heresies must all be put to flame."

"Let this be over soon."

In this matter, She Who Was First was generous.

The captain of Mirtiin's personal guard walked into the Stahaan camp unarmed, flanked by Stahaan minotaurs aiming tridents, just in case his intentions were impure. "Tekrax," said Betalem when she saw him. "Mirtiin's right hand."

Captain Tekrax crouched low and touched his lips to the ground before Gynnalem. "Humbly do I greet you, Stahaan, source of the All, first hearth, first Well, Speaker of Stone." He looked up. "Most Revered Living Mother, your soldiers stand at our gates. As if all minotaurs were not sprung from the same First Mother, an army of your soldiers stands as if to bring ruin to our halls. Most Revered Mother, has Mirtiin done aught to offend you?"

Betalem snorted. Gynnalem said, "Stahaan's priestess was driven from your halls."

"Most Revered Mother, I beg to tell you, Mirtiin does not offend. Mirtiin stands not in rebellion."

Betalem snorted again and said, "What of Mirtiin's violations of scripture? What of the *flakkach* that we have caged here, that were suffered to live when they had seen within the Halls of Mirtiin? What of the battles offered in resistance to me, Stahaan's priestess and representative?"

Gynnalem noticed that the captain did not look at Betalem, but kept his gaze on Gynnalem herself. "Misunderstandings there have been," he said.

Betalem snorted for a third time. From the outskirts of the Stahaan camp, Gynnalem heard upraised voices, cheering—no. Not cheering. *Jeering.*

The captain bowed lower. "We do not deny that grievous crimes were committed. Dark the days that these things were done. Very dark. But I tell you, Most Revered of Living Mothers, that Mirtiin did not commit these crimes against you." He looked up. "It was the doing of Myrrax, who *was* Mirtiin. No longer."

The jeering had grown louder now, and closer. Stahaan warriors in the camp were on their feet, crowding around some approaching procession. The warriors shook their tridents. Some laughed and hooted.

"He comes in chains, who offended you, Stahaan. Speaker of Stone, do not punish all of Mirtiin for the crimes of one!"

"Of one!" shouted Betalem, incredulous. "Of one!"

The crowd of Stahaan warriors parted, and Gynnalem saw that Myrrax came walking between four Mirtiin guards. Myrrax wore not the colors of all eleven houses, nor even the purple he'd been born to as Shade-in-Ice. He did not even wear the pink and turquoise of Gems-in-Hand, the house he had married. No. As if none would have him, he wore undecorated gray.

From his bearing, Gynnalem knew at once that he had not been overthrown. He stood unbowed, proud. This was Myrrax's idea, to stand alone for the punishment that all of Mirtiin would otherwise bear.

It was a gift. And Gynnalem was eager to accept.

"He did not act alone!" Betalem insisted. And Gynnalem knew that others would feel the same, that there would have to be more deaths than Myrrax's before Stahaan's wounded pride would be healed. Scaraya would have to die. And Myrrax's daughter. Perhaps a few more. Certainly, for the sake of sacred law, the human and the goblin must die in a memorable way.

But then it would be over, and things could be as they had been before.

Not that *that* was a pleasant thought, entirely. There would be more debates about a single word of scripture, about the interpretation of chapters that seemed—bless us, Great Mother, for our eyes that see flaws where none can be—*seemed* to contradict one another.

Better the despised routine. Then at least part of the day could be occupied with private thoughts.

Myrrax's guards brought him close.

"Thou art well come, Myrrax."

He bowed low. "Stahaan, I am in your hands."

CHAPTER

25

HANGING LIKE BIRDS IN THEIR CAGE, AYESH
and Tlik had a good view of the trial, though they had to
alternate sitting and standing as there was not room
enough in the cage for both to sit. Betalem had ordered
the cage to be hung at the back of the Assembly
Chamber, high on the wall where the black-and-blue banners of Rock-in-Water hung. It was a gesture Ayesh
understood well. She could read the sting of it in
Deoraya's expression.

Indeed, Ayesh was surprised at just how easily she followed the trial, dissected the strategy of it as it unfolded.
Minotaurs, which had once been unreadable to her, had
become easier and easier to understand.

Even before all the Mirtiin minotaurs had entered the
Assembly, a Shade-in-Ice rose to address Gynnalem.

"Stahaan," she said, "I humbly ask, wherefore were our
axes and tridents taken from us as we entered this chamber? For look upon us, First Among Mothers. We are
Shade-in-Ice, a house ever loyal to your temple."

From her perch on the Mirtiin throne, Gynnalem
looked at Myrrax, who knelt in chains at her feet. The

guards who stood watch over him were still his own. Captain Tekrax held a rope that was tied to the chains. But the Mirtiin guards were unarmed, and Stahaan guards with tridents stood nearby. "Until the guilty are judged," she said simply, "all must be suspect."

Betalem, who paced the floor beneath the throne, said, "What was done was not the work of one minotaur alone. Mirtiin's temple is ruined. House has fought house, and house has fought temple. Can one minotaur do all this?" She looked at the Shade-in-Ice. "Your house defended the temple. But were all within your house loyal?"

"Aye," said the Shade-in-Ice. "I tell you, Most Revered Mother, that we were ever loyal. All of us who wear the purple of our house. When you remove our axes, so too do you remove the badge that we would wear proudly. We are the house that stood faithful to you."

"As were we," said an Ants-Below, standing. "Trust us to hold our weapons, that we may serve you with them."

Gynnalem shook her head, and Betalem spread her arms in a gesture to the whole chamber. "It will be resolved in this Assembly who shall keep her axe . . . and her head. Sit thee down, Ants-Below. Do thou likewise, Shade-in-Ice. Sit down, and think well on the crimes that were done in Mirtiin. *All* the crimes."

She relishes the role of inquisitor, thought Ayesh. But Gynnalem seemed aloof every bit as much as Betalem was glorying in the trial.

Ayesh turned away from the proceedings. She said to Tlik, "Do you want a turn at standing?"

He nodded, then bit his lip as he pulled himself up by the bars. His legs trembled. Ayesh sat and looked at the bandages she had wrapped around his legs. "I wish I could clean your wounds and change your dressings, Tlik."

Over his shoulder, he said, "You would send me well healed to the axe. You are always seeing to the details, Teacher Ayesh."

"Ayesh. We are student and teacher no longer," she reminded him. "And we are not dead yet." She touched the bandages. "Does that hurt?"

"A little."

"Perhaps there will be no infection," she said. "The wounds were deep, but clean." She looked at the flute in his hand. "It would have been easier to play for her. There are times to resist, but there are also times—"

"Ayesh," he said, "if you would not have me call you Teacher, then cease to instruct me."

"But why did you not yield to her?"

"Because," he said, "I *would not yield* to her. I have been a leaf on the river of minotaurs. Is that not reason enough? I have power over my own fear. Is that not reason to do what I fear to do?"

"But if you act in futility—"

"What is *not* futile now?" He shook the bars of the cage.

Ayesh could not counsel him to hope, for looking out of the cage, she saw no friendly face looking back. Had Tana been here, perhaps. But he was too young for Assembly. He did not yet have his name.

"Gynnalem will hear no defense," Betalem was saying. "The Most Revered of Living Mothers has not ears for any excuse or softening. Accuse. Confess. These are the things she should hear. But any who offers apology offends her." She looked at Gynnalem, who gave a slight nod.

The throne turned slowly, and her gaze passed over one house after another. But it was Betalem's gaze that burned. Gynnalem seemed bored. The throne stopped as she faced Rock-in-Water. "What have the minotaurs of this house to say?" Gynnalem said.

No one moved for several heartbeats. Then Deoraya stood. "In our hearth," she said, "were we ambushed by those we had bid enter as guests."

Gynnalem nodded. "Who did attack thee, Rock-in-Water? What house?"

"No house, Most Revered Mother. The priestess Betalem and her guard, they attacked us."

Betalem stamped her hoof. "As they did shelter *flakkach* did I attack! Aye, with good reason!"

Gynnalem raised her hand. "Silence, priestess. Thou mayst not be prosecutor and witness at once."

"But I was acting by authority of—"

"Silence!"

Betalem's mouth did not close, but no more words came out.

"Accuse and confess. Did Betalem not urge this?" She smiled. She was, Ayesh thought, enjoying Betalem's discomfort. "Accuse and confess. I brook no pleadings or ameliorations. What is crime must be exposed as crime." Then she nodded to Deoraya. "Thou hast laid open a black crime, Rock-in-Water. Not even the temple is free to break the sanctity of hearth and hospitality. Hast aught else to say?"

Deoraya shook her head and sat down. Gynnalem looked long and hard at her, then at Zhanrax. Betalem glared at them. At last, though, the throne moved on to the next house, Ants-Below. "Has this house any crimes to name?"

The orange-and-gray-clad matriarch rose. "Grave crimes, and many," she said.

"Speak, then. Stahaan listens."

"This Myrrax," said the matriarch, pointing, "this one who was Mirtiin, he supported science born in heresy!"

"His crimes are already widely known," said Gynnalem. "Tell what is undiscovered."

"He supported the experiments of Iron-in-Granite that were done by Scaraya and by Myrrax's own daughter, Cimmaraya. They plotted to raise goblins above their wretched state. Why? That we might have enemies more dangerous than now? Goblins plague us from time to time, but if they were elevated in reason, would they not plague us all the more?"

"This is known," Gynnalem said wearily. "His crimes are black. He will be punished. As for Scaraya and Cimmaraya . . . tell who remains unpunished, yet is stained with evil doings. For a divine hand has stilled those two hearts already."

"'Tis a pity," said the Ants-Below matriarch, "that ashes such as those may not be called up from the Well. They mingle, alas, with the ashes of my worthy Mothers."

At that, Zhanrax stood up. Ayesh could not see his

face, but his fists were balled. Deoraya tried to pull him down, but he shouted, "It is you, by your attacks upon your own cousins, who does dishonor to our Mothers!"

There was a general stir. Some minotaurs shouted agreement, others shouted Zhanrax down.

"Ants-Below speaks," said Gynnalem. "I would hear her out."

When order returned, Ants-Below said, "As you would ask of crimes unpunished, so would I tell you of Rock-in-Water. That one who stands there, Zhanrax, brought the human *flakkach* into Mirtiin. He sheltered it in his house."

"That is no right of a son," observed Gynnalem. "The house where he lives is not his to grant as sanctuary."

"True," said the Ants-Below. "It was his mother, Deoraya, who opened her hearth to the human."

Deoraya stood. "The human asked sanctuary by the proper forms! Mirtiin ruled it proper! How could I do aught but—"

"No softenings," said Betalem. "No excuses. This Assembly is about your *crimes*!"

"Another son of their house, the one called Tana, was instructed by the human in human ways. As were the goblins. Who knows what pollution taints his young mind? Who knows if he might ever be cleansed of it?"

"Tana is a *child*!" Deoraya protested. "He has not yet taken his name!"

"I say again," said Betalem, looking sternly at Deoraya, "and let this be the last time. We shall brook no defenses or pleadings. Tell the Speaker of Stone only who is blackened with what crime. Accuse. Confess. That is all she needs to hear."

"Hast more to say?" asked Gynnalem of Ants-Below.

Ants-Below's matriarch shook her head and sat down.

The throne turned next to Flame-in-Void. Ceoloraya rose to denounce those who had been safely denounced already.

From house to house turned the throne. Neshiearaya denounced Myrrax for Grass-Above. Dzeanaraya said the same words for Stones-Afalling.

The matriarch for Horns-of-Gold said, "There were three houses that supported Myrrax in his crimes. Not only Scaraya's Iron-in-Granite is to blame. Guards from Grass-Above and Gems-in-Hand served to protect the goblins and human, *protect* them from those who would do justice by slaughtering *flakkach*." She glared at each house in turn. "Then did they darken their crime. They let the goblins escape! Only this day, an hour before this Assembly, was the last goblin caught in the corridors of Mirtiin, not far from this very chamber."

Tlik stood a little taller and pressed his face to the bars.

"This goblin's head was filled with the windings and twistings of our corridors. Such secrets did it know! Such secrets might it have escaped with had it gone but a little further and escaped the halls. Now, those secrets remain in the goblin's head, though head and body are severed."

Tlik said quietly to Ayesh, "I would sit again." His legs had begun to shake.

Ayesh stood to make room for him.

"How black a crime," continued Horns-of-Gold, "to dangle knowledge of our secret halls before our enemies! These houses, to the last, are traitors to all of Mirtiin! Iron-in-Granite! Grass-Above! Gems-in-Hand! All deserve to inherit the sky!"

There was grumbling from the accused houses.

"Black crime. Black indeed," said Betalem. "And black punishment suits it. Now more! Confess! Accuse! Tell our Most Revered Mother all!"

At last, Gynnalem's gaze had come full circle. She stopped before Rock-in-Water again and said, "But I have heard only accusations. Will none confess?"

Ayesh scanned the crowd of shaggy faces. Most eyes were downcast, most expressions blank. But sitting high in the rows of Grass-Above, Ayesh saw Phyrrax looking about with exaggerated curiosity, as if eager to see who would finally have something to confess. As if he alone was sure of his own innocence.

Don't overplay it, you fool, Ayesh thought.

"Surely, some will confess," Gynnalem said. "*Mercy likes confession!*"

"I will confess," said Deoraya. She stood. "Our house sheltered the human. And when Betalem demanded that we surrender her, pride kept us from doing so. We held honor above piety."

There was some fire in her voice as she said this, and resignation, too, as if she were just now concluding what Ayesh had already decided—that all houses would be found guilty of something. "We offended the temple."

"So you did," said Gynnalem, and she passed on to Ants-Below. "What has this house to confess?"

The matriarch rose. "We were ever loyal, Stahaan. To Stahaan, to temple, to scriptures."

Betalem stalked near the matriarch, eyes narrowing. "Yet did you not tolerate the goblins? When the human was brought into this chamber, how many of Mirtiin's guards did your house strike down in fury? When that goblin . . ." She pointed at the cage. "When that *flakkach* was brought into this room to play music, to *mock* the sacred music of our Mothers, how many axes did your house raise against the sacrilege? Even as I, your priestess, pleaded with you?"

"We—we did not know how many would stand by us! It was prudent to bide our time, to strike when we might be sure—"

"So sayeth the *Book of Knowing*: 'Caution in Righteousness is no Virtue, nor Outrage to counter Sacrilege a Curse.' Your house did tremble and waver while misrule did guide Mirtiin! I had to coax you into the proper fury and righteousness!"

Ants-Below opened her mouth, then looked down and closed it without uttering a word.

"Dost dare deny thy crime?" asked Gynnalem. "Dost dare say thou wert not liberal?"

Ants-Below shook her head. "I confess it. We were not resolute. Too late we raised out axes. Too late." She raised her gaze. "Yet was this not a lesser crime?"

"To spurn the guidance of scripture and your priestess? A lesser crime?"

Ants-Below raised her hand before her face. "A black crime! 'Tis a black crime!" she agreed, and she sat back down upon her cylinder of stone.

Gynnalem rotated for a second time through the houses, and each house confessed some sin against Stahaan. When she got to Iron-in-Granite, Rillaraya stood. "I confess that this very morning, when Stahaan's guards came to burn Scaraya's books, in my heart did I resist them, even as I bid them enter. In my heart, I opened the door only for the tridents that they bore. But there is no True Book but scripture. Stahaan's books and scrolls contain all the needed knowing. The discoveries of Scaraya were heresies."

"Books burned," Ayesh said softly. "They're letting her destroy all that makes Mirtiin different."

Tlik said, "Did you not council me just now not to act in futility?"

"They might have fought!"

"See how they express their unity, these minotaurs of Mirtiin," Tlik said. "They'd have turned to murdering each other even before this Stahaan got her war started up. A goblin's mind is fearful, but tell me not that a minotaur's is less so."

"True words," Ayesh said, hanging her head. "Like goblins, minotaurs might be more than they are."

"Are not humans the same?"

"Aye. Fear rules all who do not master it."

"We die anon," said Tlik. "But we die wise." He snorted.

Ayesh said nothing.

"Might not all justly die?" Betalem said when she and her mistress had extracted confessions of some sort from every house. "Might the very stones not crumble with shame?" She looked at Myrrax. "And yet all shall not die, for here is one whose crimes *are* blacker than the rest. Stand, Myrrax of No House."

He stood. Ayesh gripped the bars of the cage. He stood so tall, his bearing was so straight, that even stripped of his colorful robes he looked more the leader than Gynnalem did on the throne. *His* throne. How could there be any doubt that it was *his* throne? Even she knew it. She did not meet his gaze.

"Black are thy crimes, Myrrax. Wicked are thy sins. Thy conspirators have died before thee, yet thou art the one who most deserves the pains of death." She said all this without feeling, as if reciting a script.

"'Tis true," he said, looking into her eyes.

"Oh, brave and noble you seem to stand," said Betalem. "Strong beyond scarring. Even death shall not touch you, is that what you think, Myrrax? For you have a secret in your heart. But I know of the conspirator who is yet unrevealed. . . ."

Myrrax made the slightest of gestures, turning his body the slightest bit and darting his gaze at Tekrax.

Betalem saw it. So did Gynnalem. Indeed, all minotaurs saw the move, and all minotaurs were good at reading subtleties.

The briefest flicker of anguish crossed Myrrax's face. And Ayesh, in an instant, knew why.

Tekrax reveals as much by allowing me to pass, Phyrrax had said. *Did I not tell you that he likely guessed my nature?*

Betalem and Stahaan didn't know who this "unrevealed conspirator" was. This was a trick: tell Myrrax that Betalem knew and see to whom he might glance.

Tekrax reveals as much by allowing me to pass.

Phyrrax, Ayesh was sure, must be the undiscovered confederate. But Myrrax had not glanced at him.

Did I not tell you that he likely guessed my nature?

Tekrax reveals as much by allowing me to pass.

Myrrax had turned not to the conspirator Betalem hoped he would reveal, but to the one minotaur who likely knew the conspirator's name. He turned to the one he thought had betrayed the secret. And the flicker of anguish was a sign: by his worried glance, Myrrax had betrayed his loyal captain.

All so subtle. Ayesh was sure she could not have understood all this had she not been living among minotaurs. No wonder people thought they could read minds!

Betalem pointed at Captain Tekrax. "In the name of She Who is First Among Living Mothers, seize him!" Her guards clapped a set of chains on the captain's wrists and ankles.

And Myrrax said, with remorse that was no act, "I am sorry, my captain."

Tekrax's mouth was tight. There was surprise in his eyes, and fear. He looked about the chamber.

Ayesh looked at Phyrrax, whose mouth hung open and whose eyes were wide.

Now will Tekrax denounce him, she thought, *to save himself.*

Tekrax looked at Gynnalem. "'Tis true," he said. "From the beginning did I whisper in his ear. I knew of Scaraya's investigations ere Myrrax did, and I did coax him to support them."

Ayesh looked at Tlik. He was hardly listening to what was happening now, and there was no sign of understanding in his expression. She looked again at Phyrrax and found he was looking at *her.*

There were four who knew or suspected the truth: Myrrax, Phyrrax, Tekrax, and Ayesh. Chieftain and captain would die to keep the secret. But Phyrrax was uncertain of the human.

She dared not give him any sign. She only turned to listen to Tekrax denouncing himself.

"Mirtiin has ever stood in the shadow of Stahaan. Will this always be so? United with reasoning goblins, goblins made worthy of alliance, we would make these mountains ours! Our hearth traditions would be our own! We would worship the Goddess in our own ways! Our science, which has ever been a blessing Stahaan could not match, our science would flourish! We'd make gardens such as minotaurs have never seen! We would be *free!*"

"Hear his confession!" said Betalem. "And tell me, is it freedom to be cut off from the Well of your first Mothers? Is it freedom to be severed from Stahaan, from the Source, from the First Stones?"

"No!" shouted a Horns-of-Gold. The orthodox houses, and finally all the rest, joined in shouting, "No! No!" Even Phyrrax shouted.

There was an aphorism of Master Hata's: *To avoid drowning, become the sea.* It had always puzzled Ayesh up to now.

"No! No!" Phyrrax shouted. Zhanrax stood and

shouted, too. And Deoraya. And the matriarchs of every
house all shouted, "No!"

But each, in the secrets of his or her heart, Ayesh realized, might shout "No!" to something different.

To avoid drowning, become the sea.

"No!" Ayesh shouted. "No!" she cried at what must
now come to pass.

The shouts subsided.

"Kill me," Tekrax said, "but Mirtiin lives!"

"Enough!" Betalem shouted.

In the silence that followed, Gynnalem said quietly,
"Bring in the executioners." She sounded almost reluctant. Or bored. Ayesh could not say which was worse: a
half-hearted death sentence, or a disinterested one.

Betalem's cry of "Executioners!" had all the lusty
enthusiasm that Gynnalem's command had lacked.

The chamber doors opened, and six white-clad minotaurs bearing tridents came in. They wore white masks
over their faces.

No minotaur spoke as the executioners strode down to
the center of the circular room.

The executioners took up positions, two with tridents
poised at Myrrax's back, two behind Tekrax. One execu-
tioner stood in front of each.

"I can't watch this," Tlik said, closing his eyes.

"Have you not seen worse in the goblin caves?"

"*Yes!*" he said. "But I was different then!"

"All might die in this manner!" Betalem cried. "All of
the Halls of Mirtiin, every house, is stained with crime!
But these two alone shall die, for Stahaan is powerful!
Remember, those who would suffer heretics, those who
would shelter *flakkach*, those who would walk upon
scriptures—Stahaan shows mercy as she chooses. *As she
chooses*, not because she must!"

She nodded to the executioners.

Ayesh closed her eyes. There were wet sounds, then the
crunch of bone. There was a great wet snort, then
another.

Something heavy hit the floor. Then something else.
There were more sounds of wet cutting, chopping, probing.

"This is mercy?" Ayesh breathed.

When at last she opened her eyes, the Assembly floor was pooled with bright blood. The executioners stripped off their robes. They wore only loincloths and masks, now. They laid the robes over the bodies, rubbed them against the bloody floor. When the robes were soaked and scarlet, the executioners held them high.

"Behold the justice of She Who Was First!" cried Betalem. "In her name are heretics unmade and heresies forgotten!"

A Shade-in-Ice stood and cried, "Stahaan! Justice!"

"Justice!" came some diminished cheers. "Stahaan!"

Then Phyrrax stood, and Ayesh knew he cried for something else altogether when he took up the call with enthusiasm. "Justice!"

"What of the *flakkach*?" cried an Ants-Below. She pointed at the cage. "They yet live!"

Gynnalem's throne turned, and the room fell silent.

All gazes were turned on Ayesh and Tlik.

And Betalem said, "Scripture tells us that *flakkach* does not enter the halls and live."

"In truth," said Gynnalem, "scripture teaches that *flakkach* shall not violate *purrah* and live."

Betalem bowed slightly. "Even as you say, Most Revered Living Mother. What I mean to make clear is that there is a lesson here for all to learn. *Flakkach* have entered this Assembly. They must not be suffered to leave alive."

Gynnalem was looking at Ayesh. Now there was no doubting it. What was the Speaker of Stone feeling? Her expression was unreadable, but Ayesh could not shake the feeling that Gynnalem felt remorse or regret. Her eyes were dull, and her heavy lips were slack.

"What course dost recommend, priestess?"

Betalem smiled and looked at Deoraya. "I would make of these *flakkach* a lesson that will not soon be forgotten."

CHAPTER
26

THE ASSEMBLY CHAMBER HAD BEEN QUIET FOR
a long time. How long, Ayesh could not say. The guards
in the entryway had been changed five times.

It was so quiet that she could hear her own heartbeat
and the hiss of the oil lamps set in the wall. She heard
Tlik's dry breath coming and going.

She measured time by the intensity of her thirst. Her
throat felt as dry as paper. Her tongue felt pasty, swollen.

For a while, she had been hungry. The minotaurs had
not fed Ayesh and Tlik since their captivity began, but
they had given them water, at least until Betalem had
passed sentence.

"In the caves where I was born," Tlik said, "there was a
seep in one wall where the stone was shaped to receive the
water. It dripped, dripped, dripped, one cool drop at a time."

"Don't," Ayesh said.

"After I had a drink there, I would sit and watch it, listen to it. Drip, drip. I can hear it now. Through these
many leagues of stone, I hear it."

"You dwell," Ayesh said, "upon what you cannot have."

"I dwell," Tlik answered, "on what I long for with all

my soul." He licked his cracked lips. Then he managed half a smile. "You wanted to return to the Halls of Mirtiin, Ayesh. Well, here we are. For a long time."

Ayesh tried to swallow to moisten her throat, but her mouth was too dry. "At least we die awake," she said. "Better to die aware than in fear."

"I am not without fear," Tlik said hoarsely. "I do not want to die."

"We are yet alive."

Tlik shook his head. "For torture. For example."

Indeed, Betalem meant to make symbols of them now, as they died, and for long years after they were dead.

As for the flakkach, *they shall remain where they are,* Betalem had said. *In time, they shall die in that cage, yet still will they remain in this chamber. They shall never be moved.*

Will they not stink? a Shade-in-Ice had asked.

It shall be a stench with a lesson, Betalem had answered, looking at Deoraya. *For all time will the human hang near the house that brought it, that all may be minded not to ignore the word of scripture.*

Tlik sat looking for a long time at the copper flute in his hands. He raised it to his lips, and they cracked when he shaped them to blow.

The first note was sour, wavering. But the second was sweet and pure.

Water, Ayesh thought. *It sounds like water.*

"Stop that!" called one of the guards.

Tlik ignored her.

"Stop at once!" The guard strode toward them, brandishing her trident. "This is a sacred room! No music but minotaur music may sound here! Stop, else will you feel the jab of my blades!"

Tlik stopped playing to chuckle softly, then took up the music again.

"Cease!" the guard insisted.

"Oh, leave off, Hyralem," said her partner, who still stood his post by the door. "They would like nothing better than for you to speed them to death."

"It is sacrilege!" Hyralem said.

"Soon enough will that goblin fall silent of its own thirst," the other guard answered. "Leave off, lest you would anger our Most Revered Living Mother."

Hyralem banged the butt of her trident against the cage and set it to rocking. "Play, then, scoundrel!" she said. "As for me, I am thirsty." She turned to her partner. "Stand your post alone a while." She looked at Ayesh and Tlik over her shoulder. "I go to drink until my belly swells. I go to drink until I can hold not a drop more. I think, too, that I shall bathe my head."

Tlik played louder.

Hyralem pounded the cage with her trident again, then strode out past the other guard and past the minotaur who had just appeared in the doorway.

Ayesh squinted. Her gaze was clouded. Even her eyes felt dry.

"Do I hear music?" the figure asked. His robes were green and gold. It was Phyrrax. He said something else, but Ayesh could not hear him from across the chamber.

"Tlik! Stop playing!"

He stopped.

"Foreign music, *flakkach* music in the Assembly Chamber?" Phyrrax was saying.

"It cannot be stopped," said the guard, "without doing them a mercy." Then he looked at the cage, realizing that the music *had* stopped.

"But *flakkach* music," said Phyrrax, shaking his head.

Tlik played one sharp note.

Ayesh said, "Hush!"

The guard agreed. "They offend to the last breath, do they not?"

Phyrrax laughed. "They will offend far beyond that. I hope you are not posted here after they have begun to rot, my friend."

The guard snorted. "As they begin to stink, there will be no Assemblies in Mirtiin for some time, nor any need for guards to bar entry."

"Ah, I take your meaning," Phyrrax said. "Our Most Revered Mother, Speaker of Stone, is as clever as she is wise."

"Of course. She Who Was First speaks through Stahaan. Gynnalem acts always without error."

Phyrrax looked at the cage. "May I look upon them? I did see them first come into Mirtiin, and I would see up close how such creatures die."

"It is not forbidden," said the guard. Then, sternly, he asked, "You will show them no pity?"

"Mothers forfend!" said Phyrrax. "To show them pity would offend Stahaan!"

"Pass, then," said the guard.

Phyrrax approached, and in a loud voice he said, "Alas, guard! They stink already!"

The guard laughed. Tlik hissed at Phyrrax, and Ayesh said, "Stop it, Tlik!"

But Tlik said, "How soon do they all turn to their new mistress! Like dogs! Like goblins!" Then he scowled. "Listen what use I make of the name goblin. What am I?"

"Soft, soft," said Phyrrax under his breath. He looked at Ayesh. "All is not yet saved."

"Aye," Ayesh agreed. "*We* are not."

"Alas," Phyrrax said quietly, "does the guard strain to hear us?"

Ayesh looked. "He does not seem much interested."

Tlik looked puzzled. "Is he going to help us?" Then to Phyrrax, "Are you?"

Phyrrax shook his head. "Goblin, I regret to say, I am no fighter. I am a gad, a goad, a prodder. Not a warrior. There are two guards in the hallway, and usually two here inside. I can do naught."

"You can gather some who would help us," Ayesh said.

"All cower," Phyrrax said. "All fear to raise their heads up where Betalem might yet chop them."

Ayesh closed her eyes. "Phyrrax, why do you come if not to help us?"

"To warn you," he said. "Betalem will come to you half a step ahead of death. She will offer water. She may even dangle the promise of freedom. Not that she would grant it. But she'll tantalize you with all manner of things, if you will but betray a secret she suspects."

"What secret?" whispered Tlik.

"Betalem will not know what she asks for, precisely," Phyrrax said. "She will only know that you may have a secret to yield."

"I do," Ayesh said.

"What secret?" Tlik said again.

Phyrrax said, "Listen, Ayesh. You must die before you would tell her. All that is worthy that you brought to Mirtiin dies now if you do not hold your tongue."

"What?" said Tlik. "*What?*"

"That the crimes confessed by Captain Tekrax," said Ayesh, "are in truth the crimes of Phyrrax. It was he who encouraged Scaraya's researches. It was he who put the word into Myrrax's ear and the dream into his head. And I recall now something that Zhanrax said when he caught me. Phyrrax, for all his protests to the contrary, had put the idea into Zhanrax's head."

Phyrrax looked over his shoulder at the guard.

"What I brought to Mirtiin dies anyway," Ayesh said. "Stahaan has won."

"Seeds do not always sprout in the season when they are planted," said Phyrrax. "You and Tlik die. But I have Cimmaraya's formula, and it is copied even now and hidden in five houses. *Five*, not the three that Stahaan knows to suspect. Stahaan's enemies grow, even as she shames us. Next time—"

"We die, you said," Tlik interrupted. "We die. *Later*, Mirtiin minotaurs are great, but now the human and the goblin, the *flakkach* must die." He started to sneer, but the gesture dissolved into a sigh. "What do minotaurs care about us? We are your tools."

Ayesh said, "Help us, Phyrrax."

"I've told you—"

"Will you always work only in the shadows? Help us, Phyrrax. We've done much for your cause."

"If I do anything, then I compromise the future. One day, there will be another Mirtiin whose ear will hear my whisperings. We have the formula. I'll see that Tana remembers your teachings, even teaches them to others once Stahaan's grip loosens."

"Goblins and humans," said Tlik, "are expendable on the way to your dreams. *Your* dreams."

"Have minotaurs not died for this dream?" said Phyrrax. "Tlik, I ask a willing sacrifice of you. In time, all the goblins in these mountains would become as you have become!"

"My dreams die with me," said Tlik. "Why not yours?"

"Tlik!" Ayesh whispered hoarsely.

Tlik said nothing, but only glared.

"Do this, at least," said Ayesh. "Remind Zhanrax of Cimmaraya. Ask him what he would do in remembrance of her."

"He won't come," said Phyrrax. "He never cared about you. It was only—"

"Ayesh was his gift," said Tlik, "a pet to win Cimmaraya's heart."

"He'll come," Ayesh said.

Phyrrax shook his head.

Tlik looked at the flute in his hands. "Zhanrax is not subtle," he said. "Words will not move him." He stretched the flute through the bars of the cage. "Give him this. Tell him that I—no, tell him that Ayesh sends it in remembrance of Cimmaraya. She made it."

Ayesh looked at him. His hand trembled as he held out the flute. It was the object that gave him at least a little power over his guards, yet he would think to give it up. "Diamond mind," Ayesh said to him approvingly.

Tlik did not take his gaze from Phyrrax.

"Do this," Ayesh told Phyrrax, "and we keep your secrets to our last breaths." She looked at Tlik. "Do we not?"

Tlik hesitated, then nodded.

Phyrrax took the flute. "Guard!" he shouted. "I have saved your ears!"

The guard was immediately suspicious. "Did you promise them aught? Water, perhaps?"

Phyrrax laughed. "What is a promise made to *flakkach*?" He looked back at the cage. "Are they minotaurs, that my word to them is my bond?"

"Liar!" rasped Tlik.

The guard laughed.

Feebly, Tlik tugged at the bars of the cage. Then he looked at Ayesh and whispered, "Would he betray us, truly?"

"Would you, truly, betray him?"

Tlik looked at the doorway where Phyrrax vanished, and he did not answer.

The delirium of her thirst was like sleep. Ayesh's eyes were open, but half the time she did not see. She drifted in and out of dreams where cataracts rumbled with their great flood and snow melted into rivulets of cold, cold water.

Tlik was collapsed on top of her in the cramped cage. His breath on her shoulder was hot and dry.

"Tlik?" she croaked. She tried to shift him. How had he grown so heavy? He did not stir.

Her legs, folded beneath her, ached where the metal cage dug into her flesh. Since she couldn't move, she let the pain be. Soon, it wouldn't matter anymore.

Her eyes closed. She dreamed.

She was in the ventilation shaft in the Roof of Lights. The stone shaft crushed against her ribs when she tried to breathe. Her breaths came shallow, fast, and dry.

Xa-On had fallen. She was the last fighter in the last city, dying in this air shaft like a trapped rat. Her dry tongue licked papery lips, and she thought of water rushing in torrents, filling the shaft. She would drown; she would gladly drown for one last taste of water before she died.

She dreamed of storm clouds growing dark and fat with rain that never fell. The clouds swelled. They grew taller and taller in the sky. They blotted the sun, but the ground beneath was yet hot and parched. No drop fell.

There was thunder, even. It clanged like the ringing of weapons, axe on trident. It rumbled and echoed like a deep, deep voice echoing in a great room, but no rain fell.

And then rain *did* fall. Drops poured onto her cheeks, past her papery lips. Water was falling onto her swollen tongue.

Her eyes opened.

"Awake!" rumbled Zhanrax's deep voice. He held a

sponge over her face and was squeezing the water from it. He wet it again from a jar and squeezed water onto Tlik's face. "Drink!"

Tlik swallowed and gasped. He opened his eyes.

"Only a mouthful each," he said, squeezing the sponge above Ayesh again. "If you drink as much as you want, you'll be sick." He squeezed the sponge for Tlik again, then lifted the goblin from the cage and onto the floor.

Tlik couldn't stand. "Just a little more," he begged.

"In time," Zhanrax said. He lifted Ayesh down. Her legs shook.

"I knew you'd come." Feebly, Ayesh grinned.

"This cage dishonors my house," Zhanrax said.

As best she could, Ayesh snorted.

Zhanrax threw a great burlap sack onto the floor. "Get in," he said. "I'll carry you over my shoulder and pray to the Mother of Mothers that no Stahaan stops to examine my burden. Hurry! Most of Mirtiin sleeps, but we must be beneath the sky before these bodies are found."

Only then did Ayesh notice how bloody his arms were. His axe, too, was smeared with crimson. She looked at where the guards lay dead. "You'd best wash," she said.

"I will," he said. "Get in the bag."

She helped Tlik stand and get into the bag.

"Did you bring my things?" Ayesh said.

"What?" said Zhanrax.

"My pack." It hurt her throat to speak. "The possessions you took from me when you captured me."

He shook his head.

"Then we must go to Rock-in-Water and get them."

"No time!"

Ayesh folded her arms and made no move to get into the bag.

"Are you thrice mad?" Deoraya seized her own horns as if she would pull them off. "Did I raise you up to be witless?"

Zhanrax stood by the front door looking helpless while Ayesh went through her pack to see that all was there. Tlik slurped water from the bowl Zhanrax had given him.

"To free them at all is insane!" Deoraya said. "Gynnalem will know that you've done this to save the house from shame."

"I do it also in remembrance of Cimmaraya," said Zhanrax.

"Mother of Mothers," Deoraya said, opening her arms, "why did You not give me daughters?" Then she cried, "Zhanrax, Stahaan will kill you!"

"Not if she does not find me."

"And she will not find you here?"

"Come," Zhanrax said to Ayesh. "All is there. Hurry!"

Ayesh closed the pack. Tlik ducked back into the burlap bag, then popped out again to say, "Do you have *my* flute as well, Zhanrax?"

"Mine," the minotaur reminded him. "You gave it to me."

"You bring it?"

"Yes, yes!" said Zhanrax impatiently.

"Where?" Deoraya said, standing before the door. "Where will you take them?"

"I set them free."

"Then where do *you* go? How can this house protect you, Zhanrax? Stahaan is everywhere in Mirtiin. None will stand with me if I shelter you!"

Zhanrax said, very softly, "I inherit the sky."

Deoraya took a sharp breath. Ayesh saw in her eyes that she knew this was the only way. Zhanrax could not stay in Mirtiin and live. But Deoraya shook her head and pointed at Ayesh. "I was cursed from the first day this creature trod our rooms! *Flakkach!* Foul *flakkach!*"

From the inner doorway came a voice that said, "I'm coming, too."

Tana's eyes were red and rimmed with sleep. He carried a bundle of clothes.

"No!" Deoraya bellowed.

Zhanrax said, "You may not, little brother. I gave you a secret to keep, and you must keep it."

Deoraya looked at Zhanrax, a question in her eyes, but he gave her no answer.

One of the copies, Ayesh realized. *Cimmaraya's formula.*

"Teacher Ayesh," said Tana, bowing, "are my studies at an end? Do you not have more to teach me?"

"Student Tana," Ayesh said, returning the bow, "thy studies are not ended, yet must thou await another teacher."

Tana frowned. "Who else can teach me diamond mind?"

"I don't know," Ayesh said.

"Let me come."

"When the student is ready," Ayesh said, "the teacher appears."

He squinted skeptically.

"Tana," Ayesh said, "did you ever expect that a human would teach you? You have not seen the end of strange days in Mirtiin."

"Mothers protect us!" said Deoraya, fingering her phial. She threw her hands in the air. "Go who will go and stay who will stay, but do not stand about while Stahaan finds her wits and comes to slaughter all!"

Tana grinned lopsidedly.

Seeds do not always sprout in the season when they are planted, Ayesh thought. She shook her head. "I would have Tana come with us," she said, "but he can't. Before long, Tana will be no more, and Tanarax will stand in his place, a minotaur come of age. A minotaur with diamond mind." She tapped her own forehead, then raised her hand as if to tap his, though he was too tall. "A teacher."

"Who knows," said Zhanrax, "but that one day he will be Mirtiin?"

The thunder of many hooves passed in the carpeted hallway outside. There was an incoherent bellow.

"They sound alarms!" Deoraya said. "You might escape in the confusion, but they will not be confused long! Go! Go!"

Ayesh took a piece of crystal from her pack and pressed it into Tana's hand. "The Roof of Lights," she said. "Keep this, and remember."

Tana hung his head.

Deoraya opened the door and looked both ways as Ayesh climbed into the bag. It was dark inside as Zhanrax lifted her and Tlik to his shoulder, and Deoraya said, for the last time, "Go!"

CHAPTER

27

TLIK LAY WITH HIS HEAD NEXT TO THE COLD stream, watching the sky. His belly was swollen with water.

"You'll get sick," Zhanrax had warned.

"I don't care." Tlik had kept drinking until he felt he would split. The cold water made his teeth ache. And *still* he thirsted.

Now at last the fire in his throat was quenched. He no longer ached to drink. Indeed, he felt a little nauseated, and his head throbbed. It was a welcome nausea, a pleasant pain.

On the bank beside him, Ayesh rolled onto her belly and washed her face in the stream. Then she asked Zhanrax, "Are we beyond the reach of patrols?"

Zhanrax for once did not snort, but glowered—an almost goblin expression. "Beyond their reach? Sooner beyond their interest than their reach. Minotaurs may range as far as they choose. Is that not so of humans? Might minotaurs have the power to range at least as far as humans?"

"Aye, humans range the world over. Wider than minotaurs. What of it? I ask a simple enough question."

They are both so proud to be what they are, Tlik thought, closing his eyes.

"Just remember," Zhanrax rumbled, "what limits minotaurs is what they choose, not what they are able to do."

"I meant only—"

"You ask if we are safe. Had they the will to pursue us, crossing a dozen seas would not save us. But Gynnalem will lose her taste for us. If the patrols search for a day or two and find us not, she will cease to care. Stahaan has greater concerns."

"What did you bring to eat?" Tlik asked. "Now that I no longer thirst, I hunger!"

"Will you not graze upon the grass and flowers?" Zhanrax asked. "She Who Was First spreads a feast upon the earth, yet humans and goblins eat it not. What better sign that you are *flakkach* and lesser creatures?"

"Teats of Ka," Tlik said, rolling his eyes. "You didn't think to bring anything, then?"

Zhanrax snorted, then picked up the burlap bag. It was empty. Besides his axe, his sling, a bag of steelstones and the clothes he wore, he seemed to have nothing else. Of course, he had Tlik's flute somewhere. "I will go now."

"Go where?" Ayesh said. "Will you not travel in our company?"

Now did he snort. "A Mirtiin minotaur travel willingly in the company of *flakkach*?"

"You're not a Mirtiin minotaur any longer," Ayesh reminded him. "Did you not say you inherit the sky?"

Zhanrax looked up at the bright blue heavens. Though the wind blew cold, there were only a few streaky clouds. "Aye, I do. I do inherit the sky." He looked down at her. "But not with you. I did save you, in Cimmaraya's memory. I did remove you from that dishonorable cage, for the sake of my house. Would I let the sacred Assembly fill with the stink of your corpses? Do not imagine, though, that I act from more than what I say. I am a son of Mirtiin. Even in exile, I keep her forms. And I do not keep company with *flakkach*."

"So you go alone?" said Ayesh.

"There are goblin caves all about here," Tlik warned. "A minotaur alone—"

Again, Zhanrax snorted. He tucked the empty bag into his belt and walked off, following the stream down toward the tree line.

"Wait!" Tlik cried. "My flute!" He jumped to his feet. Water sloshed in him, and he felt sick. "Zhanrax!" he shouted. "My flute!"

The minotaur ignored him and kept walking.

"Get up," Tlik said. "We follow him."

"Why?" said Ayesh. "Let him go."

They watched as he disappeared among the dark pines. Tlik stood up. "We track him."

Ayesh shook her head.

"We track him!" Tlik insisted.

"No. What's the point?"

Tlik gritted his teeth, but then focused his thoughts. It would do no good to argue with her. She would command or balk until she had her way. Just like the minotaurs. Tlik and the other goblins had been mere vessels, repositories for dreams. Minotaur dreams of peace and prosperity. Ayesh's dreams of teaching all things Oneahn. What of goblin dreams?

Goblins did not matter. "Goblin mind," Ayesh called the fear mind. But did humans not have it? and minotaurs?

"Very well," Tlik said, pretending to give in, "but we must follow the stream anyway." He stood and gestured for her to lead the way.

Ah, now that she was granted the lead, now did she stand and follow Zhanrax. Behind her, where she could not see, Tlik shook his head.

Tlik had mastered his fears. Could humans and minotaurs see that he was their equal?

No, they could not. Except for Tana. He at least had joined Ayesh's class at the bottom—the new student beneath the older students, not the minotaur who expects a place above goblins as his birthright. Tana was not simply "open-minded" about goblins. Without effort, he treated them as his fellows.

With the elixir, with Tana and a hundred minotaurs like him, then might Tlik realize his own dreams. He would have no creatures—not humans, not minotaurs—

bow down to goblins. Nor would goblins kneel. They would build cities as great as Oneah's. *Greater*. But they would be goblin cities.

The day was growing late when he and Ayesh found a meadow where wild strawberries grew. They were tiny fruits, and tart, but it was food. Tlik tried eating the leaves as well, and soon Ayesh followed his example, plucking and chewing leaf, stem and berry all together.

The sky was orange when they went back to the stream, and Ayesh soaked loose the dressing and bandages on Tlik's legs. It hurt, but only a little. The wounds had knit closed already and did not bleed much as she cleaned them. She covered the wounds with strawberry leaves and wrapped the bandages tight.

Tlik heard something—light feet padding the ground?

"What's that?"

He stared into the shadows among the trees. Ayesh looked, too, though he knew she didn't see well in any but the brightest light.

A twig snapped. Ayesh closed her eyes.

"Oh, gods," she said. "Not now."

He kept peering into the shadows until he saw them. "Goblins."

He said it, he thought, as a human would. He felt ashamed, but he felt a kind of disgust for them. He wanted to be left alone.

"Do they not tire of this?" Ayesh said. "Creeping and ambushing, thieving and murdering?"

"They know no other way," said Tlik. Then he shouted, *"Ounyit! Klirr moinay ketchtkin!"*

Ayesh looked at him, doubt crossing her face.

"I tell them to go away, that you are my prisoner."

In his own language, with a good accent, she said, "I know what you say."

Ayesh was still full of surprises.

He shrugged. "It's what they will understand."

But the goblins did not honor his claim. Five of them with black-bladed daggers bolted from the trees. All five made for Ayesh. Tlik was unimportant, a competitor they would quarrel with after the dust had settled.

Stop this! Tlik thought. *I could lift you up! I could make you better!* But he knew there was no point in speaking the words aloud.

When they were almost upon her, Ayesh dropped to a crouch.

Tlik let one of the goblins nearly pass him before he tripped it. It sprawled over the pine needles. Tlik whirled to kick another in the ribs. He wanted to shout, *I don't want to hurt you!* but they would see that as a sign of his weakness, his fear.

Ayesh sidestepped, controlled the arm that thrust a knife at her. She twisted. There was a *pop*, a sound that sickened Tlik. The goblin shrieked, went limp, and cradled his dangling arm.

Tlik dodged a blade. The goblin he had tripped was up. "Ours!" it hissed.

Tlik kicked him in the face.

He heard Ayesh grunt. A goblin blade had pierced the quilting of her jacket. She grabbed the dagger and yanked it out. "Gods!" she shouted.

The goblin who had stabbed Ayesh was flailing at her with bare hands. Ayesh punched him in the throat. He went to his knees, hands clutching at a broken windpipe.

The goblin Tlik had kicked in the ribs was holding her side, but she flung her dagger at Tlik. He dodged easily.

She shrieked. He shrieked back.

Then, holding up her empty hands to admit defeat and puzzlement, she half grinned. With that expression, she reminded Tlik of Kler. Kler, who had been the last to die.

She turned her back on him.

The ones who could move were limping back into the shadows.

A word caught in Tlik's throat: *Wait!* He did not utter it, but he took a step toward the retreating goblins.

"Tlik!" said Ayesh. He looked at her.

Ayesh was trembling over her whole body. "Help me," she said. And then she fell.

*   *   *

That she did not die that first night, shivering in the
bushes where he had dragged her, was a good sign. But
she did not come fully awake in the morning. That was
bad.

He dragged her to the stream. He could see depres-
sions in the soil—signs of Zhanrax's passing. He bit his
lip. The minotaur would put many leagues between Tlik
and his flute now. If he had to care for Ayesh . . .

But he did have to care for her.

He soaked a strip of cloth, then wrung it out over her
face. He did it again. And again. She opened her eyes and
blinked in the bright sunlight.

"Yusha!" she cried out. "Mashala! Khairt!" She stared,
unseeing. Or seeing ghosts.

"Where do I take you?" Tlik asked. "Where is a human
healer?"

She squinted into the sun. "Hata? Telina Hata?"

"Ayesh, though your eyes are open, you dream! It's
me! It's Tlik!"

She squinted some more. Then she seemed to recognize him. He smiled.

"Goblin!" she cried in Voda. She kicked him, sent him
sprawling into the bushes.

"Ayesh!" he said, picking himself up. "Listen! You've
been poisoned!"

She sat up, but swayed from side to side.

"A healer!" he said, approaching her cautiously. "You
must tell me where to find a healer!"

"Stay away from me, you rotter!" she shouted. She
tried to stand, but tumbled.

"Ayesh," he said very softly. "Teacher Ayesh, please."
He eased her onto her back.

"Healers," she said in the minotaur tongue. "Healers,
in the wrestlers' longhouse."

"No," he said. "This is not Oneah."

She blinked. Her eyes seemed to see more clearly.
"Bathtown," she said. "Elder Laik."

"Bathtown, aye." He knew where that was. "How will I

know the house?" He couldn't very well ask the neighbors.

She was trembling again. "Tlik?"

"Yes, yes," he said. "It's all right." He laid his hand on
her forehead. She seemed to tremble less. "Tell me how I
will know the house."

"Two doors on the black and white," she said. "Hands."

"What?"

"Two hands. Black hand. White hand."

"What did you say about doors?"

"Black and white. Twins. Hands . . ." Her eyes lost
their focus.

"Ayesh," he said, "that makes no sense!" He shook her
gently.

"Hands."

Then she was out cold again.

When he roused her again, he got her to stand up. She
couldn't balance on her own, but if Tlik started walking,
she'd put a foot out to keep from falling. One step at a
time, he moved her along that way.

It would be a slow trip to Bathtown.

"Thirsty," she said in Voda when they had gone a little
ways. She groped blindly before her. "Water."

"We'll come upon the stream again soon," he said. She
turned, then moved her head, trying to focus on him.

"Olf," she decided. "Townsman Olf." She began to
weep. "I'm sorry. I'm sorry for the things I said."

"Shhh."

"You're not Olf," she said. "Too small."

She staggered on in silence for a time, then said,
"Oneah! Oh, for the cities!" She wept again. "Oh, Cities
of the Sun! They are ashes of the sun, now."

She stopped.

"Keep walking," Tlik said. "I can't carry you."

But she wouldn't go on. "Ruin! Ruin!" she cried. "All
is in ruin! All that was beautiful is gone!" She licked her
tears. "I thirst, Master Hata. *Aisaka ni kraleensec. Tan
kraleensec . . .*"

"There's water ahead," Tlik told her.

She was silent until they crossed a field of scree. The

rocks on the slope slid from beneath Tlik's feet and clattered together like potsherds. The sound was almost musical.

Music, Tlik thought. *Ah, music.*

He carried Ayesh's pack on his back. There were two flutes within. If he really wanted one so badly, and since Zhanrax's trail was getting colder, harder to find . . .

No. They were her flutes. There was much that the minotaurs had stolen from him. Ayesh, as much as she failed to recognize who he truly was, at least had not stolen his liberty, sacrificed him for what *she* wanted. She had given for selfish reasons, but she had given. It would not be right to steal her copper flute.

Ayesh turned to look at him. "Tlik?"

He smiled. "You know me."

"Elder Laik and Elder Alik," she said, "are the healers." She panted. "I thirst."

"Water soon," he said. "Tell me about the healers."

"On their door . . . two hands."

"A black hand and a white hand," he said.

"Yes." Then she was crying again. "You gave your flute away!"

"Aye," he said. The scree went sliding beneath their feet, and Tlik had to scramble to keep his feet. "Aye. I gave it."

"I have the one you gave me. I'll give it to you."

"Does it mean nothing to you?" he said.

"Ah, my arm! It yet burns."

"It's not bad. Keep walking."

"Don't you want the flute?" She stopped walking, lost her balance, and slid to one knee. Scree went sliding, clattering. "Does it mean so little?"

"It's not mine. Zhanrax has mine."

But she seemed not to hear him. "They died! They all died that you might have a flute!"

"Stand," he said. "You must keep walking."

"Scaraya! Cimmaraya! Myrrax! How many others? And you don't want it?" She angrily reached to her shoulders as if to loosen the straps of her pack. She was startled to find the pack missing. Then she squinted and saw it on Tlik's back.

"Please stand," he said. He offered her his hand.

She swatted his hand away. "Goblin!" she cried. She clutched at her arm, then yelped at the new pain that came when she touched the wound. "Ingrate!" she shouted. "Ungrateful rotter!"

Then she passed out again.

You named the wrong ones, he thought as he struggled to drag her across the last of the scree. Beyond, there was more solid ground, and it sloped down, down into the valley. When it was dark enough, he'd get her into Bathtown.

Scaraya, Cimmaraya, Myrrax. Aye, they died. And what of Gur and Murl, Mok and Rip, Wlur and Kler? She had not thought to name them. Were their sacrifices any less?

Nightfall brought them to Bathtown. He waited with her still form in the underbrush, and he watched the lanterns of the watchers as they walked inside the palisade. He counted it a blessing that humans grew sluggish and clumsy in the dark. With stealth, he could sneak into their midst.

When the watchers were on the far walls, Tlik dragged a windfallen tree close to the spike-topped palisade. He leaned the tree against the barrier. Then he went back for Ayesh and tied her limp form onto his back with the strips of cloth she'd used to bandage his legs.

He could scarcely walk with her. As he climbed with her, the whole tree shook with the trembling of his arms and legs.

I'll die here, he thought, *for the sake of this human. And what am I to her? Why do I not leave her here for them to find in the morning? Why do I not keep her flutes for myself? My need is the greater.*

Then he stopped his thoughts. *Diamond mind,* he reminded himself.

No matter how he jostled her, she did not stir. The poison was killing her. He must get her to the healers this night, *now.*

At the top of the wall, he untied her, then used the

strips of cloth to lower her most of the way. The last bit, he had to let her drop. Then, so that the watchers would not see the branches leaning over the palisade, he balanced on top of the sharpened poles and pushed the tree away. He dropped down beside Ayesh.

Getting in was easy, he thought. *By the Teats of Ka, may I find an exit before the humans kill me.*

He hid her in the shadows of some barrels. Then he began to slink across the dark lanes and alleys, keeping to the shadows. Moonlight at this hour was dim. Only the Glittermoon shone overhead, yet Tlik guessed that even humans, with their day-seeing eyes, might be able to see him if he stood in the open.

In a few high windows, the yellow light of candles shone, but most were dark. Most of the humans slept.

He had searched half the town before he found the door with the sign of hands upon it: one was white, the other black.

Tlik returned for Ayesh. Her feet made a sound as he dragged her across the cobbles and pebbles. Let the hearing of the humans be as bad as their vision!

No one challenged him or raised the alarm.

He laid Ayesh at the door, tapped softly, then realized that humans might not hear such a subtle sound. And if they slept, he needed to rouse them.

He took a breath, then cringed as he rapped *hard.*

He turned and darted for the shadows.

Just before he made the safety of the darkness, he looked over his shoulder. A white-haired human was at the open window of the healer's house. He aimed a crossbow at Tlik. The bolt's metal point glinted in the dim moonlight.

CHAPTER

28

AYESH DREAMED OF EMERALD DRAGONFLIES, of zephyr falcons, of basilisks and an azure drake. She dreamed of talking birds of paradise and a bird maiden who longed not to fly but to swim. She dreamed the smell of sulfur, and all through her dreaming, a voice spoke to her in Voda.

"In a house made of stars lived Osterman and his beautiful consorts, Scintyl and Fallah. They had been together since the sun had been made, so long that even the gods were getting gray hairs and crow's feet by their eyes, yet Old Osterman and his consorts were still young and beautiful. It was obvious to the gods that something odd was going on, so they sent Ant Lord, the smallest among them, to Osterman's household as a spy . . . "

Ayesh dreamed of a dwarven weaponsmith who loved a haughty human maid. She dreamed of a northern paladin who tricked a wicked hedge wizard to disenchant a sword. She dreamed of magnetic mountains, of a bell that rang the dead to life, of sea serpents that danced upon the waves and sang. She thirsted. She longed to wake and drink, but she couldn't. She dreamed, and the voice continued to guide her dreams.

"A very long time ago, a young woman lived on the shores of a distant sea. She had an exceptional talent for speaking to animals . . . "

Always, the smell of rotten eggs.

"There once was a goblin chieftess even more wicked than most . . . "

"Tlik," Ayesh groaned, and then she said, "Water."

"Laik, come! She wakes! Bring water!"

Ayesh blinked. Her eyes felt filmy, and her vision blurred. Elder Alik, an enormous blur, bent over her.

She reached into her mouth and drew out the black leech leaf. She let it drop to the floor.

"Ah, she wakes, she wakes!" boomed Laik. "Back from the dead a second time! Either she is lucky or my skill is great!" He chuckled. "Or both!"

Ayesh sat up.

"You ought not rise so soon!" Laik said, pressing her shoulders to urge her back onto the cot.

"Oh, leave her be," Alik said. "You know she's stubborn." He gave her a wooden bowl. "Here."

Ayesh sniffed at the water to make sure it was no tincture or infusion. Then she drank.

"Tlik," Ayesh said. She rubbed her eyes. Her vision began to clear, and she could see doughy Alik and hale Laik standing before her. "The goblin that brought me . . . "

Laik looked at Alik. "Did I not tell you, brother?"

"Aye, aye, I must believe it now," Alik said.

"I saw your goblin," said Laik. "Late at night, someone rapped. I went to the door, but no one called out to say who he was. I took up the crossbow that we keep by the door. Then not a rapping, but a great thundering sounded at the door. I looked out the window. What did I see but a goblin, slinking off into the shadows. But the street is wide and offers little cover. Though he meant to hide, I see well in the dark. I raised the crossbow up and sighted . . . "

"No!" Ayesh cried.

"Aye, sighted," said Laik. "But then something seemed odd to me about him. I cannot say what. He did not have the bearing of a goblin, though his ears, I saw plain enough, were pointed."

"What did you do?" Ayesh said. She grabbed the old man's tanned arm. "Tell me, healer, what did you do?"

"I let him go. Not even did I sound alarm and raise the guard."

Ayesh closed her eyes and lay back on the cot. "Gods, I am grateful. Bountiful gods, 'tis a blessing!" She turned to Laik. "Thank you for not shooting him."

"He'd have missed," said Alik. "He's a terrible shot."

Laik frowned. "I might have been lucky," he said.

"Ill luck that would be," said Ayesh. "Of all goblins that ever lived, that one deserves pity. Aye, and gratitude."

"I thought it best I had not shot," Laik said, "when I went to the door to see what mischief he'd been doing. I found you upon the cobbles. I did not know you at first in the dark. I wondered if he'd not brought a goblin for healing!"

"I never heard of one goblin caring for another in that way," said Alik.

"Aye," said Laik, "but far less caring for a human being!"

Alik crossed his arms. "Is there not a story in this? And will you not be telling it to us?"

"Aye," Ayesh said, sitting up. "Tell I will." She saw where her pack lay against the wall, its flap tied tight. She smiled. "My possessions, I see, sit unexamined."

"We learn," said Alik, and Ayesh laughed.

"Come," said Laik. "Evening falls anon. Let us sup. Can you stand?"

They gave her, as before, bean soup in a copper bowl.

"Were you among goblins all this time?" said Laik.

"None could be so long among goblins and live," said Alik. "She was hid somewhere this time where goblins did not find her."

"So you've speculated while she healed," said Laik, "and I ask you as before, where do goblins not find a traveler? To what hollow tree or narrow ravine will their noses fail to lead them?"

"I was . . ." Ayesh said as she chewed a thick slice of bread.

Alik and Laik were leaned toward her, waiting for the next word. She said, "What do you know about minotaurs?"

"Some say," said Alik, "that they eat human flesh."

"Do you believe that?"

"They do live in caves," Alik said, "as goblins do. And goblins eat flesh. In any case, I do not doubt that they are bloodthirsty creatures. Few men in these mountains have seen minotaurs and lived to tell of it."

"Human flesh?," said Laik. He shook his head. "Will you believe every story you are told, brother? They graze. Do they not have heads like cattle and teeth the same? Therefore do they graze. They are no more vicious than cattle and secretive only because they are shy."

"You're both wrong," Ayesh said. "And you're both a little right."

"Well, if you know better," said Alik, "will you set us aright?"

Ayesh scraped at the bottom of her bowl, then noticed how dark the room was getting. Bathtown was already in the mountain's shadow. The sun was setting soon.

"I will tell all," she promised. "As soon as I return."

"Not again!" said Alik. "Next time we heal you, we'll have your stories *before* we feed you!"

Ayesh laughed. "I'll not be gone long." She went to the other room and rummaged in her pack until she had found the goblin flute.

"Be back before full dark," said a guard at the gate. "None may enter the palisade by night. There are goblins about."

"Aye," said a second guard. "And be mindful of the patrol. They walk the woods to scour them of goblins. Speak up if you are spoken to. If they do not see you clear, they may mistake you for the enemy."

Ayesh looked into the scrubby woods around Bathtown. Trees at this level provided little cover. "Have any goblins been killed these last few days?"

"One or two skulkers," said the first guard.

"Not enough to make a difference," said the second.

Ayesh pulled her quilted jacket close. Already it was cool in the mountain's shadow. Summer in this high northern country was almost gone.

"Tlik!" she called into the scrub and shadows. "Tlik, are you here?"

She could see the Bathtown patrol walking the slopes on the far side of the town. They carried crossbows.

"Tlik?" The tangle of stunted pine and mountain scrub oak looked like the best cover, the best place for someone to wait and hide. A ravine ran through the middle, and it was strewn with boulders.

"Tlik!"

Maybe he had given up on her.

She felt a chill in her heart. Though she could not recall just what she had said or done in her delirium, she knew she had called him ungrateful.

"Tlik! Where are you?" She squinted into the shadows. "I'm sorry for what I said, Tlik. Are you here?"

What if the patrols had killed him while he waited? But he'd have the calm, the patience to let them pass near without bolting, the way they'd expect a goblin to.

She sighed and looked at the opposite slope. There was nowhere there that would be an obvious hiding place. The distant peaks, glazed with snow, were turning orange as the sun went down. She must get back to the town gate soon.

I hurt him, she thought. *I have wounded him with words I did not mean, and he is gone.*

"Here," said a voice in the shadows.

She spun, smiling. "Where? Tlik, show yourself!"

"The patrol might see me."

"I'll come to you. Where are you?"

"No. Stay there."

"Oh, Tlik," she said. "I'm so sorry for the things I said. It was the poison. I didn't know what I was saying."

"Are you wrong to call me ungrateful?" the goblin said. "What cause have I for gratitude?" There was ice in his voice.

"What do you mean?"

"I have no world, Teacher Ayesh. Once I was a goblin among goblins. Now I alone of goblins do not think with the mind of a goblin. Do I inherit the company of humans, then?" He was silent for a moment. "Look at them, over there, hunting with their crossbows. Do they want my company, do you think?"

Ayesh looked, then hung her head. "I would have your company," she said.

He did not answer for a long time. "That is a gesture I did not expect."

"No gesture, Tlik," she said. "I mean it."

He was silent.

"Among my kind," he said at last, "you would die. Among yours would I. We must part. But diamond mind shines in me. You taught me much. For that, I am not ungrateful."

"I brought your flute," she said, extending it toward the deep shadows.

"That's not mine," Tlik said. Then he said, "I think that even among goblins, I will be lonely for a long time."

"Tlik," she said, "how can you even think of returning to such a life?"

"I am a goblin," he said. "I cannot live among humans, and I cannot live alone. But more than that, I would teach them. I will live among fearful goblins, and I alone will not know fear."

Ayesh shuddered. "Consider instead the Hurloon," she said. "I could take you there. They are generous. I know they would take you in."

"Take me there? On a leash, so that humans will not set upon me as we travel? And how would the Hurloon keep me? What would I be among them?" He hissed. "I am a goblin, not a pet. I am a goblin! Will you never understand?"

"Tlik, think what you are saying."

"I have done much thinking while the healer had you, Ayesh. I must be among my kind."

"Every day will your heart ache," Ayesh said. "To turn from goblin mind to diamond is liberation. To turn back . . . "

"My diamond mind *is* goblin mind!" There was a wildness in his voice that half threatened. "One day there will be more of us. I don't care how long it takes. I'll teach diamond mind."

"No," said Ayesh. "If you live among goblins, you'll have to act like one. That's what it will take to survive. And if you act in goblin mind, you dwell in goblin mind." She set the flute down on the ground.

"No," he said. "Keep it."

"It is yours," she said. "It was made for goblins."

A few low flute notes came from the shadows. Ayesh opened her eyes all the wider.

Tlik chuckled. "While you healed, I caught up with Zhanrax and asked him to return my flute. As he was sleeping, he did not answer. I took that for assent."

She didn't know what to say.

"Keep yours," Tlik said. "One day, some child who sees the world with new eyes will say, 'What is a goblin?' Show her that flute. Play it for her, before she learns anything else of my race. That will be a beginning."

Then, after the space of a few heartbeats, he said, "Good-bye, Ayesh of Oneah."

"Good-bye to thee, Tlik of goblins," Ayesh said. "Good-bye to thee, diamond mind of thy tribe."

Brush rustled, and he was gone.

She stayed there, listening, until the shadows grew deeper still and the first star shone in the sky.

CHAPTER
29

"I WAS AMONG MINOTAURS."

Both brothers looked at her sternly across the breakfast table. "Come, Oneahn. We have labored to heal you, and in payment we expect at least the truth."

Ayesh laughed. "The truth is a fluid thing, Elder Alik. Did you not labor to tutor me in that?"

"That is so, it is so. But what happened to you just now, in the mountains, is memory fresh and firsthand. And that is as near to truth as one may stand." He shook his head. "Minotaurs?"

"Mirtiin minotaurs. I had been among the Hurloon before. But these minotaurs, yours here, are . . . different."

"I apologize," said Laik. "It may seem insult to disbelieve you, but the minotaurs in these mountains certainly entertain no guests!"

"Or if they do," said Alik, "they entertain them cruelly. Come, Oneahn. Tell us a story we might believe, not some fancy that softens the brutish man-cows!"

"You slander a great race," said Ayesh. "I speak the truth. I was with minotaurs."

And then, slowly, stopping to explain and convince on

the points they would not first believe, she told them the
whole story. When she had finished, she played them a
goblin tune upon the copper flute.

"Well," said Alik. "Well." It seemed he could think of
nothing more to say.

"That they are herbalists, that I might have guessed,"
Laik said. "Would that I might have met Scaraya. We
each might have had something to teach. Pity I never met
her when I was out gathering."

"'Tis true?" Alik said. "'Tis truly true?"

"I ask you," Ayesh said, standing up from the table,
"how else would you explain that a goblin breached the
stockade and brought me into Bathtown? How else to
explain that one goblin would brave the guards alone,
and not for his own gain, but for me?" She went into the
other room and then brought her pack out into the front
room. She emptied it onto the table and began to sort
through her things.

"It might be shaped for a tale," Alik said.

Ayesh stopped sorting to look at him. "Shaped? It *is* a
tale as it stands. Aye, and one worthy of telling. Should
the people who live so near to minotaurs not know their
nature?"

"Who will believe?"

"I'll tell it enough times that people around here will
have to believe." She went back to sorting her possessions.
She had the usual odds and ends common to travelers: an
oil cloth, steel and flint she never used, a folding knife.

The important things were the book of verse, Master
Hata's sash, the two flutes, and the tinderbox of unsmoking fire. Ayesh eyed it all speculatively. Then, carefully,
reverently, she picked up the silver Oneahn flute.

"Elder Laik," she said, "I would have you keep this."

"No, no!" he protested. "You paid enough for two
healings the first time."

"Aye," said Alik, "and have paid us more with this
story. Again, I am not sure how I will have to change it to
make use of it, but—"

"Change it not at all!" Ayesh said. "Does no one have ears to hear truth?"

"Truth wrapped nicely and packaged fine, aye," said Alik.

"Take it," Ayesh said to Laik.

He received the flute uncertainly. "Silver? And so fine the workings!" He held it out to her. "I can't even play it," he said.

"You'll play," she said. She opened the tinderbox and spoke the word. The flame leaped to life. She sent the flame into the flute, then showed Laik where to hold his fingers. "Think the tune," she said, "and blow."

"But I don't know *how*!"

"Pretend," she said. "If you did know how, what would you do?"

Laik brought the flute to his lips and played the first bars of a tune. Astonished, he held the flute at arm's length and marveled at it. "Oneahn, this is the payment for healing a king!"

"No," said Alik. "An emperor, his empress, and his consort for good measure. I have never seen such a marvel, not even in Nul Divva."

"Too much," said Laik, holding the flute out to Ayesh.

"I'll not leave with it," Ayesh said. "Accept it as gift, not payment."

"But why?"

"You sighted on the goblin," Ayesh said, "and yet did not loose the bolt." She gathered the rest of her things and returned them to her pack. "He lives. And I am grateful."

The tavern was busier than it had been the first time Ayesh entered, those many weeks ago. There was the buzz of half a dozen conversations.

"Ash!" said a young woman who stood near the fire. "Ash! The Oneahn!"

"Ayesh," said Ayesh, straining to see into the far corners of the dark room.

"It's Juniper," the girl said. "I met you upon the road."

"I remember."

"Olf and Tull said you would be dead. Did you not go

north into the mountains? The goblin caves hole every mountain like a cheese!"

"I went," Ayesh said. "And, aye, there were goblins. And minotaurs."

"Minotaurs!" said a voice at a table. "If you say you saw some of those blood-drinkers and lived to tell the tale, then do I know you for a liar!"

Ayesh had grown accustomed to the dark. It was Townsman Olf. Half a dozen townsfolk sat with him.

"I more than saw them. I lived among them."

Olf brayed. "A woman lives among minotaurs and lives! All the ice on Cryvern Peak will melt on the day that happens."

"Then the melt has long since gone to the sea," Ayesh said. She put her hands on her hips. "Come, stand and call me liar again."

Olf shook his head. "I have seen you fight," he said, "and though I am no coward, I would not call you liar. Nay, not for all the world. Forgive me, traveler. I am in my cups, and my tongue is loose. I mean you no offense." He made room on the bench. "Come, I'll buy you a cup of wine. Let us see your magical flute."

Ayesh hesitated, then went to sit with Olf. From within her quilted jacket, she drew the goblin flute.

"Is that it?" said a townswoman at the table. "Olf, did you not say it was silver? Aye, and Juniper said the same, did she not?"

"Stories grow," said another townsman. "This year's lamb is next year's sheep, and next year's sheep is a cow, as the saying goes."

"No, no," Olf said. "This is not the one. The flute of wonders, I mean."

"But this flute is more wondrous than you dream," Ayesh said. She played one of Tlik's tunes upon it.

"That's strange music," said Juniper, standing behind her.

"Aye, and not the miracle that I remember," said Olf. "Come, traveler, I mean the silver flute, and the box with the flame. The *magic*."

"Ah, that," Ayesh said. "I gave them away. There is more miracle here." She began again to play.

"Nay, nay," said Olf. "That's but common music!"

Ayesh stopped playing. "It is music made by woman, and by minotaur, and by . . . "

She stopped herself. Now her eyes were fully adjusted to the tavern's firelight, and she could see the expectant faces at the table. Bathtown faces. The faces of townsfolk who lived every day in fear of goblins. And with good reason, for the goblins around them knew nothing of diamond mind, could not even imagine it. They were fearful goblins, not unlike the ones that had overnumbered the Oneahn wrestlers at the Roof of Lights.

Say the word goblin, *and they'll stop listening,* she thought. *Say that you knew a worthy goblin, and they'll drive you out of Bathtown.*

She looked at their eyes, glittering with firelight. Their expressions were half amused. They did not truly believe she'd had aught to do with minotaurs. No one ever had aught to do with minotaurs.

Why did the stories of Oneah change? To so many distant shores, she had taken her true history, her memories. And whenever she heard the tales told back to her, everything was changed. Everything but the notion that Oneah was grand.

They could only remember the tales told of a world they already believe, she thought, *or want to believe.*

Well, Alik had said, *who will believe? It might be shaped for a tale.*

Around the table, the townsfolk's' eyes glittered.

"But I have told tales a many in my years," Ayesh said, "and heard too few. Townsman Olf, have you a favorite story? One that sings to you?"

"I know a good many tales," Olf said.

"He knows a good many bawdy ones!" said a townswoman.

It was hard to tell in the firelight, but it seemed Olf blushed. "A few such," he said.

"But what of heroes?" Ayesh asked him.

"Of heroes," he repeated, and rubbed his head. "Of Tembrook, king over the Golden Lands, do you mean? Such as him?"

"That's a good one," said one of the townsfolk.

"Aye, I like it, too," said Juniper.

"Then that's the sort I mean," said Ayesh. "Tell it me, will you, Townsman Olf?"

"Well, it begins . . . How to begin it aright?" A distant look came to his eyes. "There was a golden country on a plain, and a city there that was made of gold. The Golden Lands, the kingdom was called, and the king who ruled it was called Tembrook. The laws of his reign were just, but strong, so that the wicked might be swiftly punished.

"Now across the plain, there was a black tower where dwelt a wizard . . ." Olf reached out his hand as if to touch the tower he saw ". . . and it rose nigh into the sky. . . ."

The heads around the tabled nodded in agreement as Olf told the story. The townsfolk looked at Olf with the gaze that Ayesh had always longed for when she told her stories of Oneah. Longed for, but did not always see.

When Olf had finished his tale about how true justice could thwart even a wicked wizard, another man at the table had a story he wanted to tell, and then a towns-woman.

And Ayesh listened as she had not listened before.

At last, when the hour was late and eyelids grew heavy even for the most exciting tales, Olf said, "But you have not told us, traveler, where you truly were, or what you truly did, or how you lived those many weeks away."

"I was learning a story," Ayesh said.

"Will you not tell it?" said Olf. And the others, though the night had worn on toward morning, nodded along with him.

"Aye," said one. "We would hear it."

"I have not yet learned it aright," Ayesh said. And she bid them good night.

The fire burned inside the wall of stones while softly, very softly, Ayesh played her copper flute.

Juniper crossed her arms. "When first I met you, Ash," she said, "you said you were a minstrel."

Ayesh stopped playing. The townsfolk within the wall were not all youngsters, as they had been the first night she had camped here, early in the summer. There were a few, like Juniper, who had been in that first group. But most were older. They held their pikes and knives with the ease of experience and rested comfortably against the inside of the wall. The pile of firewood was high, easily high enough to keep a blaze going long through the night atop the stone pillar in the center. On the top of the wall, Townsman Olf and two others walked with their crossbows, but with an ease they had not had on that other night.

Twigs cracked and dead leaves rustled in the forest beyond the wall. Goblins skulked and waited.

The Glittermoon was high. Ayesh squinted. It moved so fast that if she watched it long enough, she could see how it crossed the field of stars. The Mistmoon, rising late, was near its first quarter. *Half moon,* she remembered Olf telling her those long weeks ago, *is for trading.*

"Are you listening to me?" said Juniper.

"I heard you," said Ayesh. "And I am a minstrel."

"But I thought a minstrel did more than play. I thought a minstrel, a real minstrel, told stories, too. But you don't ever tell any. You just *listen* all the time."

"I'm trying to learn a new kind of story," Ayesh said. "I have to hear a lot of other stories before I know how to tell this one."

"Oh," Juniper said, as if she did not believe her. As if Ayesh had told her, as elders often do, something that made sense only to elders, that excused some failing that would not be excused in the young.

In a low voice, Ayesh said, "Well, how's this? I will tell you a tale that I'm still learning to tell." She looked at the townsfolk around her, the people who would not have ears for the truth as it had happened. But what if she left out the parts they would object to most?

Juniper knelt close. "Yes!" she said. "Tell me!"

"It is the truth," Ayesh said, "but if betimes you come to doubt me, only say so, and I shall end the tale."

"Is it . . ." Juniper said, lowering her voice and looking to one side first, then the other. "Is it about minotaurs?"

"Aye," said Ayesh, smiling. *About minotaurs, entirely,* she thought.

"I thought so," said Juniper with a conspiratorial grin. "Tell me it, then, beginning to end. I have ears for it, Ash."

"Would that you had ears for my name," Ayesh told her. And she began the tale of her time among the minotaurs.

She told it true, save that she left out one thing.

Goblins.

She contrived to tell the story without them.

Ayesh woke to shouting.

She saw pikes rising on all sides, men and women drawing knives. Raspy voices hooted and jeered.

Goblins swarmed the wall.

As Ayesh watched, a crossbow bolt pierced a gray throat.

A goblin landed near Ayesh and swung its black blade at her face.

No more, she thought. *I've had enough killing for one lifetime.*

She seized the goblin's arm and twisted. The dagger fell to the ground, and the goblin howled.

A boy seized the dagger, and before Ayesh could say a word, he sliced the gray neck from ear to ear. Then he grinned at Ayesh as the goblin crumpled.

She knew the boy. He was Ilif, Juniper's friend.

"I've learned a trick or two since you saw me last," he said. Then more goblins clambered over the wall, and he turned to kick at them and slash with the captured blade.

Ayesh looked at the goblin. "Oh, Tlik," she said softly, and she hoped he was far, far away from this place.

Then she dodged a goblin blade that was aimed at her shoulder. She spun and landed what she knew was a killing blow to the goblin's head.

"We've got 'em on the run!" shouted Townsman Olf. He shot a bolt into a retreating goblin's back.

*   *   *

In the morning, Juniper walked beside Ayesh toward the sea, swinging her bundle as she walked. At last Townsman Olf cried, "Those are not silks alone, you carry, girl, but Nul Divva glass as well! Be careful! Mind what you do!"

Juniper stopped swinging the bundle and held it close to her body.

"Where will you go?" Juniper said.

Ayesh shrugged. "The world is wide."

"But is there no one who waits for you? No one who misses you?"

The valley had opened out, and from here they could see the sea and the rocky shore, barren within reach of the night-feeding moonswimmers. There was a ship coming full sail from the open sea.

"I don't know," Ayesh said.

"What does that mean?" Juniper said. "If someone was waiting for you, if there was someone you left behind, wouldn't you know?"

"There have been many leave-takes in my years," Ayesh said. "Who feels my absence? Much can change even in the space of days, Juniper. Is that not one of the lessons my story teaches?"

Juniper stopped and looked back at the mountains. "I would lief meet them one day," she said.

"Who?"

"The minotaurs."

"If you met the Mirtiin outside of their labyrinth, 'tis not likely they would harm you," said Ayesh. "You must enter the halls to violate *purrah*. But were they Stahaan, I would not wish you such a meeting."

"There was a ship's captain who asked after you," Juniper said, starting to walk again, "at the trading of the last half moon."

"There was? What country?"

"In this country," Juniper said.

"No, where from?"

Juniper shrugged. "I don't know. Somebody told me." She stopped walking again. "Do you really think he might grow up to rule?"

"Who?"

"Tana, of course."

"Girl, your mind takes such turnings and makes such leaps, is it any wonder I am lost behind you? Yes, I think he might. Or he may teach other minotaurs, and one of them might one day rule. Though rule is the wrong word. Mirtiin does not rule. He rides and tries to steer."

"Orvada," Juniper said. "I think he was from Orvada."

"Did he smoke a pipe?" Ayesh asked.

"*You* told the story," Juniper said, "but I don't think you said anything about the minotaurs smoking. Wouldn't Tana be too young?"

"Gods and gashes, girl! If you can't lead a thought by the straight path, won't you at least follow one?"

The ship in the bay was not Orvadish. Ayesh could see that much. If she took passage, if she made a search, she had the whole of the Voda Sea in which to go looking. And even if she found him . . . he had only given her passage and heard her stories, after all. It was not a thing to put any hope in.

"Look," said Juniper. "They lower the boats." Wistfully, she added, "I wish I could go with you. It must be wonderful to go places."

"Aye," said Ayesh. "But it is fine, too, to have a home. It is fine, finally, to rest."

The sailors in the boats dipped their oars. Juniper, watching them, sighed a great sigh. And Ayesh, for other reasons, sighed, too.

EPILOGUE

AFTER SHE HAD HELPED TO CLEAR AND WASH
the breakfast dishes, Aleena returned to the table where
her father sat sharpening his scythe. She sat beside him
and sighed a loud, dramatic sigh.

"It's no use, daughter," he said. "You have your task
for the day, and I'll give you no other."

Aleena said nothing. It wasn't seemly to complain.

Her mother hung up the towel and said, "This is the
last day anyway, Aleena. Just show them around for one
more day, and tomorrow you can help me dig up the
potatoes for the cellar."

Aleena smiled. Now that was an important job, much
better than introducing the storyteller and her husband to
all the neighbors. "Can't I help dig potatoes today?" she
said. "Corey could show the storyteller around."

"Corey has to bind and stack the sheaves," said her
father.

"What troubles you so about the storyteller?" asked
her mother. "Does she speak harshly to you?"

"No," Aleena said. "But couldn't she show herself
around?"

"She's a guest among us," said her father. "We'll do her every honor. Don't you want to hear new stories?"

"But she hasn't told any!" Aleena said. "All she does is *listen*! And her husband says even less. Besides, the turnips have to come in, and the potatoes, and there's grain that needs threshing . . . "

Her mother smiled, as if she understood. "Do you think it's an unimportant job, daughter, to introduce the storyteller to our neighbors?"

Well, wasn't it? And that was the thing she didn't like. The storyteller wasn't unpleasant, but showing her around was such easy work when so many other things needed doing. *Honorable* things that would let Aleena show off how hard she could labor.

"If it's as important as bringing in the harvest," said Aleena, "then why doesn't Father do it? Or Uncle Payter?"

"Because, daughter," said her father as he felt the edge of the scythe, "each takes the task he is suited for."

"Am I suited to only lead these strangers about and stand idly while the storyteller asks her questions?"

"Hush, daughter," her father said. "I hear footsteps upon the path. One day more of what you've been doing, Aleena, and then you may do work that pleases you more. I'll even let you swing the scythe, if you like."

"Oh, yes!" she said. He'd always said she was too young before.

There was a knock on the door. It was the storyteller and her husband returned from their ablutions at the stream.

Aleena watched them from the corner of her eye as she led them to Farmer Shohn's house. This was her third day with the couple, and she still could not stop noticing how strange their clothes were. The husband wore blue silks the like of which Aleena had never seen. The storyteller herself wore the same color, but in a jacket and leggings that were sewn in squares like a quilt. They each had more gray in their hair than Aleena's mother, but less than her grandparents.

The storyteller looked hither and yon as she walked,

marking the scorched roofs and battered walls, the broken pigpens and the tipped-over granaries. Everywhere, men, women, and children were working to set things aright and bring the harvest in.

The captain looked, too. He seemed to take in as much as his wife, but he rarely remarked on what he saw. Aleena decided that when the time came, *she* would not take a husband who knew so little how to use words!

"Was there ever a time," asked the storyteller, "when orcs did not plague this land?"

"Aye," said Aleena, "but that was long ago, before I was born."

The storyteller's captain laughed. The storyteller said, "That cannot be long. How many summers have you seen, girl?"

"Eleven," Aleena said, then added with pride, "Enough that on the morrow, my father lets me swing the scythe!"

"Is this Farmer Shohn?" the storyteller asked as they approached. The man was up on his roof, tearing out the remains of burned thatch. Below, his son and daughter were binding new thatch to replace what the orcs had scorched.

"Storyteller Ayesh and her husband, Captain Raal," Aleena said. "This is Farmer Shohn."

"I bid you welcome," said Farmer Shohn.

"We thank you," said the storyteller, and she began to ask the sorts of questions she asked of everyone. It led, always, to, "What story, of the ones you know, is your favorite?"

Aleena let her arms hang at her sides and tried to look thoroughly bored, which she soon would be, listening to yet another story that she already knew.

"My favorite story?" said Farmer Shohn. "Well . . ."

He chanced to look at Aleena, then said, "Willem's daughter, will you help Jaylin and Mineena to tie thatch?" He winked at her.

Aleena smiled a grateful smile. Jaylin and Mineena made room for her on their bench, and Aleena set to work.

Now no one who chanced to pass would think she was lazy!

"Let me think," Farmer Shohn said, "my favorite story. Ah, well, there's this one." He cleared his throat. "When the world was first made, there were a great many more kinds of stone than there are today. There was a kind of stone that would heal any wound you touched it to, and another stone that would hold as much water as you poured into it. There was even a pebble that would let people understand the speech of animals. All you had to do was put the pebble in your ear.

"Now one day, a farmer was plowing in his field, and his plow struck something hard. . . ."

All through the telling, Farmer Shohn kept working. He was tying down the first new thatch when the story was finished. Captain Raal lit and smoked his pipe.

"I thank you," said the storyteller. "I will repay your story with one of my own tonight at Farmer Willem's fire."

They visited Farmer Emill's house near the cliffs, where the orcs had done their worst raiding. Farmer Emill was fixing his sheep pen where the orcs had knocked it down. He had lost a lot of sheep in this year's raid. It wasn't surprising that his favorite story was about a farmer who was a great slayer of orcs.

At Farmer Glenny's house, all were winnowing grain. That was easy labor to join uninvited, and Aleena did so. Farmer Glenny could think of no story he liked best, but his wife told one. "Once there was a farmer who planted corn, but when he collected the ears at harvesttime and began to shuck them, he found not a single grain upon the cobs. Instead, they were covered with nuggets of gold. Thought he, 'There's riches here, but naught to eat. I'll have to take some of this gold and go trade in town.' So he filled a bag with the gold. *But what if I am robbed?* he thought. So to be on the safe side, he filled another bag with vipers and scorpions. He tied the bags on their end of a pole, and set off for town with the pole on his shoulders. . . ."

They visited the hovels of Farmer Quincil and Farmer Breck, of Farmer Dacks and Farmer Maurris. At last, the storyteller said, "That's enough. I've heard what I must hear and seen what I must see." The captain nodded.

On the way back to her father's house, Aleena said, "Do you do no more work than this? Listening and telling?"

The storyteller smiled. "At times."

"You and yours love work," observed the captain—the most words he had spoken all day!

"By work are we worthy of our God, who labored to make the world," she said. "Orcs love sloth. That is why they are wicked."

"Ah," said Captain Raal, and that was all he said.

A great fire was made for the storytelling that night, and there were many little fires built around it. People needed light to see by while they listened. The women brought embroidery, and the men brought their knitting. Young children brought their toys, and older children brought their carving knives or needles for making new toys.

When the storyteller came out to tell her stories, she wore a cloak of many colors. Aleena had never seen anything so beautiful. She marveled to think of how many days it would take to dye, weave, and sew such a garment.

"That is a fine-made cloak," she said. And to be sure, she asked rather a rude question. "Did you make it yourself?"

"Aleena!" said her mother.

But the storyteller smiled. "Yes," she said. "I made it. It is the Robe of the Eleven, and I will tell you a story about it. But not now. I'll tell it next to last. The best stories come last."

So she does *do more than stand and listen,* Aleena thought. *She can sew. Well, that's a noble labor.*

"Here is a tale," the storyteller said. Her husband sat beside her and lit his pipe as she began:

In a region of the Hurloon Mountains, there lived a band of Pradesh gypsies called the Band of Three, though there were far more than three of them. Now just why they were called the Band of Three, none could say.

One day, a beautiful princess who lived nearby found

herself wondering, for no particular reason, why some twenty gypsies should have a name that so undercounted them. The more she thought about the question, the more curious she became, until finally . . .

Aleena found herself lost in the tale. And in the next.

Once upon a time, there lived an old ferryman whose hut lay on the banks of a great river. Now one year, the rains poured down for weeks and weeks, and the river had swollen to the very door of the hut. The current was so swift, that the ferryman was grateful not to have any customers.

One morning, there came a knock on his door and a deep voice said, "Open and ferry, fetch and carry, I must to the other shore go!"

When the ferryman opened his door to see who it was that summoned him, there was no one there. "That's curious," he said to himself. "I was sure I heard someone." Now the ferryman chanced to look down at his feet, and what should he see there but . . .

The stories were about all manner of creatures. Besides the brass man who was no bigger than an ant, there was a cockatrice that danced a dust cloud that seven knights mistook for rain. There was a stone giant that fell in love with the Mistmoon and almost sang her down to earth. There was an elvish queen who found a flying carpet, Balduvian bears who had the gift of speech, a sailor who learned to make stones rain from the sky. There were will-o'-the-wisps that lured with light, a thicket basilisk with a dangerous stare, and Uthden trolls that boiled out of the ground hunting treasure. . . .

"It grows late," said Aleena's father, and to her surprise, Aleena said, "No!"

"We've work to do with first light," her father said. Aleena looked about and saw that all of the youngest children were asleep.

"Then it is time we told our last two tales," said the storyteller, "and the best. First is the Tale of the Eleven."

Long, long ago, she began, *in a country between sea and cliffs . . .*

*   *   *

"Like ours!" said Aleena.

The storyteller smiled.

. . . there lived a king and his eleven princes. The land where they lived was fruitful for those who worked it, and neither rulers nor subjects of this country were lazy. Even the king and his princes worked all the day through when the season demanded it. You can even know by their names what sort of men they were. The king's name was Swings-the-Hammer. The eleven princes, from eldest to youngest, were called Milks-the-Cow, Plows-the-Field, Plants-the-Corn, Fetches-the-Water, Shoes-the-Horse, Mends-the-Fence, Tends-the-Fire, Racks-the-Hay, Stacks-the-Sheaves, Thatches-the-Roof, and Winnows-the-Grain.

You can see by their names that these were no ordinary princes who would live in idle luxury. No, not these. When they saw what needed to be done, they would do it themselves. But labor was not the only thing they loved. They had a passion, too, for beauty, as you can see by the Robe of the Eleven. Such a robe was worn by their king.

As I've told you, theirs was a rich land. Sun, rain, and soil rewarded the labor of the princes and their subjects. Alas, one thing stood between them and happiness. A tribe of hill giants lived in the cliffs. Often when a shepherd drove his flock to the good grazing near the cliffs, the giants stole his sheep. In the winter, the hill giants would even raid the country's villages, tear open the barns, and devour the cattle and pigs.

"Like orcs," said Farmer Maurris.

Each spring, the king and princes would put on their armor and fight with the hill giants, but it seemed that no matter how many they killed, there were yet many giants alive in the next season. Fighting took as much time as plowing, and with less to show for the effort.

*One day, an old peddler woman came to the castle.
Though her bag was small and her clothes were tattered,
it amused the king to bid her enter and display her wares.
He called to his sons, and they all stood in the throne
room while the old woman laid her offerings upon the
stone floor.*

> *She had a thimble and a comb,*
> *an ancient moldy tome,*
> *a candle and nine beads of glass.*

> *She showed a spindle and a broom,*
> *the shuttle from a loom,*
> *a bottle and a mat of grass.*

> *She had a handle for a spade,*
> *a poker for the fire,*
> *three stones and eleven pins.*

> *She showed a hilt without a blade,*
> *a strainer made of wire,*
> *a file and some tarnished tins.*

"*Is that all?*" asked King Swings-the-Hammer. He had
expected her offering to be meager, but not so disappointing as this.

"*There is treasure here for him who sees it,*" the old
woman said.

The eleven princes laughed at this, but the king looked
hard at the items. "*What, I pray thee tell me, is in the tins?*"

"*Naught but air and darkness,*" said the peddler woman.

"*What is the subject of the book?*" asked the king.

"*Tis written in a tongue no longer known,*" she
answered.

Prince Milks-the-Cow, who was the oldest, said, "*There's
naught of value, father, and work yet to do this day.*"

But King Swings-the-Hammer waved him to silence
and asked, "*What is in the bottle?*"

"*That is Adun's balm,*" said the peddler woman. "*A*

*potion of uncertain nature. Drink it, and it may bring
destruction. But if not destruction, then it brings all-
seeing wisdom."*

"I'll buy it," he said, and when they had agreed upon
a price, he unstopped the bottle.

"If not wisdom, then destruction," she reminded him.

The princes urged him not to drink, but King Swings-
the-Hammer said, "What use is a king if he be not
wise?" And he drank a third portion of the potion. It did
not kill him, at least not at once.

The peddler woman was putting away her things, but
the king smiled and said, "Not so fast, if you please.
Those three stones that look so ordinary, what makes
them worth peddling?"

"Nothing much," the old woman said. "Only touch
them to the tongue, and they banish all fear."

Aleena saw Farmer Shohn nod and smile.

The king said, "I see a use for them."

"What use?" asked Plows-the-Field, the second eldest.
"Are your sons not brave enough already?" And it was
true that his sons were brave, indeed, in battle.

"Another use," the king said, and he paid the peddler
the price she asked.

When the peddler had gone, the king explained that he
would go to the hill giants and convince them to touch
the stone to their tongues. "For all evil is done from
fear," he said, "and if the hill giants do not fear, then
may we trust one another and bargain for peace."

The sons thought this was a terrible idea, and it was so
unlike their father to propose such a scheme. Obviously,
the potion's evil effect was working its way with him. But
he would not be talked out of going to treat with the
giants.

"He goes to his death," said Milks-the-Cow.

"Worse!" said Shoes-the-Horse. "What if he succeeds?
Hill giants that are without fear will be no less wicked!

We will never be able to put them to flight! They will be unstoppable."

"Well," said Milks-the-Cow. "I'm the eldest, so I'll see what I can do."

The next day, the king sent a messenger to the cliffs. The messenger did not dare to stand close to the cliffs, but stood at a distance to cry out that the king was coming at noon to treat with the leader of the hill giants. "And the king declares that the giants will be well served to listen to him!" the messenger cried before he ran off.

"Well served to listen, is it?" said the chieftess of the giants. "He'll be up to some trick. There's no trusting humans. Let's kill him." And the other giants agreed.

Before King Swings-the-Hammer came before the hill giants, he touched one of the stones to his tongue. Sure as sure, it banished all his fears. He marched right up to the cliffs. Milks-the-Cow, though, refused to use the stone. Though his legs shook with fear, he nonetheless stayed near his father.

"Well, well!" said the chieftess of the hill giants. "What bargain do you have for us?"

The king and prince drew their swords, and the hill giants drew back a little. But not much. There were many of them against only the king and one prince. "We would offer you tribute," said the king, "but ere we speak of how many sheep or pigs we shall bring to you, touch this treaty stone to your tongues. If you do that, then we can come to an agreement that benefits all." He touched his own tongue to the stone to show that it was not poisoned, then held it out to the chieftess.

The hill giant chieftess was suspicious. She had never heard of a "treaty stone." Still, she liked the idea of her dinners coming to her without any work. Just as she was about to take the stone, Milks-the-Cow snatched it from his father's hand and dashed it to the ground. He cried, "No! Run! Save yourself!" And he spun on his heels and ran as fast as he could go back to the castle.

The king, however, stood his ground. He tried to pick up the stone, but before he could, one of the hill giants killed him. "Remember," the giant told his chieftess, "you can't trust them."

Now Milks-the-Cow felt terrible. At first he said to his ten brothers, "It was the potion he drank. It doomed him." But with time, he grew less certain that this was true. Before long, when he had come to wear his father's robe, he ached to know if he had done the right thing. For the consolation of all-seeing wisdom, he drank a portion of Adun's balm, even though his brothers urged him not to take the risk.

"Oh, the ache of my heart. I see that our father was right," he told the others after he had swallowed the potion. "We must let the hill giants taste one of the stones, and thus lose their fear."

"No, no!" said the others. "The potion warps your mind and will send you to your doom! Hill giants made fearless are only made dangerous."

"All evil springs from fear," said young King Milks-the-Cow. "I am determined."

The other ten discussed the dangers amongst themselves. "Don't worry," said Plows-the-Field. "I'm the next oldest. I'll go along and stop him."

With Milks-the-Cow and Plows-the-Field, it was just as before. Milks-the-Cow touched the second stone to his tongue, but his brother refused. Milks-the-Cow was calm as they approached the hill giants, but Plows-the-Field felt his legs trembling.

"We don't need a treaty," said one of the hill giants when they approached. "We already take what we want."

"I'll make it easier still," said Milks-the-Cow to their chieftess. "Only touch this stone to your tongue, and we'll discuss how much tribute peace is worth to my people."

But just as the chieftess was about to take the stone, Prince Plows-the-Field knocked it out of his brother's hand. He cried, "Run for it, brother!" and ran as fast as he could go back to the castle.

Poor Milks-the-Cow was killed as his father had been.

The robe passed to the next brother.

Plows-the-Field had no doubt that the whole scheme had been foolish. "Now that I'm king," he said to his brothers, "we'll have an end to this!" He made ready to pour out the last portion of Adun's balm. But before he could, the youngest prince, Winnows-the-Grain, seized the bottle and drank down the last third for himself.

"Ah," he said, grabbing the third stone and touching it to his tongue. "Now I'm with wisdom and without fear, and I can see that our father and oldest brother were right. I'm going right to the hill giants to bargain for peace."

"No, you don't!" said Plows-the-Field. "I forbid it!"

But the youngest prince ran off toward the cliffs before anyone could stop him.

"Don't worry," said Plows-the-Field. "He has to obey me. I'll put a stop to this." And he chased after his youngest brother.

Now when the giant chieftess saw a prince and a king running toward the meeting place, she said, "If they keep coming and we keep killing, there will be an end to them, and who will raise cattle and sheep and pigs for us?"

The other hill giants said, "All right, we'll listen to them. But any tricks, and we'll kill them. There always seem to be plenty around."

Just before Prince Winnows-the-Grain arrived before the hill giants, he stooped to pick up an ordinary rock from the ground. He held the rock in one hand and the magical stone in the other.

He stopped at the feet of the giant chieftess, and his brother the king was a few strides behind him. Prince Winnows-the-Grain held out the rock to the hill giant and offered the same bargain as before. Just as he did so, his brother, the king, slapped the stone out of his hand, then spun and ran off crying, "Save yourself, you fool!"

"Well," said the prince, "this stone, then."

Now Prince Winnows-the-Grain had run off in such a hurry that he didn't even have his sword. The giant chieftess could easily have snatched him up and killed him, but by now she was getting curious about this stone business. So very gingerly, she touched the stone to her tongue.

"Listen," said the prince. "We will feed all the hill giants a tribute of cows, pigs, and sheep. You won't have

*to raid us any more. All we ask is that you stop raiding us
and help protect us if another enemy attacks."*

The chieftess considered this.

"You can't trust him!" cried another giant.

*"It's a trap!" insisted a third. "They won't keep their
bargain!"*

*But the chieftess said, "How many cows? How many
pigs?" In an hour, they had concluded the terms of a
truce. The other hill giants didn't like this much until the
giant chieftess made each of them touch the stone to their
tongues. Then all agreed that it would be as the prince
proposed, and the hill giants would live by tribute, not by
raids.*

*Alas, the story did not end there. Young King Plows-
the-Field was furious that he'd been upstaged. When
each of the other brothers not only touched the stone to
their tongues, but endorsed the peace, he flew into a rage.
He went about the castle chopping things with his sword.
In his fury, he chopped off the hand of his youngest
brother, the hand that still held the stone. In his rage, the
king then chopped at the stone. It shattered, though a
tiny splinter of it flew up and pierced his tongue.*

*The king dropped his sword. Without his fear, his
anger died. But now that he saw what he had done, he
began to weep. None could console him, and he wept so
many tears that the drops gathered into rivulets and the
rivulets into a stream, and the stream surged into a river.
He wept so hard that he dried up from the inside and
died. But the river still flows to this day. Anyone who
drinks of its waters remembers harm done in fear, and
grieves.*

"And that," said the storyteller, "is the end of my tale."

No one said anything at first. At last, Aleena's father
said, "Would that orcs were like hill giants."

And Aleena asked, "Could there be such a stone as
that?"

"There once *were* such stones," said Farmer Shohn,
"when the world was new."

"I ask your attention for but one tale more," said the
storyteller. She opened a long, skinny sack and took out a
copper flute, the like of which Aleena had never seen
before.

Her husband, the captain, cleared his throat. "This is
the one tale I tell," he said. "It will seem a marvelous
fancy, yet it is true, true as may be. It is the story of a
land called Oneah."

The storyteller then played a few beautiful notes on the
flute before the captain began.

"There once was a people blessed and beloved by the
sun," he said. "They are no more. But in their time, they
built great cities upon a black-soiled plain, and they
called their country *Oneah*."

He said the name of the place with such music in his
voice! *Oneah. Oneah!* Even before she knew anything
about this land, the name enchanted Aleena. She looked
at the storyteller, and she saw that she must feel the
same. Surely she had heard this tale a hundred times, yet
the captain's words put dreaming into her gaze.

"There were Seven Cities of the Sun in this country,"
said the captain. "And their names were Onirrah, Onlish,
Onmarakhent, Onnilla, Xa-On . . . "

In his voice, Aleena heard a longing deeper than any
she had yet felt. She heard the despair of months-long
voyages far from land, the dream of landfall, the ache to
see the sun on grass again . . . but not just any grass. Oh,
Oneah! The captain said the names so that everyone who
heard him would ache for all things ever lost.

He had been there, Aleena decided. This magical place
that made one's heart ache must be the country of his birth.

The storyteller played her flute, tunes of longing, when
the captain paused in his tale.

"I tell you now of the Roof of Lights, and how the sun
danced colors across the skin of wrestlers . . . "

Aleena dreamed this place, this wonder, this Oneah.
And she felt its loss when the captain told of the
unnamed enemy who overran the borders. With such passion did he tell his tale that tears wet even his wife's
cheeks as he finished.

The storyteller played a few nostalgic notes on her flute. This was the captain's tale for the telling, but her music at least echoed the feelings of his words. The last note trailed into silence.

The fire crackled.

For a long time, no one stirred.

At last, families began to put away their knitting, their embroidery, their wood carving. They gathered up their children, and each farmer brought a small gift for Storyteller Ayesh or Captain Raal. They brought things they had made, or things their wives had made. Gifts of labor. Ayesh and Raal accepted each with a bow.

The fire burned low. Aleena stayed outside, watching the embers, even when her parents and two guests had gone inside. Wouldn't it be wonderful to live in such a land as that? Ah, but even the Oneahns had their problems. Wouldn't it be wonderful to live anywhere, even here, *without raids*! People spoke often of how grand it would be if all the orcs were dead, but wouldn't it serve just as well if instead the orcs were not wicked? But was it fear or sloth that made them what they were?

At last, the chill of the night, and perhaps a few thoughts too many about orcs, sent her inside.

"Today," promised her father, "you bring in potatoes. And you can help to mow the hay."

"Thank you, Father. But first, may I walk the storyteller and her captain to the sea?"

"I thought I would do it," her father said, "since you seem to want another task."

"No!" she said. "Let me take them!"

He smiled. "As you will, daughter."

Walking through the farms of her neighbors, Aleena asked every question of the storyteller she could think of, except the one she longed to ask. "What manner of clothes are your jacket and leggings? Do all Orvadish men wear silks as your husband does? Were you always a storyteller?"

My own manner. Yes. No.

There was smoke lying close to the fields, and orange flames licked the harvest stubble.

They walked nearer and nearer the shore. Already, the ship that returned for the storyteller and her husband was on the horizon.

At last, Aleena said, "Is it true?"

"Is what true?" asked the storyteller. "The story of Oneah?"

"Oh," said Aleena, glancing at the captain, "I know *that's* true."

"Then what?"

"Is it true that evil begins in fear? Could something as evil as an orc be less so, if it learned not to fear?"

"It is a true story I told," said the storyteller. "That evil begins in fear, that is the most true thing about it."

Aleena walked on with them, thinking.

Captain Raal stopped for a moment to light his pipe. He spoke so seldom that it surprised Aleena when he asked, "Why do they burn the fields?"

Aleena didn't know how to explain it. "They plant in the ashes."

"Ah," said the storyteller. "So do we."

And she and her husband looked at Aleena with gazes so unwavering that Aleena finally had to look away.

The storyteller laughed gently.

"So do we."